THE
LAVENDER HOUSE
❧ MOB ❧

THE
LAVENDER HOUSE
MOB

ANNIE CRUX

buried
river
press

© Annie Crux 2015
First published in Great Britain 2015

ISBN 978-1-910208-13-7

Buried River Press
Clerkenwell House
Clerkenwell Green
London EC1R 0HT

www.buriedriverpress.co.uk

Buried River Press is an imprint of Robert Hale Ltd

2 4 6 8 10 9 7 5 3 1

Typeset in Palatino
Printed and bound in Great Britain by
CPI Antony Rowe, Chippenham and Eastbourne

CHAPTER
ONE

Tipping Tabitha, the eldest of the four cats, from her lap, Louise willed herself to continue writing on her laptop as she sat in the garden. She tried to concentrate again, but found it difficult. Perhaps it wasn't such a good idea taking work out into the garden as it invited distractions. From where she sat she could see that two slates were slipping on the roof.

'Damn,' she muttered. 'I'll have to get Kevin round again. Hopefully he can nail them back in place without it costing too much.' She jotted a note down on the pad beside her, RING KEVIN, then decided she might as well do it straight away and get it over with and rang him on the mobile. 'Hi, Kevin,' she tried to sound bright and friendly. 'It's Louise Gregory.'

'Yes.' Kevin didn't respond to her friendliness.

Louise was not surprised, he very rarely did, which was why she usually put off ringing him. 'I've noticed a couple of slates slipping on the roof,' she said, 'and I wondered when you have the time, if you could …'

'Come round,' interrupted Kevin. 'Yes all right, I'll be there when I can.'

'Thank you,' said Louise meekly. 'I'm very grateful.'

Kevin cut her off without saying goodbye, and Louise felt annoyed with herself. I pay him, for God's sake, why do I feel guilty about asking him? But the truth was she was rather frightened of him. He was always scowling and surly, and she never knew when he would turn up, and when he did arrive he had a nasty habit of taking off his cap, scratching his head and pronouncing that the whole roof needed replacing. Then he got on and did the job and never charged much, and in Louise's permanently precarious financial situation cheapness counted for a lot. So she put up with his bad tempered ways.

That was the trouble with old houses. They looked wonderfully romantic, with wisteria and roses climbing over the walls, but something was always falling off, breaking or collapsing from sheer age. Lavender House was about two hundred and fifty years old, and had once had two farm cottages at the bottom of the enormous garden, only one of which remained. Everyone called it the pottery cottage, as it was where John, her husband, had done his potting after he'd lost his money in Australia. Louise came back with him to England, a very young wife with a 2-year-old daughter. It was a struggle, he was demoralized and depressed, and had no qualifications for anything except art, and decided to become a full time potter. The only good thing about coming back to England was Lavender House, which Louise had inherited from her Godmother so at least they'd had somewhere to live. Her daughter Penny was only four when John had a heart attack and died. Louise didn't linger long with that particular memory. It was all so long ago, twenty years in fact. Poor John, he'd made wonderful pots but not much money. She was better off as a widow, with the small allowance he'd organized for her through an insurance policy, than she had been when he was alive.

There must have been other outbuildings once, which someone, not Louise or John, had knocked together making one enormous house. It was a rabbit warren of a place, with rooms shooting off down corridors in all directions. Much too large for Louise living there alone, but she loved it, although it stretched her finances to the absolute limit. She looked at the slates again, and hoped Kevin wouldn't cost too much when he came. But age was creeping up on him, and she knew his roof climbing days were numbered; finding another Kevin would be difficult. It was hot, and pushing her hair back out of her eyes she gritted her teeth and continued typing, ignoring Tabitha who was determinedly trying to climb back onto her lap, and pushing the two dogs away who were snuggling up to her as if it were a cold winter's day, then panting heavily because they were so hot.

'Go away, idiots,' she said fondly. 'Go and sit in the shade you silly things.' They looked at her with brown soulful eyes and stayed where they were.

Louise frowned and continued typing. She had to finish it, because she needed the money. Her last book had just sold enough copies to earn her some small royalties, so now she was desperate to earn something from this one. Her agent, Dottie LeClerc, forever the optimist, was always hoping one of her authors would write a bestseller, so was always breathing down her neck every week asking her how it was going. Louise knew why, she'd just lost one of her biggest authors, Anita Bliss, who'd been poached by another, better organized agency. Dottie was nice, but eccentric, but her organizational skills were zero. Not once, to Louise's knowledge, had she managed to sell on the film rights of any of her authors, not even bestsellers like Anita Bliss. Rumour had it that Anita Bliss had moved because of that. If Louise had been in the enviable

7

position of being in the best-seller list, she might have thought of going to another agent, but as things stood she doubted another agent would want her. Oh, if only she could earn vast sums of money like Anita Bliss!

Staring at the words on the screen, the uplifting finish which she wanted eluded her. Actually, if she were honest, it was rather a miserable book, but one which she needed to write. She'd written from the heart and felt better for it, and hoped someone would buy it. She doubted her agent would agree, Dottie liked blood and guts, or happy endings, and this book had neither.

Her mind wandered, thinking of her only daughter, Penny, wishing she were down with her in Hampshire. There was a heat wave, and Louise thought it was far too hot for her to be in London with two small children. They needed fresh air; and the last time she'd spoken to Penny, on her twenty-fourth birthday, she'd sounded so tired. But at least she was in a settled relationship with David, although Louise did wish they were married.

She, herself, had married young; people did in those days when they wanted to sleep together. So she'd married John; given birth to Penny when she was nineteen a year later. They'd been happy although broke most of the time, and Louise being a realist had accepted life as it was.

But Penny was different. She wanted perfection, but not marriage, despite having two children. 'Mum, you're so old fashioned to feel that way,' she always said.

But Louise did feel that way. She was of the school of thought that liked children to have a mother and father with the same surname. 'It shows commitment to each other,' was her stock answer. But she knew, of course, that both Penny and David would ignore her.

Dragging her mind back to her fictional characters,

Louise wondered whether to kill off the grandmother in her story, giving the novel a bit of heartrending drama. To tell the truth she didn't much like the grandmother anyway. She'd modelled her on her own mother, who'd been a hard-hearted, demanding woman, and was now dead so she couldn't be offended. It would, of course, be more heartrending to kill off the family dog, but she couldn't bring herself to do that. No, she had to think of a suitable, quick but final ending for the grandmother who up until this point in the novel was in rude health. It would have to be a car accident, or something equally disastrous. A car accident, she eventually decided, with all the drama that involved. Her fingers tapped busily over the keys, and she was just beginning to enjoy herself when the sound of a car being driven up the gravel drive to the house distracted her.

She looked up, and her heart sank. It was Jane, her elder and only sister. She always managed to turn up at the most inconvenient moment, and never phoned first.

Louise finished the sentence, hit the full stop key abruptly and ended up with a whole line of dots.

'Hi,' said Jane breezing into the garden. 'I was passing, and thought I'd pop in.' She stood at the gate on the other side of the lawn for a moment, then advanced purposefully. 'You know,' she said breathily, Jane always spoke breathily, as if she were about to make some very exciting, momentous announcement, 'I can't understand why someone hasn't snapped you up, Louise. You look so attractive sitting there with your blonde hair up, have you dyed it again? And in that skimpy top and shorts. Of course, I'd never dare wear shorts; I'm not the right age.' She paused for breath and Louise knew what she really meant was, *what on earth are you doing wearing shorts at your age* – Jane was very good at back-handed compliments. She, of course, Louise noted, was looking immaculate as usual in an oatmeal coloured linen dress and jacket, and a pair of elegant sandals that looked, and probably had, cost a fortune. Geoffrey, Jane's husband made a lot of money and always made sure Jane looked the way he thought a wife of his ought to look, hence the expensive outfits. Louise was never quite sure how he made his money, and she knew Jane had absolutely no idea; she didn't bother to think about things like that. Now, she stood in front of Louise and said – her voice dropping to a sympathetic note – 'it isn't right that you should be on your own.'

'I'm quite happy on my own, and I don't want to be snapped up. But thanks for the compliment anyway.' Louise shut her laptop, and got up; there was no point in trying to finish anything now. 'I'm going to print off what I've done. I'm running late with this book.' She crossed the lawn towards the room next door to the kitchen, which served as her office. If she was very firm, Jane might take the hint and leave.

It was a vain hope.

'Oh, don't mind me,' said Jane airily, determinedly not taking the hint. 'I'll amuse myself while you do that. Oh, and by the way I've bought some fresh pasta for lunch. I thought you could whip up one of your marvellous sauces and we could have a leisurely lunch together.'

Jane was one of those women whose kitchen could have been used as an advert for a *Home and Country* magazine; it was a gleaming homage to the god of gourmet cooking. However, very little cooking of any type happened there. Jane hated toiling over a hot stove. She preferred working in her state of the art shed in the garden making her lavender and calendula soaps, which even Louise admitted were gorgeous. However, she had a good appetite and was not averse to eating other people's cooking, especially Louise's.

Later, as Louise was rather grudgingly whipping up one of her marvellous sauces, listening with half an ear to Jane wittering on about Geoffrey, she wondered why she always did the hard bit. The chopping of the onions, tomatoes and basil, grating the cheese etc., while Jane did the easy part, waltzing into the supermarket and picking up a packet of fresh pasta from the shelf, presenting it when she arrived, with a flourish that suggested she had personally laboured long and hard and made it herself by hand.

Once the ingredients were sizzling in the pan, Louise concentrated on what Jane was saying. 'I meant it when I said you should be snapped up,' said Jane, gazing at Louise. 'Your hair looks so lovely, as if you've just washed it.'

'I have,' said Louise, wanting to add *and yours would look better if you washed it more often*. But she didn't, knowing it would be a waste of time. Jane was one of those women who went once a week to the hairdresser and had her hair washed and set, the result was that most of the time it looked lank and unhealthy.

Jane ran her fingers through her drab locks. 'I know mine looks awful,' she said. 'Geoffrey said so this morning. I think he prefers Sharon's hairdo. You know, bouffey.'

'Bouffant,' corrected Louise.

Sharon was the blonde barmaid at the Ring of Bells. She had a forty-two inch bust, was a D cup, always wore low cut tops, and had a reputation to match her appearance.

Louise grinned at the thought. 'I doubt that Geoffrey's eyes ever reach her hairdo. Most of the men around here get stuck at bust level. As for my hair, none of them are likely to look at me. I don't stand out from the crowd like Sharon, and I meant it when I said I don't want to be snapped up, as you put it. I'm quite happy living on my own. It's been twenty years since John died. I've got used to it. I like pleasing myself, and I certainly don't need a man.'

'Of course you do,' said Jane, running her finger along the spatula and tasting the sauce. 'Every woman needs a man, especially someone as young as you. You're only forty-four, and even Geoffrey says you're quite attractive.'

'Only quite?' Louise raised her eyebrows. She'd never liked Geoffrey, and to her 'quite' sounded like an insult.

'And you're such a good cook,' added Jane hastily. 'Geoffrey says that as well. It's a pity though that John lost all that money in Australia, because you'd be better off than you are now if he hadn't. Geoffrey always said there was something fishy about that mining deal John put his money into. Of course I know Geoffrey put money in as well. He took a risk too, because he knew the man who was leading the project.'

'Yes, but Geoffrey got his money out in time didn't he, without mentioning anything to John,' Louise said sharply. It was something that had always rankled. John had come back from Australia a broken, penniless man, whereas Geoffrey had actually made on the deal before the whole thing went belly-up. Louise had never understood why, and Geoffrey had always refused to talk about it. The only good thing to come out of the whole affair was that after John's sudden death, Louise started receiving a small monthly allowance from Hinks and Hillier who were acting as Administrators for the firm's assets in Australia. Apparently John had set up some kind of insurance policy before the firm crashed. The money came, and it was Louise's lifesaver, enabling her to continue living in Lavender House. She got by on that, and the little money she made from writing, which was just as well as she wasn't qualified to do anything else. She could have sold the house, which would have broken her heart, and anyway where else could she live with the cats and dogs she'd acquired over the years. No, she got by, and that was sufficient for her. Lavender House was her haven.

'I'm sure Geoffrey didn't know that firm was going to go under. He would have warned John if he had,' Jane said in a halting voice, which didn't ring true, and Louise knew she felt guilty too.

'Well, that's water under the bridge, no point in thinking about that now. Wine?' she asked briskly.

She fished out half a bottle of Chianti from between two spider plants and the half dozen African violets on the windowsill. There were far too many and she hated them all. They collected dust and needed constant attention. Aggie Smethurst, the old lady down the lane, propagated them at the rate of knots and then dispersed them to the church fete, friends, and neighbours including Louise who never had the heart to tell her she didn't like them. Besides, Aggie made the most melt-in-the-mouth scones which she often presented to Louise along with the violets.

'Of course, darling.' Jane took the glass Louise proffered and continued with her theme of Louise and a man. 'Geoffrey and I were only saying the other day, that if you'd come up to the golf club you could meet some of the men there. Quite a few of them are divorced and looking for new partners.'

'Forget it,' Louise, took a fortifying gulp of wine. 'Golfers are boring.'

'Geoffrey's a golfer,' said Jane.

'Exactly.' Jane bristled, and Louise hastily added, 'but he's your husband, and therefore out of the equation as he's not divorced. Unless,' she took another sip of wine and looked at Jane, 'you are thinking of getting rid of him.'

Jane looked shocked, and Louise grinned, it was so easy to shock Jane. 'Of course not,' she said in horror struck tones. 'How would I manage financially without Geoffrey?'

True, thought Louise. Geoffrey provided the money and Jane spent it. Although he kept her on a pretty tight rein where housekeeping was concerned, which Louise always thought rather odd, as he never seemed to mind what she spent on clothes.

'Anyway,' Louise said, vigorously stirring the tomato sauce, 'I don't want someone else's cast-off. Men are usually divorced for a very good reason.'

'I think you're being very old fashioned. Shall I put the pasta on now?' Jane's hand was poised over the pan of boiling water with the box of fresh pasta at the ready.

'Yes.' Louise changed the subject. 'By the way, I'm trying to persuade Penny to come down for a few days with her two little ones.'

'Good idea.' Jane concentrated on dropping the pasta in piece by piece. 'Shall I use all of it?'

'Might as well. I'm not on a diet.'

Jane threw in the rest. 'That'll be company for you,' she said, adding, 'by the way, is Sam potty trained yet?'

Sam was Louise's eldest grandson; he was just coming up to four.

'Not yet.'

'Oh, Wendy's little Leon has been for ages. Of course he's very forward for his age. One can't expect all children to be like that.'

Resisting the urge to hit her with the wooden spoon, Louise gritted her teeth and said, 'no, one can't.'

Leon, Jane's only grandson, could write his name, go to the toilet on his own, and always kept his clothes immaculate. All of which Louise thought most unnatural. But she knew the heavy sarcasm of her tone of voice would go right over Jane's head. She was not one to pick up subtle nuances. Besides she thought Leon the most wonderful child in the world, which Louise had to admit, was natural for most grandmothers.

In the large London house she shared with her partner, David, and the two children, Penny sighed and mopped up after Sam yet again, changing his pants and trousers and longing for the day when he'd tell her in advance when he wanted to wee. Why was it she did nothing but clear up after people? The kitchen was a mess; David had made breakfast for her and the children, as a special treat, but hadn't cleared up. She felt suicidal. What was the point of a treat if it meant two hours of hard work to clear up the debris? And now Sam had made a mess. She loved him dearly; at least she thought she did, although sometimes she felt like strangling him. Mothers weren't supposed to feel like that, not according to the books she'd read, although she suspected they were all written by 'experts' who'd never had any children. But Sam did seem to take a perverse pleasure in outsmarting her where poo and pee was concerned. When he was in pants he wet himself, and when he was in nappies he behaved perfectly normally and asked to use the toilet or potty.

'Never mind, darling,' she said now, forcing a benevolent smile in his direction, 'everyone has accidents sometimes.'

'Does Nanna have accidents?' asked Sam, standing

legs wide apart while he waited to be cleaned up and changed for the second time that morning.

'Probably.' Her mother would kill her if she said that in front of anyone. She grinned at the thought. 'You'll have to ask her when you see her next time.'

'I want to ask her now,' said Sam, bottom lip jutting: always an ominous sign.

'OK we'll give her a ring.' Penny felt like having a long chat with someone. She needed to moan about David, and never dared do it to her girlfriends, all of whom claimed to have perfect lives, until they suddenly separated or divorced. Her mother was a good listener, and lived, what Penny often thought, was an idyllic life. She was all alone in a big house with a lovely garden, doing what she liked when she liked, because she never had to please anyone but herself.

'Now,' said Sam loudly. 'I want to speak to her now.'

'Just as soon as I've fed Jacob.' Penny picked up 9-month-old Jacob who was screaming with hunger. The moment he was in her arms he began tearing at the buttons on her blouse to get at her nipple. Penny knew she really ought to think about starting to wean him on to solids, but the breast was so easy, and always shut him up.

With the baby firmly attached to her breast, and Sam snuggled in beside her on the sofa, Penny clicked on her mother's number.

'Hello,' her mother sounded far away, and preoccupied, and she could hear the clatter of pots and pans.

'Mum. It's me.'

'Yes, dear, I know. I can't talk for long, I've got Jane here.'

'Oh God, is it lunch time already?' Penny knew Jane's habits of turning up at mealtimes. Penny never wore a watch and lived her life by what time she thought it might be, which very rarely tallied with the time it actually was. This, as Louise had pointed out on numerous occasions, would have been all very well if she lived in a cave and her husband was a hunter gatherer, but was very inconvenient in London where trains, shops and everyone else lived their lives according to Greenwich Mean Time. 'I suppose you haven't time at the moment to have a good gossip,' continued Penny on a slightly mournful note, wishing she too was sitting with just one other person at a kitchen table, a bottle of wine between them.

'No, not really, darling, and when Jane goes, I must get down to finishing my book. I'm nearly there, and my editor is making noises, which are not encouraging. She says they have to cut back on titles, which probably means they are thinking of getting rid of me because I haven't got a signed contract. And as for Dottie, well you know Dottie, she's hassling me because she's short of money as usual and wants to sell my book to someone, anyone.'

'I need a break,' Penny rushed on hardly listening to her mother. Like everyone else in the family she thought her mother's writing was a nice little hobby, nothing important. 'Is it all right if I come down the day after tomorrow and stay for a bit longer than I usually do?'

'Is that OK with David?' Louise always thought David was a tad possessive, although she never voiced her thoughts out loud.

'What bloody difference does it make to David? We're not married. I can do as I like.'

Louise opened her mouth about to say that perhaps that was not the right attitude then closed it.

'Well, darling,' she said, doing a quick mental calculation; if she stayed up most of tonight, and worked all day tomorrow, she might get the book finished and be able to send it off to Dottie. 'Of course, you can come. You know I love having you. I'll expect you and the children on Thursday. Perhaps we can take them to the Dairy Farm while you're here, Sam always likes that.'

'Great,' Penny breathed a sigh of relief. She just longed to get away from the grime of London, and David. Sam nudged her and whispered, and she remembered her promise. 'Sam wants to ask you something. I'll pass the phone to him.'

Louise waited then heard Sam's small voice echoing down the line. 'Nanna,' he said.

'Yes, my darling.' Louise adored Sam. Jacob was as yet an unknown quantity. He slept, smiled, wailed when hungry as all babies did, but hadn't developed a real personality. 'What do you want to tell me?'

'I don't want to tell. I want to ask,' replied Sam, who could be quite pedantic when it suited him.

'Yes?' said Louise and waited.

'Do you sometimes have accidents?' Sam stumbled over the long word.

Louise was surprised. She immediately thought of car accidents, or dropping cups and smashing them. 'Well, I ...' she began, then said, 'what sort of accidents?'

'Wet ones.'

'Oh,' Louise guessed there had just been one such accident. 'Well, sometimes. Everyone does sometimes. We just have to be careful, darling. But it's nothing to worry about.'

'Oh,' there was a long silence, and then a quavering voice said, 'I've had two this morning.'

Louise's heart went out to him. She knew Penny was struggling with a new baby, while Sam was still in babyhood himself. 'Never mind, darling,' she said, 'you and Mummy and Jacob are coming to stay with me the day after tomorrow. We'll go to the farm one day, and you can give milk to the calves. How would you like that?'

'I like it.' Sam passed the phone back to his mother.

'He'll like what?' asked Penny.

'A visit to the farm.'

'Oh that. Well, but I don't know whether I can manage both of them, this double buggy is so hard to push.' Penny sounded very tired and bad tempered.

'I can take Sam on his own,' said Louise, 'and you can stay in the garden and have a rest.' It was no use telling her daughter that small children only stayed small for a very short time, and when they were grown up you looked back on those innocent days with regret that you hadn't treasured them more. Penny would only flare back at her and say that she didn't know what it was like now and that life was different. To be truthful Louise found it difficult to remember exactly what it had been like. The years had flown by; full of laughter, tears and various crises and now she was alone living a peaceful life. Well, peaceful most of the time, it certainly wouldn't be when Penny arrived.

There was a loud wail from the other end of the line and Penny said quickly, 'I've got to go, Mum. See you on Thursday about lunchtime. I'll drive down in the morning.'

Louise returned to Jane and the pasta feeling slightly uneasy. She did worry about Penny, despite the fact that she seemed settled and happy most of the time. But lately she thought she'd changed; the girl who'd always been so positive and full of life, seemed to have had the stuffing knocked out of her by two babies in quick succession.

She could imagine the scene in the house now. Toys littered everywhere, dirty cups and plates piled in the sink. David was loving and kind, he worked hard at his computer business; Louise was never quite sure exactly what it was that he did, only that apparently he was an IT wizard, and he seemed to make enough money for them to live on. The downside was he was totally undomesticated. He still lived like a student, playing loud music, getting absorbed in a book, never picking up a sock or cup, just leaving them where he'd put them down, asking friends round without telling Penny, which made Louise seethe with annoyance. She could see that her daughter was battling to look after two small children and keep some sort of semblance of order in the house. She would have liked to have told David to help a bit more, but kept quiet. She'd had an interfering mother, and didn't want to turn into one herself.

'Problems with Penny?' asked Jane. She'd set the table in the kitchen ready for lunch, and put the bottle of Chianti in the middle of the table. Louise's heart sank. Jane was obviously hoping for a long gossipy session.

'Not really.' Louise didn't want to admit that all was not perfect with Penny's life. 'She's coming down earlier than planned, on Thursday, which means I've got to get on with my book. So don't give me any more wine, Jane, I'll have to work this afternoon and this evening, and too much wine befuddles my brain.'

Jane looked disappointed, as Louise knew she would. 'Geoffrey's gone up to London again,' she said. 'He didn't tell me what for. He never tells me anything. So I'm on my own again.'

Louise felt a stab of irritation and wanted to say I'm on my own most of the time, but didn't. Married friends never thought of what it was like to be alone, until they were widowed or divorced.

'Well, I expect you've got plenty to do,' she said briskly.

'I know I have. What's Wendy doing? You could go and help her with Leon. He must be a handful sometimes.'

'He's never a handful,' said Jane. 'He's at nursery every day while Wendy works. She's been promoted to Practice Manager at the surgery so often has to stay late. When Leon comes home he's so tired he goes straight to bed. He hardly sees Wendy, and as for his father, sometimes I wonder if he knows who he is. As a politician he's never at home, or very rarely. He's either in London, Brussels or at some other meeting. Since he became an MEP the two of them don't have much of a home life.'

'That's nice,' said Louise vaguely, who wasn't listening but thinking about the next, and hopefully, final, chapter of her book.

'It's not nice,' said Jane fiercely. 'I never see Leon. He's my only grandchild and I never see him.' Then she promptly burst into noisy, hiccupping tears. 'And I never see Geoffrey either. If he's not in London or abroad, he's always playing golf or down at the pub because he says the cooking there is better than mine. How can a microwaved steak and kidney pie be better than my cooking? I ask you.'

Not difficult, thought Louise, who knew her sister's culinary prowess. It was then that she realized that beneath her expensive outfit and pearls, Jane was deeply unhappy with her lot.

With a sigh she drained the pasta and poured herself another glass of wine. The final chapter was never going to get written this afternoon. She couldn't leave Jane in tears. She wasn't quite sure what she could do, but knew it would involve more than one glass of wine.

The wine bottle was empty, and Jane was still talking. Distraught she might have been, but she nevertheless managed to eat two plates of pasta, drink several glasses of wine as well as talk non-stop. But now she had ground to a halt. Well, very nearly. Her final words were, 'well, what do you think I should do? Shall I challenge Geoffrey and ask him if he's having an affair? Shall I confront Wendy and demand to have my share of Leon, and also tell her that I don't always think her husband is in London or Brussels, but that he is having an affair as well?'

'You do seem to be a little paranoid about affairs, without much evidence other than your suspicions,' observed Louise. She looked at Jane's blotchy red face; tears were never becoming. As sisters they'd never been very close emotionally. Jane was the successful one, married well, or so they all thought at the time. She was chairwoman of practically every association in the district, and had, up until now, always kept a very stiff British upper lip. Louise had been the impetuous volatile one, and thought Jane's life dull. She thought now for a moment, and then said, 'Personally, I think unless you have proof about affairs, the least said soonest mended. Let's deal with Leon first. As grandparents we don't really have any rights to share, as you put it, but you can invite Leon to stay in the holidays instead of being packed off to nursery and child-minders. Point out to Wendy that she'd be saving money, and that you'd love to have him to get to know him better. You might find Wendy is quite pleased with an arrangement like that. But I certainly wouldn't advise interfering in her marriage, that's for her to sort out.'

Jane sniffed and wiped her eyes. 'Yes, I'll try that. But what shall I do about Geoffrey's affair? What would you have done if it had been John?'

Louise tried to imagine John having an affair, but

couldn't. 'Do you think fidelity is essential in a marriage?' she asked.

'Oh yes, definitely,' Jane replied without a moment's hesitation.

Knowing she was being devil's advocate Louise said, 'Then if you have proof that he's shagging someone else, you must divorce him.'

Jane shuddered gently. 'I can't bear that word, shag. It's so … so.'

'Descriptive?' suggested Louise wickedly.

'Unladylike,' said Jane, a prim note creeping into her voice.

'There's nothing ladylike about sex,' said Louise. 'Not unless you're one of those women who lay back, study the damp patch on the ceiling, and think of England.'

'We haven't got a damp patch,' said Jane.

'Ah, that proves you've been looking at the ceiling,' teased Louise. 'Maybe that's your trouble. Perhaps Geoffrey has got a little bit bored. He's just the age for a mid-life crisis. Perhaps you should go out and buy some really sexy underwear at the Ann Summers shop, then surprise him one night by wearing it.'

'I couldn't.' Jane shuddered. 'I'm not the type. You could, I can imagine you in a pair of crotchless knickers.' There was a note of envy in her voice. 'But not me.'

'Then it's divorce,' said Louise firmly, rather wickedly enjoying the expression on Jane's face, and ignoring the remark about the knickers. 'Get the proof, and then divorce him. Of course, you'd have to move, as the house would be divided, and you'd probably need to go out to work until you reached retirement age, which I believe has just gone up to sixty-seven for women.' She knew perfectly well that Jane would never consider such a thing.

'You haven't had to give up your house.' Jane waved

around at the large comfortable kitchen petulantly. 'And you've got seven bedrooms, which you don't need, and a huge garden with a cottage in it, which you don't even use.'

'Ah, but I wasn't divorced. And anyway this house was always mine. John didn't leave me much money, but I can manage. So I shall never need to give it up.'

Jane picked up the bottle to pour another glass of wine but stopped when she saw it was empty, and banged the bottle back down on the table. 'Oh, all right. I'll go home. But I'm not getting divorced, even if he is sleeping with that barmaid, Sharon Murphy. Those boobs of hers cannot be real; she must have had them done. At least everything I've got is natural.' She picked up her handbag and car keys with an exaggerated flourish. 'And I want to keep the house.'

'And Geoffrey?' asked Louise

'I suppose so.' Jane didn't sound so convinced about that. She lurched to her feet waving her car keys. 'I'm going home.'

'In a taxi,' said Louise, taking the car keys away from her, and picking up the phone. 'You are in no fit state to drive. You can get Geoffrey to bring you back tomorrow and pick the car up, or walk here if he's not back.'

'But what shall I say? I can't tell him I've had too much to drink.'

'I don't see why not. There's no crime in that. But tell him you had a migraine and had to leave suddenly to go to bed, if you must.' Louise made Jane sit down on the bench outside in the garden to get some fresh air while they waited for the taxi. 'Of course,' she continued, as they sat side by side surrounded by an army of bees buzzing busily in the lavender, 'I think you're quite mad. Geoffrey just isn't the type to go lusting after women.

Money and golf are his passion, not women.'

'Any man is the type,' muttered Jane. 'I'm always reading articles about it in my magazines. I've got to do something to get him interested in me as a woman again. I've just read an article which says: *Seduce your husband on the stairs.*'

'Bloody uncomfortable I should think, not to mention you'd need frequent visits to the chiropractor afterwards. For God's sake stop reading those rubbishy magazines and read a decent book for a change.' Louise felt irritated.

Luckily Jimmie Garnier the local taxi driver arrived that moment. 'What's the problem?' he asked. 'Car broken down?'

'No, a severe migraine,' lied Louise. 'She's in no fit state to drive.'

By now Jane certainly did look as if she were suffering from migraine, she was pale and slumped sideways on the bench. Louise was hoping that Jimmie wouldn't notice the strong smell of alcohol, but if he did, he was too polite to mention it, and solicitously helped Jane into the back seat.

As the taxi was turning to drive out, Jane suddenly opened the back window and stuck her head out. 'Will you come with me to buy some sexy knickers?' She shouted. 'I believe they do crotchless ones.'

Jimmie swerved violently, nearly mowing down the lavender hedge at the side of the drive. Louise grinned. She doubted crotchless knickers were a common item of underwear in East Willow.

'Certainly not,' she shouted back. 'I've got my reputation to think of.'

What the hell was wrong with Jane? Obsessed with affairs and sex, was this what a mid-life crisis was like?

CHAPTER
❧ TWO ❧

Louise worked through that night until 2 a.m. the next morning. Then she had a very late, luxuriously scented, hot bath to relax, and firmly banished residual twinges of guilt for not being more sympathetic to Jane about Geoffrey. But for the life of her she just couldn't imagine Geoffrey having an affair. Although she'd never liked him, he was such a solid man, in more than one sense of the word, she'd always thought he and Jane were well suited because they were both devoid of any sense of adventure or humour. No! Geoffrey having an affair was definitely not possible. Jane's imagination was working overtime. Moreover as for Wendy, she hardly knew her niece. She had always been a quiet little thing, and Louise had only met Dennis, her husband, at the wedding and later on, the night he'd been elected as an MEP. Louise thought him pompous, but that was Wendy's problem, not hers.

Dispensing with family matters, she concentrated her mind on the rest of the book, so by the time she climbed out of the bath, found an ancient, but clean, nightdress in the airing cupboard (all her nightdresses were ancient as it seemed a waste of money to buy new ones because no one ever saw them) and padded across the landing and fell into bed, the book was very nearly finished in her head. She always felt relieved when she knew for certain where she was going. Not for her the tightly written synopsis, with every stop along the way planned, although when she occasionally taught at creative writing courses she always told her students to do that. Settling down cosily in bed, pulling the nightdress down about her knees she tore it, right across one shoulder, but couldn't be bothered to get out of bed and find another one.

If the book sells well, maybe I'll treat myself to some new ones, she thought sleepily. Thank goodness she'd get it on paper tomorrow before Penny and the children arrived. Her heroine's life had been sorted out, not happily, but realistically which was what she'd wanted. She was glad she wasn't the actual heroine, but that was what books were for, manipulating other people's lives on paper. Your own life, she reflected, could very rarely be manipulated; it usually just happened.

The high pitched whine of the milk float followed by a clatter of milk bottles woke her, reminding her that it was seven o'clock. It was Daniel delivering the milk. He was nothing like the Daniel in her novel. Milkman Daniel had one front tooth missing, and the rest were heavily stained with nicotine, he wore a milkman's cap, which had definitely seen better days, on the back of his head, and his shirt and jeans always looked as if they could do with a good wash, or a 'boil' as Louise's mother would have said. However, no one complained, as he was the last of a dying breed, delivering milk to every house in the village and to all the outlying farms and cottages in the district. It was only the newcomers, the people with holiday cottages, who didn't use him, preferring to bring with them their organic milk in cartons, and Italian food from trendy little delicatessens in central London. When they stayed for longer in the summer or at Christmas, they drove twenty miles to the nearest supermarket in Salisbury.

Louise sat up in bed at the same moment as Tabitha climbed in through the open window with a wriggling mouse in her mouth. Despite her great age, Tabitha was an inveterate mouser. She jumped on the bed, the mouse still in her mouth, Louise screamed, Tabitha dropped the mouse, which promptly shot off the bed and scampered across the scrubbed pine floor, disappearing down a hole in the wainscot. The dogs, hearing the noise, thundered up the stairs from the kitchen to join in the fun.

'You all right, up there, Mrs Gregory?' Daniel shouted.

Louise poked her head out of the window, then remembering the torn nightdress, covered one boob with a handful of bunched up material. 'Yes thanks, Daniel. The damned cat just brought a live mouse in, and it surprised me a bit.' Aware that his eyes were firmly fixed on her bosom, quite a lot of which was still showing, Louise hitched the nightdress material higher. Maybe it *was* time to buy some new ones.

Daniel threw back his head and cackled. Not a pretty sight, thought Louise, wondering if his wife ever kissed him. 'That cat should be getting rid of the mice in the house,' he observed, 'not adding to them.' He looked pointedly at Louise's bare shoulders, and grinned, 'and there was I thinking to myself that you'd got a man up there.'

'Of course not.' Louise backed away from the window.

'Pity,' said Daniel. 'Would have given me something to gossip about.' He deposited a single milk bottle inside the front porch, and crunched a three-point turn in the gravel before humming his way down towards the lane.

Louise leaned out of the window again. 'I'll need at least four bottles tomorrow,' she shouted. 'Penny and the children are coming to stay.' She assumed Daniel had heard, as a weather-beaten hand waved back her as he drove out of the gateway.

Tabitha took up residence by the wainscot, her nose glued to the hole. The dogs sat close behind her.

'This bedroom is far too crowded,' said Louise, fondly pulling the dogs' ears, before making her way down to collect the milk and make herself a coffee. If the chapter was to be typed and the manuscript sent off this morning, she'd need a good dose of stimulating caffeine to get going.

Getting out her ancient sit up and beg bicycle, Louise shoved the finished manuscript, which she'd carefully sealed in a re-used jiffy bag, and put it in the basket at the front, before wobbling off down the drive and out into the lane. She was not the world's best cyclist, but had started cycling again for two reasons: one was to save money, and the other was to try and keep her figure. Jane had gloomily informed her that according to the women's magazines she read avidly, cycling made your bottom get bigger, and men didn't like big bums. But unlike Jane, Louise didn't believe what the magazines said, and anyway she knew her rear end was quite trim. Unlike Jane's; now she really *could* do with some extra exercise.

'I don't have a man to please,' she'd told Jane. 'I just want to keep fit, and cycling is cheaper than going to the gym.'

Arriving outside the post office, she leaned the bike against the wall, never having quite got the knack of balancing it on the kerb with the pedal, and puffed her way in to join the queue. They'd recently erected steel railings in the post office, which forced customers to queue in a grid like fashion. It reminded Louise of the cattle market which used to be held once a month in East Willow. She felt the customers should all have tags in their ears and have their numbers and breed shouted out when they reached the front. She could just imagine she'd be announced as 'Lot No. 10, a barren cow, good condition for age.'

'What's this then, Louise?' said Mrs Bernard, the village postmistress, when she eventually arrived at the counter. 'A new book? I thought it was about time you should be posting off another one. I only said so the other day to Mrs Perkins, you know how she likes your books, always borrows them from the library.'

Yes, and I wish she'd buy the wretched things, thought Louise. Borrowing books was all very well, but didn't do the author a lot of good from the financial point of view. Buying them was much better, but it was no good explaining that, so she managed a smile for Mrs Bernard's benefit, and hoped she wouldn't ask too many questions. She hated taking her manuscripts to the post office, but couldn't send the whole thing by email, as Dottie, her agent, was not in the twenty-first century yet, and Louise doubted whether she ever would be. So it still had to be sealed into a jiffy bag and posted.

'Yes,' she said, answering Mrs Bernard, and keeping her voice down. The trouble was that everyone in the village thought she was filthy rich, but eccentric, because she never spent any money. They assumed all authors must be millionaires. It was no use how many times she told the local writers' circle that this was not the case, they never believed her. They had no idea of her apprehension that anything she wrote could come winging its way back, rejected. People could never understand that. At the moment that was Louise's main fear, as she was out of contract and Dottie hadn't secured a new one before the book was finished.

She'd been up to Dottie's London office to discuss her options. 'Don't worry, darling,' Dottie had said, through the haze of cigarette smoke which always surrounded her, and moving aside a mountain of paper so that Louise could sit down. Other people's manuscripts Louise thought gloomily, surveying the muddled pile. Dottie waved her cigarette, scattering ash in all directions. 'I'll get you a better contract, if you write a better book. You've got to write something different, something that grabs editors by the throat. A breakthrough book.'

Louise had drawn a deep breath at this point and gritted her teeth. The only throat she felt like grabbing at that particular moment was Dottie's, but she kept smiling. How many times had she heard that phrase and Dottie followed it up with the inevitable punch line, 'Editors are always looking for something different, and they don't know what they want until they see it.'

This, of course, was true. They'd had this conversation many times before. Louise knew she had been stuck in the mould of happy endings, with not much explicit sex. Her earlier books had been sexy, but she'd run out of different ways to describe sexual intercourse, although this book was different. It had sex, but it was different, and she thought it would probably surprise Dottie. She mentally crossed her fingers as Mrs Bernard stuck the strip of paper, which passed as stamps, across the parcel, and wrote out the proof of posting slip.

'What's it about?' Mrs Bernard asked pushing the receipt beneath the glass grill.

'A woman,' said Louise. 'Her life, her lovers and her losses.'

'Not too serious I hope. Now, what I like is a really good romance, with plenty of sex. Of course, my husband always reads your books, so you have to be careful; he was quite shocked at the bad language in your last one. He said to me, "you wouldn't think a respectable woman like Mrs Gregory would know those words."'

'I'm sorry about that. Hope he approves of this one if he reads it.' Louise made her escape, and dashed across the road to the butchers. She made it just in time before he closed. 'Half a kilo of best minced steak,' she said. 'I'm making a cottage pie tomorrow, the grandchildren are coming down.'

'One pound of mince coming up,' said Mr Jones, who firmly resisted entering the metric age, even though his scales had been changed. 'Anything else?'

Louise got some of his homemade pork sausages, then changed her mind and added another pound to the mince, and some green back bacon. 'That'll be all.' She fished in her purse hoping she had enough money; Mr Jones didn't believe in cards either and only took cash.

'Just the children coming?'

'Good heavens, no, I couldn't manage them all on my own. My daughter's coming as well.'

Mr Jones beamed. 'Ah, I remember her. Penny isn't it. Pretty little thing she was; always skipping and laughing. Why does she have to live in London? Nasty noisy place.'

Louise smiled. No point in arguing with him, Mr Jones's ideas were set in stone. 'Perhaps you're right,' she said. But her mind sped back to the time when Penny *was* a small blonde girl racing around the garden. Always skipping and laughing, yes, that was how she had been.

'Penny is now a harassed housewife, coping in a house on three levels with two small boys,' she told Mr Jones. She knew mothers shouldn't regret their children growing up, but if she were honest she had to admit that sometimes she did. But it was only sometimes, when she allowed herself to think too much.

Mr Jones parcelled up her purchases into a brown paper bag. That was another thing Louise liked about him. He didn't go on about being environmentally friendly, and she doubted he knew what a carbon footprint was, but he hated plastic, and always used white paper to wrap the meat in, before putting it in a brown paper bags.

Cycling back towards Lavender House, thinking about Penny and the children, and wondering whether she had enough potatoes in the sack in the outhouse to make a cottage pie, she didn't hear the car coming up behind her. The lane was narrow, and the driver of the large white sports car was going much too fast. As it whizzed past, she lost her balance, wobbled to a halt with one foot in the ditch, the shopping falling out of the rickety basket on the front of the bike. The driver, a man, screeched to a halt, and came rushing back, solicitously helping her out of the ditch, picking up her shopping and dusting her down.

'These lanes are too narrow for bicycles,' he said.

'Nonsense! They're too narrow for maniacs like you,' said Louise crossly and feeling at a distinct disadvantage because she could see a large streak of mud down her leg and wondered where else she might be muddy.

Once she was upright, she realized how tall he was, and large. He had the physique of a rugby player. Definitely not local, thought Louise, feeling even more cross that he should be driving so fast. He looked as if he were on holiday as he was wearing jeans and an open-necked shirt, and was tanned.

'Is there anything else I can do?' he asked, retrieving one packet of mince, which had fallen to the bottom of the ditch amongst the nettles. He handed it to Louise.

'You mean apart from running me over?' He opened his mouth to reply but Louise carried on, not letting him get in another word. 'Yes, there *is* something you can do. You can drive more slowly in future.'

Her snappy reply seemed to unsettle him, as he took a step backwards. 'Well, I'll be going then, if there's nothing broken. Sorry.'

'Yes,' said Louise, 'but please take more care in future. I could have been a child. They also ride bikes round here.' She watched him drive off. The sight of him climbing back into the car and driving off stirred up some long distant memory. Had she seen him before or was it her imagination? It worried Louise, she hated not being able to put names to faces, and she had the oddest feeling that she had met him before but he'd been dressed differently and it certainly hadn't been at Lavender House. Maybe he was one of Geoffrey and Jane's golfing friends, although he didn't look the type. She cycled home, feeling uneasy.

However, she forgot everything when she opened the kitchen door and saw the pile of post on the floor. Maybe there was a royalty cheque amongst the post, she did sometimes receive a nice little cheque from some foreign deal Dottie had done with one of her books. That always cheered her up. The postman put the post through the kitchen door, as it was the only door in the house with a letterbox. Once it had been someone else's front door, but had been retrieved by Louise from a skip in the next village when her original kitchen door had disintegrated with age.

There was no cheque from Dottie, the rest was junk except for one in an official looking envelope franked with a stamp she didn't recognize. Binning the junk mail, she looked at the interesting looking one, but before opening it, she put all the brown paper packages from the butcher in the fridge away from a crowd of very interested animals. They didn't get near that much meat very often! Sausages and mince safe, Louise sat down at the kitchen table and opened the envelope.

At first she thought it must be a mistake. But then she read it again. There wasn't a lot to read, and it wasn't a mistake. Definitely not. It consisted of just two pages, which told her, in stark, official language, that Hinks and Hillier had gone into liquidation, and there was no money left in the insurance fund. They regretted any inconvenience that this might cause, and should she have any queries these should be addressed to the Official Administrator, whose address and telephone number was given at the bottom of the letter.

No money. Nothing left in the fund. That meant no money coming in on a regular monthly basis. It was unbelievable. She had years and years to go before she was old enough for a proper pension from the state, which wouldn't be much anyway. Recently she'd relied more and more on that small amount of money every month from Hinks and Hillier because it enabled her to go on living in Lavender House. The income from her books hadn't been much lately; apparently she was not in vogue with the book buyers of Asda and Tesco who either went for absolute rubbish (in Louise's opinion) or highbrow literary stuff (also rubbish in Louise's opinion) recommended by TV book shows. Louise stopped thinking and just sat. The silence of the house overwhelmed her, and then, slowly, the awful realization struck her. She'd have to sell the house.

Tabitha, unaware of the crisis, climbed on to her

lap, rumbling happily, while the two dogs panted at her feet; the other three cats slid out through the open window into the garden as no food was forthcoming. None of them were worried. Outside she could hear the hum of insects, busy around the lavender bushes, and the chirruping of birds, even the house itself seemed to be breathing. She felt as if it were wrapping its ancient bricks and mortar around her, strong familiar arms, holding her. Then she burst into tears.

'I can't sell the house,' she muttered, and burying her head in her arms on the table, she let the tears stream down her cheeks, knowing it was stupid talking to herself, but there was no one else there one to talk to. 'I can't sell the house, I couldn't bear it,' she repeated.

'Then why should you?'

Startled, Louise looked up. There leaning in the open kitchen doorway was the man from the lane. The one who'd nearly knocked her off her bike.

'What do you want?' Louise searched for a handkerchief but not finding one wiped her eyes with the back of her hand. 'And who are you?'

'Panda eyes,' he said proffering a clean white handkerchief. 'Not becoming.'

Ignoring the handkerchief, Louise tore a piece from the kitchen roll on the windowsill. She knew her mascara had run and that panda eyes were not becoming, but didn't need to be reminded by a man who'd appeared from nowhere. 'What do you want?' she snapped. He was interrupting her misery and she resented it.

'Bed and Breakfast.'

'I don't do bed and breakfast.'

'I didn't mean you. I mean do you know of anywhere near here where I could stay the night, or several nights. I've driven all around and not found anywhere, and I need to stay in the district for a while. Business matters,' he added.

Louise finished mopping up the excess mascara. 'There's the Stag and Beetle in the village, the other pub, the Village Bells doesn't do B and B.'

He rolled his eyes heavenwards. 'The Stag and Beetle, what sort of a name is that? Is it a stag, is it a beetle, or is it a stag beetle?'

Against her will, Louise smiled at his expression. 'No,' she said, 'I'm afraid it is called the Stag and Beetle. It was called the Oak but it's been taken over by two young men from London who've got three pubs in the area all called the Stag and Beetle. I doubt that their natural history knowledge extends to the fact that there actually is a stag beetle in existence. Apparently they've refurbished it in reds and gold, and imitation oil lamps, and the food is quite good I've been told, if you like foie gras and oysters. Hardly any of the locals in East Willow use it; they prefer microwaved pie and chips at the Village Bells.'

'Good heavens, it all sounds ghastly. I was hoping for country food, stolid and comforting. Steak and kidney pudding with mashed potato, you know the sort of thing.'

'Sorry, that's all there is.' Louise wanted him to go. She needed to think about money, the future, the house, everything. She pointed down the drive. 'If you turn left at my gate and keep going until you reach the village, you can't miss it. It's right in the middle, opposite the duck pond. Well, it would be a duck pond if we had some rain, but at the moment it's a muddy hollow.'

'OK. I'll be off.'

She followed him to the door and watched him climb back into the sports car. He did a rapid three-point turn which churned up her gravel, started off down the drive, then stopped. 'You never did tell me. Why you've got to sell the house?'

For a moment Louise was tempted to say that it was none of his business, then common sense prevailed. Why pretend. She had to face facts. 'Because I need the money,' she said simply.

He didn't reply, in fact, he looked distinctly disinterested. And why should he care? It was her misfortune, not his. He was just a passing stranger looking for somewhere to stay. Perhaps she was being hypersensitive, but it seemed to Louise that he couldn't get away quickly enough as he drove out of the gate.

Once he'd gone, she looked at the letter again, before putting it carefully in the letter rack of things to do. She'd ring the number as soon as she'd prepared for Penny's visit. Maybe there was something she could claim from somewhere. John had put a lot of money into that insurance scheme. She'd been told that after his death, although he'd never mentioned it when he was alive, and she'd been touched that he'd put money aside for her, something she knew he could ill afford to do. She'd been assured after his death that the money was safe. So what had happened to it? Surely all that money couldn't just disappear?

Later on that day Louise rang the number, and talked to a young man at the Administrator's office. He sounded sympathetic, although, she thought, rather evasive. This wasn't the only scheme he was dealing with, he told her. She was just one of many, although her case had had a slightly different financial element to it. A lot of people in other schemes had also been affected, he'd told her, and there was nothing he could do. He doubted that she'd ever get another penny.

'Do you mean never, ever?' Louise asked.

'I'm afraid I do mean never,' he replied briefly. 'I'm very sorry, Mrs Gregory.'

He sounded genuinely sorry, and Louise found herself feeling sorry for him. It couldn't be a pleasant job always having to give bad news to people. 'Never mind,' she said, trying to sound cheerful. 'You know what they say, one door closes and another door opens. I'll have to get a job.' The question was, what kind of job?

She put down the phone, and as if on cue Penny stuck her head round the kitchen door.

'I'm here.'

The announcement was not really necessary as Sam came bursting in immediately afterwards like a miniature whirlwind.

'I'm starving, Nanny. Beans on toast, please,' he demanded.

'Sorry, Mum, but he really is hungry. I was,' Penny hesitated, and then repeated, 'I was a bit rushed this morning, so I just bunged him in the car, gave him a biscuit, and set off. You don't have to worry about Jacob, he's still on the breast, and I've brought some jars of baby food.'

'Good.' Louise was still thinking about the young man at the Administrator's office, imagining him sitting in the City. He would be sitting on a swivel chair in front of a blinking computer screen, surrounded by large pot plants, and looking out over the River Thames through enormous, tinted, plate glass windows. Her mood changed, and she felt bitter. He didn't care that she, and thousands like her, had suddenly been cut off without a penny. She was filled with rage at the injustice of it all. Standing by the kitchen window she glowered at a fat thrush skittering across the lawn, a snail impaled on his beak. Life is bloody unfair, she thought; the thrush had got his lunch, but her sympathies were all with the snail that had only moments to live.

'Beans, Mum,' Penny reminded her.

Louise remembered her hungry grandchild. 'Oh, yes.' She got down a tin of organic baked beans, Penny always insisted on everything organic, and fished in the drawer for a tin opener.

'You OK?' Penny sounded anxious.

'Of course.' She'd tell Penny later. Feed the children first, then they'd have some time to themselves.

'Bread,' demanded Sam loudly. 'Can I put it in the toaster? Mummy always lets me.'

'He'll need a chair to stand on to do it,' said Penny, sitting in the chair usually occupied by Tabitha, with Jacob firmly attached to one nipple.

Louise could see his little jaws working rhythmically, his eyes closed a blissful expression on his round baby face. She felt a stab of nostalgia. Once she'd been like that, with a small child, not terribly well off, but happy. Somehow not having much money hadn't seemed so bad then, and they'd always managed. But how on earth was she going to manage now? She'd only just scraped enough cash together to pay the council tax bill last year. Please God, let Dottie sell the manuscript, she prayed silently as she tipped beans into a saucepan.

'Mum.'

Louise suddenly noticed that her daughter didn't look her usual self. She was pale and thin. Haggard almost, Louise thought. 'Mum,' Penny repeated, 'I've got something awful to tell you.' She looked at her mother, and then at Sam. 'But perhaps I'd better wait until they've both been fed.'

They fed both children, and afterwards Sam played happily in the sandpit, which luckily Louise had just had refilled especially for a future visit, while Jacob rocked in his baby bouncer. Louise and Penny sat side-by-side drinking tea. All the time the something awful hung in the air between them; Louise could almost feel it like a blast of cold air rushing through the warm spring garden. She sneaked a sideways look at Penny, only to find that she was doing the same thing to her.

Their eyes met and Louise tried to smile in a comforting, motherly way, because that was what she felt she ought to be doing. But the thought of her bank balance, the bills that would soon be coming in, and the fact that there'd be no money going into her account at the beginning of the month made even Penny's problem, whatever it was, seem unimportant.

She took refuge in thinking about food. Something she always did in times of crisis. 'When we've got the children settled, I'll make an asparagus risotto for us, there's plenty popping up now in the old asparagus bed, the new bed won't be ready for another couple of weeks. And I've got half a bottle of Pinot Grigio in the fridge.'

'Half a bottle won't be enough,' replied Penny gloomily. 'I need more than that to drown my sorrows.' Then she turned and looked at her mother quizzically, 'and you, if I may say so, don't look exactly full of the joys of spring.'

'Old age,' joked Louise. She decided there and then she was not going to mention her own troubles. At least, not until she found out what Penny's problems were, so she merely said, 'I've just finished a book, and you know how twitchy I always get about that. Not one of my best, because I rushed it. But Dottie has been putting pressure on me, I think she's got a cash flow problem, and wants another contract, any contract, as soon as possible.'

'Dottie's always got a cash flow problem,' said Penny, who'd known Dottie for years. 'And what do you mean by any contract?'

'I'm out of contract with my regular publisher,' Louise said, 'so Dottie's going to have to work hard to get me a new deal. It's not easy these days. I'm not young with a high-powered column in *The Times* to boost my publicity, and Dottie says I'm a middle class woman, which seems to be almost a crime. At least it does in Dottie's eyes. She tells me that editors want young beautiful women, who know about life in the fast lane, sleep with the right people, and wear the latest fashion. Then they can do big financial deals, because they can be promoted.'

'I'm sure you're exaggerating,' said Penny. 'The books I read aren't about women like that, and anyway you are quite good looking.' Penny eyed her mother up and down. 'Those shorts and that T-shirt do absolutely nothing for you though.'

'Thanks for your vote of confidence,' said Louise wryly. 'However, I may tell you that Jane thought my outfit suited me, and that I should be snapped up by a man instead of enjoying widowhood.'

'Jane's mad. Always has been,' was Penny's opinion. 'I don't know how you can be related because you're so different. Why do you let her keep coming round?'

'Habit,' replied Louise. 'And she is my sister.'

'I want tea please,' Sam emerged from the sand pit clutching a plastic teapot. Louise duly obliged and poured some cool milky tea into the teapot, so that he could pour it into his cup himself. 'Jane thinks Geoffrey is having an affair,' she continued. 'Geoffrey of all people! He'd never know how to go about it, even if he had the energy, which he hasn't, because he's put on so much weight. The last time he came here he could hardly struggle up out of the armchair on account of his huge stomach.'

Instead of laughing as she thought she would, Penny merely looked more gloomy and bad-tempered than ever. 'I wouldn't put it past him. There's not a man in the world who can be trusted.'

'Including David?' asked Louise cautiously.

'Especially David,' said Penny. 'But I'm not talking about it now.' Her mouth closed in a tight line.

Finishing her tea, Louise stood up. 'I'll get some more wine up from below the stairs for this evening. You start persuading Sam that it's time for bath and bed.' From the look on Penny's face Louise decided that probably a glass or three would be needed during the evening, and crossed her fingers that she had some left in the cobwebby space below the stairs, which she called the cellar.

Cautiously venturing down between the cobwebs and resident spiders, who scuttled away alarmed at their quiet homes being disturbed, Louise found that there were three more bottles. Two red Chianti and one white Orvieto, left over from her last splurge on Italian wine. These will have to last, she thought; wine is now on the luxury list.

Clutching the bottles to her chest on her way back to the kitchen, she met Penny in the hall with Sam in tow and Jacob balanced on one hip. 'I'm just taking these two guys up for bath and bed,' said Penny eyeing the bottles. 'We'll start on those when I come down.'

'I'll come up and read Sam his story.' That was a task Louise loved. Reading about snails and whales and magical jungle creatures to a wide-eyed small boy. She felt like a fairy godmother able to create a magic world with words.

Once the boys were in bed, Louise started the risotto. It bubbled quietly on the stove, Louise getting up every now and then to give it a stir, and half the Pinot Grigio disappeared before the risotto was ready while Louise waited in silence for Penny to tell her what the awful problem was.

Penny sipped the wine and sat looking out of the window. 'It's lovely here,' she said at last. 'A perfect early summer's evening. There are long shadows on the grass, birds fluttering about collecting food for their young to keep them going through the night, bats swooping silently down on the midges. Not a sound except those sheep bleating in the field by the stream. Not like London. There it's impossible to escape the background sound of traffic, and there's always a police or ambulance siren blaring somewhere near, and then there are the diesel trains which hoot every time they race through on the line at the bottom of the garden.'

'Is it London that's the problem?' asked Louise. She added a little more wine to the risotto and kept stirring, dropping the last of her saffron into a cup to soak before adding it to the risotto. Real saffron will have to be taken off the shopping list, she thought mournfully, much too expensive.

'Yes, partly.' Penny swung round in her chair and faced her mother standing at the stove. 'That, and the fact that I've left David. I mean left for good. I think he's been two-timing me because he's always home late, and when he is home he drives me mad. He's untidy, inconsiderate, and useless. He can't even find a pair of socks without asking me. He wants me to wait on him hand and foot. And to cap it all, now he wants us to get married.'

'Wanting to get married is hardly the act of a man

who's two-timing you,' said Louise mildly. 'Anyway, you know I've always thought you should get married.'

Penny sniffed. 'I bet it's all to do with money and his business and tax concessions. Nothing to do with love.'

'And, of course, you've talked to him about this.' Knowing her daughter's impulsive nature, Louise doubted that this was the case.

There was a long silence. Louise continued stirring the risotto, carefully adding the asparagus and saffron.

'There's no point in talking to him,' said Penny confirming her suspicions. 'We always argue lately. He says I fly off the handle at the slightest thing.'

'Maybe you do sometimes.'

'Oh God, not you as well.'

Louise bit her tongue and wished she'd kept silent. Penny had always taken offence at the slightest thing, even as a small child. It was a habit she'd not lost. Now, she flounced across the kitchen, splashing herself another glass of wine, before turning back to Louise. 'Perhaps I'd better find somewhere else to live. Is there a women's refuge near here?'

Now it was Louise's turn to fly off the handle. 'For God's sake, don't be so melodramatic. David hasn't beaten you up has he?'

'No,' Penny mumbled.

'So you've come home to me. Does that mean you want to live here more or less permanently?'

'Well, yes … er … no.' Penny hesitated. 'Well, not permanently, not forever, but for the time being. I thought you wouldn't mind if I stayed here. You've got plenty of empty bedrooms.'

'How are you going to manage about money? Is David going to give you an allowance?'

'I won't accept a penny from him.' Penny flung herself

back down on a chair, spilling some of her wine. 'Not a penny,' she repeated.

Louise hardened her heart. She'd always bailed Penny out as a teenager and a student. But much as she would have liked to spoil her now, the stark truth was she couldn't afford to.

'I think you may have to accept financial assistance from David,' she said quietly. 'Much as I'd like to be able to, I can't afford to keep you and the two children. I haven't got the money.'

Penny sat up straight and stared in disbelief. 'What do you mean? Can't afford to. You're a writer. You earn money from your books. I see loads of them in the library. And, you've got Dad's insurance money every month.'

The Pinot Grigio finished, Louise took the bottle of Orvieto from the fridge, opened it, poured herself a large glass, drank some of it, then topping up her glass, she sat down opposite Penny.

'Now, I've got something awful to tell you,' she said. 'I'm virtually penniless. The insurance company paying out the monthly allowance has gone belly-up, there will be no more money from that source, and my books are not making much money.'

There was a long silence while Penny stared at her mother in horror.

In the distance there was the baaing sound from the sheep in the far field. It sounded as if they were laughing.

CHAPTER
❧ THREE ❧

DAVID MADE HIS way back to the house near Blackheath. Actually it was nearer Lewisham but David thought from the business point of view Blackheath sounded better, so he always gave the address as Blackheath near Lee. He'd had a late business lunch, which had lingered on until the evening because he'd forgotten the time, as he always did, when he was busy demonstrating the latest technology. He knew Penny said he must have another woman, but of course she was joking. She must know that the only things he was attached to besides her and the children were computers; they were voracious beasts gobbling up all his time. His web designing business was going well, most people were thrilled with the designs he did for them, and because they had no idea of how the Internet or, indeed anything else to do with computers worked, were pathetically grateful and usually paid whatever he asked. But the client he'd lunched with today, before demonstrating his skills that afternoon, had acquired a little knowledge, and was picky and difficult, and had very specific ideas on how his website should look and function, not all of them practicable. As soon as David put forward an idea, he wanted it modified, which meant using alternative software. David, normally a laid back person, at least that's what he prided himself on being, came back to the house he shared with Penny and the children, in anything but a laid back mood.

He felt bad tempered and moody, and all he wanted to do was to slouch in front of the TV with a glass of wine and then have something to eat. As usual, he'd hung around in the Irish bar near the station, with his friends after leaving his office, just long enough to put off having to help put the children to bed. He hated the chaos of nappies, water, plastic ducks and trying to dry small, slippery children, especially Sam whose idea of fun was to race around the house naked while he raced after him trying to put him in pyjamas. No, that was definitely Penny's job, because she'd had nothing to do all day. By 7.30, he reckoned they would be safely out of the way and finishing his drink swung around on the bar stool, shouted, 'I'm off,' and started to leave.

'Kids in bed now?' Brian, the barman gave a knowing wink, and flapped his hands expressively. 'Don't blame you, or any of the rest of them, for hanging on.' He nodded towards David's friends who were all finishing their drinks and picking up their laptops. 'Bath time is murder.'

David paused, and turned back. He felt unsettled. Was he that transparent? Anyway how did Brian know? He was gay. 'How do you know?'

'Ducky, I may be gay, but I'm living with my sister until I move, and she's got four kids. I can tell you I'm glad I work in the evenings. I love my nephews and nieces, but at a suitable distance. When I move to the country I shall feel even more affectionate just as long as they don't visit me too often.'

'Moving? You?' David leaned on the counter. Brian

had been a fixture at O'Hanlon's wine bar for as long as he could remember.

'Yes, moving from here, thank God. Down to a lovely little place called East Willow in Hampshire, I'm buying an old cottage with a friend. It's near to …'

'I know where it is. Penny's mother lives there. She's got a big house on the edge of the village, it's called Lavender House.'

Brian's jaw dropped. 'Oh,' he sighed. 'I know it. I've seen it from the road. It's a gorgeous house, must be worth a fortune. Wish we could afford something like that. We've bought this cottage, it's all we could afford, and needs some renovation, but it's got a big garage and we're going to run an internet antique business from there. We're both fed up with London, the noise, the crowds of people.'

David slid off the barstool. 'Small world,' he said. 'I might run into you down there when we're visiting.'

'Look us up on the internet,' Brian shouted after him as he left the wine bar. 'I'm off next week. We'll be trading under WillowAntiques.com.'

David took a detour and walked back along the side of the heath. It was crowded as it was a sunny spring evening. Brian was right, London was crowded, but that was how he liked it. He didn't particularly want to do anything exciting himself, but he felt he was part of the crowd, and liked hearing the voices of all the different nationalities as they swirled around him.

However, the road where he lived with Penny and the children was fairly quiet, except for the constant roar of traffic as cars took the short cut between Lewisham, Blackheath and Greenwich. The speed humps, which the council had put in, had actually increased the noise level as cars changed gear every time they crossed one.

When he got home, the first thing that struck him when he opened the front door was the silence. Normally there was some noise from upstairs. Sam and Jacob never settled quietly; one of them always roared in complaint at being put to bed. But tonight there was silence. Then he noticed the absence of any smell of cooking. Usually there was something in the oven spreading a warm smell throughout the house. David complained on numerous occasions that the only things Penny cooked were casseroles or pasta. Only to be told by Penny, that was all she had time for.

'Casseroles can be put in the oven and forgotten,' she'd snapped at him, 'and pasta can be organized and cooked in ten minutes if I use a sauce from a jar. All you've got to do is grate your own parmesan on top of it. So be thankful there's something hot on your plate.' She snapped a lot these days, David had noticed.

However, it seemed there was neither casserole nor pasta tonight if smell was anything to go by.

Hanging his jacket in the hall, on top of a mountain of other coats, he loped along the passageway leading to the kitchen. Theirs was a long, narrow London house, with the kitchen at the back, leading out into a miniscule garden.

There was no one in the kitchen. The coffee machine was still switched on, just as he'd left it that morning, which was strange as Penny always switched it off and cleaned it out ready for his next fix of coffee. The plate covered with his toast crumbs was still in the sink along with his coffee mug. Nothing had been touched. David began to feel uneasy. The place was like the Marie Celeste. What had happened to them all? Had they been kidnapped?

Then he saw the note. It was pinned with a large, bright yellow drawing pin to the middle of the kitchen table. It said:

David,
   I cannot go on living the way we are. I am leaving you and taking the children. I have gone to live with Mum in Hampshire for the time being. I will get in touch later about getting the rest of our stuff. Don't try and do anything. As we are not married, but are only partners, you have no legal rights over me, or the children. I don't want any money from you; in fact, I don't want anything more to do with you.
   Penny.

David read it three times, each time with growing disbelief. What have I done wrong, he wondered? What's she on about, 'can't go on living the way we are.' Everything is fine. He looked around the kitchen in bewilderment, hardly noticing the detritus of the family breakfast which lay all around him. It all looked perfectly normal to him. Seeing the remains of breakfast made him feel hungry. David had an enormous appetite, and not even the greatest tragedy in the world would have made a dent in it, and anyway, Penny and children leaving did not rate as the greatest tragedy in the world, merely a puzzling blip. He always prided himself on his logical mind; in his line of work, logic worked miracles. Logic, that was what he needed now, he reasoned. He would eat first, then telephone Penny, reassure her that nothing was wrong, and once he'd done that she'd see reason, then she'd come back and they'd go on as before. This was merely a slight error in the order of their lives, like an irritating fault on a computer, which disappeared once you'd clicked on the right box. He'd fix it later.

However, fixing something to eat proved to be more difficult than sorting out computer problems. For a start he couldn't find anything. There were a few tins in the cupboard, mostly baby food, and frozen meat and vegetables in the freezer. But nothing was ready.

'Penny always has everything ready and something hot and in the oven,' he muttered to himself plaintively.

Then he realized that it had never occurred to him where she'd got it from or how it was prepared. The normal pattern was that ten minutes after arriving home David was sitting down in the kitchen with a glass of wine, the London Evening Standard, which he always picked up on his way home, at his elbow, and a plate of something cooked in front of him.

Now he couldn't even find any plates, not unless he counted the dirty ones in the sink. The fridge was empty, apart from a soggy packet of fish fingers. For a moment he was tempted to grill them, then thought that no, they should be frozen, not soggy, so he crammed the box into the waste bin with difficulty as it was already overflowing with rather nasty smelling nappy sacks. He tied them up in a bag then dropped the bag in the wheelie bin outside the kitchen door. That was overflowing too. Which day did the bin men come? He had no idea, but it looked as if they were due to visit pretty soon. Did they come through the side gate and collect it, or did Penny put it out? Again he had no idea, so he left it where it was. Supper came before wheelie bins. Searching for a plate he opened the dishwasher to find it was full of clean, sparkling china and cutlery, which cheered him up. He started to unload it, only to realize that apart from the knives and forks he hadn't a clue where any of it went. Penny had always done that. He'd only ever slung dirty things in the sink, in fact, he suddenly realized he'd never actually switched on the dishwasher, and started worrying. Why was that light still on? Was it on standby like a computer? Or should he do something? He decided to leave it; Penny would know what to do when she came back.

Opening various cupboard doors, he managed to get rid of the contents of the dishwasher although he doubted that he'd ever find anything again. That also would have to wait until Penny came back. Some little niggles of worry settled at the back of his mind and began to grow in size. Was it this that Penny couldn't stand? In the process of stuffing plates and pots into the cupboards, he found an opened bottle of Corbières, minus a cork, and poured himself a glass. It was sharp and vinegary, but he drank it anyway, sitting at the kitchen table staring down into the long narrow garden with the line of lime trees at the bottom. They were too tall and effectively took all the evening sunlight from the garden. Penny had been on at him for ages to get someone in to pollard them, but he'd always put it off.

Without really thinking, he rang his mother. He couldn't ring Penny, not at the moment, because he didn't fancy talking to Louise if she answered the phone. What could he say? He was pretty certain she didn't really like him, although she'd never said so and anyway she'd be bound to take Penny's side, whatever that might be.

His mother answered the phone just as the answer phone started to cut in. 'Maggie West, here. How may I help you?' Her piercing voice drowned the answer phone. She'd been an actress, still was when she could get a part suited to her age, and had been trained to throw her voice in the days before body mikes were invented. She still threw it, all the time, deafening nearly everyone around her, which was the reason she rarely got parts in TV dramas unless they needed a harridan of some sort who had to shriek. Her best part had been Lady Bracknell in *The Importance of Being Earnest*, at the Haymarket Theatre about twenty years ago, a part that had been written for her, so she had told everyone. David held the phone away from his ear. Perhaps ringing his mother had not been such a good idea. 'Who is it?' she boomed. 'If you're a heavy breather you might as well give up. I'm not at all impressed by that sort of thing.'

'I'm not a heavy breather. It's me, David.'

'Oh, you. What do you want? What's wrong?'

'What makes you think something is wrong?' David felt defensive. His mother always made him feel like that.

'Well, darling, you never ring me unless there is some problem. In fact you hardly ever ring me at all now that you've got plenty of money. When you were hard up you always kept in touch.'

'That's not true …' David began to say.

But his mother interrupted him. 'Just a minute, I must sit down.'

David felt a tinge of anxiety. Was she ill? After all she was over seventy. 'Why?' he demanded.

'Because I'm standing up, of course,' snapped his mother. 'I'm exhausted, darling, totally, totally exhausted,' she continued dramatically. 'I've just come down from the attic where I've been searching out some of my old costumes. The local Am Dram is doing *My Fair Lady* and I'm loaning them some of my black and white costumes for the opening of Act Two. You know, the Ascot scene. Now what is it you want?'

'I don't actually want anything really,' David hesitated. Should he tell her? Then decided he might as well.

'Penny's left me and taken the children. She's gone back to her mother.'

'Very sensible of her.'

'What do you mean, very sensible? What about me? She's left me here all alone, and the house is in a terrible state.' David slumped lower over the kitchen table, and took another sip of the wine, which tasted more disgusting with every mouthful.

'Your house is always in a terrible state,' said his mother in a matter of fact tone of voice, 'and that's hardly surprising is it. Penny's got three children to look after.'

'We've only got two. Sam and Jacob.'

'Three, dear,' said his mother. 'She's got you as well.'

David didn't listen. He was thinking, should he tell her or not? He decided yes, so said, 'I've asked her to marry me and now she's left me.'

His mother burst into laughter, which both surprised and annoyed him. 'Marry you!' she choked. 'She'd be mad if she did.'

'Why do you say that?'

His mother stopped laughing, and said very seriously. 'If you have to ask that, my darling, you're even more hopeless than I thought you were.'

A high-pitched buzz told David she'd put the phone down. Irritably he wondered why on earth he ever bothered to phone his mother. She was never any help. Now, he felt more muddled, forlorn and hard done by than before. Why wasn't she sympathetic, why did she think Penny would be mad to marry him?

He rang her back.

'Yes?' she said. 'I know it's you, David.'

'I know why you said that,' he blurted, stumbling over his words in fury. 'You're anti men. You don't like men, not even me, your own son. You've had three husbands and never kept any of them. Even your current one is held at arm's length.'

'Seth chooses to work in New York because as a celebrity chef he has his own TV programme and earns plenty of dollars. I hate New York. I ...' she paused, a calculated moment of drama, then said, 'I am an English rose. New York doesn't suit me, Seth knows that. And as for you, you're thirty-seven and haven't managed to get one wife yet, let alone divorce one. At your age I'd already divorced two husbands.' His mother slammed down the phone once more.

He had no answer to that, so David gave up, and in desperation poured himself another glass of the disgusting red wine.

About the time Maggie put the phone down on David, a thoroughly over-excited Sam was racing around Lavender House wearing one sock, and a paper crown left over from Christmas that he'd found in a drawer upstairs. He'd been put to bed once, but had got up, taken off his pyjamas and started dressing for the next day. He loved staying with Nanny Lou, as he called her, because her house rambled all over the place. Three steps down, and two steps up and each set of steps led into another room. What was more, he'd been allowed to choose his bedroom. He always chose the same one, the little one at the top of the stairs where the ceiling and window sloped down to the floor.

Penny objected when he first chose it. 'He could fall out of the window!'

'You slept here and you never fell out of the window,' said Louise. 'Besides I've had a catch put on it now so that it only opens halfway.'

So the attic room became Sam's and gradually over

the frequent visits to Lavender House he had accumulated his special things that were always there, ready to greet him like old friends whenever he came to stay.

Jacob was a very easy baby, he didn't care where he slept so long as it was warm, and he was full of milk and had his sucking toy.

After they had settled Sam again, Louise poured out two glasses of wine, and she and Penny sat outside the kitchen door in the last of the warm evening sunshine. The sun slanted at an angle illuminating the white flowering candle blossoms of the horse-chestnut tree at the bottom of the garden.

'The garden looks beautiful,' said Penny, sipping her wine.

Louise didn't reply, she was wondering what to do about Penny and David, then gave up thinking about it and said, 'Only five minutes before the risotto is ready.'

'We're two penniless women, so perhaps we shouldn't be drinking wine,' said Penny.

'You're not really penniless,' said Louise who was feeling exhausted. She'd forgotten just how tiring an over-excited toddler could be. What she really wanted was to be alone and work out how she was going to manage on virtually no money. But she was not alone; she had Penny and the children to deal with. Sending up a silent prayer that Dottie would be able to sell her book quickly, she turned to Penny and said more severely than she'd intended, 'You've run away and made yourself penniless, whereas it happened to me without warning.'

'I won't take any money from David.' The set of Penny's mouth indicated her obstinacy.

Oh, she looks so like her father, thought Louise, when he'd made up his mind about something and there was no budging him; the thought suddenly overwhelmed her with sadness that he wasn't here to enjoy his grand-children. She missed him less these days, but every now and then the loneliness still hit her when she was least expecting it.

'I'm not telling you to go back to him,' she said, 'but I am telling you not to be selfish. The children are half his and you can't deny them material things just because you've fallen out with their father. How are you going to live without money? It's no use depending on me; it's something you've got to sort out with David.' Louise paused for a moment and thought of Sam. 'Now I come to think of it Sam didn't mention him once. He never asked where Daddy was. I suppose he thinks he's going back home soon.'

Penny sniffed derisively. 'He doesn't ask about him, because he hardly ever sees him, except at weekends, and then David only pays him absent minded attention in-between fiddling with some new electronic gizmo.' A tear trickled slowly down her cheek and Penny wiped it away with the back of her hand and sniffed. 'That's why I left, Mum. We didn't have a relationship. I can't remem-ber the last time we made love, not that it's David's fault on that score. It's me. I'm so tired. Jacob is always waking in the night. Sometimes I think I can't go on, so that why I came home. I wanted to see you.'

Louise squeezed Penny's hand. 'I think we'll talk about your problems tomorrow. Maybe the country air will keep Jacob asleep and you'll get a good night's sleep. We're both tired. I'll just pop down the garden and get some fresh rocket to go with our supper.'

Penny leapt to her feet. 'I'll go and pick the rocket. Oh, it's so lovely to have a real garden, with real earth and things growing in it. Not a horrible London garden with dry sandy earth full of poo from the cat next door.' She started off down the brick path, which led between the herb garden and the vegetable patch, then stopped. 'But, Mum, we haven't talked about your problem. How are you going to manage without that insurance money Dad set up?'

Louise eased herself wearily from the bench, and picked up the wine glasses. I'm forty-four, she reflected, the age that some women are only just starting to have babies. But I've had mine, and the only babies around are grandchildren. Maybe that's the reason why, at the moment, I feel like one hundred and forty-four.

She answered Penny's question. 'I don't know. But I'll think of something.'

Penny scuffed her foot on the moss covered bricks of the path. 'Don't sell Lavender House, Mum, please.'

'Why not? It's the obvious thing to do. It's a bottomless pit as far as money is concerned. There's always something that needs doing in an old house like this, and I really don't need all this room.'

'But you can't sell the house,' Penny wailed. 'It's my home. Where will I go when I want to come home?'

'You are grown up. You have your own home. I was thinking that perhaps I might sell Lavender House, partition off the garden, and move down into the old cottage at the far end of the garden. I'll need planning permission and the cottage needs sorting out. The kiln is still there, and the place is full of your father's pots, which he made after he came back from Australia. Some of them are quite lovely, and I suppose I could sell those.'

For a brief second her mind lingered on that difficult time of their lives. John had been moody and bad tempered, blaming everyone but himself. Louise remembered screaming at him that it was his fault, and that he'd put the family in jeopardy because he'd taken all their hard earned money and got involved in some hare-brained mining scheme in Australia. She'd been the main breadwinner then with the money from her writing, right up until his premature death. In those days her books had sold well. Then the surprise monthly insurance payment had turned up after his death. There was no point in thinking about the bad times, she always made herself think of the good days. Those memories were like golden pebbles to be slipped into her pocket and fingered whenever she felt down. She needed those golden pebbles now.

'I know it wasn't easy for you then, Mum, and it's even worse now,' said Penny thoughtfully. 'Maybe we could let the cottage out to a potter, then you could still live in Lavender House because you'd have money from the rent coming in.'

'I don't know any potters now. Besides, all the potters that I did know when your father was alive were all hard up. Making pots might seem glamorous, but it's not a lucrative business, as I know only too well. It was your father's hobby, not his livelihood; we could never have managed if it hadn't been for my books.'

'And now all the money he paid in for you to live on after his death has disappeared down a black hole.'

'Yes. But I'm not the only one. Think of the people affected who are too old to work, and who have no houses to sell. I'm young enough to get a job, so I must look on the bright side and be positive. I'm going to earn some money somehow. You never know, this time next year I may be a millionaire.'

'Yes, I suppose so,' said Penny disappearing along the brick path in the direction of the rocket, but she didn't sound convinced.

Twenty minutes later, they were sitting at the kitchen table. 'We should both have a deep dreamless sleep,' said Louise, 'with all this food and wine inside us.'

The asparagus risotto was melt in the mouth perfect, and the rocket piled in one of her ancient tureens, and dressed with olive oil and balsamic vinegar, was delicious.

'I'll sort my finances out tomorrow,' said Penny. 'I promise I won't be silly and I will accept money from David, but I'm not, definitely not, going back to live with him.'

Louise didn't reply, but thought she saw in her daughter's eyes a gleam of fatigue and worry, and guessed she wasn't quite as determined or hard hearted about David as she appeared. It gave her hope. David wasn't perfect, but then who was? In her opinion, young people too often saw things in black and white and refused to compromise. She thought back to her life with John. If the truth were told, their life was one long compromise, but they'd managed somehow, and the last few years of their marriage had been happy, in a strange way, despite lack of money. They'd got used to one another and were comfortable in their companionship. It hadn't been passionate, but it was adequate. That was what counted, that and remembering the good times.

She put her hand over Penny's. 'I won't be silly either,' she said. 'Selling the house will be a last resort. I shall try to think of other ways to raise money. But I'm going to sleep on it. Let's not talk about it now.'

'Agreed,' said Penny picking up a spoonful of rocket.

The sound of a car coming through the gates and crunching to a halt on the turning circle at the front of the house disturbed them. Louise had a horrible premonition. She recognized the sound of the car.

The next moment there was a knock on the kitchen door, and then it was pushed open. Her premonition had been correct; it was the man with the white sports car. He stood in the opening. 'I know I've got a cheek, but I've brought a take-away with me and wondered if I could eat it here,' he said. 'A homemade steak and stilton pie from the butcher's shop in the square, some chips and a good bottle of burgundy. I thought perhaps, that if I could eat here then maybe you could do me bed and breakfast. You've got a very large house, and I know you've got your daughter staying so you're not alone.'

'How do you know that?' Louise was surprised and annoyed.

'Mr Jones, the butcher told me. He also suggested that I should throw myself on your mercy as I can't possibly stay in that poofter's paradise, the Stag and Beetle.'

Penny laughed. 'That's a terribly un PC thing to say.'

'Mr Jones' words, not mine.'

Penny laughed again, but Louise didn't laugh. She felt exasperated at the interruption, and cross with Mr Jones. 'I told you I don't do bed and breakfast,' she said. 'Neither do I do dinner.'

'You don't have to do dinner, I've got it.' He eyed the risotto and the tureen of rocket. 'Maybe mine has a little more cholesterol than yours, but it's good old English fare, and this is an emergency.' He remained in the doorway in a way that seemed far too permanent for Louise's liking. 'You can't throw me out into the dark on a cold and windy night,' he said.

'It's not cold and windy, nor dark. The sun has only just gone in.' A gut feeling told Louise that this man had the potential to disrupt her already disrupted life even further. 'No,' she said firmly. 'You'll have to find somewhere else. Go on to Rumsey or Salisbury.'

'But I want to stay in East Willow for sentimental reasons which I can't go into now.'

'No,' said Louise.

'Mum, how can you?' Penny seemed delighted at the interruption to their meal. She got up and pushed the door right open and waved him through. 'Come in,' she said 'we've just started dinner but you're welcome to join us.'

'Penny!' Louise was taken aback. How could Penny be so rash? They didn't know this man. Her imagination ran riot. He might be a murderer or a prisoner on the run, and she didn't like his self-confident air. No, not self-confident, smug, was a better word she thought, however, she had to admit he didn't look much like a prisoner on the run. But he could always be a murderer. One never knew these days. She wanted to kick Penny under the table, but couldn't as Penny was already standing up at the door and out of her reach.

Penny was shaking hands and saying, 'I'm Penny Gregory, and this is my mother Louise.'

'Ah yes,' he said. 'I've met Louise before, when she ...' Louise thought for a moment he was about to say when she was weeping, but he didn't, he said, 'she directed me to the Stag and Beetle, when I told her I was looking for somewhere to stay. But I can't possibly stay there. It's too camp for words, and having seen the menu I have a feeling their food will be the same. Little twirls of this and that, not enough to satisfy a gnat, and all set off with a pansy on the top.'

'I don't do bed and breakfast,' said Louise again. But no one was listening to her.

Penny was unwrapping the pie and had already turned on the oven. 'We'll have this after the risotto. Mum, would you pop down to the veggie patch and get some more rocket.'

'I don't do bed and breakfast,' repeated Louise, but knowing she was fighting a losing battle.

'Mum, for God's sake don't keep repeating yourself. You sound like a parrot. The very least we can do is to offer Mr ...' she paused, and Louise realized that they didn't know the name of the man now sitting at the kitchen table and uncorking the burgundy he'd brought with him.

'Jack,' he said, raising the bottle in a toast to them. 'Jack O'Leary.' He looked at Louise. 'I can show you my driver's licence to prove who I am, and it doesn't even have points on it.'

'Unlike yours, Mum,' said Penny. She turned to Jack. 'She's got six points for speeding.'

'Obviously a reckless woman.' He raised his eyebrows expressively. 'But here I am, at your service,' with that he uncorked the bottle of burgundy.

'At our service!' Louise was feeling more indignant by the minute. 'It seems to me that we're at your service.' But as she spoke she had a eureka moment. Of course, that was what she had to do to keep Lavender House. She'd do bed and breakfast. The New Forest was always full of visitors in the spring and summer, and quite a few in autumn and winter too.

Louise turned and walked out of the kitchen towards the rocket bed, clicking her fingers for the dogs to follow her. But they, the traitors, had decided they approved of the new visitor, and had each placed a head on his knees while he fondled their ears. Behind her she could hear Penny and Jack talking animatedly.

Jack O'Leary, yes, well, she'd let him stay for tonight, and charge him ... her thoughts ground momentarily to a halt. Charge him what? She had no idea. But it had to be something that would put him off from staying longer. If he were actually as desperate as he said he was, he'd pay whatever she demanded, even if it was double what the Stag and Beetle charged.

Walking back to the kitchen up the moss covered garden path, Louise's mind raced ahead. Jack O'Leary could stay in the big room at the front, which had its own bathroom. Thank goodness she'd given the house a thorough clean when she knew Penny was coming. All that particular room needed was a flick over with a duster, some fresh towels in the bathroom and new soap in the washbasin. She had plenty of Jane's handmade lavender soap, which would give it a rural touch, and some bath gel and shampoo and conditioner she'd pinched from a hotel in France years ago and never used.

She'd make it look as professional as possible. It would be good practice for when she began letting out rooms in earnest, although she wouldn't let Jack O'Leary know she was practising on him. She wanted everything to appear as effortless as if she did this kind of thing every day of her life. The problem was, how much should she charge?

CHAPTER
⋙ FOUR ⋘

Later that evening, Louise flung open the window in the front bedroom and inspected everything in the room, making sure it was ready for her paying guest. Outside, a tractor growled up the lane, its headlights illuminating the creamy cow-parsley blossoms in the hedgerow. Queen Ann's Lace, old Aggie Smethurst called it. Louise paused and smiled. She knew the tractor driver was Bert Hackett who had a small organic farm at the end of the lane; he'd given her a paper bag containing four huge field mushrooms that morning, they'd be useful for breakfast. He always took his tractor to the pub. Not the newly refurbished Stag and Beetle, who didn't want him in with his muddy boots, but to the Ring of Bells, which had one public bar, presided over by Sharon, the girl Jane hated because of the size of her bosom, and which was always crowded with locals. It was a pity, thought Louise, but people and places like Bert and the Ring of Bells were fast disappearing in the rush of the modern world, and she determined there and then that Lavender House would remain comfortable but old fashioned, and become known for its good, organic food. That would be her marketing point, when she went to see the bank manager. If all her guests were as generous as Jack when it came to paying, then she'd manage very well. Not make a fortune, but certainly make a comfortable living. She thought of Jack again; he was attractive, no doubt about that, in a buccaneer kind of way, and Penny was obviously very smitten. Louise decided that he must either be mad or very rich, thinking one hundred pounds a night in a lovely, but shabby house, a bargain.

During their supper, he'd looked at Louise and said, 'You'd better tell me how much you're going to charge for bed and breakfast.'

Louise, who'd been mulling this over in her mind and hadn't yet reached a decision, said on impulse, 'One hundred pounds.'

Penny's eyes had grown round with amazement, and grew even rounder when Jack said, 'Fine. Sounds very reasonable to me. Do you want a cheque or cash?'

'Cash,' Penny said quickly before Louise could even open her mouth. So cash it had been.

Liberally spraying lavender wax polish on to a duster and flicking every surface in sight, so that the room smelled as if it were polished every day, Louise went into the bathroom. It was clean, thank goodness; all it needed was a quick wipe over with an antibacterial spray and a set of clean towels. Rummaging in the cupboard for the clean towels, Louise wondered why Jack O'Leary (and that was his name because she had checked his driving licence when he'd offered it) wanted to stay in East Willow. It was a pretty village, but out of the way, and not so pretty that lots of tourists visited to take photos. But still, she thought, no accounting for taste. She found the fluffiest towels she had – for a hundred pounds she supposed she ought to give him decent towels – and draped them over the towel rail. In the bottom drawer of the towel cupboard, she had Jane's lavender soap, and then found the individual shower, bath gels, and shampoos, which she taken from a hotel in France on her last short holiday. They were tall thin bottles, *Gel Cheveux et Corps and Shampooing* and *Conditionneur avec huile essentielle pour vitalité*. They looked very nice standing on the end of the bath, pale primrose and purple, although Louise was a little doubtful about the need for *vitalité*: he seemed to have quite enough of that already.

Downstairs, she could hear Penny shrieking with laughter, not sounding at all like the girl who'd arrived downtrodden and weary with two small children in tow a few hours ago. Had she given any thought to her impecunious predicament or the future of her life without David, Louise wondered? She doubted it. Penny was a great one for not thinking about things, she just did them, and it had always driven Louise mad. Especially when it was something important, like falling headlong into a relationship, as she had with David, and then producing two children in quick succession. It was only now the hard facts of motherhood and being tied to a house and family were beginning to sink in.

'Why wait, Mum?' she'd said, when Louise had queried the wisdom of two children in quick succession. 'You didn't wait; you had me when you were only nineteen.'

Louise couldn't argue with that because it was true. It was only years later that she regretted not having sown a few wild oats before settling down.

She took one last look around the bedroom, and then went slowly downstairs. She wanted to talk seriously to Penny, about David, about money, about the children. But all of that would have to wait until Jack O'Leary went to bed. Louise had no intention of discussing such private family matters in front of him. She hoped he'd go to bed soon. But when she entered the kitchen, it was glimmering by candles casting a soft light. Penny had scattered them around liberally, and Jack looked as if he had taken root.

'I thought I'd save on electricity,' said Penny, 'and Jack suggested the candles to save money.'

'Did he?' Louise was determined not to be too friendly.

'I gather you've got a cash flow problem,' he said.

'Temporarily,' said Louise in a tone of voice, which she hoped would preclude any further discussion on the subject.

Penny, however, had other ideas. 'I've told Jack all about David and me, and you,' she said. 'He says I should sue David for everything he has if I'm determined to go solo.'

'Did he?' said Louise again.

Jack must have caught the ominous note in her voice because he looked up momentarily as he poured himself another drink. A whisky this time, *my* whisky Louise noted with annoyance, as he tipped the bottle, obviously given to him by Penny. But she couldn't help noticing either, how muscular and tanned his arms were, and the width of his shoulders. Not unattractive in a hunky way, probably a rugby player in his youth. She could see how some women might find him attractive, although he was definitely not her type. She liked sophisticated men, not that any men like that had come her way lately, although she supposed there was always hope once she started having guests on a regular basis. Sophisticated and wealthy, that was the kind of man she needed if she was going to have one at all, otherwise she preferred being single. Penny, however, seemed rather dangerously smitten. But he was much too old for her, and besides she had a partner, even if he was temporarily out of favour.

'It's much too soon for Penny to be thinking of a permanent break in her relationship,' she said firmly. 'They've only been separated five minutes, and there are the children to consider.'

'Penny tells me you're a widow,' said Jack, ignoring her remark.

'Penny tells you too much.' Louise felt cross at Penny's indiscretions. 'What about you?' she said, determined to steer the subject away from what she considered were her own very personal affairs. 'You know all about us and we know nothing about you. What are you doing here for a start?'

Louise wondered if it was her imagination that Jack hesitated for a moment before giving a slow smile, and saying, 'Oh, me, I'm not very interesting. I've been married, now I'm alone, and have been for six years.' He shrugged, 'I'm homeless, at the moment as I sold up my place in South Africa and thought I'd come back to the old country and look up a few friends.' He pushed a full glass of wine across towards Louise, and she could have sworn it was a roguish glint she was seeing in his dark eyes. 'But now I'm thinking perhaps I'll put off the search for a bit. It's such a lovely spot here; I feel I could stay for ever.'

Louise felt uneasy. 'You can't stay here for ever.'

'Why not?' demanded Penny. 'Plenty of people live in hotels all their lives.'

'This is not a hotel,' said Louise firmly. Why did she have this feeling that she was being out-manoeuvred? 'I've decided to run it as a bed and breakfast, with occasional dinners for special parties, so neither of you can stay here forever, as I'm not keeping a refuge for people on the run. I've got to get things organized and put it on a proper business footing.'

'But, Mum, I've got nowhere else to go,' wailed Penny. Louise could see her casting despairing 'help me' looks in the direction of Jack.

He, damn him, to Louise's fury, roared with laughter, throwing back his head revealing beautiful teeth. Not natural in a man of his age, thought Louise, feeling decidedly grumpy, consoling herself with the thought that they were probably all capped. 'You can't throw your own daughter out,' he said, between guffaws, 'and what's all this about a refuge for people on the run? You make it sound as if Lavender House is harbouring criminals, and the whole outfit is an illegal operation.'

Penny hiccupped and giggled. The wine and Jack were having a very bad effect on her. It seemed she was incapable of taking anything seriously. 'It *is* an illegal operation,' she giggled. 'Mum, you have taken cash in hand, no tax to pay, nothing official, all under the counter. At this rate, in no time at all you'll be a millionaire, and you won't want to stay here, you'll be off to the Costa del Sol with some perma-tanned man who you will have met at a business conference and who, of course, will be filthy rich.'

'Don't be so silly. I shall never leave here; I've got all the animals to think of.' Louise sat at the kitchen table, and on cue the dogs nuzzled her thighs with their wet muzzles. She sat watching the candlelight flickering through her glass of red wine, feeling exhausted. Sam and baby Jacob had taken their toll, she'd got out of practice with the noise and mess young children made, plus there was the worry of how she was going to make ends meet. A one off paying guest, even if he was paying over the odds, was hardly going to make her a millionaire. She wondered if Dottie had got the manuscript, and whether or not she liked it and thought she could sell it. But even if a publisher did want it, the advance wouldn't be much. Maybe a thousand pounds if she were lucky, the absolute maximum these days and that wouldn't last long. She'd put the hundred pounds, which Jack had given her in cash, in the old teapot on the kitchen dresser. That wouldn't last long either, not at the rate Jacob and Sam were going through disposable nappies. She wondered briefly if nappies would make good compost. Tomorrow she'd look it up on the Internet; it was amazing what one could find out there. But at the moment, all she wanted to do was to get to bed. Penny might as well have been in bed, as by now she had her eyes closed and her head on her arms on the table.

Jack got up and strolled to the window looking out into the darkening garden. Bats were flitting madly about, wheeling and diving after invisible insects. Through the open window, Louise could hear a loud grunting sound and knew the hedgehog family from the bottom of the garden were out and about ferreting for slugs and snails.

'I can hear hedgehogs,' said Jack. 'Reminds me of my boyhood. I was raised on a farm in County Kerry and got used to the sounds of the creatures of the night. Where I lived in South Africa it was virtually a desert, and at night I'd hear the barks of hyenas but no snuffling hedgehogs. Nothing comforting like that.' He turned suddenly, and sat down opposite Louise. His face illuminated by the candlelight seemed softer, not quite so much the scrum-half look, and in fact, thought Louise, surprisingly gentle. 'I can understand why you don't want to leave this house,' he said. 'I suppose you've lived here for ever.'

'No, I lived in London before I was married. This house belonged to my Godmother, and now I feel that it's my responsibility to look after it. Silly really, I suppose.'

'Not at all. You've put down your roots here, and I envy that. I've never had roots. Never stayed anywhere long enough.'

'Once it was full of people and very busy,' Louise continued her mind full of memories. 'John's mother stayed with us for a while, then there was Penny and her friends during the summer holidays, plus our friends. It was always full of life.'

There was a sudden roar from upstairs. 'Sounds full of life now,' said Jack.

'It will be Jacob, he always wakes about this time wanting a feed, just as everyone else is about to go to bed.' Louise nudged Penny. 'Your son needs you.'

Penny groaned, and staggered towards the kitchen door leading into the hall. 'Breastfeeding is all very well,' she complained, 'but it does mean you can't hand them over to anyone else. If he was on the bottle you could do it, Mum.'

'But he's not. So go upstairs and feed him, and then go to bed yourself,' said Louise firmly. 'You've had far too much to drink, that poor baby will be getting undiluted alcohol.'

Penny giggled and went upstairs.

Left alone in the kitchen Louise tried to observe Jack more closely without making it too obvious.

'I'm not a danger to you,' he said, obviously aware of her observation, 'and I really would like to stay for a while. It's so peaceful. If,' he added, 'we can come to a more sensible arrangement about the cost. I'll pay you fifty pounds for bed and breakfast, full English mind, and ten pounds for dinner in the evening.'

Louise did some quick mental arithmetic, never her strongest point, and couldn't work it out. 'Well, I'll think about it,' she said, wishing she had a calculator or a piece of paper on which to do some calculations.

'That'll be four hundred and twenty pounds a week,' said Jack. 'Better than a smack in the eye with a wet kipper.'

Louise laughed, 'I've never heard that expression before, but it's certainly true.'

Jack leaned forward. 'Do you know that's the first time I've seen you look really cheerful since I met you.'

'It's the thought of all that money,' Louise confessed. 'I never expected a middle-aged angel to turn up in a sports car.'

'Hold fire with the middle-aged bit, but take advantage of me while I'm here,' replied Jack, looking serious. 'Angels are apt to take off and fly away.' He got up and made for the door into the hall. 'I know where my bedroom is. I notice that you've put me as far away as possible from you and Penny. You were worried about me weren't you?'

'No,' lied Louise. To her chagrin she felt herself blushing guiltily. It was true. She had felt uneasy about allowing a complete stranger to sleep in her house, despite Penny's enthusiasm. 'That's because I didn't want you disturbed by the children,' she said hastily.

'And here was me thinking it was because you didn't trust me,' he said, with a grin. Then he left the room, picked his bag up from the floor by the kitchen door where it still languished, and went upstairs to his specially prepared bedroom.

Louise levered herself from the chair and clicked her fingers at the dogs. 'Time for you to go out for a last wee, my darlings,' she said.

Seamus and Megan uncurled their long legs from their comfortable positions beneath the table, and loped unenthusiastically over to the back door, which led out into the garden. They're both getting old, thought Louise sadly. That was the trouble with animals; they wormed their way into your heart and then left you heartbroken far too soon.

Following them down the garden, Louise paused and breathed in the night air. It was warm and still, not a breath of wind. Somewhere in the woods, which backed on to the far side of the garden, an owl hooted; a long drawn out melancholy sound. She could hear the dogs rustling about in the long grass next to the clump of nettles, which Louise let grow especially for the butterflies. Jane thought she was mad. Everything in her garden had its place. Nettles were weeds, and therefore were not allowed to grow. Louise thought Jane's garden looked like a regimental parade ground, but Jane and Geoffrey liked it, so she kept her thoughts to herself, and let them think she was slightly eccentric or lazy, or probably both. At the thought of Jane, Louise smiled to herself. What a storm in a teacup about Geoffrey. Mentally crossing her fingers she hoped she'd heard the last of Jane's suspicions and would not be dragged off to an Ann Summers shop to buy sexy underwear.

When the dogs padded back from their brief forage amongst the grass, Louise turned and walked slowly back towards the house. She didn't worry about the cats; they went in and out of the cat flap at will, or climbed up the wisteria and through open bedroom windows. Too late, she realized she should have warned Jack about that. Toby, her fat black and white cat was especially fond of sharing warm beds. The light was on in her paying guest's room on the far side of the house, spilling a golden rectangle on to a dark patch of lawn. The kitchen lights were on too, the candles having long ago burnt themselves out, and from where she stood, the inside of the kitchen looked beautiful. Like an advert in one of those homes and gardens magazines, thought Louise. There were fresh flowers, buttercups and forget-me-nots, picked by Sam, and stuffed into an old blue enamel jug by Penny, the plates and cups on the welsh dresser gleamed rose and gold in the light. They'd been a wedding present from her parents years ago, and from a distance looked perfect. The chips and cracks from years of use disappeared as if by magic in the light. Another light suddenly came on in Penny's room above the kitchen; the curtains were pink and added a rosy glow to the garden. Tonight, the house looked loved, and lived in, and this is how it should be, thought Louise. I shouldn't be here rattling around on my own. Perhaps having to do bed and breakfast is not such a bad idea after all. Suddenly she felt peaceful. She'd give it a go, and what was more, she'd make a success of it.

She entered the kitchen after the dogs, who immediately flopped into their beds, and closed the door behind her. Then she heard Penny's voice echoing down the stairs. She was on her mobile, in the corridor outside her bedroom. Louise couldn't help overhearing Penny say, 'No, I won't marry you, David. Do you think I'm mad? I wouldn't marry you if you were the last man on earth. Besides, I think I've found myself another man. Yes, here. Where do you think? Goodbye.'

The door clicked as Penny went back into the bedroom next door to the boys' room.

Another man? Surely she couldn't be referring to Jack O'Leary? He was much too old. Besides, David was the father of her children, even if Penny had fallen out of love with him and thought he was lazy. The sense of peace Louise had felt a moment ago evaporated. When did children stop being problems?

CHAPTER
≫ FIVE ≪

L OUISE HARDLY SLEPT that night. She worried about
Penny and David. But in the morning she decided to
concentrate on more immediate matters. She was determined to prove that even if she was inexperienced she
would be the hostess with the mostess when it came to
doing B and B, but first of all she must ring Kevin. Better
get that roof fixed if she was aiming to have more guests,
and anyway she could afford it at the moment, if she
used some of the money from Jack. She hated ringing
Kevin again, but it had to be done.

Preparing herself for his grumpy reply she put on her
most cheerful voice. 'Hallo, Kevin. How are you?'

He didn't respond to her greeting, merely said, 'More
slates slipping?'

'Well, it's the same ones and I was wondering ...'

'I'll be round later this morning. Said I would. Got to
do a job on old Mrs Smethurst's roof. You women and
your roofs,' he huffed.

'Yes, I'm sorry.' Louise felt guilty, as if she personally
were responsible for the slipping slates on her own and
Aggie Smethurst's roof.

Kevin snorted. 'Don't be sorry, Mrs Gregory. I'd be

out of work if it wasn't for women like you. You're me bread and butter.'

'Oh,' Louise cheered up. It was the first time to her knowledge that he'd ever said anything positive. 'Well, I'll see you later this morning then, and I'll make some of those rock cakes you like.' Bribery she knew, but anything to get the roof fixed.

Grabbing her normal huge cup of coffee she started preparing a big British breakfast, eggs, bacon, mushrooms, two of the ones Bert Hackett had given her, tomatoes, and black pudding which she fished out from the freezer, in fact, the lot.

'Smells delicious.' Jack entered the kitchen.

'High cholesterol I'm afraid, but that's your full English for you.'

'Who cares,' replied Jack, watching her slice the field mushrooms. 'I don't agree with all this agonizing over what's good and what's not. I never go to the doctor, and look at me, the picture of health.

Louise looked over her shoulder as she went into the dining room. It was true he did look the picture of health. She turned her attention to the dining room, which was only used for Christmas these days, so the table needed laying before Jack could eat there.

'You don't expect me to eat in here on my own do you?' boomed Jack, standing right behind her and making her jump. He walked over to the table and said again, 'I'm not eating in here.'

'But you're a paying guest,' said Louise, putting out a cut glass cruet set which hadn't been used since the Christmas before last.

Jack picked it up. 'Nice piece of glass, pity about the salt.'

'What do you mean?'

Jack held the saltcellar upside down; the salt was rock solid and remained where it was. 'I'm not eating in here along with the museum pieces; it will make me feel like one myself.'

'But ...' Louise started to protest.

'No buts about it.' Taking hold of her shoulders and firmly steering her back to the kitchen, he said, 'I want my breakfast in here, woman.'

'My name is Mrs Gregory, not woman!' she said with as much dignity as she could muster, as he was still pinning her down by holding her shoulders.

Blatantly unrepentant, Jack gave her one of his wicked grins. 'For one hundred pounds a night I think I'm entitled to call you "woman."'

Louise opened her mouth to protest then decided against it. He was right, in a way, she had scandalously overcharged him and he was getting his own back a little. But only a little. The thought of the money still safely stuffed in the teapot on the dresser was cheering.

'By the way,' continued Jack, 'I've been out for a walk, and took your dogs, but they, lazy things, decided the walk was too long, and came back by themselves. However, on my way back to the house I met a woman who looked as if she intended coming in, but when she saw me, she drove off in floods of tears. Very strange. I don't usually have that effect on women.'

'What did she look like?' Louise had a sense of foreboding.

'Well dressed, wearing an expensive looking raincoat. She looked anxious, and was wearing her handbag diagonally across her front as if she were carrying the crown jewels. If there's ever anything guaranteed to put a man off, it's a woman who wears her handbag firmly strapped across her bosom.'

Louise laughed and breathed a sigh of relief. 'Can't think who that can be. It can't be my sister, she's the epitome of a genteel countrywoman, never wears her handbag like that. No it can't be Jane.'

She dropped the back rashers into the pan, where they spat and sizzled, and drew in a contented breath. It did smell delicious. She hadn't cooked bacon for breakfast for years. Her contentment, however, was short lived as the kitchen door burst opened and a distraught Jane, with her handbag strapped across her chest, staggered in.

'That's the woman I told you about,' said Jack backing rather apprehensively further away from the door.

'Who is that man?' screeched Jane. 'How dare you tell me you're not interested in men, when you're sleeping with one, and he's still here in the morning.'

Louise, about to tip the mushrooms in with the bacon, stopped, mushrooms poised mid air, and stared. Jack had said he'd seen a strange woman. This woman her sister, Jane, didn't look strange, she looked unhinged. Her eyes were red and puffy, her normally so neat hair was awry, and her expensive raincoat was creased and looked as if it had been slept in.

'I'll take those.' Jack took the mushrooms from Louise and pushed her away from the stove, 'you'd better look after her. She seems to know you.'

'It's my sister, Jane.' Louise stepped towards her. 'Whatever is the matter?'

'Don't touch me,' shouted Jane. 'It's all your fault. You were the one who told me to buy those crotchless knickers.'

Jack began to look interested and stopped stirring the mushrooms. There was silence broken only by Jane's heavy breathing, then he said nonchalantly, 'Shall I add the tomatoes?'

'You're sleeping with a man,' wailed Jane.

'He's paying me,' said Louise.

'Paying you! That's even worse.' Jane's wails got louder. 'You get paid for sex and I don't even have the opportunity to say I've got a headache. Geoffrey just isn't interested in me.'

'This is Jack O'Leary,' said Louise hastily before there could be any more misunderstanding, 'He's stayed the night as a bed and breakfast guest at Lavender House because there was nowhere else to go. The pub was full up, and Penny is upstairs with the children, I'm not here on my own.' Why on earth am I justifying myself to my own sister, I must be as mad as she is. Louise felt cross with herself. God only knew what Jack O'Leary was thinking.

Jane's wails subsided into sniffs, alternating with hiccups. 'Sounds like a steam train revving up to go,' muttered Jack, tipping the contents of the frying pan on to a plate which he put in the oven, before sloshing the pan with a liberal amount of olive oil and putting in two slices of bread. 'This oil is good for cholesterol,' he said seeing Louise's disapproving look.

Ignoring him Louise put her arm around Jane's shoulders. 'Come on,' she said gently steering her out of the kitchen, 'let's go into the dining room and you can tell me all about it, and you can make us a pot of coffee and bring it through,' she shouted at Jack over her shoulder.'

'Ok, but only if I get a rebate for being a waiter, and you promise to protect me,' he shouted back, grinning widely.

Louise poured Jane a large brandy. True, it was only 7.30 in the morning, but Jane looked as if she could do with it, and Louise reckoned the coffee, when Jack brought it in, would sober her up if necessary.

Putting the balloon glass of brandy down in front of Jane, Louise sat down beside her and said severely, 'Now, Jane. I think you owe me an explanation for your rather ...' she hesitated, then said, 'bizarre behaviour this morning.'

Jane took an enormous glug of brandy, hiccupped again, and said, 'Well, you remember the other day when I said I thought Geoffrey was ... was ...'

'Having an affair,' prompted Louise.

'Yes, that. Afterwards I thought about what you said. Mid-life crisis and all that, and maybe ...' She gulped. 'Perhaps it was true that I was boring.' She took another slurp of the brandy, hesitated then said in a rush, 'Well, to tell you the truth I have never really enjoyed sex. There is always a lot of fiddling about, by Geoffrey, not me, and then nothing much for me at the end of it. I've read about orgasms, but I've never had one. At least, not that I know of.'

'You'd know if you'd had one,' interrupted Louise, trying not to look amazed at these revelations.

'But Geoffrey seemed to enjoy it, and I suppose if I'm honest it gave me a sense of power. I could always say no, and sometimes I did. But I never have to these days, and that's the problem. Anyway, you said I ought to go to an Ann Summers shop and buy some sexy knickers.'

'I don't think those were my actual words,' said Louise hastily.

'Yes, they were. Exactly. You suggested that I go to one of those Ann Summers shops and buy some ... some,' she took another large gulp of brandy, and waved a limp hand vaguely across her stomach.

'I said sexy underwear, not necessarily from Ann Summers,' said Louise, wondering what Jane had bought. 'You were the one with crotchless knickers on the brain, although God knows why. Anyway, go on.'

'Well, I went to … you know. Going into that shop was bad enough. All the girls were so slim and sexy, and they knew all about everything. Things I've never even heard of. They,' she put her head in between her hands, 'they even suggested that it was very common for a woman of my age to buy a vibrator so that I could have some fun on my own. They said middle-aged men often went off the boil.'

'Off the boil! I can assure you this water was boiling when I put it in the cafetière.' Jack came through with a tray, containing the coffee and two cups and saucers. 'I've done you a couple of pieces of toast,' he added.

'Thanks.' Louise wondered how much he'd heard.

Penny put her head round the door. 'Hi, Mum. OK if I make the boys some porridge? Jack is starting on solids now and porridge is OK. I promise not to burn the saucepan.' She spied Jane and noticed the now nearly empty brandy glass, and Jane's ravaged face. 'Hi, Jane,' she said cautiously.

'Yes, yes. Do whatever you like.' Louise waved a dismissive hand, wanting them to leave her and Jane alone. It was obvious that Jack had warned Penny, judging by her expression.

She could hear Sam's voice in the background demanding to be let out in the garden and Jack saying, 'But don't you think you ought to put some clothes on first?' Penny was still staring at Jane in a puzzled way, and Jane was still sniffing, although the hiccups, thank heavens, thought Louise, had died down.

'I'll see you later,' Louise said firmly. 'Jane and I are having some breakfast in here. We want to talk.'

Penny withdrew her head somewhat reluctantly. She was obviously dying with curiosity, and so, if she were honest, was Louise. 'Let's get back to the vibrator,' she said, trying to make Jane smile, 'you've got me interested.'

It was obviously the wrong thing to say as Jane burst into tears again. 'Well, that's why I was so angry when I thought you and that man in there were … were …'

'Having sex?' suggested Louise. Why was it Jane could rarely bring herself to actually say the word?

'Yes,' said Jane. 'Well, I did buy sexy knickers and a bra in red and black silk lace. Cost me a fortune, and they were both terribly uncomfortable, but I thought anything to get Geoffrey interested.'

'What about the vibrator?' asked Louise?

'I didn't get that.'

'Pity, I've always wondered what they were like.' Louise poured the coffee, and pushed a cup towards Jane, at the same time furtively removing the brandy. 'I could have had a character use one in my next book.'

'Louise,' said Jane. 'This is serious.'

'Yes, yes, of course. Go on.' Resigning herself to hearing the whole sorry tale, Louise took a piece of hot buttered toast and crunched into it. 'Have some,' she said through a mouthful of toast. 'It's delicious.'

But Jane was too upset to eat. 'I hung around in the bedroom wearing the knickers and bra. I was freezing, and as I said they were so uncomfortable. They cut into me everywhere, and my breasts sort of spilled over. The girls in the shop said that was the whole idea.'

Louise tried to imagine Jane in red and black lace, spilling over everywhere, but gave up trying as the only thing she could come up with was not a pleasant sight. 'Perhaps they were the wrong size,' she ventured eventually.

'They were the biggest size,' said Jane indignantly. 'My size, so the girl said. Anyway I had them on and

Geoffrey came into the bedroom.'

'And?'

'He didn't even notice. He just cleaned his teeth, put on his pyjamas, got into bed and got out his laptop and started doing some accounts.'

'Oh,' said Louise, desperately trying to think of something comforting, or suitable to say, but failing miserably.

'I busied about. You know, getting things out of drawers, and putting them away again, I kept walking past him so that he'd notice what I was wearing.'

'Or wasn't,' muttered Louise, trying again to imagine Jane in black and red skimpy underwear, then hastily giving it up.

'He just didn't notice me,' continued Jane. 'I might as well have been invisible.'

'Didn't he say anything?'

'Nothing. Not even good night. He just switched off the laptop, turned out his light and went to sleep.' Jane stopped sniffing, gave her nose a good blow and sat up straight. 'My marriage is over,' she said in a sepulchral tone. 'I shall ask Geoffrey for a divorce.'

'But you can't divorce him because he didn't notice you. That's hardly grounds for divorce, Jane,' said Louise gently, pushing a piece of heavily buttered toast towards her. 'Have some,' she said firmly.

Jane took it, sipped the coffee before munching her way dolefully through the toast. 'I suppose the girls in that shop were right,' she said eventually. 'Geoffrey has gone off the boil.'

Louise felt she had to ask. 'Are you desperate for sex, then, Jane?'

Jane took another piece of toast, and ate it slowly. 'No,' she said at last. 'I told you I've never much cared for it.

But I do feel that there must be something wrong with us or with him at any rate. According to all the magazines I read, everyone's having fantastic sex even in their eighties. So if Geoffrey isn't having it with me, he *must* be having it with Sharon from the Ring of Bells.'

Louise laughed out loud. 'What rubbish you are talking. People get paid to write those silly articles. They have to make it sound as if everyone is having a fantastic time otherwise they'd never get published. Look at me, I'm always being told to put more sex in my novels, even when I feel, personally, that it's not appropriate. And I do it. Anything to earn a crust of bread.'

'I thought you said when you talked to the Women's Institute that you had to believe in what you were writing, so I've always thought you were terribly sexy.'

'I hope the rest of the WI doesn't think like that.'

'Oh, they do, because your sex scenes are so real.'

'They only seem real because of the way I write them, but they're not real. There is a limit. I make them up.' She eyed Jane who was staring at her through dirty spectacles, which matched the rest of her attire. 'Tell me, did you go to bed? Or spend the night in the car?'

'I got up at four o'clock this morning, went for a long walk. In the rain,' she added unnecessarily as Louise could see she was still pretty wet. 'Then I drove around, trying to pluck up courage to come and see you, and then just when I had, I saw that gorgeous man coming out of here, and ...'

'You jumped to the wrong conclusion.' Louise stood up and looked towards the kitchen. Jack, gorgeous! She couldn't see it. He was pleasant enough, attractive even, but not gorgeous. Then she remembered overhearing Penny's conversation on the phone the night before. Perhaps there was something she'd missed. Penny was apparently attracted to him, but that was a problem she'd have to sort out later. Jane was her priority now. 'Come on,' she said. 'Let's go up to my bedroom and smarten you up, then you can go back home looking like the old Jane we all know and love.'

'You mean back to being me, boring old Jane,' said Jane.

'I'm sure Geoffrey prefers you that way,' said Louise, crossing her fingers behind her back, and making up her mind that if a suitable occasion arose she'd try and find out in a tactful way what it was that Geoffrey really thought. Although on second thoughts the chance of finding the right moment seemed fairly remote.

'But all the magazines say ...' began Jane.

'Stop reading those magazines. Just listen to me for a moment. I shall need your help.' Louise steered Jane through the hall and towards the stairs. 'I haven't told you yet of my plans. I'm going to run Lavender House as a B and B, and it's going to be an organic B and B, so I shall need plenty of your lovely lavender soap and bath gel for my guests.'

'Oh! Really? I can make bath salts as well you know,' said Jane, noticeably perking up. 'And herbal cushions so people can have a good night's sleep. And I've just started making calendula cream which is marvellous for the skin.'

'Great. I'm sure I'll be able to sell all of it.' Louise ushered a much more cheerful Jane into her bedroom. She hadn't yet told Jane about her loss of the monthly allowance, which was the reason for opening the house to paying guests, but as Jane hadn't asked the reason she decided to leave that for the time being. There was quite enough going on for the moment without complicating matters even more.

*

In the kitchen, Penny was enjoying the company of Jack. He had an engaging flirty way about him, which boosted her morale and made her feel more feminine and attractive than she had for ages. She and David hardly ever spoke to each other these days. He was always working, and when he did come home she was too tired for small talk. Well, to be truthful too tired for much talk at all. She was usually to be found slumped in front of the TV in the evening, watching whatever rubbish happened to be on, with a glass of wine in her hand.

David did remark on her wine intake once. 'Do you think all that alcohol is good for you and the baby?'

'You have to drink a lot when you're breast feeding,' Penny had said, defensively. 'And it's good for me.'

David had given a snort of disapproval. 'But not good for the baby if you ask me.'

'I'm not asking you,' Penny had snapped back

After that episode, David had subsided into a heap on the settee, muttering something about Jacob growing up to be an alcoholic, but hadn't mentioned it again. Penny, feeling guilty, had tried to ration herself to two glasses per evening. But their days of animated conversation seemed to have died a death, which was why she was finding the company of Jack so entertaining.

'What did you do before you became a full-time mother?' asked Jack.

He'd made the porridge for her, without making it stick to the bottom of the pan, Penny noticed, and was dishing up platefuls for the boys. 'You'd make a perfect father,' said Penny, not answering his question.

Jack tousled Sam's blond head. 'I'll never be one,' he said. 'All my wives have hated children.'

'All! How have many have there been then?'

He laughed, and again his eyes twinkled wickedly. Penny felt herself drawn more and more to him. 'Three,' he confessed. 'I'm serial husband material. They were all gold diggers.' He sighed dramatically, and ate a spoonful of porridge. 'I suppose you could say I'm stupid. Always choosing the wrong women.'

'Not stupid at all,' said Penny, 'though I suppose you must be rich.' She thought about the one hundred pounds he'd parted with so easily. 'Anyway, how old are you? You don't seem old to me.'

'I'm forty-nine, which is old enough,' said Jack, 'and for your information I've given up on marriage.'

Louise and Jane returned to the kitchen and caught the end of the conversation.

'That's a pity,' said Jane, who had recovered sufficiently to be back to her breathy, slightly sanctimonious self. 'I've been worrying about Louise for ages. She shouldn't live here on her own. It's not good. I'm always telling her she should get married again.'

'And I'm always telling you I like being on my own, and have no desire to end up washing some man's pants and socks.' Louise felt cross, wishing Jane wouldn't try to match make when she should be concentrating on her own marriage, which appeared to be in a perilous state, not to mention downright strange.

'You could do with a rich man, though,' said Penny shamelessly. 'But then, so could I.' To Louise's horror she saw her daughter flutter her eyelashes at Jack. 'How do you fancy an unmarried mother with two delightful children?' A remark rather marred by Jacob choosing that moment to choke on his porridge, and then throw up. 'And I'd like more children,' added Penny.

'I'm not rich,' said Jack. 'Three ex-wives have seen to that, and I'll never have children. Apparently my sperm are not the right kind. They swim too slowly and tend to stop outside the egg and fraternize with each other instead of getting on with the job.'

'There you are then,' said Louise firmly. 'He's not rich and he's too old for you and me. So stop trying to marry him off.'

'Amen to that,' said Jack with a wide grin, which for some reason annoyed Louise immeasurably. 'Although, I wouldn't have said that I'm too old for you, Louise, because you can't be *that* much younger than me, and if you are, then you've not worn very well.'

If he hadn't left the kitchen that very moment with Sam in tow, Louise would have thrown something at him.

CHAPTER
❧ SIX ❧

ONCE JACK AND Sam had disappeared, Louise started clearing the breakfast things, and glowered at Penny.

'This is something you can do to earn your keep. Do a bit of tidying up and cleaning. I meant it when I said I can't afford to keep you and the boys.' She saw Jane's slightly shocked expression. 'I'm not being hard hearted, I'm being realistic, which is how I'm going to be from now on, and the reason is,' she addressed this to Jane who as yet was unaware of her financial situation, 'I've just heard that my monthly allowance from the insurance scheme has gone belly-up, the way of many others. So I have to think of other ways to make money.'

'Oh.' Jane's eyes opened wide. 'But can't you …'

'I haven't got time to go into all the details now, just take it from me that the bottom line is I'm hard up. And by the way, Jane, don't you think you should be getting back home to Geoffrey? He must be wondering where you are at this time of the morning. You're not usually up, let alone out.'

Jane shrugged. 'Well, it won't hurt him to wonder; always assuming that he's noticed I'm not there.'

'Yes, that is the trouble, isn't it,' said Penny. 'They become so used to you that you're invisible.'

'You're so right.' Jane turned to Penny, tears at the ready.

Louise stepped in abruptly; she felt a brute but knew she had to do it. 'Go home Jane, you can't stay here commiserating with Penny for the rest of the morning. I've got to go to the bank and tell them why my monthly payment won't be going in and how I'm going to pay all the direct debits, as well as getting some advice on how to set up a business.' Direct debits were the bane of Louise's life. She imagined them like black, clawing hands, coming in from outer space and snatching what little money she had.

Although doing her best to appear brisk and businesslike in front of Penny and Jane, Louise felt sick with apprehension. She hated visiting the bank, and always felt guilty even if she did have money in her account. Once, many years before when she was young, and bank managers had enormous power, or so it seemed to her, she'd been hauled before one because of her overdraft. Ever since she'd been afraid of banks and only visited them when absolutely necessary.

A clatter outside the window announced the arrival of Kevin, the roofer. Louise rushed outside. 'No need to tell me, Mrs Gregory,' he said, sounding remarkably cheerful for him. 'I've had a wander round and I can see where they've slipped by that front chimney again. Did you know you've got another five or six slipping at the back by the other chimney, I'll have to get at those over the outside lavatory roof.'

'Oh dear.' The hundred pounds was going to disappear before she knew it.

'You got them rock cakes ready? I'll be down for a coffee and a cake when I've finished here in the front.'

'Oh dear,' repeated Louise. 'I'm afraid I haven't had time to make them.' She looked back at Jane. 'I've had such a lot of interruptions. But I can do you a bacon sandwich if you like.'

'Well, I suppose that'll have to do.' Kevin sounded back to his grumpy self.

She was still thinking about the roof, direct debits, the bank manager, and her as yet unformulated business plan, as she walked back into the kitchen. Penny was stacking the dishwasher, and Jane was still there telling her about Geoffrey, when they were interrupted by the loud roar of an engine followed by several deafening explosions. Then there was a scream from Kevin as the ladder whizzed down past the window.

'Oh my God! He's gone down the chimney like little Bill in Alice in Wonderland,' said Penny.

'Who was Bill?' asked Jane in an interested voice, 'I've never read Alice in Wonderland.'

'Never mind that,' shouted Louise rushing outside to find Kevin clinging perilously to the chimneystack. 'Where is Jack? Why are men never around when you need them? Come on, Penny, Jane, help me with the ladder.'

Between them they managed to put the heavy ladder back in place, and a very shaky Kevin climbed down. 'Never mind the coffee, I think I'll have a brandy if you don't mind,' he said breathlessly. He waggled one arm. 'I think it's broken.'

'Rubbish,' said a woman in a loud voice, it boomed from the culprit of Kevin's demise. Picking up his arm, and ignoring his groans, she wrenched it from one side to the other, and then pronounced, 'It's not broken. I've been in lots of hospital films, one gets to know these things.'

'You've only ever been a patient, you've never been a doctor,' said Louise crossly. Kevin was clutching his arm to his chest, and she thought if it wasn't broken before it might very well might be now.

'Who is that?' whispered Jane staring at the tall thin woman. The new arrival was wearing dark glasses, had skin the colour and texture of a wrinkled walnut, was wearing an emerald green trouser suit, with a cerise scarf around her neck. Enormous gold hoop earrings finished off her outfit.

'Maggie West, my mother-in-law,' said Penny. 'Well, nearly my mother-in-law, she would be if David and I were married. She's a terrible driver.'

'Tell me about it,' muttered Kevin tottering past with Louise into the kitchen.

'You're not married?' Jane was horrified. 'But you've got two children. Louise never told me you weren't married. What about the children's surname?'

'Oh, for goodness sake, Jane, don't let's go into all that now.' Louise lost patience. 'Go home and get your husband his breakfast. And, Maggie,' she shouted at the woman who was going back to lock her car, which was a vintage cream and black Bentley, 'for Heaven's sake do please remember to put the handbrake on, we don't want the car ending up in the rose bed like last time.'

'I don't know whether I can face Geoffrey.' Jane's voice quavered, and she started back towards the kitchen.

Louise grabbed her by the shoulders and turned her round. 'You have to. Go now, and get it over with. Go now, and get out of my way, there are far too many people here, I just can't stand it.' Firmly pushing her back into the garden towards her car, Louise knew she was being brutal, but she'd reached the end of her tether. Maggie turning up and knocking Kevin off his ladder was the last straw. In the background she could hear Jacob starting to roar just to add to the general mayhem.

Jane backed away nervously. 'All right,' she said meekly. 'I'll let you know how I get on.' But she didn't go, she lurked around anxious to see what would happen next.

Louise didn't notice, she was too busy administering a generous brandy to Kevin who was sitting, ashen faced, at the kitchen table, in stark contrast to that of Jacob who was puce with rage because Penny had taken away his porridge. 'Let me feel your arm.' Kevin held it out and Louise gently ran her fingers along it. How did one know if an arm was broken? 'I don't think it's broken,' she told him with more confidence than she felt.

Kevin moved his arm and opened and closed his hand. 'No it's OK, I think,' he said, and took another gulp of brandy. 'But that woman shouldn't be allowed on the road, she's a menace.'

'Amen to that,' replied Louise with feeling.

Penny peered out of the window watching Maggie taking a case from the car. 'I think she's come to make me go back,' she said, and tried to get out of sight behind Louise.

'For goodness sake, you're a grown woman. You can make your own decisions,' said Louise. She liked Maggie, eccentric though she was, and despite her terrible driving, she had a heart of gold, and Louise knew she found her son David as exasperating as both she and Penny did. Maggie said he took after his father, her second husband, and that it was a great pity that her present husband wasn't his father. He, the present husband, Seth Weinberger, was a chef in New York, where he had a restaurant and a TV show on some minor TV channel. He and Maggie only met about three times a year, which suited them both because they were always so pleased to see each other on these rare occasions that they never had time to argue.

'A good marriage is one conducted on a long distance basis,' Maggie was fond of saying, usually immediately contradicting herself by adding that Penny and David should spend more time together bonding.

Louise went out to help her with the case.

'Darling,' boomed Maggie, her emerald coloured trouser suit contrasting beautifully with the lavender bushes at the side of the path, 'I've come to see what all this nonsense with Penny and David is about.' She spied Penny looking at her through the kitchen window, Jacob by now attached to one breast to shut him up. 'I'm with you, of course, darling,' she called. 'All the way.'

'I'm don't know whether I'm with her or not. I've hardly had time to talk to Penny properly,' said Louise, 'and I'm not sure whether it is a good idea to encourage the break-up of a partnership when two young children are involved.' She followed Maggie along the path towards the kitchen. 'Penny and I have not really had a moment to ourselves, at least not long enough to discuss it properly, since she arrived.'

Maggie swirled round to face Louise, a mass of flying beads and bangles. 'But of course you must be with her. It's we women against the men. We must stand our ground, fight our corner, and demand our rights as liberated women.'

'It's not easy to be liberated when you've got two young children tugging at your skirts,' observed Louise. But she knew Maggie wasn't listening as she flung open the kitchen door, and planted a kiss on the top of Jacob's head, which left a large lipstick mark. She never listened to anyone. She also wasn't that liberated. At least, not in Louise's book. Her acting days were virtually over, as parts for rather wrinkled old women rarely came up, unless it was a drunk propping up a bar in something like *EastEnders*, which Maggie despised as being too downmarket. She was not, however, averse to playing corpses, and did quite well by making brief appearances; usually on a trolley with so many drips and machinery attached she looked like a petrol pump, in the many and various hospital dramas on TV.

Kevin eyed the emerald and cerise vision rather apprehensively.

'This is the man you nearly killed when you ran into his ladder,' Louise told her.

Maggie registered Kevin in one all embracing glance, and then dismissed him as unworthy of a second look. Louise knew she liked her men tall, dark and handsome, and Kevin didn't come up to standard in any of those categories. 'Sorry, darling,' she beamed at him, before turning back to Jacob and tickling him under the chin, 'but you must admit it was an awfully silly place to put a ladder.'

'I was on the roof, replacing slates,' said Kevin peevishly.

'Yes, and he always does a wonderful job,' interrupted Louise quickly. The last thing she wanted was to lose the services of Kevin. He was looking better now. 'Do you want to do those at the back now, or leave them until another day?'

'I'll do them now.' Kevin got up, wobbled a little, and then brushed a hand across his forehead in a dramatic gesture. Louise had never seen him so animated before; perhaps giving him the brandy hadn't been wise. 'I'll have a coffee now, I'll take it round the back out of everyone's way,' he added, skirting around Maggie nervously.

'I'll bring it round,' Louise ushered him out, and put on the kettle for a fresh cafetière, and worried: should he go up the ladder after all that brandy? But then mentally crossed her fingers hoping that Kevin knew best.

'I'm not going back to him,' said Penny, trying to rub the lipstick from Jacob's head with the sleeve of her cardigan. 'He asked me to marry him last night, and I said no.'

'Quite right too, darling,' said Maggie. 'I'd have said no too.' She sat herself down on a kitchen chair, in a floating motion, so that her scarf spread about her in the most becoming manner. Ever the poseur, it was second nature to Maggie. Her hair was looking terrific, Louise noticed. Much too good to be real, must be a wig. 'I could do with a drink,' she said.

'I'll make a cup of tea.' Jane, who'd sidled back into the kitchen, darted forward. Louise could see she was absolutely fascinated by the exotic creature that had just arrived; somehow she and Maggie's paths had never crossed before.

'I said a drink, darling. Tea is not a drink. I fancy a Bloody Mary. I need something to set me up for the day. I was up at the crack of dawn.'

'Oh!' Jane tottered back nonplussed. People didn't drink Bloody Marys at nine o'clock in the morning in her social circles.

Louise took over. 'There's no vodka, Maggie. You'll have to make do with the remains of last night's white wine.' She got it out of the fridge and plonked it on the table with a large wine glass.

Maggie peered at it. 'But it's from Tesco,' she said plaintively.

'Yes, it's all I can afford. We don't all have wealthy husbands to support us.'

Maggie dismissed that remark with a wave of her bejewelled hand. 'Well darling, you're a writer. You don't need a husband. Look at Jeffrey Archer. He's made millions, even when he was in prison he made money.'

'I'm not in the same league as Jeffrey Archer, and I'm not sure I want to be,' said Louise sharply, pouring hot water into the cafetière for Kevin's coffee, before cutting some bread for his bacon sandwich. 'Do you want a piece of toast?' she asked Maggie.

'I'd prefer a croissant.' Maggie looked enquiringly at Louise, and then added, 'but a piece of toast would be lovely.'

Louise rammed the slice of bread, which she'd cut much too thickly, bad temperedly into the toaster, which immediately started emitting smoke and a strong smell of burning, and put two rashers into the frying pan.

'Can I help?' Jane was hovering about again.

'No!' Louise exploded. 'Go away. Go home and get your husband's breakfast. I thought you'd gone ages ago.' She opened the kitchen door and waved Jane through into the garden, watching as she climbed reluctantly into her car.

Jane wound the window down. 'Well, I suppose you're right, I've got to face him some time.'

Louise smiled in what she hoped was an encouraging manner, then shut the kitchen door very firmly.

'Where's Sam?' asked Maggie.

'Sam? Oh Heavens, I'd forgotten about him,' said Penny. 'Jack took Sam out ages ago. I hope they're OK.'

As she spoke, Louise looked out of the kitchen window and saw that Jack and Sam were indeed OK, and were coming through the gate at the bottom of the garden. Sam was carefully carrying a basket and looking very pleased with himself.

'We've got some fresh eggs from a Mr Hackett,' called Jack. 'Sam's going to have one boiled for his lunch.'

'And I picked them up,' shouted Sam excitedly. 'They were all warm from the hen's bottom.'

Louise opened the door and stepped outside.

Jane wound down her window again, and Louise felt like leaning in and throttling her, but resisted the temptation. 'What are you going to do about Maggie?' she asked through the open window.

'Nothing, she'll go in a couple of hours. She usually does. Now go! Go! Go!' Just as Louise was on the point of losing her patience, Jane put the car in gear and finally drove off.

It was true, Maggie did normally disappear after a short time, usually after dispensing the most inappropriate advice, which luckily no one took any notice of. Louise always thought her heart was in the right place, but had doubts about her brain. But as she was always here, there and everywhere at the drop of a hat, it never seemed to matter.

Louise hoped that this visit would run true to form, although the fact that she'd unloaded her suitcase was ominous. But at least, she reflected, her book was finished and sent off to Dottie so she didn't have that to worry about. She could concentrate on Penny's problems and try and get her reunited with David. Much as she loved her daughter, and both Sam and Jacob, Louise didn't feel she could go back to having children permanently in the house. Her child rearing days were over, and she must make that clear to Penny. Besides, she had to get her moneymaking scheme under way, and couldn't turn into a baby-minding nanny while Penny went out to work.

In London, David got up late and decided to work from home that day, something he never did normally. Even though he ran his own business, he always felt more comfortable in his rented office, with its serried rows of electrical equipment, and neat filing cabinets stuffed full of perfectly filed information. Although he worked in what was nowadays euphemistically called the paperless environment, and urged all his clients to cut out paper and rely on their websites and online order systems, he personally, could never quite bring himself to rely exclusively on the sometimes unpredictable whims of the computers at his beck and call. Not something he ever told his clients.

The house was eerily quiet. No Jacob howling and shaking the bars of his cot, no Sam shouting that he needed the potty, and no warm smells of toast or porridge. Wandering moodily into the kitchen David decided to fix breakfast. He fancied porridge and got out the big plastic container that Penny kept the oats in, and then realized he had no idea of how to make it. He knew Penny mixed it with something and put it in the microwave, but there were no recipe books lying around to help.

But no problem, he thought. These days a computer had the answer to everything, so getting out his laptop he typed in the word porridge. One could find out anything on the Internet, he'd show Penny he could manage without her. Sure enough, some recipes popped up. The first one he looked at recommended stirring the porridge in a clockwise direction using the right hand to avoid evoking the Devil. That didn't sound right, and he was pretty certain that Penny had never worried about evoking the Devil, neither had she used a straight wooden spoon known as a 'spurtle' or 'theevil'.

'Bloody hell, this porridge business seems a bit complicated,' he muttered, wishing more than ever that he was surrounded by the usual family racket with Penny in charge. He thought about ringing his mother again, but dismissed that idea. He doubted that her porridge making abilities were any better than his, she'd probably launch into the witches incantation from Macbeth.

Clicking into another site, he found one which seemed eminently sensible. Half a cup of oats, one and a half cups of water, and three minutes in the microwave. The result was something closely resembling glue, but with plenty of sugar, not salt as recommended, it was almost palatable.

After the porridge he made himself a strong espresso, at least he knew how to work the espresso machine, and then he sat down and looked around. The place really was a terrible mess, something he hadn't noticed before. There was wet washing in the washing machine, a huge basket of dirty clothes beside it obviously waiting to be washed. Toys scattered everywhere, the detritus of yesterday's breakfast on the floor where Sam and Jacob had thrown their porridge bowls and toast. All in all, the house needed a thorough clean. Slowly a thought filtered through into his brain. Was it from this that Penny had fled? Surely not. Housework was, after all, an unskilled job. Merely a question of putting things away, turning on the vacuum cleaner and wiping over a few surfaces. Penny was an intelligent woman. She had a first class honours degree in history and had got job in a trendy house and gardens magazine, but then the children were born. David had always thought she should have kept the job and got someone else to look after the children, not taken the easy route. But Penny had wanted to be a full-time mother and stayed at home.

His mobile rang. David answered quickly hoping it was Penny, but it wasn't. It was a client trying to reach him. He should have known, of course. She would have rung on the landline, not the mobile.

'David,' said the voice on the other end. It was one of his most trying clients; a woman running a trendy boutique in Chelsea who wanted to change her website every five minutes. Just the sound of her voice made him feel bad-tempered. 'I'm not happy with the latest layout of the site,' she said. 'The way you've done it makes my clothes look too expensive.'

'They are expensive,' said David, omitting the word 'too' which he actually thought was appropriate. 'I thought that was what you wanted. Exclusivity.'

'Not so exclusive that nobody will buy the bloody things,' she replied huffily. 'I have an idea for some major changes; I'd like you to come round this morning to discuss them with me.'

'Sorry, no can do. Not today.' He looked around the kitchen and, balancing the phone behind his ear, started making himself another espresso. 'I've got a big job on today, and I may not be free tomorrow.' Tomorrow he'd go down to Hampshire and fetch Penny and the children back to where they belonged. 'Just email me your ideas and I'll have a look at them as soon as I can.'

'I don't pay you a fortune to be put off for two days.'

David could just imagine her expression. She was one of those middle-aged women who'd had one too many face-lifts so that she looked permanently surprised. Coat hanger thin, with her perma-tanned complexion and dyed blonde hair, he found her almost frightening. She reminded him rather of his mother, although to give her credit she'd not had facelifts.

'I'm afraid you don't pay me enough to secure my

exclusivity,' he said, keeping his voice as polite as possible. 'You send me your ideas, and I'll do the best I can.'

'There are other web designers,' she shrieked.

'True. Perhaps you'd better find one.' David pressed the off button. Damn and blast it, he'd lost a client, and it was all Penny's fault. If she'd been at home, and he hadn't been sitting alone in the kitchen, this would never have happened.

He yanked the phone down from its place on the kitchen wall, and began to tap in the number of Louise's phone, then stopped. No, he'd do the house first. Looking at his watch he saw it was 9.30 in the morning already. OK, he'd ring Penny at 10.30 when he'd finished.

By twelve noon he hadn't got beyond the kitchen. He'd hung one lot of washing on the long line in the garden as it was a lovely sunny day, and ended up with aching arms and what felt like a dislocated shoulder. Penny must be stronger than he'd thought. Then he put another lot of dirty clothes in the washing machine, but soon realized he'd done something wrong. All the clothes he could see swirling round through the glass front were bright pink, and they definitely weren't that colour when he'd put them in, and he also suspected that perhaps he'd overdone the soap powder as there were bubbles emerging from every crack in the machine, forming small, pink mountains everywhere. But the kitchen floor was clean, and he felt quite proud of that. Everything was put away, not necessarily in the right place he had to admit, but at least out of sight, and the surfaces had been washed and the sink scoured. That had been difficult, and took him three pads of wire wool. Now he knew why Penny always shouted at him for throwing his coffee dregs and tea bags in the sink.

Staggering through into the sitting room, he flung

himself down on the settee for a rest. Maybe he'd have to ring Penny tomorrow and tell her how he'd cleaned up; he didn't think he had the energy to finish the rest of the house today. Designing websites was definitely much easier. In less than five minutes, he was snoring on the settee.

At Lavender House, Maggie West was in full swing vamping Jack the moment he'd entered the kitchen with Sam and his eggs.

'Darling, how wonderful,' said Louise, carefully taking the eggs from Sam and putting them in the fridge.

'I'm having one for lunch,' said Sam importantly. 'It's organic.' He stumbled over the unfamiliar word, adding 'And it's from a hen.'

'All eggs are from hens, darling,' said Maggie, swirling her cerise scarf around her neck in a come-hither manner.

Penny raised her eyes heavenwards. She was used to Maggie's way with men. The fact that she was on her third husband and over seventy, although nobody knew by how much, made no difference. She still regarded every man she met as a challenge to her femininity and powers of seduction.

Louise felt annoyed as well. Heaven only knows what Jack must think of my family and friends, she thought, everyone seems to have gone stark, staring mad today. Was it only Monday she'd been sitting so peacefully in the garden, thinking vaguely about whether or not to call Kevin in to fix the slates, and feeling secure in the knowledge that she really had nothing much to worry about. Then suddenly the money had dried up, a bombshell out of the blue; Penny and the children had arrived announcing they intended to stay for the duration, and then there was Jane, who was definitely having more than one senior moment, and now Maggie who was always absolutely unbearable when there was a new man about. Not that there'd ever been one on Louise's premises before, but she'd seen her in action at various soirees she'd been dragged to by Penny when she was desperate for a night out in London, and had got a freebie via Maggie for a gallery opening, or a first night preview.

She looked surreptitiously across to Jack to see how he was reacting to Maggie, and felt a small frisson of illicit pleasure, as he seemed to be ignoring her and concentrating on Sam.

'It's because this egg is fresh,' he was telling Sam seriously. 'That's why it'll be a different colour. A lovely pale yellow. The ones you buy in the shops are always old ones.'

'I can see you are a man of the land,' said Maggie, fluttering her heavily mascared eyelashes.

'Definitely,' said Jack, 'and I can see you are a woman of ...' he hesitated, and Louise wondered what he was going to say. Then he said, 'A woman of infinite experience.'

For a moment Louise wondered how Maggie was going to take this two edged compliment. But she was pleased, and made a great show of taking Jacob from Penny and playing at being the doting grandmother. Louise knew she was being mean, but couldn't help hoping that Jacob would spew up some of his breakfast down the emerald trouser suit.

But Jacob merely gave a seraphic smile, and snuggled himself into Maggie's rather sparse bosom.

CHAPTER
⋙ SEVEN ⋘

LOUISE HAD NO intention of mentioning her financial problems to Maggie. She'd made up her mind that she was definitely not going to become obsessed about money, and therefore was not going to talk about it. But Penny had no such inhibitions, and over yet another pot of coffee – all this is costing me a fortune, thought Louise forgetting her rule about obsession and feeling slightly desperate – she told Maggie of Louise's allowance disappearing into thin air, and about being out of contract with her publisher so that there was no guarantee of any money coming from that source either.

Maggie listened, while dandling Jacob on her knee and letting him play with her golden hoop earrings. When Penny had finished the story, she turned to Louise. 'You'll just have to use your savings,' she said complacently. 'That's what I'd do.'

Horribly aware of Jack listening to everything being said, and being too proud to admit that she didn't have any savings, Louise determined to put a stop to the discussion of her financial affairs. 'I'm going down to the bank in Rumsey to discuss my options this morning. As you know I've decided to run Lavender House as a bed and breakfast guesthouse. It was Jack who gave me the idea by turning up on my doorstep.'

He pulled a face. 'I'm glad you think I've been of some use.'

'I'm surprised you haven't thought of it before. I would have done,' said Maggie airily, 'but then, of course, I've never been broke.'

'I'm not broke, and you've never had to think of how to support yourself,' said Louise abruptly, then immediately regretted sounding so waspish. But the truth was she didn't have any savings to speak of. She and John had spent their money on the children, the animals and holidays, and they'd only repaired the house when absolutely necessary. John had not been an ambitious man, which was the thing Louise had loved about him. The only time he had been ambitious was when he'd gone off to Australia with Geoffrey to invest and dabble in mining, and that had turned out disastrously. Sometimes they'd made vague plans for the future. Maybe to sell Lavender House and downsize, but neither of them really fancied that, and anyway, they always told each other, they were too young; besides there was plenty of time.

But life had other plans, and there was no time. John died unexpectedly of a massive heart attack. Louise had found him lying amongst the bean sticks, a trug full of freshly picked runner beans in his hand. She'd never grown runner beans since; although Penny had urged her to, telling her it was silly to be so sentimental about beans. But Louise couldn't bring herself to plant them. Not yet anyway, 'maybe next year,' she always said.

Louise dragged her thoughts back to the present and heard Penny saying 'I think it's silly letting all these empty bedrooms go to waste. They're all furnished and ready. She could put up a sign and open immediately.'

Jack joined them at the kitchen table. 'As your first paying guest I second that.' He looked across at Louise, and added, 'I don't think it wise to dip into your savings. You will need those for a really rainy day.'

'Yes, I suppose you're right,' said Louise. She was pretty certain that Jack had guessed her savings were non-existent. Well, very nearly, she had a few shares, which she didn't bother to keep track of, as the annual payments were so small, and also some premium bonds, which had never delivered anything in the way of prizes.

'Tell you what, darling,' said Maggie. 'I'm resting at the moment, and the country is so much healthier than Notting Hill. Ever since they made that damned film with Hugh Grant and Julia Roberts it's so full of traffic, tourists and drug dealers, it's become unbearable. I'm thinking I'll let my house there, and become your second paying guest.'

'A hundred pounds a night,' Jack said quickly.

'Good heavens! For that I shall expect champagne for breakfast.' Unexpectedly though, Maggie appeared unfazed by the price.

'Cash in hand, Maggie,' added Penny. 'Mum's not legit yet. She hasn't got a double drainer or anything like that. You know all this health and safety business, so we'll have to be discreet for a while.'

'Pity,' Jack lolled back in his chair looking amused. 'I was going to offer to put up a board outside today, saying "B and B, vacancies."'

It was all too much. Louise stood up. 'Stop organizing my life,' she said fiercely. 'It's not definite. I'm considering it. I have to talk to the bank manager, and anyway I'm not sure I want to let the house out. It won't be mine any more if I do that.'

'It won't be yours any more if you can't afford to live

here,' Jack pointed out with unerring logic.

Louise didn't want logic. She wanted a solution, but what had appeared so simple yesterday, now had obstacles in the way. As Penny had said, there were health and safety regulations, and registration and loads of other things she hadn't even begun to unravel. Help in the house, redecorating, and a million and one other things. She looked at Jack, lolling back on one of the kitchen chairs as if he owned the place. 'Sit up', she snapped. 'You'll break that chair, they are very old.' Jack sat to attention. 'And stop trying to organize me. This time yesterday I didn't even know you. You were just a man who made me fall off my bike, and now you're trying manipulate me into going into a business I know nothing about.'

'Anyone can make a bed and cook breakfast,' said Maggie blithely, waving one of her heavily ring-clad hands. 'I'll help you in the kitchen.' She paused, then added, 'For a deduction in the going rate.'

The thought of Maggie helping in the kitchen was one nightmare too many. Louise couldn't bear it. 'I'm going into Rumsey to see the bank manager, and talk over things with him. I've already made an appointment so I've got to hurry up.' It was a lie, but they weren't to know that, and she wanted to get away from the family and think things over before she did see the bank manager.

'He'll tell you to get a business plan, and then come back,' said Penny gloomily. 'I know David had to do that before they'd even let him open a business account.'

'Talking of David,' said Louise severely, 'I think it's about time you rang him and sorted your own life out before you try and sort out mine.'

Penny looked mutinous. 'I don't need sorting out, and I don't need David. If I'm really desperate I could always go on the game. I believe it's quite profitable.'

'Not round here it wouldn't be, darling,' said Maggie. 'Too many twitching lace curtains for the men to dare stray, and those who might would probably smell of manure. No, London's the place to do it. But you'd have to smarten yourself up, and farm out the children. Nothing so off putting as a toddler appearing when you're heavily involved with a client. However, that aside, I can tell you, my dear, that high class call girls live in luxury.'

'You speak as if you have first hand knowledge,' observed Jack slyly.

Louise hid a grin as Maggie flushed, then said in a sulky tone of voice, 'Of course not me, personally. But I have quite a few girlfriends, actresses, who have done it when they've been resting. One has to do something when there's no money coming in. Luckily for me I've always had a rich husband.'

'Or two,' said Penny maliciously.

Louise left them to it before Maggie had a chance to reply. She had no wish to be involved in an argument between Penny and Maggie and went upstairs to get ready for her encounter with the bank manager. She decided to wear something businesslike, so that he'd think her a sensible woman who had a chance of succeeding with running a guesthouse. The more she thought about it the more sensible it seemed. She could do bed and breakfast, occasional picnic lunches if required, that would be easy, and maybe evening dinner sometimes. It would mean that she could stay in the house, and hopefully it would also give her time for writing, if Dottie could get her another contract. And if income from writing did dry up completely she'd just carry on with the bed and breakfast business; she put aside the niggling doubts that told her that having paying guests was likely to be very hard work, because, she reasoned, there was no point in worrying about problems before they arose.

But she wished Dottie would ring and tell her what she thought of the latest book. It was vital that she liked it and thought she could sell the damned thing. But Dottie was unpredictable; it depended on the time of month, what was happening in her chaotic love life, and whether or not one of her cats was pregnant. Louise crossed her fingers and hoped that Dottie's next lover, she was always referring vaguely to her lovers, would be someone in the upper echelons of publishing who'd take and publish every and any manuscript she pushed his way. All, dreams, dreams, dreams, Louise knew. The reality was that Dottie would either rave about it and say it was the most wonderful thing she'd read for ages, but then not be able to sell it, and ring back to say 'Forget it, darling. Just get on with the next book, and try and think of a new angle. Editors are always looking for something new.' Or she'd reject it out of hand and say the middle, beginning, or end, whichever bit she didn't like, needed rewriting. Louise didn't mind any of this, it was par for the course with Dottie, but she did need to know.

Anyway, meeting the bank manager came first in her list of things to do. So she applied discreet lipstick and mascara, and drew her hair back into a tidy looking chignon. What to wear had been a problem. Louise didn't get out much socially these days, and mostly wore jeans and a T-shirt. The dresses she did have were not terribly fashionable. She'd worn them at her book launches in her more affluent days, but none of them were suitable for riding a bike to the bank, which she intended to do. Eventually she chose a red shirt-waister, a positive colour, with a nice stiff collar, which looked good with a string of pearls, and had a well cut, fairly narrow skirt.

She made her way downstairs and let herself out of the front door.

Then she hesitated. Perhaps she ought to take the car, it looked more professional. But the petrol gauge was flashing orange when she turned the key in the ignition, which meant she had just about enough petrol to get to the garage outside of Rumsey, and no further. It certainly wouldn't take her to the bank and back. She looked in her purse and calculated petrol or food. If she'd been on her own it would have been different, but extra food for lunch and dinner had to be bought for four adults and two children. The garden was a wonderful provider, but unless they survived on rocket, spinach, spring onions, and early potatoes, she needed to buy something else.

'Sorry darlings,' she said, tipping a couple of disgruntled dogs from the car. They'd leapt in the moment she'd opened the door. 'I need food, and I'm taking the bike.'

Might as well start as I mean to go on, she told herself, struggling down the lane, her tight red skirt hitched up to her thighs. Cycling is good for the figure and health, and also saves money. Besides, she suddenly remembered, it was the day for the farmers' market in Rumsey, and there'd be nowhere to park, so a bicycle was definitely more practicable.

She arrived at the bank, hot and sweaty, having negotiated the farmers' market stalls, and stopped off in the public toilets in the village square to tidy herself before entering the bank. Not a very reassuring experience as it turned out, because the glass mirror had been vandalized and replaced with a metal one which had been bent. Her reflection made her look physically deformed. If I were auditioning for the *Hunchback of Notre Dame* I'd be in with a chance, thought Louise dismally, but I'm certainly not looking at all like the businesswoman of the year.

Back in Blackheath, David woke up with a start and dragged himself up from the sofa. He was desperately missing Penny and the children and was longing to ring Lavender House again, but pride forbade him to until he'd finished cleaning the house. Nothing before had presented him with such a physical challenge. He'd had no idea that housework could be so tiring, and now he realized that Penny had tried to do it with two children demanding her constant attention. Well, to be accurate, one small boy and a baby, with Sam being more demanding than the baby who, at the moment was always satisfied when full of food and milk, although he knew that wouldn't last. Soon Jacob would be running about and demanding extra attention like Sam. I must bring her back to a clean house, full of flowers, and the promise of a cleaner to come in every week and help, thought David, as he tried to vacuum the steep stairs, struggling with the hose of the cleaner, which seemed to have a mind of its own.

The telephone rang again. David hoped it would be Penny. But it wasn't, it was another customer wanting elaborate changes to yet another website. As he had a lucrative contract with this particular firm he needed to keep them happy and couldn't put off the work, so leaving the cleaner halfway up the stairs, David went into his study and after linking his computer to the one in his office, began working on the changes. By the time he'd finished it was five o'clock in the afternoon and he'd dealt with several more calls and managed to tie everything up neatly. A profitable day's work. Normally if the calls and emails dried up, he'd walk from his office across the road in Blackheath High Street and join his mates in the Irish bar for a drink, before going home to a cooked dinner. Now he picked up the vacuum, wrestled with the hose again before finishing the stairs, then had beans on toast.

David watched a blackbird hopping across their miniscule London lawn looking for something to eat. The hawthorn bush at the bottom of the garden glowed white in the last of the evening sunshine, and the blackbird had some luck with a worm in a damp patch beneath the hawthorn. Nothing much would grow in the dry sandy soil of their garden, although Penny had mulched it like mad since they'd been there, and last year even tried with some broad beans. But they'd come up long and straggly and only produced enough beans for one small portion. David knew she missed the lovely garden of her childhood home in Hampshire, and would have much preferred to live outside of the city. But he was a Londoner, through and through, and the thought of stagnating in the country horrified him. There was nowhere to go, nothing to do. Whereas here, in London, there was a myriad of places to visit and things to do, although now David thought about it, he couldn't remember the last time either of them had gone to an art gallery, museum, or theatre, or in fact, done anything together. Their life was a cultural black hole even though they did live in London, one of the most vibrant cities in the world.

Feeling depressed, he put his supper plate in the dishwasher, remembering to rinse it first, as this morning all the plates he'd put in yesterday had needed to be redone because every scrap of food was baked on. It took him ages to scrape off porridge, beans and egg, before reloading them again. He had no intention of doing that again! He'd always thought Penny made an unnecessary fuss about rinsing plates before loading, now he knew why. Closing the dishwasher door, he threw on a jacket and walked the half mile up to Blackheath High Street and into the pub.

'Hi,' Brian, the bar man, greeted him cheerfully. 'Half a pint of Murphy's as usual?'

'Thanks.' David perched himself on a bar stool and looked around for some familiar faces, someone to chat to who was as hooked on IT as he was. Most of his friends were in IT or accountancy, and were married with children and, like him, put off going home until the children were safely out of the way; the few women in his circle were glamorous but older, and usually held down jobs far superior to their husbands over whom they had an iron grip. If they had children, they had nannies and cleaners, and if they didn't have children, they had cleaners. David was secretly frightened of them, and was glad Penny wasn't like that. He couldn't imagine any of them cooking their husbands' suppers; it would be takeaways or eating out. However, tonight he was later, and it was a different crowd spilling into the bar. Younger, noisier, with nowhere in particular to go, unless it was the pizza place next door, so they were drinking more and enjoying themselves.

David suddenly felt very old.

'You're in late tonight,' said Brian, when he had a moment in between serving. 'Something wrong?'

Brian was very easy to talk to and for a moment David was tempted to tell him that Penny had left him, but then decided not to. 'No, I just finished work later this evening,' he said. 'Looks like I missed everyone.'

Brian shrugged expressively. 'Oh, the middle-aged crowd have all gone home.'

Middle-aged! Did Brian mean him?

'I do prefer your lot,' Brian continued. 'I know they're not going to get drunk and abusive, but this crowd.' He shrugged again, and ran a cloth along the top of the bar, 'They're never ready to go, and now the manager has decided we're staying open till midnight. I tell you it's killing my feet. I've been standing all day you know. At my age I've got to think of my health, if I'm not careful I'll be getting varicose veins or piles. Or with my luck, both. And my partner's fed up with me coming home too exhausted to even talk to him, let alone, *you know*,' he raised his eyebrows expressively. 'I can't wait to give in my notice and move to Hampshire.'

'Oh, yes, I remember now you told me.' David looked more closely at him. He'd never thought about Brian's life before. He was just the gay guy who served drinks. 'Do you think you'll like living out of London?'

'Oh my God, yes.' Someone called for a drink, but Brian ignored them. 'You know I told you about the cottage we're getting in East Willow, well, I've already been promised a part-time job in a pub there, the Stag and Beetle, which will tide us over until the antique business really gets going. I can't wait to give in my notice. As soon as we've sold our flat here, we're off.'

'Oi,' called a tall youth from the other end of the bar. 'Is there any service in this place?'

'Coming, sir, coming.' Brian dashed off to the other end of the bar.

David watched him. At my age, he'd said, as if that were old. He supposed Brian was about the same age as him, thirty-seven or in that region. That wasn't old. But he had to admit that today, after all the housework he'd done, he was aching all over and felt old. The crowd grew thicker, young girls piled in, giggling loudly, permanently on their mobiles, and all with skirts so short they were barely decent. Most of them had bare midriffs showing silver rings in their belly buttons.

'Is this stool free?' a young blonde perched next to him, smiling and tossing her long hair over her shoulders in a seductive manner. She was very attractive.

David cheered up. Life wasn't that bad if a blonde was prepared to flirt with him. He hadn't done any flirting in years. He smiled back, suddenly feeling much more cheerful, and about ten years younger. 'Yes it's free, and it will be a pleasure to have you sitting next to me,' he said in a gallant manner which had always worked fifteen years before.

The girl looked him up and down and the smile faded. 'Thanks,' she said, and turning her back on him began to text furiously.

Down at the other end of the bar, David saw another girl reading her phone, then looking at him and laughing. He was sure they were texting about him, and felt embarrassed. Draining the last of his Murphy's, he left the bar and wandered back through the empty streets to the empty house, thinking miserably that he was an old married man with responsibilities. As he put the key in the lock it suddenly struck him. He had the responsibilities, but he wasn't married. He and Penny had never got round to it. She had mentioned it years ago, but he'd never been that keen, then the children came along, and he'd been even less keen, but when he'd asked her she'd said no. All these years of not being married had given him a sense of freedom, but now he realized it was only an illusion. He and Penny were as tied to each other as any married couple, only not legally.

He remembered his mother saying once that if he didn't marry Penny he would have no legal rights over the children. But he'd ignored her, as his mother was always advocating marriage, either her own or someone else's. His mother liked the security of marriage, even though she was not too keen on the till death us do part bit. And, anyway, he'd never for one moment thought that Penny would leave him. However, she had, and now he was alone, and what was even worse, when he had asked her to marry him last night on the phone she'd turn him down flat yet again, and told him there was someone else. Who was it? And when did she find time to form a relationship with anyone else? David decided that Penny must have hidden depths that he knew nothing about.

He made a decision. He'd go and get Penny back. He'd go now. No time like the present. Charging up stairs, he tripped over the vacuum cleaner, which he'd forgotten he'd left on the landing, rushed into the bedroom and threw a few clothes into a holdall. Not much, just a T-shirt, sweater, pair of pants and one pair of socks, reasoning he'd not need much for just one night. He picked up his laptop on the way out, and then thought of Penny. She was always saying that if it were possible he'd have his laptop surgically attached to his body. She exaggerated, of course, but one never knew when it would be needed. He had to be available for his customers. David couldn't even remember what life had been like before the electronic age.

Jumping into the car, he drove off towards the M25. The drive to Lavender House should take about two hours, so, with any luck, they'd all be up when he arrived. Yes, this was the right thing to do. By tomorrow night, his life would be sorted. He'd make sure of that.

CHAPTER
⊰⊱ EIGHT ⊰⊱

ONCE SHE'D GOT there, Louise wished she'd decided to go into Rumsey any day but market day, because everyone she knew seemed to be there. She became horribly aware of the shortness of her red skirt as she negotiated her way through the market trying to avoid catching her wheels in the drains and squeezing past the stalls.

Old Miss Haringey, the jewellery lady, who Louise had never seen sell anything, but who was always there come rain or shine, called out in her high, rather wobbly voice, 'Mrs Gregory, how nice to see you. I've got some new earrings I think you'd be very interested in.'

'Sorry, can't stop,' puffed Louise, which was true as the brakes on her bike were worn, and she could only stop if she put one foot down and skidded along for a bit.

She rode past the big butcher's van and he gave a loud wolf whistle, making her even more aware of her skirt, which by now had ridden well up her thighs. Then she saw Jane, standing beside the home-made bread stall, in her country casual clothes, immaculate as usual, quite different than the last time she'd seen her. She had a large wicker shopping-basket on her arm. 'Good heavens,

Louise,' she said disapprovingly as Louise whizzed past, 'you are showing rather a lot of ...'

But Louise had gone, knowing the last word was almost certainly 'leg'. Damn Jane! Then she smiled, at least she'd got whistled at, which was an uplifting experience. Men didn't whistle at respectable looking women in country casuals; she felt a youthful frisson of pleasure.

But by the time she'd negotiated the rest of the stalls, and parked the bicycle against the wall of the bank, she knew her face was as red as her dress.

'Here, ducks,' said a woman she didn't know, who was selling organic cider and wine outside the bank, 'have a glass of this. It'll cool you down. You don't have to buy anything.'

'But I've got to go into the bank.' Louise pulled the skirt of her dress down, vainly trying the yank out the creases, and make her appearance look as businesslike as possible.

'Going in for a loan is it?' the woman looked sympathetic. 'I know what it's like to have one of those appointments.' She sniffed and pulled a face. 'I'm always in my bank; it's that one over there, that's why I'm here. I don't want them seeing how much business I don't do.'

'No, no,' Louise said hastily. 'Not a loan, but it is business, yes. But no appointment, I'm just going in on spec hoping I can talk to someone.'

'Then you've got time to sit down and drink a glass of this. If it's business you'll need to collect your thoughts together.' The woman put a glass of ice-cold liquid into Louise's hand.

Before she knew it, Louise was sitting on a wobbly chair in the sun, gratefully drinking the cider, and telling the woman, who wasn't selling much, her troubles.

'So,' she finished, by now on her second glass of cider

and feeling definitely more cheerful, 'I thought that taking in paying guests would be the easiest thing to do as I've got a large house, and I can add that money to any I might make from my writing.'

Angelica James, by now Louise knew her name, nodded her head sympathetically. Another nice thing was she had actually read some of Louise's books and liked them, so Louise felt a warm bond of friendship with her.

Angelica James was also very practical. Louise learned that she had to be. Her husband made the cider and wine from their small organic orchard and vineyard, and her job was selling what she could prevent him from drinking. 'The important thing to do,' she said, 'is to start collecting receipts for everything. Food, electricity, every-thing, and I know you are allowed to let a room and get the money tax-free up to a certain amount. The man in the bank will tell you. And if you really get going I could always supply you with cider and wine for your organic dinner parties.'

'I'll remember that,' Louise promised. Her plan, now mapped out in her head, seemed sensible and realistic. She felt like a proper businesswoman already. Finishing off the cider, she made her way unsteadily into the bank. That sun was strong, she thought, I feel quite heady.

It turned out the bank did not have a resident manager, but a visiting one two days a week, a Mr Norman Long, and he was in that day.

'I know I haven't got an appointment but I wonder if I could see him. I won't take up much of his time.' Louise smiled what she hoped was her most winning smile.

It was wasted. The girl at the counter didn't look up but continued tapping the keys on her computer with two fingers. Eventually she informed her in a deadpan voice, 'Mr Long could see you in ten minutes if you wait. Otherwise he's very busy. In fact,' she continued in the same disinterested tone of voice, 'we're always busy on market day.' Louise could see from the card stuck on the window opening in front of her desk that her name was Tracy Blake.

'Yes, I expect you are,' Louise ventured sympathetically. Trying to elicit some kind of response.

Tracy didn't raise her eyes from her keyboard. 'Yes, it's just one wretched thing after another. Things we could do without, as we're always busy anyway.' She gave Louise the impression that she was one of those wretched things she could do without.

'Thank you, I'll wait. Is there a toilet here?' Louise was wishing she hadn't drunk two glasses of cider.

'Not for customers,' said Tracy firmly, still not looking up from her computer.

Louise knew there was one on the other side of the market square, which she'd used before. There was no alternative; she'd have to make a dash for it. 'I'll be back,' she said as she left the bank. 'Ask Mr Long to wait for me.'

Mr Long turned out to look young enough to be her son, and had spots all over his face, which were red and angry. Louise immediately felt motherly, and longed to tell him not to squeeze them, but give them a good scrub with some natural, unscented soap. But Mr Long, not Louise, was the one dishing out advice.

She told him of her predicament and what she thought could be the solution, although not as succinctly as she would have liked. The cider seemed to have made her mind a little sluggish. Louise hoped he wouldn't notice.

But he seemed preoccupied as he looked at her account on the screen. 'I can see there will be a problem without your ex-husband's allowance,' he said.

'He's not my ex-husband, he's my dead husband,' said Louise. 'Ex sounds as if I've got rid of him from choice, which is not true. And I know we've, I mean I've, never been a good customer for the bank. I've never made you any money.'

Mr Long actually smiled. 'You've never caused any trouble either,' he said, and pressed a buzzer on his desk. A girl, not Tracy, popped her head around the door. 'Two strong coffees, please,' he said.

'I'm not drunk, you know,' said Louise horribly aware that her breath must reek of cider.

'You're not the only customer to get waylaid by Angelica,' he said. 'Thank goodness she's not one of my customers; she must give away more than she sells.'

'And her husband drinks the rest, apparently,' said Louise.

They both laughed, and then Mr Long looked serious, and said, 'I know, but we both need clear heads to sort this out.' He turned the screen of the computer slightly so that she could see her account record. 'We've got lots of customers like you, I'm glad to say, who jog along with just about enough money to see them through the month.' He paused for a moment, then added, 'My mother's a widow, so I know how difficult it can be to manage on very little. Have you got any family who could help you out initially, or loan you something at the beginning?'

Louise thought of her daughter. Penny had not a bean to her name, so no help coming from there. And she couldn't possibly ask Jane and Geoffrey, pride forbade that. It was the bank or nothing. 'No and I don't have any other relatives. Besides I don't think I actually need much money to start with. I've got all the rooms furnished, I've got masses of good linen and towels, there are enough bathrooms and toilets, and two of the bedrooms are en-suite. I can give the guests the best bedrooms, and move to the back of the house myself. That's not a problem. So you see it won't be a large business, it will only be a little one, to start with at any rate. I just need to know really if I can have an overdraft if necessary and some advice of what's entailed in setting up a business. Of course, if it goes well I can always expand.'

'It's always good to be ambitious,' said Mr Long, and then rather spoilt it by adding, 'that's what they always tell me to say. Make the customers stretch themselves by offering them a loan.'

'And do you?' asked Louise. He didn't answer, just pulled a slight face.

The coffee arrived and Louise sipped it gratefully. It was strong and hot and began to clear her mind. Mr Long drank his too, then opened a drawer and took out a sheaf of papers. 'This is about starting a business from scratch,' he said. 'Here are some flow charts, and instructions on how to set up a spreadsheet. But I expect you know that.'

'Flow charts,' said Louise faintly, her mind reeling at the sight of the boxes and arrows, which appeared all over the sheets of paper. 'I've no idea of how to do a flow chart, let alone understand one, and I've never done a spreadsheet.'

'It's really quite simple.' He sounded soothing. 'It's to help you get sorted out in order of priority.' He flicked through it, ticking various items, while Louise hastily gulped back some more coffee; the mere sight of the

126

forms filled her with panic. 'The boxes I've marked,' he continued, 'are the most important ones to start with. You can look at the other matters later.'

'Thank you.' Louise took the bundle reluctantly and scanned the papers he'd passed over. The headings alone struck fear in her. Health and Safety, Fire Certification, Environmental Issues (Disposal of Effluent and Recyclable waste), Design of Letterheads and Stationery. Her head buzzed. It seemed letting other people sleep and eat in her house was much more complicated than she, or any of the others, had ever anticipated. 'And then there's tax, I suppose,' she said, bringing up the subject reluctantly. She'd fallen foul of the taxman once when she'd been making more money from writing than she did now, and was anxious not to do that again. 'I suppose I ought to open a separate business account, and get an accountant. At the moment I just put my writing money into a building society account and do the tax return myself.'

'Very sensible,' Mr Long reassured her. 'We'll keep the B and B money separate by opening another account here for you. A number 2 account. There's no need for an accountant for the moment, but I've got an uncle who's a retired accountant, Archie Dewar is his name. I'm sure he'll be glad to keep an eye on things for you. I'll speak to him.'

'Thank you.' This was better, someone to keep an eye on the money, it was more than Louise had ever hoped for. Her heart warmed to the spotty faced young man before her.

'Of course,' he added, 'if you are very successful, I can help you form a company. It's not expensive; you can be a limited company, with a bank account, VAT registered, and a website with a domain name. You can have the works for a few hundred pounds, or even less if we do it simply.'

By the time Louise left the bank, she was feeling both elated and apprehensive. Writing books and paying in a cheque when one was received occasionally, was quite different from running a proper business with a continual stream of income and expenditure, at least she hoped it would be a continual stream of income. Mr Long had taken his time explaining things; so long that Tracy had knocked on the door twice to remind him that he had other appointments. But he hadn't hurried, and Louise was grateful.

Louise shook his hand before leaving. 'Thank you so much,' she said. 'You've been an enormous help. I'm glad now, that I plucked up courage to come and see you. Once I'm really into doing evening meals, you must come and have dinner one evening with your wife.'

'I'm not married. Haven't even got a girl friend,' he replied gloomily, adding, 'it's these.' He pointed to his spots. 'Puts girls off.'

'Never mind, come to dinner anyway,' said Louise. 'And, don't be offended, but I've got some very good, pure herbal soap, it's made by my sister, and with a good scrub and a massage, it could very well do the trick for those ...' she hesitated.

'Zits,' he said, with a sigh.

'Yes, that's what you call them isn't it,' agreed Louise. 'But I was trying to think of a polite word.'

'There isn't one,' said Mr Long, as he opened the office door for her.

After cadging a plastic bag from Angelica James's stall for all the paperwork Norman Long had given her, Louise cycled home, her mind buzzing with things to do. She'd keep chickens, there was plenty of room at the end of the garden, and that way she'd have fresh eggs for her guests' breakfasts. She'd get Jane to make her special small individual herbal soaps and bath oil to put in the bathrooms. She wouldn't even try to be big; instead she'd concentrate on being as organic as possible, and different. That was what Mr Long had said, to succeed in business one had to find a niche market and then go for it. Her niche, she decided, was to be natural, organic and slow. What was it Jack had mentioned last night about the Slow Food Organization? She'd look into that she decided as she cycled slowly back. She didn't feel the need to hurry, instead she felt surprisingly contented.

As she came round the corner and Lavender House came into view, it seemed to Louise that it had come alive. Louise could almost see it ruffling up its feathers and stretching like a big contented bird, as she cycled towards it, the carrier bag with the flow chart in it, dangling from the handlebars. The house is going to enjoy being full of people again, she thought. Maybe Jack had been right. She had been stuck in a rut, and now she was about to climb out of it and do something really positive. Something she should have done years ago.

Whether it was the weather, which was beautiful, the comparative tranquillity as both the boys were playing happily outside the kitchen door, Sam digging up one of her mother's flowerbeds and Jacob concentrating on putting pebbles into a bucket, or the fact that she'd had an uninterrupted night's sleep, Penny felt full of energy, and filled with the urge to cook. A state of affairs that she hadn't felt for months, she decided, she would do lunch. Lunch for everyone, and it definitely wouldn't be a casserole.

'Jack,' she called, interrupting him as he pored over

The Times crossword in the armchair by the window. 'Can you go down the garden, find the old greenhouse, and pick me a huge bunch of basil? I know Mum always grows it there. I need it for lunch.'

'Do you want a hand with anything else?' he asked.

'No, thank you. I'll do it.' Penny was quite firm. 'But after you've picked the basil you can pop up the lane to Bert Hackett and get me a couple of rabbits. I know he'll have some because I heard him shooting yesterday evening. Just make sure you get skinned ones with their innards cleaned out.'

'Oh Heavens! Rabbit!' said Maggie with a delicate shudder and much shaking of bangles. 'You're not proposing that we should eat rabbits are you?'

'You needn't, but we will. However, I can tell you my recipe is delicious.' She waved Jack away. 'Off you go and get the basil, while I find the rest of the ingredients I need from Mum's cupboards.'

Jack disappeared down the garden path, and Penny pointedly put a chair outside in the garden. 'You can keep an eye on the children for me while I do lunch,' she told Maggie.

'But I haven't had time to put my face on yet,' Maggie grumbled. 'I never feel dressed unless I've got at least two layers of mascara on. Also I haven't used my skin tightening cream this morning, the one with collagen and vitamin E in it. Terribly expensive but does wonders for the skin.' She tilted a wrinkled cheek towards Penny.

'You look lovely as you are,' lied Penny, thinking that judging by the wrinkles Maggie was wasting her money. She practically pushed her through the doorway. 'And the kids don't worry about mascara.' She watched with amusement as the children greeted her arrival with gleeful cries; any adult to play with was always welcome, even Maggie, slumping unwillingly in a chair. But Penny noticed that despite her reluctance to play with them, her expression softened as Jacob tried to stagger, then crawled, towards her, eventually emptying his bucket of pebbles in her lap.

Penny heard her muttering, 'Thank you, darling,' and then turned her attention back to the kitchen and the preparation of lunch.

By the time Louise arrived, Penny had organized the meal for everyone, which smelled delicious. The children were in their high chairs, and Jack and Maggie were sitting at the kitchen table ready to start.

'Jack found your wonderful basil in the old greenhouse, Mum,' said Penny, 'and I found your good virgin olive oil and some pine nuts. I thought you said you were hard up, that oil must have cost a fortune. Jack dashed into Rumsey and bought some fresh parmesan and more garlic, so I made some pesto. Luckily you had a cupboard full of pasta; I suppose you keep that in for when Jane comes round.'

'Right,' said Louise. 'How did you guess?'

Penny thought her mother looked lovely. Quite different from the way she had only the day before. Her hair was windswept, but it suited her, and her complexion had a healthy glow. There was an exuberance about her and she didn't look a day over thirty-five, and that was without the masses of mascara and collagen enhanced face cream, which Maggie swore by. True, despite her age, Maggie looked glamorous, but to Penny's eyes her mother looked naturally beautiful, and she preferred it that way.

'Sit down, darling,' said Maggie to Louise, drawing up another chair, 'and have a glass of this delicious wine which Jack bought.' She poured Louise a large glass and pushed it into the extra place she was in the process of setting out. 'I can see why David wants to keep hold of Penny,' she said, 'she's a marvellous cook, and mother.' She beamed at Penny, who immediately thought that perhaps Maggie was not so bad after all, and beamed back. 'By the way,' Maggie continued, 'I've definitely decided to help you get off to a flying start with your new venture. I've put the Notting Hill house in an agent's hands to rent out, and I'm staying on as a paying guest. I've chosen my room, the other one with the en-suite bathroom. Penny and Jacob have moved out for me, and she said you'd give everything a good clean this afternoon.'

'Oh, did she.' Louise left the wine, and poured herself some water. She'd had enough alcohol for one day from Angelica James. Then she picked up the plastic bag containing all the information from the bank.

Penny suddenly realized that her mother was tired; she could see her positive mood evaporating. 'Sorry, Mum,' she said, 'perhaps I have rushed things a bit.'

'No,' said Louise. 'You're right. If I'm to make a go of this I can't hang around.' She drank the water.

'Try this.' Jack waved the wine bottle in her direction. 'Vino Nobile, Montepulciano.' He raised his glass to Louise. 'Thought it went well with the pasta.'

'Thanks, I will in a moment.' Louise felt momentarily confused. It seemed he'd decided to stay on as well, so she'd have to sort out the prices soon. She looked at the wine, it all seemed a little crazy, having paying guests who provided the wine, but then thought, who am I to complain?

'Try it,' urged Jack.

Louise obediently took a tiny sip of the dark red liquid, and had to agree it was delectable.

'Of course I shall pay the going rate, so you don't have to worry about that, darling.' Maggie spooned a mouthful of pasta into Jacob's mouth, which was open as usual, with his small, hungry bird impression.

'I haven't made up my mind what the going rate is,' Louise confessed.

'Well,' Penny hesitated, and wondered whether she should tell her mother she'd been discussing it with Jack, and then decided she might as well go ahead. 'We thought forty-eight pounds for a single room, and fifty-eight for a double en-suite, that's per room per night, and includes breakfast, of course. You need to be cheaper than other places as you haven't got all the luxury things, and it is an old family house. Then we can knock off ten per cent if they stay a week, because you'd have fewer bedclothes to change. Evening dinner, ordered in advance would be sixteen pounds per person, for three courses, and wine would, of course, cost extra.'

'Don't you have to have a licence for wine?' asked Louise, remembering something she'd seen fleetingly in the mass of paper Norman Long had given her.

'Not if it's included in the overall price for dinner,' said Penny. 'I looked it up.'

Jack passed her a generous plate of pasta. 'What do you think of that?' he said. 'We've done it all for you. I've even started designing your headed notepaper; I hope you don't mind me using your computer. I must say I found it a bit of a struggle. That computer was designed when dinosaurs roamed the earth.'

'It's all I can afford,' said Louise, 'and it suits me very well,' not sure that she wanted Penny and Jack rushing ahead and organizing everything.

'Don't be cross, Mum,' said Penny. 'We wanted to do something to help.'

'But I wanted to do it myself,' said Louise. 'You're making me feel useless.'

'Nonsense, if we help it will leave you some time for writing as well as running Lavender House.' Jack looked at Louise sternly. 'I read one of your books in bed last night. It was surprisingly good, and I can't think why you don't earn more money from your books. Maybe your agent isn't much good.'

'She isn't,' said Penny quickly. 'Her name is Dottie, and it's very appropriate, as she is dotty. Totally disorganized, I delivered one of Mum's manuscripts to her office once, God! It's a tip. I don't how she ever finds anything.'

'Dottie always says she knows where everything is.' Louise felt she ought to stand up for Dottie who she'd known for years.

'I'm sure she does know where everything is,' Penny always felt outraged when she thought of Dottie who she thought had treated her mother badly. 'She knows where everything is, because it's all on the floor.'

'Hmmm,' said Jack thoughtfully. 'I have a few friends in publishing from my university days. Maybe I'll ask around a bit. Perhaps I could get you a better agent.'

'There's no need,' said Louise huffily. 'Do you think I'm an airhead? I can manage my own affairs. Anyway, people outside of publishing never understand how it works.'

Penny put a plate of pasta before Maggie, and raised her eyebrows at Jack signalling for him to shut up. She knew the warning signs. Her mother was getting angry. 'Although I say it myself,' she said, 'the pasta is delicious, so eat up. But not too much as there's rabbit and salad to follow.'

However, Jack was not to be silenced so easily. 'Of

course I don't think you're an airhead. It's just that I can't understand why you don't make more money from your writing.'

'Because as I said, you don't understand, and I'm not a best-seller, that's why,' Louise spluttered through a mouthful of pasta. 'You may know some people in publishing, Jack, but you obviously know nothing about the industry. Everyone outside of publishing thinks that if you're a writer you should be rolling in money, when the fact is that most writers earn less than five thousand pounds a year, if they're lucky. And the agent takes 15% of that.'

'Anyway, Mum.' Penny sat down opposite her, and began feeding Sam who was messing about with his pasta, getting more up his sleeve than into his mouth. 'If you let all six bedrooms for a week you'd take in two thousand, one hundred and seventy pounds. Then after you knocked off, say, one hundred and seventy pounds for breakfasts and washing etc, that would leave you with two thousand pounds profit a week.'

Louise waved towards the welsh dresser on the other side of the kitchen, upon which lay the plastic bag with all the paperwork Norman Long, the bank manager, had given her. 'There are additional costs you know nothing about, and neither did I until this morning. Public liability insurance, health and safety things.' She looked at the sink. 'I'll have to get a double drainer for a start.'

'Oh, Mum.' Penny said crossly. 'Don't be so negative.'

'And anyway,' Louise was determined not to be too enthusiastic. 'How am I going to let all the bedrooms with you and the boys staying here? And where am I going to sleep?'

'We've thought of that too,' said Jack, and gave a devastatingly wicked grin. 'Stop being bad tempered woman, listen, and eat up your pasta before it gets cold, because I can't wait to get to the rabbit, and neither can the dogs by the look of it.' He pointed to Seamus and Megan who were sitting as close to the stove as possible looking hopeful. He put an arm around her shoulders and gave her a quick bear hug. 'Cheer up.'

Louise looked at the dogs and laughed, and Penny looked pleased. Louise shrugged her shoulders away from Jack's embrace, she didn't want them thinking he fancied her. It flattered her ego that perhaps he might, but there was a problem. Maggie! She was making a great play for him, the fact that she already had a husband in New York did nothing to deter her. Any moment now she's going to distract him, she thought.

True to form, Maggie laughed, one of her sexy throaty laughs. 'Darling,' she said to Jack, 'could you possibly get me the teeniest, weeniest bit more pasta? I know there's rabbit to follow, but I think the dogs can have my share. I prefer my bunnies frolicking in the fields.'

'Not if they're eating your lettuces, you wouldn't,' replied Jack. But he took her plate and moved across to the cooker. Maggie smiled; mission accomplished, Jack waiting on her, thought Louise and hid her amusement.

Then she went back to their original conversation about the bedrooms and repeated, 'You seem to have worked everything out, but where am I supposed to sleep?'

Penny giggled. 'Don't worry, Mum. You won't have to sleep with Jack.'

'Although I'm game, if you are,' said Jack, grinning as Louise blushed.

'You're going to sleep in the garden,' said Maggie, a slightly acerbic tone to her voice. 'It's all been worked out.'

'Yes,' Penny whipped away the pasta plates, and put the casserole dish containing the rabbit in the middle of the table. 'We've been down and had a look at Dad's old pottery cottage. It's in quite good nick. The roof is sound, the bathroom works, no hot water, but Jack says we can get one of those combustion things, which are very easy to install and as all the radiator pipes are there it just needs connecting up. There are three bedrooms if you count the downstairs dining room, which we need not use as a room for eating, because the kitchen is quite big and has a cooker and tables and chairs. All a bit shabby, but perfectly OK, and anyway most of the time we'll be in the kitchen here. You can live there, and I'll be there with the children, of course. Sam can give up his attic room here, and we can use that as the clean linen room which will free up another bedroom.'

'It seems that you have completely organized my life,' said Louise.

'Yes,' said Jack. 'And I can tell you something, I haven't had this much fun for years. We're going to give the cottage a good spring clean this afternoon.'

'And I'm helping too, darling,' said Maggie, determined not to be left out. 'Cleaning is very therapeutic, so they tell me.' She saw Louise looking at her long red nails. 'I may need some rubber gloves,' she added thoughtfully, flexing her fingers. Penny took the lid off the casserole and the aromatic smell of rabbit cooked in white wine and sage wafted around the kitchen. 'And I might just try a tiny piece of that rabbit too.'

Jack caught Louise's gaze across the table and grinned. After a moment's hesitation, Penny noticed Louise grinning back. The dogs sat by Louise, knowing she was a soft touch when it came to titbits, nuzzling their whiskery chins in her lap, while Tabitha lingered purposefully on the windowsill.

Penny hid a smile. Her mother looked relaxed, and she felt very happy. Life without David was perfect.

CHAPTER
NINE

D AVID ARRIVED AT Lavender House at just gone eleven o'clock that night. He'd expected Penny to be asleep, because he hardly ever saw her that late in the evening. At home she usually fell into bed between 9 and 9.30, saying she was exhausted. But tonight it seemed she was up and definitely not exhausted, as he could hear her laughter; something he'd not heard much of recently. Stupid of me to feel guilty, he told himself, trying to bolster his courage, it isn't my fault the children tire her; and stupid of me to feel jealous. But he couldn't stop the wave of envy washing over him. Who was it making her laugh so much? He tried to remember the last time they'd had a good laugh together, but couldn't.

Walking across the gravel drive towards the house, he noticed there were more cars than he would normally expect at Lavender House, then he spied his mother's gleaming sports car. It was parked untidily, the way she always parked, rear end sticking out. He stopped dead in his tracks. No! Surely she couldn't be here. Why would she come to Lavender House? She never went anywhere unless it was to interfere in something, and she usually caused trouble. No, he told himself firmly, I must be mistaken, it was dark and there were no lights outside the house – Louise didn't believe in security lights and said they were too expensive – so to make certain, he went to have a closer look.

Unfortunately when he got close to the car there was no doubt about it. It really was his mother's car. So what the hell was she doing here? Causing trouble for him. Sure to be. She always did, and because she was so unpredictable you never knew what the trouble was going to be. That fact, more than anything was an anathema to David; he liked a routine. He and Penny had a routine, at least, up until two days ago they'd had one, and it was a routine he'd liked. He'd lived comfortably, the house was well looked after by Penny, as of course it should be because that was her job. He went off to his office, had a drink with friends after work then came home to a warm, well cooked meal, and saw the children occasionally during the week and at weekends. That had been their routine and it had suited him down to the ground. But it had not, as he'd only just found out, apparently suited Penny.

Hearing Penny's voice again, then more bursts of laughter, sent him scurrying across to peer in at the kitchen window. An amazing sight met his eyes. For a start, the kitchen was exclusively lit by candlelight, which did something magical to the room. All the chipped crockery and cracked paintwork had faded into a golden glow. There were bottles of wine on the table, and dishes of steaming food, which made his mouth water. The whole place had turned into an Aladdin's cave. Penny, who he'd last seen wearing an old T-shirt and jeans, was now wearing one of his mother's glamorous dresses in brilliant red and gold, with a tight belt around the waist, and showing a dangerous, in David's opinion, amount of cleavage. She was wearing dangly earrings and had put her hair up in a French style topknot which made her look as if she had just got out of bed, and not to change a nappy! She was leaning forward seductively, and laughing at a man he'd never seen before. He was large and tanned, and attractive in, what David thought, a brutal sort of way. In fact, he was the kind of man that made David horribly aware of his blond hair, pale skin, and spindly figure, which Penny, when she was in a good mood, called lithe, but which David knew was the result of too much time spent indoors, huddled over a computer. This man looked like an ex-rugby player, and had a mop of untidy black hair streaked with silver. He was wearing a white open necked shirt, which showed off his tan. He looked like a pirate, thought David; all he needed was an earring! His mother was there as well. Of course, she was fawning over the man, which was inevitable, and was wearing a deep purple top with birds of paradise fluttering across it. Her heavily blackened lashes were fluttering so violently that David thought she ought to take off and buzz around the kitchen. He felt his usual stab of indignation. Why couldn't she be dignified like other people's mothers, and why did she have to flirt with anything in trousers? She was married for God's sake, even if his stepfather was working in the USA, and anyway she was too damned old at seventy-two. She should have given up flirting years ago. Why couldn't she be more like Louise?

Then he did a double take. Louise was wearing what looked like a French maid's outfit, a tight fitting, short-skirted black dress, with a frilly white apron. She looked as if she had stepped straight out of a French farce, and was carrying a tray on which was balanced a magnum of champagne, plus four champagne flutes, and was prancing round the kitchen to hysterical laughter.

He pressed his face closer to the window. Had they all gone mad? Then Penny jumped up and screamed. 'Oh, my God! There's an awful man at the window.'

They all turned and looked at David whose nose, by now, was rather flattened, as he was so close to the pane of glass.

'It's not an awful man,' said Louise briskly, putting down the tray and going across to the kitchen door. 'It's your husband.' She pulled the bolt back and lifted the latch, then paused. 'Oh no, he's not your husband is he. You're not married. He's a ...'

'He's just a man,' said Maggie dismissively, with a wave of her hand, long red nails and chunky rings glittering in the candlelight. 'But I suppose you'd better let him in. He is the fruit of my loins, God help me.'

'I don't want him in,' shouted Penny. 'I came down here to get away from him.'

Louise let the latch drop back down. 'She doesn't want you in,' she said, speaking to the flattened face at the window.

'I can't stay out here,' said David. He was beginning to feel very vulnerable and excluded. It was dark in the garden, and he could hear noises in the bushes. He was used to London noises, sirens, roar of traffic and the clickety-clack clatter of trains in the background. Comfortable noises because he knew what they were. The noises in Louise's garden were alien and made him feel uneasy.

Louise, taking pity on him, opened the kitchen door, and let him in. 'It's no good,' said Penny sullenly, all her previous sparkle evaporating as she glowered at David. 'I'm not coming back to you. So you might as well go away.'

'It's too late to go back now.' David slumped down in

142

the nearest chair. 'I've driven through the night to get here, and I'm tired after doing loads of housework.'

'There was nothing to do.'

'There was plenty to do, you'd just left everything.' He saw Penny open her mouth to argue and quickly changed the subject. Motioning to the bottle of champagne and the glasses, he asked, 'What's the celebration?'

'Nothing to do with you,' said Penny huffily. 'Jack was just going to open the bottle when you interrupted us.'

The pirate stretched out a large hand. 'Hi, I'm Jack.'

'Hi.' David tried not to wince as Jack crushed his hand in a painful handshake. 'I'm David.' He took his hand away, surreptitiously flexing his fingers under the table, wondering if any of them were broken.

Jack eyed him curiously. 'I take it that you are,' he hesitated, then said carefully, 'the father of Penny's children.'

'Yes.' Penny answered for David before he could open his mouth. 'But not my husband,' she added. 'I'm a free agent.'

'We all know that, dear,' said Louise, hastily getting another champagne flute from the cupboard, and turning to David. 'Would you like some champagne?'

'He doesn't deserve any champagne. He's done nothing to help.' Penny had a mulish expression, one that Louise recognized from her rebellious childhood.

'Don't be silly. Now he's here, he can join in.' It had been such a lovely evening so far, the last thing she wanted was Penny and David being disagreeable to each other. They could save that till tomorrow, when they were alone. 'Join us in a celebratory drink, David.'

'What are you celebrating? And why are you dressed up like a French maid?' David had to ask. Louise looked very different from her normal appearance but he had to admit that she did have fabulous legs.

'Oh, that's just a joke. We all felt in the mood for being silly.'

'We're celebrating Louise's new business venture,' his mother told him. 'She's going to open Lavender House for bed and breakfast and evening meals. We've all been helping sort out the pottery cottage, that's where Louise and Penny will live, and rest of Lavender House will be let out to paying clients. Jack and I are the first ones. I'm letting the house in Notting Hill and staying here for a bit, bed and breakfast.'

'Bed and Breakfast?'

'Yes.'

'You're staying here?'

'Yes, I've just said that. Don't keep repeating me, dear, it's a nasty habit you've got, and it makes you sound like a parrot.'

Penny laughed. 'That's what I always tell him.'

'And Penny's living in the pottery cottage?' stuttered David.

'Yes,' said Maggie.

'The pottery cottage!'

'Pretty Polly!' squawked Maggie. David glowered at her. His mother could be so infuriating sometimes.

'The one Dad used to do his potting in after he came back from Australia. We've sorted it out, found a few good pots too. It's perfect for me and the boys,' said Penny. 'But there won't be room for you. I'm sleeping on a single bed.'

'Could be cosy,' Jack said, and popped open the champagne bottle with a flourish.

Penny flashed him an irritated look. 'Don't interfere.'

David slumped further down in his seat, feeling totally defeated. Why had he come? He didn't usually do things on the spur of the moment, but then the last couple of days hadn't been what he would call usual. Worse than that, it was unusual not to feel in control of things, which was how he was feeling now. 'What about me?' He heard his own voice, childlike, whiney, and hated himself for being so weak.

Louise poured him a glass of champagne. 'Drink up,' she said. 'There's room for you in Lavender House tonight. Jack and Maggie only take one bedroom each, and Penny and I haven't moved into the pottery cottage yet. You can have the little study at the back of the house, there's a Z-bed there. I'll make it up when we've eaten.'

Suddenly aware of a delicious smell emanating from the dishes on the table and the oven, David cheered up and took a sip of champagne. He'd be able to work out something with Penny tomorrow. Of course he would. She couldn't stay down here with her mother forever. It wasn't right. Her place was with him and the children. 'What's for supper?' he asked.

'Melon and prosciutto, then wild mushroom risotto, followed by melanzane parmigiana,' replied his mother. 'Jack made it. He's a fabulous cook.' She threaded her gold earrings through her fingers and fluttered her spiky eye-lashes in the direction of Jack. David's heart sank again. He knew that routine. She was preparing to change husbands again. Maggie in action was like a glittering steamroller, even if Jack wasn't particularly interested, she'd have him snared before he knew it. David liked his stepfather, Seth. He was amiable, and tolerant and kept Maggie in the manner to which she'd become accustomed. He'd telephone Seth tomorrow and suggest that he should come over from New York and spend a little time in the wilds of Hampshire. Or even better, take his wife back to New York and find her something to do. He had TV contacts; surely there was something in New

York for Maggie, anything to keep her happy and occupied. David didn't think he could live through another
divorce, the weeping histrionics for hours on the phone,
the quarrels about money, which Maggie always won.
Although Seth might prove himself to be made of sterner
stuff than his predecessors, as during their ten year marriage Maggie hadn't always got her way. 'And David,'
his mother's voice dragged him back to the present, 'I
found this marvellous cheese shop down a side street
by Rumsey Abbey, so I bought a selection. I must have
second sight and have known you'd be here, because I
bought your favourite, the runniest brie with a marvellous smell.'

David managed a smile. There, she'd done it again.
One moment he disliked her, the next moment she'd
managed to touch a soft spot in his conscience.

'That brie is so marvellous,' said Louise re-entering
the kitchen dressed now in jeans and a sweatshirt, 'that
I've had to put it out in the old scullery until we eat it,
as it was on the verge of walking out of the larder on its
own.'

After the meal, Louise left Maggie still fluttering her
heavy black eyelashes at Jack, and making a great show
of domesticity by stacking the dishwasher in a higgledy-
piggledy manner. Maggie fancies Jack, she thought
crossly, although she's much too old for him and married
already. And, Penny fancies him as well and she's much
too young for him, and has a partner and two children.
It was irrational she knew, but she felt annoyed with Jack
for arriving at Lavender House and, without any effort
managing to set all the feminine hearts aflame. Even Jane
had been smitten, and would have hung around if Louise
had let her, but she'd sent her packing back to Geoffrey,

and Jane had gone eventually, albeit reluctantly.

Just as well I'm not similarly afflicted, she thought, and even if I was, which I'm not, I've got other things to think about. Lavender House, and all those things such as damned business flow charts, health and safety rules, all the minutiae of planning for guests, plus eventually trying to get three rose signs from the relevant authority. This, she'd been told, was essential as it signalled a well-run guesthouse. Playing around pretending to be a French maid, (Penny's idea) and drinking champagne was all very well, but tomorrow she'd have to get down to real business. She wondered whether Jack was attracted to Maggie, or whether her flirtatious attentions would drive him away. She hoped not. He'd been so useful, and had a lot of good ideas.

Later in the evening, when everyone had disappeared to bed, even David to his Z-bed in the study, Louise wandered down through the garden with Seamus and Megan shuffling after her. She stopped and breathed in the cool night air. There was just enough light to see a bat swooping silently down through the branches of the trees, and one lone bumblebee lumbered in and out of the foxglove flowers.

'You're out late,' said Louise, watching the bee's velvety behind as it burrowed into another foxglove. It must have agreed with her for it extricated itself and flew off into the night. Living on her own she'd got used to talking to the animals, or anything else, which happened to be around. It was a comforting sort of conversation because no one ever answered back or argued.

The dogs came back from the undergrowth at the end of the garden, bumping their heads against her legs to indicate they wanted to go back to bed. Louise pulled their silky ears, and heard them breathing heavily in pleasure. They were ecstatic at having their ears massaged. That's what I need, she thought, someone to give me a nice relaxing massage. But there was no one. She stopped thinking then. No point in allowing herself to wallow in self pity. It was something she always hated in other people. She had nothing to be gloomy about. She had Penny and two grandchildren. They were her family, but somehow the affection she felt for the dogs was a different deeper emotion than that which she felt for her grown up daughter. Not something she would ever have admitted to anyone. The dogs, and to a lesser extent, the cats, had grown closer to her over the years, they depended on her, and showed her unconditional love, whereas Penny had grown up and moved away. Maybe it is the dependency that triggers that warm loving feeling, she reflected, the necessity to feel needed. She felt the same about Penny's children, Sam and Jacob. They were vulnerable and needy, and she loved both of them with a passionate intensity, which was quite different to anything else.

Ignoring the dogs' wish to retreat back to the kitchen, Louise carried on until she reached the end of the garden. Leaning on the rickety wooden fence that separated the garden from the overgrown wilderness of the wood on the edge of the field, she looked out into the darkness. Although it was dim, Louise knew every tree and bush by heart, and could recognize the sounds of the night creatures going about their business.

'There's another world coming alive out there.' Jack appeared from nowhere and stood behind her.

A roosting bird nearby, rustled and shuffled around then was quiet, and a cow coughed, a rasping, whooshing sound in the field off to the left. 'All we need is an owl to hoot,' said Louise, glad that it was Jack who'd come down, and not Maggie.

An eerie, rasping cry drifted through the night air. 'Right on time,' said Jack, and Louise could tell he was smiling in the darkness. 'A barn owl, I think.'

'They are nesting in the Rumsey Abbey tower,' said Louise. 'I worry about the chicks being deafened by the bells when they ring the changes.'

'Perhaps we should organize some earplugs for them.'

Louise laughed. 'It would be terribly difficult to find their ears.'

'And they'd probably eat the plugs anyway.'

They stood for a moment in companionable silence. 'You know, I do love it here,' said Louise. 'That's why I was weeping that day you came to the kitchen door. I don't think I could bear to leave Lavender House.'

'You are leaving,' Jack pointed out. 'You are moving to Pottery Cottage.'

'That doesn't count. It's not far away, only down at the bottom of the garden. Anyway, if Dottie sells my book for a huge advance maybe I won't have to let rooms at all, and I shall stay in the house and let Pottery Cottage as a holiday place.' Louise knew it was very unlikely that Dottie would get her a big advance, but there was no harm in hoping. She always dreamed of making the headlines in one of the national newspapers: Louise Gregory settles for a million advance! 'People do get enormous advances sometimes,' she added, as much to convince herself, as for his information.

'Hmm ...' Jack didn't sound convinced. 'Everyone has to move on sooner or later,' he said. 'Even you. Maybe writing books is not your future.'

Louise turned and looked at his profile, or what she could see of it in the dark. At their feet, the two dogs padded about in the damp grass getting impatient, wanting to get back to the house, and their warm, dry baskets. Louise ignored them and continued her surreptitious study of his profile. His nose must have been broken at some time, she decided, the big lump in the middle of it couldn't possibly be natural. She wondered about him. What did he do? Where had he come from and why was he here? It was strange. She felt as if she had known him for years, and yet she'd only met him two days ago, and knew nothing about him, except that he had a vintage sports car, and appeared to have plenty of money.

'What are you moving on from?' she asked curiously, momentarily forgetting her own problems.

'Oh, all kinds of things.' Louise thought he sounded evasive. He took a deep breath, and added, 'Too many things.'

'Things?'

'Yes. Things, like my ex-wife.'

'Are you … er?' Louise hesitated, not quite knowing how to put it.

'Divorced?' replied Jack, second-guessing her. 'No, we're still married, but separated. Once the finances have been sorted, we'll divorce.'

So he was still married. Louise felt a quick pang of regret, but firmly stamped on it. 'Oh,' she said, the only comment she could think of in the circumstances. She shrugged her shoulders, trying to loosen her neck. Jack put his hands on her shoulders and began massaging her neck. Louise knew exactly how the dogs felt. 'Oh, that's lovely,' she said.

Jack, however, carried on as if she hadn't interrupted. 'To be honest, I married her for her looks and her big boobs. She was, still is a model, plus she was fun, and she married me for my big bank account. Now she's gone off with a much better looking man, with a bigger bank account; divorcing me for mental cruelty, and threatening to take me to the cleaners.'

'Were you cruel?'

'Only if you count shouting at her because she'd never heard of Charles Dickens, and insisted on playing pop music all day in the house, full blast.'

'I'm sorry,' said Louise.

'Don't be. To tell you the truth, I'm relieved. I won't have to worry about keeping my stomach in all the time and I can eat what I like. She only ever ate salad without the dressing. Having a model wife can be very boring. I've just got to sort out the money situation before the divorce, that's the biggest problem.'

Louise couldn't help it. She laughed. 'Oh dear,' she said, 'the man who hates women.'

'Is that what you think of me? A man who hates women?'

'No, of course not,' said Louise. Jack leaned closer, and Louise instinctively raised her face to his. Soft as silk, she thought but couldn't be sure, his lips brushed hers in the briefest of kisses, and suddenly she felt both elated and vulnerable at the same time, and wanted more. But then her innate common sense came to her rescue, as the dogs' wet noses nudged her again. Drawing in a deep breath, she drew away and said, 'The dogs want to go to bed, and so do I. So I'm going back indoors. Thanks for buying the champagne tonight, and your encouragement with my new venture.'

Jack didn't reply, so Louise went back to the house leaving him leaning silently on the fence.

Had he meant to kiss her? Was it a kiss? Or was it her overactive imagination?

CHAPTER
❧ TEN ❧

LOUISE HAD DIFFICULTY in sleeping that night. A few months ago she'd never had any problem sleeping, but lately sleep often evaded her as she was always worrying about something. But tonight was different. She relived the moment of Jack's hands on her shoulders, and realized that it had been a long time since any man had caressed her, and it was a caress, no doubt about that. Then she told herself not to be so fanciful, it had merely been a friendly gesture and should be forgotten; she turned over in bed, bunched the duvet around her and willed herself to sleep. But the memory of Jack's face so close to hers was unsettling. What would she have done if he had really kissed her properly? Would she have enjoyed it? The answer, Louise had to admit, was probably a definite yes.

In the small room next door to her boys, Penny tossed and turned as well, knowing that David was not far away. *Do I love him?* She wasn't sure, not for certain. The only thing she was certain about was that she did not want her life to continue in the same way as it had for the past few years. Babies, housework and cooking, never an adult to talk to unless it was another mum in the park, and then the conversation always consisted of potty training, feeding difficulties, and which store or shopping mall had the best baby-changing facilities. There was never any discussion on the latest novels or films, because none of them had time to read a book or get out to a film. Apart from one other mother, Amanda, who was different. She put in an occasionally appearance in the park when she wasn't at the gym. But she had a nanny who came in three times a week while she worked out, and although her conversation hardly fitted into the category of intellectual stimulation, as her main interest in life was dieting and exercise, at least she told them the latest gossip from the gym; who was sleeping with their personal trainer, and the latest routine designed to flatten a stomach and tighten a bum.

'I shall never be a normal shape or size again,' was one mother's doleful response.

'Rubbish,' Penny had responded firmly, with more conviction than she felt. 'Of course you will.'

Penny was convinced Amanda was anorexic. She had to be as she'd got her figure down to a size eight, which made her appear like an alien species in comparison to the rest of them, most of whom were still, or had just finished, breast feeding, and had squidgy thighs and buxom breasts.

'You and the others are normal,' Louise had said when Penny told her about Amanda. 'A size eight for a woman who's just had babies is not normal in my opinion.'

I might be normal but my life is dull, thought Penny now, miserably turning her pillow over to the cool side, and punching a hole in it for her head. I need to get my brain working again, get a job, and meet interesting people without babies in tow. The problem is, how to do it? She sat up in bed to consider the problem. 'Go on,' the walls of her bedroom, seemed to say. The faded cabbage roses of the old fashioned wallpaper seemed to come alive and whisper, 'Yes, *do* something.'

Penny flopped back on to the pillow. 'But what *can* I do?' she said out loud, willing the cabbage roses to answer back. 'I can't go back to working on a magazine, which was what I loved. I wish I hadn't got pregnant so soon.' It's all David's fault, she thought irrationally. If only he hadn't been so tall, good looking, in a pale and interesting way. In those far off days he had reminded her of a cross between a saluki and an afghan hound with melting brown eyes fringed by long lashes, a combination she'd found irresistible. Of course, that attraction had worn off now, and she merely thought of him as thin and weedy, and the melting brown eyes were usually hidden behind glasses, plus he was absolutely hopeless around the house. She supposed he was still good in bed, although these days she was too tired to be bothered to find out. Then she thought of Sam and Jacob, and couldn't envisage life without them. She had David to thank for them, and the more she mulled things over the more confused she became.

Telling herself she must think positively, she started going over her list of accomplishments. They were very few; a degree in History didn't count for much these days, lots of people had degrees. She could cook, but then so could most other people. She wasn't good on the computer, and couldn't type, not unless you counted typing with two fingers, and she certainly couldn't add up, at least not with any degree of accuracy. Although, she thought, cheering up a little, I did work out what Mum's finances would be through letting Lavender House, albeit with the aid of a calculator. I could get David to teach me to really use the computer, he's a whiz at that. Then she remembered grumpily that as they weren't really on speaking terms, getting him to teach her would be rather difficult.

Her contemplations were disturbed by Sam crying out for her from the room next door. Penny sighed, he was not a good sleeper, never had been, the night before had been an exception. Tiptoeing across the bare boards outside her room, trying not to step on any creaky ones, she went into the boys' bedroom.

'Mummy, it's dark,' whispered Sam. 'There are no street lights.'

'I know, darling. This is the country,' Penny whispered back. 'They don't have street lights here. But it's quite safe, and you've got your little night light on.' Outside the barn owl, which Louise and Jack had heard, called again.

'What is it?' whispered Sam, shivering. 'I don't like it.'

Penny wrapped her arms around her small son and held him close. 'Nothing to worry about,' she said. 'It's an owl. I heard them all the time when I lived here as a little girl. There are not so many about now, and we must be glad we can still hear them here. I'll show you a picture of one tomorrow morning. They're lovely, like flying pussycats.'

'What's it doing?' Sam asked. 'Why does it make that noise?'

'It's out hunting for its supper. A tasty mouse, and then afterwards he'll hoot for a mate. He's looking for his ladylove. Now go back to sleep.' She settled Sam back down, snuggling the duvet around him and found Binkie, a much loved soft toy which was a cross between a dog and a kangaroo, and gave it to him.

Sam took Binkie, and burrowed down, closing his eyes, then he opened them again and said, 'Daddy's looking for his ladylove. He told me.' He shut his eyes again.

Penny was startled. 'When? You haven't seen him since we came down to Lavender House.'

Sam's eyes stayed closed and he said sleepily. 'Yes, I have. He came in to kiss me and Jacob goodnight just now. Jacob didn't know he came because he was snoring, but I was awake, and I asked him why he was here.'

'Oh,' said Penny, not knowing what to say.

'People marry their ladyloves, don't they?'

'Sometimes,' said Penny carefully, wondering what Sam knew about marriage and the state of his parents' relationship.

'Always,' said Sam firmly. 'In storybooks the prince always marries his ladylove, and she's always a princess. Do you think Daddy will marry a princess?'

'I think princesses are in pretty short supply these days,' said Penny.

'Oh!' Sam considered this. 'Well, he could always marry you.'

Penny remained silent and stroked his head. Sam burrowed further down beneath the duvet and mercifully, for Penny, was silent.

When she was sure he was asleep, Penny crept out of the room and back to her lonely bed feeling more confused than ever. The only certainty in her life at the moment, were the boys. Whatever she did in the future, they had to be part of it. She couldn't imagine life without them. But as for David, now he was another matter.

In the box-room at the back of the house, over what had once been the milking parlour in the days when Lavender House had been a farm, David also thrashed about uncomfortably in the Z-bed put-u-up. He would

156

have tossed and turned, had it been possible to turn, but the bed was very narrow, and David, although thin, was a large man. Every time he moved he felt as if he were undergoing hip surgery without an anaesthetic.

The mobile phone on the bedside table beside him lit up. He'd put it on silent mode; the light meant someone was trying to get him. He looked at it for a moment. Who the hell was it? He didn't recognize the number, which he couldn't read easily as his glasses were somewhere under the bed and he couldn't find them. Of course it might be someone from the States, he did have a several good accounts there, and they never adjusted to English time when they flitted across the pond. So he answered it.

It wasn't a client; it was one of his single, or to be more precise, divorced friends, who was obviously drunk. 'Hi Dave, it's me, Guy.'

'What are you doing ringing me in the middle of the night?' David whispered not wanting to disturb the rest of the house.

'Ish not the middle of the night, ish's …' Guy's voice was slurred and difficult to understand. 'Ish's, only early and the party here has jush got going. I mished you tonight in the pub. Met this fab girl there, we're all at her place now. Thought you might fancy a break from babies, poo and all that yuk.' Guy had walked out on his wife two weeks after the second baby's birth to live with his secretary, Fiona. It lasted a month, then he ended up in a bedsit when she'd thrown him out because of his untidy habits, and because she found out he was sleeping with someone else as well as her.

'I'm not in London, and even if I were I wouldn't want to go to a party with people I don't know.'

'What do you mean, not in London?' Guy sounded

very puzzled. David knew that he never ventured out of London, unless it was for a skiing holiday or a trip to the Bahamas. Primrose Hill and Greenwich meant the country to a city boy like Guy.

'I'm in Hampshire,' David hissed, 'with my family. So piss off Guy and leave me alone.'

'Family, Oh God! A fate worse than death.' Guy gurgled down the phone. 'Get in the car and come here, I want a mate with me because I'm outnumbered by all these women. They're pretty hot stuff I can tell you, and I don't think I'm up to it.'

'Then go home.'

'I haven't got a home,' said Guy with the plaintive tearfulness of a drunk. 'I'm kipping on Jerry's sofa at the moment, and his girlfriend isn't too keen, so I think I might stay here if they'll have me.'

David clicked the off button with his thumb and put the phone down. 'I haven't got a home.' Guy's voice reverberated around in his head. He'd sounded desperate. What had happened to the freewheeling, single bloke, who'd left his wife and children to have more fun?

It didn't take a genius to work it out. David remembered the girl next to him in the pub. He couldn't pass for 25 any more, he was too old, and so was Guy. But Guy had burnt his boats and was up the creek without a paddle, and socializing with a nefarious crowd of boozers and drug takers, whereas…. Here, David started to feel muddled, not only because his brain was mixing metaphors, but because he felt frustrated and angry and had drunk too much champagne and wine at supper. Penny had put him in this situation, by leaving him. He didn't want to end up on someone else's sofa. He moved, and let out an involuntary groan as the metal edges of the put-u-up dug into him. They had a lovely king-sized bed in their house in London, which was where he should be, with Penny, and with Sam and Jacob safely tucked up in their bedrooms. He didn't want to be in a box room in this old draughty house, lying on a bed which could easily double as a torture rack. Outside two owls hooted, first one and then the other on a slightly higher note. It was with difficulty that David restrained himself from sticking his head out of the window and hooting back at them.

Instead he decided that in the morning he would talk to Penny. Make her see sense. They would get married, go back to the London house, and everything would be all right. But he couldn't sleep, and realized that he was hungry. He hadn't felt much like eating with his mother one side of the table, shaking her earrings and glowering at him, and Penny on the other stubbornly refusing to speak to him, not even a 'Pass the salt, please.' Louise, he remembered, had remained serenely impervious to everything around her, and Jack had been the life and soul of the party, with his mother and Penny hanging on his every word. Anyway, now he was hungry, so he decided he'd go down to the kitchen and get something to eat, reasoning that there must be something left in the fridge.

Creeping downstairs, wearing only his underpants, a pair which Penny had washed in with a Tweeny Dressing up outfit of Sam's, so that they were streaked, rather unbecomingly, with green and yellow, he made his way to the kitchen. He hadn't brought his pyjamas, because he couldn't find them, but wished now he'd looked harder and hoped no one else was up. He knew one of the stairs creaked loudly and prayed he'd miss it; but found it, trod on it, so that it creaked, long and loud, echoing through the house. But there was nothing for it, he had to carry on, hunger pangs drove him forward, and he made for the kitchen.

There was a bottle of whisky on the Welsh dresser. Jack must have had a snifter before going to bed, thought David, pouring himself a generous glass. Perhaps it would help him sleep on that bloody bed. Then he looked in the fridge. There was a ceramic pot of pâté, which he took out. In the bread bin was a fresh uncut baguette, which smelt delicious. In no time at all he was spooning generous dollops of pâté on to a plate and tearing at the bread, stuffing it into his mouth in-between glugs of whisky.

'Just what do you think you are doing?'

David nearly choked. 'I … er … um … felt hungry,' he managed to say through a mouthful of bread and pâté.

'So I see,' said Louise, standing in front of him with her arms folded, a very fierce expression on her face. 'Did it not occur to you that I might have had plans for that food tomorrow?'

'No,' replied David truthfully.

'I'm not made of money,' continued Louise in the same severe tone of voice. 'With a house full of people I have to plan ahead for meals and stretch what money I've got as far as it will go. Penny made that pâté with some chicken livers the butcher gave me.'

She was wearing a blue gingham dressing gown, pulled in tight at the waist by an old blue tie. David thought it made her look very young. Very much like Penny in fact. Tears welled up in his eyes, what was he doing down here stealing from the fridge, and feeling vulnerable and guilty like some 14-year-old schoolboy? 'You look like Penny,' he said, and sniffled unhappily.

Louise's expression softened. 'I'm not that much older than Penny, and not in my dotage yet, so I'm bound to look like an older version of her,' she replied. 'I had her when I was very young, much younger than Penny is now.'

She sat down opposite him and David pushed the whisky bottle across towards her. 'The pâté is very good.' He said spreading another lump on the bread.

'Penny's a good cook.' Louise glowered at him. 'As you should know.'

With a shamefaced expression, and feeling more than ever like a guilty schoolboy, David put the pâté back in the fridge, and returned the baguette, or what was left of it, to the bread bin, then sat down again opposite Louise. 'Why have you come down?' he asked.

Louise didn't answer straight away. She got up and took a glass from a shelf on the Welsh dresser and poured herself some whisky. 'Same reason as you I suspect. I couldn't sleep, and then I heard the stair creak, so I knew someone was up.'

'Why couldn't you sleep? You haven't got any problems. Not like me.' As soon as he'd uttered the words, David knew it was a stupid thing to say. Louise did have problems, but for the life of him he couldn't remember what they were at this precise moment in time. Two glasses of whisky, and lack of sleep, had befuddled his brain.

Louise was annoyed. He knew that from the way her mouth set in a straight line after she'd taken a sip of whisky, which she didn't look as if she were enjoying. 'The trouble with you, David,' she said, 'is that you are totally self-centred. I suppose you take after your mother in that respect, although to give her some credit she does recognize the fault in you, although she fails to recognize it in herself.'

'I didn't come down here for psychoanalysis,'

muttered David, feeling indignant. 'How dare you libel me and my mother.'

'It's true, and if it wasn't it would be slander, not libel,' said Louise.

'Anyway,' continued David, determined to and get the upper hand of the conversation. 'I came down to get my wife and ...'

'She's not your wife,' cut in Louise quick as a flash. 'You've never shown any sign of being committed to your family. You've bought a house, true. You sleep with Penny, and occasionally notice you've got two sons. But Penny works hard, keeping that large house going with no help and two small children to look after. She cooks for you, washes and irons your clothes, and you just saunter in when you feel like it after drinking with your friends in the pub, when you should be at home bathing the children sometimes, and giving her a hand.'

'Has Penny told you this?' David spluttered through his last mouthful of bread and pâté.

'She didn't have to. I've stayed with you. I've seen it with my own eyes. My daughter is a drudge, and she's had enough.'

David choked on his bread. 'Drudge!' he squeaked, 'what an old fashioned word. The trouble with you, Louise, is that you think everyone should be like you, which is impossible. You live in a lovely old house, which you inherited, so you've never had to pay a mortgage or rent. You've got nothing to do all day, so you do a bit of writing when you feel like it and get paid for it. Penny doesn't have to stay at home and be a drudge, as you call it. If she were a bit more organized she could go to work if she wanted to and meet people. Housework doesn't take any brainpower, all it takes is organization.' Even as he was speaking David remembered the backbreaking effort he'd made with the washing and kitchen, and even more worryingly remembered the mess he hadn't got round to finishing in the house at Blackheath. Louise was looking at him with a quizzical expression, which made him feel she could see right into his head. 'Well, that's what I think.' He said, tailing off lamely.

Louise began to laugh, in a way that made David feel very uncomfortable. He knew everything he'd said was untrue, why the hell hadn't he kept his mouth shut?

'You just don't get it, do you?' she said. 'About Penny or me. You haven't even realized that besides worrying about my daughter and my grandchildren, my life hasn't been that easy. True, I inherited the house without a mortgage to pay, but old houses need constant upkeep, there's always something going wrong which needs money. After John lost all our money in that stupid Australian adventure, we struggled along, hand to mouth all the time. I'm not asking for sympathy, but I can tell you I've worked bloody hard at writing, which mostly paid the bills, and I did housework, and painting, and decorating as well as gardening. Lovely old houses don't stay lovely on their own; they need time and money spent on them.'

'I suppose so,' said David sulkily, 'but as far as Penny and the children are concerned, you don't have to worry. I can look after them'

Louise carried on speaking as if he hadn't interrupted. 'And now, besides worrying about the usual problems, there are others. I have to decide how I'm to manage my life, now my monthly income has disappeared, and I'm out of contract for my next book, because there's no guarantee that Dottie will be able to sell it. That's why I'm starting the Bed and Breakfast business.'

'But I thought your books made loads of money, you've never said.'

'You've never shown the slightest interest nor asked,' snapped Louise bad-temperedly.

Everything was beginning to whirl in his brain. His mother flirting with the Jack man, who instinctively he didn't like; Louise playing at being a French maid, Penny being very hostile, Jacob snoring through his furtive bedtime visit, and Sam being tearful and asking if he loved his mummy.

'I'll tell you now, so that you know the true state of affairs,' said Louise. 'My books just chug along, earning a few hundred pounds here and there, certainly not enough to keep this house running. I relied on that insurance money John had set up for me, because I'm not old enough to get any kind of pension, and apart from stacking shelves in a supermarket I'm not qualified to do anything else. I could train for another career but that takes time and money, and I'm short of both. In other words I've got to earn some money fairly quickly. Now do you understand why I couldn't sleep?'

David opened his mouth but Louise carried on, not letting him get a word in. 'And what is more to the point, my troubles are not of my own making, but yours are. If you had treated Penny differently she would not have left you.'

'Do you think she'll come back?' David mumbled his head in his hands.

'I've no idea, that's up to her.' Louise stood up and removed the whisky bottle. 'One thing is certain. I will not be persuading her one way or the other. She must make up her own mind, and she can stay here with the children for as long as she likes, and you must pay maintenance for your children. The country air is better for them anyway, no pollution, and plenty of room for them to play.'

'No intellectual stimulation,' said David mutinously, feeling as if he were being run over by a steamroller and making a last ditch attempt to stand his ground.

'They can get all the stimulation they need at this stage by playing in the garden and learning about the world around them,' said Louise sharply. 'Now get to bed, and mind that stair on the way up. I don't want the whole house awake.' She removed his plate, and deftly swept the breadcrumbs off the table, put the glasses in the sink, and stood by the kitchen door, which she opened and motioned him through.

David obeyed. There was nothing else he could do; he put his hands down by his sides hoping to hide as much as he could of his hideous pants which he knew Louise had noticed. Halfway through the door he hesitated. 'My mother,' he said.

'Yes,' said Louise, an ominous expression settling across her face.

'She's flirting with Jack isn't she?'

'Yes,' said Louise.

'What shall I do? I like Seth. I don't want her to get another divorce, and end up being on the phone to me for hours. I've been through it twice.'

'If it's any consolation I don't think Jack is encouraging her, he'll make up his own mind. But anyway,' Louise continued briskly, 'there's nothing you can do. Maggie's her own woman. Even though she is scatterbrain and flighty, she's not bad. And as for Jack, I don't know much about him, but as I said, I think he'll make up his own mind without any interference from us.'

With that pronouncement David had to be satisfied. He made his way upstairs groping for the banister, trying to avoid the creaking stair. He thought it was the fifth one so he counted, but it wasn't, it was the sixth. He trod on it and a loud groan from the protesting wood reverberated through the house.

Downstairs, alone in the kitchen, Louise sighed, then winced as she heard the stair creak as David stepped on it. What next, she wondered. It was said that troubles always came in threes. So far she only had two, her own financial worries, and Penny's state of flux, so what else could happen? Jane's problems didn't count, she ought to be able to sort those out herself, and common sense told her there was nothing she could do about her own now. She should go to bed and stop worrying, because worry in itself achieved nothing.

There was a list of shopping to be done written by Penny and pinned to the notice-board by the kitchen door. Seeing the list and thinking about Jane reminded her that she must ring her tomorrow, and get her to make her a batch of lavender and oatmeal soap and flower essence for her guests' bedrooms for when they came. Jane could come round tomorrow and get more lavender and gather the marigolds which were now flowering in abundance to make the calendula cream which Louise thought she could sell on to her guests at a profit if she made special labels saying it was organic and came from Lavender House, East Willow. At the moment, Jane sold them in plain pots for £3 a pot, but, with a well-designed label, Louise was sure she could sell them for at least £5. No, £5.50 she thought, that would cover the cost of the label and make her £2 profit.

A sudden surge of excitement engulfed her. She would succeed, she *would*. This was a real challenge. She'd coasted along living easily, if frugally, for far too long. It was time she came out of hibernation and did something really positive. It was spring after all, and she suddenly imagined herself as one of the creatures in the woods, a dormouse waking after the long winter sleep, or a hedgehog perhaps. I'd better be a hedgehog, she decided. They snuffle and wuffle determinedly searching out what they want, and roll up in a ball when threatened. That's the way to survive.

She went back upstairs and climbed into bed and heard Penny in the next room, whispering to Jacob who was still waking at night for a feed. Louise couldn't hear what she was saying, but it was a comforting mother and baby sound. She felt nostalgic, remembering what it was like suckling a baby at the breast. She remembered the time when she and her baby were in a tiny enclosed world, she remembered the warmth and the scent of a clean baby. No one else intruded, it was a special bond between mother and child, and Penny must be allowed to treasure and enjoy it, even if it did mean leaving David out of the loop for the time being, she thought. She felt more relaxed, things would work out. They usually did, even if it wasn't always the way you'd envisaged. I suppose, she thought sleepily, this is something, which happens. You gain the wisdom to expect the unexpected and to accept the inevitable, whatever it is, if there's not much you can do about it. Banging one's head against a brick wall is a waste of energy, and achieves nothing.

Louise turned over, and pulled the duvet up around her ears. The whisky did its work, and she fell asleep. Tomorrow was another day. She'd tackle whatever it threw at her when it arrived.

CHAPTER
❧ ELEVEN ❧

TWO MONTHS PASSED by in a few moments, at least that was how it seemed to Louise. The delicate pale green of spring gave way to the lush, darker green of summer. Wild vetch and goose grass scrambled skywards at the bottom of the garden, and Sam would come running in with purple foxglove flowers on the end of his fingers announcing that he was a fox wearing gloves. Jacob was beginning to scramble about and both he and Sam turned a nut brown colour from playing in the garden dressed in just shorts and T-shirts and Louise wondered how she had ever enjoyed living on her own. Lavender House was a whirl of activity these days.

Both Maggie and Jack had stayed on as paying guests, although Louise often thought she should be paying Jack because he did so much for her, and although he appeared to have forgotten about that brief embrace, she hadn't, and it crept into her mind every now and then. However, she didn't allow herself to dwell on it.

He enlarged the vegetable patch, so that the house was almost self sufficient with vegetables during that summer, and had even managed to plant some late main crop potatoes for later in the year. He'd made a sign, nailing it firmly to one of the gate pillars saying: 'LAVENDER HOUSE, Bed and Breakfast', and then he'd made two other smaller signs saying 'Vacancies' and another saying 'Full'. To Louise's amazement and gratitude, the 'Full' sign was the one most often swinging from its spot on the pillar. People liked Lavender House, even though they had to share bathrooms when the house became full. They loved Louise's cooked breakfasts, often supplemented with the large field mushrooms Jack and Bert Hackett had gathered early in the morning before anyone else was up and about; Bert often adding a large paper sack of his new potatoes every now and then. But sometimes Jack disappeared for a couple of days without warning. 'Important business,' he always said when he came back, but never explained where he went or who he'd seen.

Out of curiosity, Louise looked at the mileage on his car before and after one of his mysterious trips, and worked out that the mileage he'd done had been about enough to get him to London and back. Why did he go to London? For some reason she couldn't explain, Louise was certain it was London. Maybe to finalize his divorce? She never asked and he had never mentioned his ex-wife again. But another strange thing she noticed was that his trips nearly always coincided with the times Jane's husband was away. He went to London. Or so Jane thought, but then told Louise she had doubts about London when she found Eurostar tickets to Brussels in the pocket of one of his suits.

Louise, ever practical, said, 'Why don't you ask him?'

Jane shuddered. 'I don't dare,' she said. 'He can fly into the most awful rage you know, especially lately. This last year he's been very edgy. I wonder sometimes if it's his hormones, and that it's all tied up with his lack of interest in me.'

'Oh, for God's sake don't let's get back on that subject again,' said Louise, then immediately felt guilty and irritated at the same time. Why didn't Jane *do* something about herself and Geoffrey? Then she remembered Jane's pathetic attempt at playing the sex goddess, and felt even more guilty; poor Jane, she had tried. 'They do say men have a kind of menopause,' she said, vainly trying to offer some words of comfort.

Surprisingly this seemed to satisfy Jane. 'Yes, I'm sure that's what it is. It's his hormones.'

Louise didn't reply, but let her mind wander back to Jack, which it did with increasing frequency lately. She knew she was growing fond of him, too fond, but it was impossible to dislike him. He was always good tempered, the children adored him, and he flirted with Penny and Maggie outrageously, but never with her. Louise wasn't sure whether to be offended or pleased about this, but admittedly it did simplify their relationship, as there were never any awkward moments. Sometimes, she thought, it was almost as if they were an old married couple, but without the sex. Now that was something she did not allow herself to think about under any circumstances, except when she slept. Then her dreams were beyond conscious control. When she was safely asleep under her duvet, Jack appeared and wrapped her in a big bear hug and kissed her again. Unfortunately her dreams had a nasty habit of stopping right when they got to the really interesting part. She took it as a subliminal message.

However, one morning after one of his mysterious absences, and a particularly nice but disturbing dream which progressed much further than usual, Louise decided to try and find out a little more about Jack O'Leary. She had a house full of guests, and had their breakfast sausages sizzling in the pan and was just adding the bacon rashers when he came into the kitchen, accompanied by Seamus and Megan whose noses began to twitch at the scent of the bacon frying. He plonked down a basket of the most enormous field mushrooms on the kitchen table.

'That rain we had last night has worked miracles,' he said. 'Do you want me to feed the dogs?'

'Thanks.' Louise started to peel a couple of the biggest mushrooms. 'I don't know what I'd do without you. Which reminds me, I've been meaning to ask you how long you intend staying at Lavender House?'

Jack looked wary. 'Do you want to get rid of me?'

'Oh no, I … er.' Louise trailed into silence, then said, 'I just wondered.'

'The answer is how long is a piece of string? I'll let you know when I have to go.'

Have to go. Not want to go. Louise thought the words had an ominous ring. It implied that his departure would not be of his choosing. But Jack quickly changed the subject and Louise continued cooking the breakfast in silence. He obviously had no intention of telling her anything.

After taking in the breakfasts to her guests, a couple of elderly ladies and a single man who went out into the forest every day to paint watercolours, Louise retreated to her little office next to the kitchen, to catch up with her accounts. She'd finally got the hang of doing spreadsheets, with Norman's (she was on first name terms with the bank manager now) assistance, and filled in with meticulous care all her income and expenditure every day. Glancing up from the computer she saw Jack walk past the window, climb into his car and drive off. That was another odd thing; he was strangely reticent about where he went in his car. If he walked he always told everyone where he'd been, but when in the car, it was a different matter.

Jack was away on one of his trips. Because there were guests in every available room, and a dinner party in the dining room that night, both Louise and Penny needed to work in the kitchen; normally Jack always helped out. It was a gorgeous day, hot and sunny, much too nice to spend indoors. 'But needs must,' Louise told Penny, 'I need your help in here today.'

'Just let me rig up something for Jacob, and I'll be right in,' Penny promised.

The previous day, Penny had found her old playpen up in the loft in the roof, or to be more precise Kevin had found it. He'd come round again the day before to fix some more slates now that the weather was good. 'But only,' he said, 'if that mad woman doesn't drive her car while I'm on the roof.'

'I promise Maggie will not be going anywhere,' said Louise, crossing her fingers and hoping that Maggie wouldn't decide to go roaring off to Rumsey, where she usually created havoc in the boutiques which abounded there. All terribly country and not Maggie's type at all, but that didn't stop her trying everything on.

Kevin's visit had been fruitful, not only for the roof which he'd patched up once again, but because he'd found the playpen. Jacob had just got to the curious stage and could disappear very rapidly, so letting him loose in the garden had become a nightmare. Someone had to look after him, and Maggie couldn't be trusted. She always had the best of intentions, but warm sunshine, combined with a glass of wine had a disastrous effect on her powers of concentration, which were never her forte at the best of times.

Penny was outside rigging up Jacob's barricade and Louise was alone in the kitchen when the phone rang. It was Jane.

'I've got Leon for the day,' she said, sounding both excited and worried. 'The nursery is closed today, not enough staff apparently, so Wendy has brought him over. I've never had him for a whole day and I think he'll be bored here. I've got no toys or anything.'

'Bring him over,' said Louise. 'One more child won't make any difference and he can play with Sam, and you,' she told Jane, 'can make yourself helpful and work with me in the kitchen.'

'I'll be over in about ten minutes.'

She was as good as her word and duly arrived with a rather apprehensive looking Leon.

'Where's Geoffrey?' asked Louise, busily putting blobs of goats' cheese and garlic in the middle of small pastry rounds before pinching them into little envelopes. She saw Jane watching. 'I've got another dinner party this evening, ten people this time. That's my maximum. And Geoffrey?' she reminded Jane. 'I thought perhaps he might want to be with his grandson.'

'Oh, yes, Geoffrey.' Jane sounded a bit vague, as she unbuttoned Leon's pale linen coat which matched his shirt and long trousers; he was much too well dressed to play in the garden, thought Louise, but she hadn't time to worry about that. 'Yes, Geoffrey,' Jane repeated, 'he's been in Brussels with Dennis, for the last two days. He's gone to some EU economics conference. It's all to do with money. They're due back tonight.'

'In other words a freebie,' said Louise, dismissively. She didn't like Wendy's husband. Dennis Mills was a smoother, oilier version of Geoffrey. Politics and money went together in her opinion, although Jane always told her that Dennis worked very hard.

'What shall I do with Leon now?' asked Jane.

'Just let him loose in the garden to play with Sam. Jacob's going to be corralled temporarily, but Sam and Leon can run loose. There's a sandpit, plenty of things to dig with, a tent, a tricycle. All the usual things children have.'

'I'm not sure Wendy will be keen on him getting sandy. Leon,' she called after his disappearing figure, 'try not to get too dirty.' But Leon, given the chance of freedom, bolted like a horse let out to pasture for the first time in spring, and Louise doubted he heard a word. She did as much preparation as she could in the kitchen with Jane and Penny's intermittent help, as they were both always popping outside to make sure the children were all right. Then she dragged Jane upstairs to help her change the sheets and clean the bedroom ready for some new guests due to arrive that evening.

'How's it going with you and Geoffrey?'

'Fine,' said Jane, 'if you can call being ignored fine. We just don't speak much, and he's moved into the other big bedroom.'

'Oh, dear.'

Jane suddenly smiled. 'Do you know I prefer it. I've never slept so well in years. Sleeping with Geoffrey was like sleeping with a hippopotamus, when he turned over everything went with him. And he farted.'

'Charming,' said Louise, and began to laugh. After a second or so Jane joined in, and they sat side by side on the half made bed laughing until the tears streamed down their cheeks.

'I've got the perfect marriage,' said Jane between hic-cupping laughs, 'a lovely house, the bed to myself, and a hippopotamus in the spare room. All I need is for him to drop dead then life really would be perfect.'

'Jane!' It was Penny's horrified voice. She was standing in the doorway. 'I came up to tell you lunch was ready. But I ...' her voice faltered, her expression a mixture of puzzlement and consternation. Then she drew a deep breath. 'Words fail me.' She started to clatter downstairs towards the kitchen.

'Hang on,' called Louise. 'In my opinion Jane was expressing a perfectly valid viewpoint, she doesn't love Geoffrey and he's not nice to live with. Wouldn't you be pleased if David suddenly disappeared from your life forever, instead of coming down here every now and then?'

'Do you mean, dead?'

'Yes. It simplifies everything doesn't it?'

'But ... but I love David,' said Penny, her mouth puckering and her eyes filling with tears.

'Then tell him, and for God's sake get together again.'

Penny didn't answer. She went downstairs to the kitchen.

After they'd both washed their faces, and applied some mascara and lipstick so that at least they'd compete a little with Maggie, Jane and Louise joined the family in the kitchen. Maggie was feeding Jacob, who was securely strapped into his high chair, and Sam and Leon were sitting up to the big table, covered in mud and sand, except for their hands and faces which Penny had obviously washed. They were only wearing their underpants.

'I took their clothes off as they were getting a bit grubby,' explained Penny, dishing out spoonfuls of cottage pie and purple sprouting broccoli.

'Grubby! That's the understatement of the year,' said Maggie. 'That's why I'm sitting well away from them.'

Strangely enough, Louise noticed, Jane didn't seem horrified at Leon's filthy condition. Instead she said, in an aside to Louise, 'I've never seen him so happy and animated.' And it was true. Pale, quiet, buttoned-up Leon was flushed from the sun, talking non-stop to Sam in-between shovelling large mouthfuls of lunch into his mouth. 'And he never, normally, eats his greens.'

It was an idyllic day, somehow the work preparing the food for the evening dinner party didn't seem as exhausting as usual, because someone was always popping in and out of the kitchen, and once she finished, Louise joined the rest of them under the fig tree for tea, jam sandwiches and lemon drizzle cake which Maggie had driven into Rumsey to buy.

During the afternoon, Louise noticed that Penny had been on her mobile for some time, and crossed her fingers, hoping the call was to David in London.

'This is perfect bliss,' said Maggie, biting into her second slice of cake, 'I've decided to stop worrying about my figure.'

'Yes, it is bliss isn't it,' agreed Jane, as a very sandy Leon still clutching a jam sandwich, climbed on to her lap, and snuggled into her.

'What is going on here?' A sharp, threatening voice cut through the buzz of bees and birdsong and severed the peace of the group beneath the tree.

Advancing towards them from the kitchen doorway was Wendy, dressed in a smart black suit, her husband, Conservative MEP for mid Hampshire, Dennis Mills, at her side, dressed in a typical European Union grey business suit and, and with them was Geoffrey, similarly attired. Out of the corner of her eye, Louise saw Jane shrink back in her chair, while Leon dropped his jam sandwich in fright.

Maggie, the least fazed of any of them, dragged another garden chair from a clump of nettles. 'Won't you join us?' she said, with a gracious wave of her hand. Louise was sure she gave an extra jangle of her bracelets. 'We're having tea in the garden.'

'Is that what you call it?' Dennis Mills had a mid-Atlantic slightly plummy accent, which he'd adopted since he'd clawed his way up the social ladder in Europe. Louise could remember a time when he'd had a distinctly Hampshire accent, and had been a nicer man than he was now.

'Yes, my darlings. Tea,' said Maggie with another jangle.

'We can't join you; I have important business to attend to.'

'Pity,' said Louise. 'You'll never know what you're missing.'

'Absolutely, darlings. Here,' Maggie waved at Geoffrey. 'Just have a try of this drizzle cake. I can see you're a man who likes his food,' she added, looking pointedly at his bulging stomach that even the expensively cut suit couldn't disguise. Geoffrey flushed angrily.

'We're on our way to Lord Burley's manor house for cocktails before discussing a confidential European business venture,' said Dennis stiffly. He glowered in Jane's direction. 'Wendy,' he snapped, and Louise noticed she jumped to attention. 'Go and get that child.'

Wendy moved across to Jane and grasped Leon's hand. He climbed down from Jane's lap reluctantly and stood by his mother's side.

Dennis walked across and inspected his extremely dirty son standing still clad only in his underpants. 'I had intended to take Leon with me,' said Dennis. 'Lord Burley apparently loves children, is very strong on the family value side of life. I wanted to create a good impression.'

Wendy stood, holding Leon's hand, and looking rather desperate, thought Louise.

Penny jumped up. 'Well, that's OK. It won't take me a minute to give him a quick wash and put his clothes back on. They are a bit grubby, but ...'

'Filthy actually,' said Louise feeling that Wendy ought to be told the truth. 'But if, as you say, Lord Burley loves children he'll know that it's natural for small boys to get themselves dirty.'

'It's not natural for Leon,' was Dennis's icy reply looking at his son with disgust.

Wendy turned to her mother. 'We'll have to go without him. Could you take him back to the house later?'

'If you can get yourself organized enough to bring him back to the house at eight o'clock,' said Dennis. 'Unfortunately Yvette, our daily maid, will be gone by then, but,' he sighed heavily, 'but I dare say Wendy can manage to bath him and put him to bed when we get back.'

'I'll do that, Wendy,' said Jane, eager to make amends.

'You've done enough damage already,' snapped Dennis. 'I think the less Leon sees of you, or these other filthy children, the better. My son is being brought up in a different way.'

'You can say that again,' said Louise, white hot rage sweeping through her.

The three of them turned to leave, and spurred on by anger at Dennis's treatment of Jane, Wendy and his small son; Louise leapt up and followed them. As they reached the house she grabbed Dennis by the arm, and pulled him round and hissed, 'How dare you speak to your mother-in-law like that. She's done you a favour looking after Leon all day, and Leon, bless him, has had the time of his life. It's not natural to keep a 3-year-old dressed like Little Lord Fauntleroy, children need to play, experience life outside, and enjoy themselves. And most of all they need love, which he obviously isn't getting from you. You pompous prick!'

Behind her, she heard a gasp from the others at her language.

Dennis stopped in his tracks. 'Pardon?' he said in his plumiest voice.

'You heard,' repeated Louise. 'Now buzz off to bloody Lord Burley's cocktails, and when you get back don't think of punishing Leon for getting dirty. I intend to see a lot more of Leon with Jane so that he can come here and have a little bit of normality.'

'I don't think Dennis will allow that,' said Wendy in a small frightened voice.

'If he doesn't, I shall have no hesitation in reporting you to the Social Services for child cruelty. My friend, Olivia Savage is the head social worker, and is aptly named Savage. She's very left-wing and she'd love to investigate the family of a Conservative MEP. Just think of the scandal, and I'd make sure it got leaked to all the national newspapers as well as the local rag.'

Dennis took two steps back and tried to shake his arm free. 'That's blackmail.'

'Exactly.' Louise let go of his arm. 'Just remember that I mean it.'

'Louise is a bad influence on Jane as well,' muttered Geoffrey to Dennis.

'I am not a bad influence. She's my sister and I love her, which is more than you do,' said Louise. She was suddenly feeling exhilarated, and all powerful. She felt as if she could sort out all the troubles in the world.

'And *you'd* better watch your step,' she added for good measure. 'Always off making more money, on the fiddle no doubt. But be sure your sins will find you out. Someone will track you down.' She had added that bit for dramatic effect, but hadn't expected the effect to be quite as dramatic as it turned out to be. Geoffrey turned a ghastly pale colour, made a noise somewhere between a gulp and a hiccup, then turned and disappeared without another word.

Now it was Louise's turn to be puzzled. What *was* going on?

Once they'd gone, the party atmosphere subsided like a pricked balloon. 'What a load of shits,' said Maggie.

'Language!' said Penny.

'My sentiments exactly,' said Jane, who'd recovered a little of her courage.

'Yes, but not expressed like that in front of the children,' said Penny. 'I'm trying to teach them not to use bad language.'

'It's hardly worth the bother.' Maggie shrugged her shoulders expressively. 'They'll learn lots of bad language the moment they start school.'

Nobody disagreed.

Once his parents had disappeared, Leon recovered and was back to a normal little boy. He took another jam sandwich then he and Sam and went off to have another game before bed. Louise went back into the house and brought out another pot of tea. 'I think we all need this,' she said, setting out some fresh cups.

'And don't worry about Leon,' Penny told Jane. 'We'll bath him here and you can take him back to his home in a clean pair of Sam's pyjamas, and I'll wash and iron that damned linen suit he wore here.'

Jane visibly heaved a sigh of relief. 'Thanks Penny.'

'I'm just glad Jack wasn't here to witness our family row. He would have thought we were all very peculiar,' said Penny.

Louise didn't reply, but she was still puzzling over Geoffrey's strange reaction to her remark about making money. Jane hadn't appeared to notice, she'd been too concerned for Leon but in Louise's opinion there was something very odd about Geoffrey's behaviour.

CHAPTER
ᚴ TWELVE ᚴ

AFTER MUCH NAGGING by everyone, especially Sam, Louise decided to take the plunge and embark upon keeping chickens.

It was really one of her guests who had finally persuaded her. Miss Smythe, an eccentric old lady who'd taken a keen interest in everything to do with Lavender House, had announced that she intended to stay for at least four weeks next time if Louise could guarantee her a fresh egg for breakfast every day. 'And I do mean fresh,' she had said severely. 'With a garden like yours there's really no excuse for not keeping chickens. Promise me that by the next time I come you will have chickens.'

Louise promised and the chickens were a 'dozen point of lay hens', so called by Bert Hackett, because they were young and nearly ready to lay. 'If they don't,' he'd told Louise, 'you can always wring their necks and eat them.'

Louise looked at them eagerly pecking the fresh grass and regarding her with bright beady eyes, and knew she'd never be able to wring their necks. Now they'd arrived at Lavender house, they'd stay forever and would probably die of old age unless a fox got them.

David took it as the perfect excuse to stay on. He

researched various kinds of poultry housing on the web, decided on one and bought it. The hens were installed.

'They seem to be very happy,' said David, watching the hens in their new enclosure, which had been set up, as recommended, in the vegetable patch. 'Look how they're eating the weeds in between your leeks, they're weeding and depositing manure at the same time.'

In an incredibly short time, the hens duly fulfilled their duty and fresh eggs began to appear on the menu, much to her guests' delight. 'I had no idea,' one of her guests told her, 'that eggs straight from a chicken could taste so different. I shall definitely come here again.'

The highlight of Sam and Jacob's day was when they went down first thing in the morning to collect the eggs. Leon went too, whenever he visited with Jane, which Louise noted was a little more often these days. She thought it strange that he was allowed to come after the fuss there'd been, but made no comment. She just made certain that as soon as he arrived, he was changed into some of Sam's old clothes, so that his own remained pristine. She knew Jane was grateful, although she said nothing, so Louise was left to wonder what was going on in the Mills and Steadman households.

It was evident that Penny loved living back in Hampshire. David came at weekends, and then started staying most of the week. He took on the responsibility for moving the chicken house and pen when the hens needed somewhere fresh to scratch and feed. He read up on poultry-keeping and fed them pellets and gravel, which he assured Louise they needed for an extra bit of nutrition as they were such good layers.

The chicken project had definitely helped draw Penny and David together but Louise noticed that he was still relegated to the Z bed in the box-room at the back of the house, although Penny did allow him to come into Pottery Cottage and share their bathroom now they'd had the hot water immersion heater installed. But as far as Louise could make out, they were not sleeping together.

'Oh, this is the life,' Penny said one day, coming in with an armful of spinach. 'I have enough to make one of my quick spinach pies for tonight. This stuff is going mad at the bottom of the garden.' She tipped the spinach on to the kitchen table. 'You know, I don't think I could bear to go back and live in grimy, litter strewn London.'

'Your part of London is not so bad; in fact it's very nice. You live in a tree lined avenue, near the heath and Greenwich Park. And what's wrong with your house there?' Louise asked her. 'Besides there is David to consider.'

'Oh, the house is just a house,' said Penny dismissively. Louise noticed that David didn't get a mention.

Sometimes she felt inadequate as a mother, wanting to bring them back together but afraid of saying the wrong thing. Grown up children didn't throw tantrums and lie on the floor kicking their legs the way Sam did, but they could be just as difficult in a different way. Being a mother never got any easier, she decided

Maggie was very sanguine about Penny and David. 'Leave them alone and they'll come home, bringing their tails behind them,' had been her only comment.

She was probably right, Louise decided, and anyway she had too many other things, including Jack, on her mind to spend too long thinking about it.

She had finally got used to sleeping in Pottery Cottage with Penny and the boys, having given up her own large comfortable bedroom with reluctance. But as financial needs dictated the move, she told herself, 'needs must.'

They shared their new house with quite a few spiders, which had been in residence for a long time before them and didn't see why they should move out now. Louise hated them, but Sam loved them, and spent quite a few hours watching them scuttle about, prodding them with twigs if they didn't scuttle fast enough. He wouldn't allow Louise to brush them out. 'This is their house,' he insisted.

'I'd rather they found another house, not mine,' said Louise, trying to brush one very stubborn spider from her bedroom windowsill. The obstinate beast dived into a corner and curled himself up into a ball, thus making the task of removing him without injury an impossibility. 'Damned thing,' she said.

'That's a naughty word,' said Sam pompously. 'Mummy said so.'

Louise gave up on the spider and turned to Sam. 'As a nanny I'm allowed to use naughty words sometimes,' she told Sam firmly. 'Just tell Mummy that.'

Sam climbed on a chair and leaned on the windowsill watching for the spider to make a move, and giggled. 'Jack says naughty words sometimes. He said one the other day when he dropped the spade on his foot. And he says, don't tell Mummy.'

'And do you tell?'

Sam looked shocked. 'Of course not. I like Jack. I wish he was my daddy.'

'But you've got a daddy.'

'I know. But he's not here.'

Louise stored that remark in her memory. Something really did need to be done about those two. Mothers shouldn't be interfering, but she wanted to interfere. David was back in London and hadn't been down for a couple of weekends, which worried her. 'Come on.' She lifted Sam down, and took his hand. 'We've got to go back to the house so that I can prepare vegetables for tonight's dinner, and then later Jane is coming round to collect some lavender heads, and marigolds to make soaps. You can help her if you like.'

Sam trotted beside her as they made their way through the bottom end of the garden. They had kept this for the family, as with a great deal of hard manual labour, Jack had transformed the other side of the garden into a space where Louise's guests could sit in peace and quiet if they wished.

'Jane's funny, isn't she,' said Sam.

'Funny? How do you mean?'

'She doesn't have legs like you and Mummy,' said Sam. 'And she wears funny stockings which only go up to her knees. When she bends over to pick the flowers I can see right up her skirt, and her stockings stop at her knees and then she's got fat legs.'

'I don't think you should look,' said Louise.

'I like looking. Her legs are all wobbly at the top, like pink jelly.'

Louise thought it time to change the subject. 'I think you might be needed in the kitchen to help Mummy with the lunch. She's making her easy spinach pie.'

'Do you think she'll let me squidge the spinach through the colander?' He let go of Louise's hand and ran towards the kitchen.

'I'm sure she will,' said Louise, stopping to pick some baby dandelion leaves for a salad, and still think-ing of Sam's remark about wanting Jack to be his father. Somehow he had become part of the family without even trying. A father figure to Penny, although Louise sensed she was still attracted to him, but also, and perhaps more importantly, she knew Penny respected his opinions; maybe she should get him on her side regarding the errant couple. He played the doting grandfather to Sam and Jacob, who had now just started staggering about. When Jack was about, the pair frolicked around him like a couple of puppies. As for Maggie, she wasn't sure. She was a mass of contradictions; one moment the hard hearted feminist, the next moment the meek little woman, and only recently Louise had heard her on the phone to Seth in New York telling him in dulcet tones how much she missed him.

The guesthouse had got off to a flying start, and most of the guests were charming. There had only been one difficult couple with a precocious son named Piers who demanded every type of melon available in the supermarket, but when Louise served him, he refused to eat any of them. But apart from that, everything had been surprisingly easy.

Every time she banked some money from the house Louise was thankful because Dottie LeClerk, after much huffing and puffing, and telling her how difficult the market was and that agents were all going broke (never mind about the authors, thought Louise crossly) had eventually sold her book to a small, new publisher, called Weatherby and Son. The son, apparently, was the editor and general factotum.

'How much for?' asked Louise.

'Five hundred. Two hundred and fifty now. Then two hundred and fifty on publication, minus my 15 per cent of course.'

'Huh!' said Louise. It was the lowest advance she'd ever been offered. 'It was hardly worth bothering to write the damned thing. Why can't you get me an advance like that girl in today's *Daily Mail*? A quarter of a million, up front, for a synopsis and three pages.'

'Because you are not nineteen, you're not a size 8 dress size and very promotable, your name isn't Millie Johnson, your father a TV star, and your grandfather a cabinet minister. Besides, as I said, you can't expect much when you've written something completely different from all your other novels. Your old publishers expected fruit and nut and you delivered plain, bitter chocolate. They didn't want it. It was very difficult to place, too highbrow, almost literary.'

'You mean I used long words,' said Louise feeling indignant, but knowing Dottie was right. Everyone, publishers and readers, always wanted more of the same. She'd taken a gamble and written something different and it hadn't paid off.

'Well, yes that too. It would never sell in Asda, or Sainsburys, the ending was too miserable. Anyway, luckily for you, Simon Weatherby, the son, loved it. Said it was just the thing to launch their new list for the thinking woman.'

Louise refused to be mollified. 'I suppose he's a hundred and ninety, and hasn't got a clue. Anyway it seems to me that all the so-called thinking women live in London and write columns for newspapers. Then they write novels and give each other terrific reviews. I'm stuck in the country and not part of that scene.'

'Now, now, now,' scolded Dottie. 'You know that's not true. There are plenty of women who are intellectual, but don't live in London or write for the newspapers.'

'None round here,' said Louise, determined not to be cheerful. She thought of Jane, her obsession with clothes, organic soaps and essences, and lately, sex. Then there were the other local women who did patchwork and lace-making and held competitions. As Louise could hardly thread a needle, let alone make anything, she wasn't a member of their group, and thought what a dull lot they were. Apart from wondering what to cook for the next meal she doubted if any of them would notice if World War Three started. Logic told her that she was being unreasonable and unfair to Dottie, but at that precise moment in time in her disgruntled state that was how she felt.

'Anyway, I have kept the audio rights,' Dottie trilled down the phone, 'as I think I can do a good deal on those. I had lunch last week with Delia Galeton and she's very interested. So you'll get a few hundred extra if I can do a deal.'

'Great,' said Louise knowing she was sounding ungrateful, and feeling it. It seemed to her sometimes that all Dottie did was have lunch, talk about money, very little of which ever came her way. 'But Dottie, I need more than a few hundred, I need a million.'

'Don't we all, darling. But stop complaining, it's a tough world in publishing, and every little helps.'

Louise thought she sounded like a supermarket advert, but said, 'I suppose so.'

'I've done the best I can. You'll be getting about five hundred pounds eventually and that's not to be sniffed at.'

'It won't be five hundred by the time you've taken your 15 per cent,' said Louise. The result was that they'd parted on slightly hostile terms, which Louise knew was her fault. Dottie did do her best for all her clients; after all it was in her own interests to do so. Louise meant to phone her and apologize for being so grumpy, but hadn't had the time. Since then, there had been silence from Dottie, apart from the contract arriving, and then a cheque for £202.50 which was the two hundred and fifty minus Dottie's 15 per cent. She'd banked that in her sparse writing account and didn't spend any of it.

She was now living from the Bed and Breakfast account, which was what she called it, although officially it was still just account number two. She also opened a deposit account, on Norman Long's advice, into which she put a third of everything for the income tax bill.

'That's far too much,' said Penny. 'You can fiddle loads of things.'

Even Jane thought she was mad. 'I don't tell the taxman anything at all about my soaps and things, and I do make money even though it's really a hobby. Anyway, Geoffrey always says fiddle as much as you can.'

'Geoffrey would,' Louise replied, and continued to put the money into the special account for tax. She'd never actually met a tax inspector. At one time she *had* got into a muddle, but managed to get everything dealt with by letter. In her imagination, taxmen were tall and dark and distinctly menacing, the mere thought of them terrified her.

However, she didn't have much time to worry about money these days as running Lavender House was hard work. Changing the sheets every day when they had 'one-nighters' as Jack called them was a hassle, and the washing machine was always on the go. But the weather was good, and the sheets blew dry on the line by the field, which was out of sight of the house and garden. David had rigged it up for her on one of his frequent trips down, before he'd gone back to London and his solitary existence. Louise felt for him, sensing, although he never said, that he really enjoyed being in the country and playing with his sons, and wished Penny would at least meet him halfway to discuss their future.

But when she'd said so, Penny had shouted and said. 'Leave me alone, Mum. I'm an adult and I can make my own mistakes.'

'That's the whole point,' Louise had replied angrily. 'I think you are making a big mistake. One you will live to regret.'

'I don't need your advice.'

The atmosphere between them remained frigid for a few days, and after that, Louise kept her own counsel. She welcomed David whenever he came without appearing too obvious in front of Penny. He still worked while he was down in Hampshire, and had actually picked up some local clients, farmers and smallholders who were diversifying and needed websites extolling the virtues of their organic produce and the beauty of the New Forest. In a small place like East Willow, word soon got around that there was someone providing a top class service. So no need to advertise. He managed very well with his laptop and phone, plus a few other electronic gizmos he brought with him which mystified Louise who resisted the latest technology. Her old computer was quite technical enough for her. David told her that he was keeping all his clients happy, having more time with the boys, and hardly any time at all in the office, plus he'd only visited the pub in Blackheath once since he'd altered his working practice.

Penny, however, refused to be won over, and was adamant she needed 'space' as she put it. Time away from David.

Louise despaired but plucked up courage to broach the subject again. 'I do think, Penny, that perhaps you are being selfish, and not thinking about the children. They love David; you must see that as they are so happy when he's around. And you loved him once.' They were both in the greenhouse picking out the side shoots from the tomatoes.

Maggie, as usual was not actually doing any physical

labour, but was outside with the children. 'I can't bear the smell of fresh tomatoes,' she said, opting to loll on the garden bench with Sam playing at her feet and Jacob pulling on her golden hoop earrings; his favourite occupation.

But Penny remained on the defensive where David was concerned. 'I'm not married to him. I can do as I like, and the children are quite happy.'

Louise persisted. 'Of course they are at the moment, because they see him often. I know you think I'm old fashioned, but I think children should have the same surname as their parents. One surname, the one you'd all have if you married David. It's not just you involved. You can't think of yourself all the time.' She waited for Penny to explode. But she didn't. However, neither did she give in.

'I admit they see more of him here but they managed all right without him in London,' Penny replied, the same old defensive note to her voice. 'They hardly ever saw him then. It would be the same if I went back. They wouldn't see him, which proves to me they don't need him.'

'A very skewed logic,' said Louise beginning to feel cross again.

'I agree with Penny,' chimed in Maggie who'd been listening. 'Children don't need fathers. They get in the way of what mothers want to do.'

'You mind your own business.' Louise stuck her head out of the greenhouse door. 'As a mother you're a very bad example.'

Maggie was unfazed. 'Yes, I suppose I am,' she said fiddling absentmindedly with her golden hoops.

Louise ignored her and turned back to Penny. 'David's made up for the London life down here,' she pointed out.

'He's helped enormously with the chickens. We couldn't have got our egg production going without him.'

'Jack could have done it.'

'Jack is not family,' replied Louise sharply, 'We can't rely on him for everything.'

'David is not family either,' said Penny.

Louise bit her tongue, wishing she understood Penny. She'd never really understood her, not even as a small girl. 'He's family, in as much as he is the father of your children,' she reminded her daughter. 'And the children adore him.'

'They adore Jack as well,' Penny pointed out obstinately. 'They adore anyone who takes notice of them.'

'Of course they do,' Maggie said. 'As I said, when you interrupted me, they can manage without David. And Penny can manage without him. Any woman can manage without a man.'

Louise felt a rush of fury; sometimes Maggie could be so stupid, so selfish. 'Tell me about it,' she said loudly, feeling her cheeks redden, a mixture of anger and heat from the greenhouse. 'I've managed without a man for years. I've *had* to. You've *never* managed without a man. Anyway, we're not talking about women. I'm talking about Sam and Jacob who are two small boys who need a father. In my book, a one-parent family is not normal, and I don't care what anybody says. It might be un-PC to say so, but I believe a family should consist of a mother, a father and children.'

'Nonsense,' Penny shouted back. 'One parent families are the norm these days. You've only got to read women's magazines or a newspaper to see that this is the case.'

'I've seen those rubbishy magazines you read, full of adverts for incredibly beautiful, unrealistic homes, not a box of Lego or a broken toy in sight. With mothers and toddlers all dressed in the latest "must have" outfits, no doubt with an illegal immigrant as a nanny, while they work full-time, and not a man to be seen anywhere.'

'Those magazines are edited by mature women of thirty-five or more who have real experience of life.' Penny stamped her foot, causing a shower of ripe tomatoes to thud to the floor of the greenhouse.

'And all with the mental age of a 16-year-old and no common sense because they've got a bag of make-up pads stuffed between their ears.' Louise bent down and starting picking up the fallen tomatoes, throwing them in an old wooden trug. Half of her was thinking this is ridiculous, what are we arguing about, and the other half was thinking, these tomatoes are ruined and will only be fit for soup, which we've had twice this week already.

During the argument, Sam had taken himself off to the far end of the garden, and Maggie had clapped her hands over a rather bewildered Jacob's ears. She drew the conversation back to herself. 'I must say I agree with Penny. I have to cope without a man. My husband is in New York most of the time, and look at me, I'm OK.'

'Rubbish!' Louise exploded again. 'For a start you haven't got two small children, what's more you are always on the phone for money or whatever else you want, and as for coping, I've noticed since you've been here that you can't even open a tin of beans if Jack is anywhere within range. Talk about a helpless female. You make me sick!'

'Mum!' Penny was shocked at her mother's outburst.

Maggie dumped Jacob on the grass, gathered up her long skirt with one theatrical sweep, tossed back her head so that her droopy earrings jangled even more loudly than normal, and stalked dramatically up the garden path towards the house.

'Mum!' said Penny again. 'You shouldn't have said that.'

But Louise was in full flood. 'Why not? I'm sick of watching her ogle Jack. It's embarrassing, especially for a woman of her age. She must be a good twenty-five to thirty years older than me.' Louise knew she had gone too far, but she was not in a mood to care. Maggie had arrived without an invitation, and was enjoying herself so much that Louise doubted that even throwing the most offensive remarks at her would drive her away. She was also landed with Penny and the boys, whom she loved, and wanted desperately to help sort out their lives, but knew, from bitter experience, that Penny would stubbornly continue to follow her own path. All she could hope for was an eventual satisfactory outcome.

But as suddenly as it had started Penny's mood changed and she apparently forgot about their row of a few moments ago, because she grinned and said, 'I think you're rather sweet on Jack yourself.'

'Nonsense,' said Louise vehemently, more forcefully than she'd intended. 'I'm not interested in him. I've no intention of becoming shackled again. I want to be free of considering someone else, and I certainly don't want to end up washing any man's underpants.'

Penny laughed, and pointed to the washing line, on which were fluttering half a dozen pairs of large boxer shorts. 'You never let Dad wear those,' she said. 'You always said there was too much dangling down to be decent.'

Against her will Louise laughed as well. 'True.' She agreed. 'But Jack is not your father, neither is he my husband, so he can dangle as much as he likes. Anyway, I don't wash them; he always does his own washing.' She left Penny in the greenhouse to finish pinching out the tomato shoots, collected the trug of damaged fruit and started towards the kitchen. 'Come and help with preparing lunch when you've finished, I've still got a couple of bedrooms to clean and polish, and I need to check up on Mrs Dickson's work, she's inclined to skimp sometimes.'

'Goodness knows why you employ that woman. She's not a good cleaner.'

'No, but she's honest, and needs the money,' said Louise, picking up Jacob and plonking him in the green-house with Penny. 'For goodness sake keep an eye on your offspring. Lately they're beginning to wander all over the place.'

Penny suddenly laughed. 'I'm looking forward to lunch. I shall be watching you with interest. You on one side of Jack, and Maggie on the other.'

'I think Jane might be coming,' replied Louise, 'so I shall put her on the other side of Jack, and you can watch her do her heavy breathing routine.'

'Your sister's mad.'

'I can't disagree with that,' said Louise and disappeared up the garden towards the house.

CHAPTER
❧ THIRTEEN ❧

Predictably, Jane turned up just in time for lunch but too late, of course, to be able to offer to help. However, today and very unexpectedly, she had Geoffrey in tow.

'Darling,' she said kissing Louise. 'Geoffrey's come with me. I knew you wouldn't mind. I had to bring him; I had absolutely nothing in the fridge to leave him for lunch.'

'Nothing new there,' muttered Geoffrey looking his usual bad-tempered self.

'I didn't want him going down to the Oak, having a pork pie, two packets of crisps and a pint of Old Peculiar,' said Jane. 'He's got to lose weight. The doctor says he's in danger of having a heart attack if he goes on the way he is.'

'I thought that's what you wanted,' whispered Louise in Jane's ear while kissing her in welcome.

Jane flushed and looked indignant, while Louise kissed Geoffrey on both cheeks as well, wondering at the same time why it was that the English had all fallen into the habit of kissing people they didn't like. Must be all those foreign holidays, she decided, dodging Geoffrey's lips as he tried to kiss her on the mouth. Should she tell him that they were having a vegetarian lunch, tomato and basil soup, followed by spinach and cheese pie? Geoffrey was meat and two veg man, but Louise decided that as he was eating a free lunch he could eat whatever was presented to him. He'd drink whatever wine there was available too, that was for certain; Geoffrey was fond of his wine. Too fond, in Louise's opinion, who knew he was often drunk at home, even though it was something Jane never mentioned to her or anyone else as far as she knew. She'd learned about the drinking from Mrs Dickson who also cleaned for Jane as well as Lavender House.

'I've seen him drunk as a lord,' Mrs Dickson had told her. 'And nasty he was with it too.'

'I'll set another two places,' she said now. 'You know you're both welcome.' Not strictly true, in fact it was a nuisance as Penny had calculated five adults and two children when making the pie. 'But don't go into the kitchen just now, it's terribly hot. Why don't you go through to the sitting room, it's much more peaceful.'

'Thought I'd better come,' Geoffrey grunted as he followed Louise and Jane through to the sitting room. She thought he could have been more gracious, but that wasn't Geoffrey's way. He was never gracious. No wonder Jane was fed up. 'Jane's always on about this Jack chap you've hired,' Geoffrey continued, 'always on about his wonderful cooking. So thought I'd come and take a deco.'

'I haven't *hired* Jack,' said Louise. 'He's staying here as a paying guest, and he doesn't do the cooking all the time, in fact today Penny is doing most of it, but as it happens he likes it and often helps out in the kitchen for me.'

'Cheap labour,' sniffed Geoffrey, sinking down into an old armchair. 'Where's my aperitif then?'

He really should go on a diet, decided Louise

looking at him and wondering if it would ever be possible to lever him out of the chair, which was very low on account of the springs being worn out. But that was another problem; the most immediate one was the food. Was there enough of it? 'Excuse me,' she said, and dashed back towards the kitchen.

'Shall I do the sherries?' Jane called, already moving across to the drinks cupboard.

'Yes, please.'

As she left Louise heard Geoffrey muttering, 'Don't want any of that pansy sherry stuff, get me good malt.' What a cheek, she thought, anyway he'll be lucky, I can't afford a good malt, and I'm not letting him get his hands on that bottle Jack bought, which luckily is in the kitchen. The thought that he'd have to have sherry gave her malicious glee.

The kitchen was very hot even with all the windows flung wide open. Penny was roasting, even Jack was red faced. He was hastily rolling out more pastry, and had a pile of dripping spinach in a bowl beside him. 'Just bung that in the microwave for two minutes will you?' he said nodding towards the spinach. 'I'm making some rough puff pastry, which will have to do for another pie.'

Penny was busy whizzing the cooked tomatoes and basil before straining the mixture, and Sam, who was standing on a pair of small steps, was busily chopping basil with a benign smile of satisfaction on his face. It wasn't often he was allowed to use sharp things.

'Don't worry, Mum. Everything is under control,' said Penny. 'Nothing for you to do here.'

Louise watched her and forgot for the moment about Jane and Geoffrey in the next room. Penny looked so happy. Oh, if only she and David made it up so that they could become a proper family again and then maybe they could even move down to Hampshire permanently. Then she reined in her wayward thoughts. Get real, she told herself; you can't organize people in real life like you can in novels. Just enjoy the moment. So she watched Penny making soup, Jack rolling the pastry, and Sam happily engaged in his chopping. It was only later that she realized that she'd included Jack in her picture of contented family life.

'Lunch in about eight minutes,' said Jack. Louise suddenly became aware that he was looking rather serious today. He was usually shouting and laughing when he cooked, but today he seemed preoccupied, and almost worried.

'I see you're coping well with the extra one for lunch.' said Louise. 'Jane and Geoffrey have arrived and I've put them in the sitting room for the time being to have a sherry.'

Jack had put too much water in the flour and it was sticking to the rolling pin. 'Damn,' he swore. Then he said, 'Can't imagine Geoffrey going for sherry.'

'No swearing in front of Sam,' Penny whispered sternly.

Jack looked up and Louise met his eyes. There was something troubling him. She was sure of it. 'You've met Geoffrey already have you?'

'No,' he said quickly. Much too quickly for Louise to believe him. He did know Geoffrey, she was sure of it. But how? 'Men, on the whole, don't like sherry,' he said. 'It's a woman's drink.' But his explanation somehow didn't ring true to Louise's ears.

'You're probably right. Sure there's nothing I can do?'

Jack flashed her a smile, but Louise thought it lacked his usual twinkle. 'No, nothing to do, although at the rate we're going maybe we should tell them lunch in twenty minutes, not ten.'

'And get Jane to do something useful, like laying the table out in the garden, it's too hot to eat in the kitchen today,' Penny said. 'Tell her, five adults and two high chairs. Jacob will be awake by then, so he can chew on some bread while he's waiting.' She sighed heavily. 'Now we've got to delay lunch it means I won't be able to eat my meal in peace. I'll have to keep Jacob happy.'

'I'll feed Jacob.' Louise put another couple of bottles of beer in the fridge to drink with the pie, then left to return to Jane and Geoffrey who had already moved outside into the garden.

Jane had anticipated Penny's command and had started laying the table outside. She took Louise by the arm and made her sit down. 'You look tired,' she sounded concerned. 'Here take this and sit in the shade while I finish off the table. Louise took a glass of sherry and sat down in an old wicker armchair, which had seen better days but was so comfortable, she was loath to throw it away. She watched Jane. She was a good sister, even though she did drive her mad sometimes. Then she looked at Geoffrey slouched in a garden chair doing the newspaper crossword. She didn't like him. She hadn't liked him when Jane had married him. But then Jane hadn't liked John and had said he was weak, which was true. But we both loved them, thought Louise watching Geoffrey. No accounting for taste, and love was such an unreliable emotion. John might have been weak, but he'd been kind and easy going, whereas Geoffrey was bad-tempered and arrogant.

Jane had obviously had at least two glasses of sherry, as she was rushing around happily, humming loudly as she put the final touches to the table. Louise thought she was humming the 'Lonely Goatherd' from *The Sound of Music*, but wasn't sure as Jane's grasp of a tune was always tenuous at the best of times, and her yodelling certainly left a lot to be desired.

Soothed by the large schooner of sherry, Louise looked at the table set out in the garden beneath the ancient fig tree. No one knew how old the tree was, it was a brown turkey apparently, and had been planted by her godmother's great grandparents; against all odds and the English weather had survived, grown enormous and in good summers fruited prolifically. Today, its deep green shiny leaves looked lovely gleaming in the sun and between the leaves were the purple smudges of slowly ripening figs. Jane had spread out the old sheet Louise used as a garden table-cloth, and then put out the old blue and yellow plates, which had once belonged to their mother. Louise loved them and had kept them, as Jane preferred everything she used to be new. She'd found some primrose coloured paper serviettes, and had filled two empty jam jars with buttercups and forget-me-nots.

'I'm taking a digital photograph,' said Jane, standing back and looking at the table. 'Thought I'd try to get you some publicity in the *County Magazine* as I know the editor, and I'll go down and take a photo of the chickens as well. Maybe they'll take both and you can be advertised as really countrified.'

'Waste of time,' muttered Geoffrey. 'The magazine won't be interested in your photos; you're not a professional. And as for the chickens, they won't live long. A fox will get them. Mark my words.'

Both women ignored him. 'Thanks,' said Louise. 'It will be good to have some free advertising, although at the moment I have to turn people away.'

'Won't be like that in the winter,' said Geoffrey sourly. 'Then you'll struggle to make ends meet.'

Louise still ignored him. 'And your handmade soaps, shampoo and bath essence have gone down very well with the guests. They like them so much they're buying more to take away with them as souvenirs of their stay here.'

'Huh,' snorted Geoffrey, 'if you're doing that well, Jane, you'd better let me take over and do your accounts. I'll keep hold of the money.'

'I thought I could do that myself,' said Jane, sounding uncertain. 'Louise was going with me so see Norman Long the bank manager to open a new account.'

Geoffrey looked up from his crossword and snorted.

But before he could say anything Louise cut in. 'Jane is more than capable of doing her own accounts,' she said briskly. 'We are keeping the running of Lavender House and Jane's cosmetic business as a strictly female only enterprise. No men allowed.'

'Yes,' agreed Jane timidly. 'Women only.' Her voice strengthened. 'Maybe if we work hard enough we could win the Businesswomen of the Year award.'

Geoffrey snorted again. 'Some hope of that. Anyway, Louise, you let this Jack help you, so it's not women only.'

'I told you before, he's a guest, and when he does help it's only practical masculine things. I do the accounts.' Louise lay back in the wicker chair to indicate that the conversation was closed, and looked up into the darkness of the fig tree. It looked as if there would be a good harvest.

Jane saw her looking up into the dense branches and read her thoughts. 'You'll be able to make some fig jam this year,' she said. 'I'll help you.'

'Yes,' Louise smiled contentedly. 'I'll be able to use

it for breakfasts, as well as selling some to my paying guests. They can take back home-made jam as souvenirs as well as your soaps.'

'Don't know what John would have said about you taking in paying guests at Lavender House.' Geoffrey held out his glass towards Jane for another sherry. 'Not quite the thing; not in my book anyway, letting complete strangers into your home.'

'Well ...' began Jane, her voice timid again. 'I think it's quite a good ...'

'You know nothing about business,' interrupted Geoffrey rudely. 'Neither does Louise. Come on, more sherry.'

'No!' Louise whipped the sherry bottle from Jane's hand. 'I know enough about business to know I can't afford to let my guests guzzle glass after glass of sherry before lunch. Especially non paying guests.' She heard Jane's horrified intake of breath. Geoffrey wasn't used to being spoken to like that, but Louise was annoyed, and once into her stride she continued. 'And what goes on in Lavender House has nothing to do with you, Geoffrey. John is not here now, so he can't say anything. I manage things on my own, the way I want them to be.' She put the sherry bottle down in the grass beside her chair, well away from Geoffrey who was jutting his bottom lip forward like a petulant child. 'And I wouldn't be running a guest house now, if John hadn't invested in that damned mining company, which, may I remind you, was due to your advice.'

John and Geoffrey had gone to school together. Geoffrey had gone on to become a solicitor dealing mainly in the finances of divorce cases. He was well known for getting the best deal for his clients when finalizing divorce settlements. He'd also become a pillar of the community, a parish councillor, a Rotarian and a Freemason, and had made a lot of money from the buying and selling of shares. Rumour had it in the village, mostly from the city folk who had weekend cottages, that some of his dealings were rather dodgy, but nothing had ever been proved. So he and Jane were wealthy, or rather *he* was wealthy, as he took care not to let Jane get her hands on too much of their money; rationing her allowance as he thought fit.

John, on the other hand, had become a potter, married Louise, and had made a precarious living. When his mother died leaving him a sizeable sum of money, he'd taken Geoffrey's advice and invested in a mining company in Australia. Geoffrey had invested as well. The firm had disappeared without trace, and John's money with it. Not Geoffrey's money, of course. He'd got his out before the insolvency was declared.

'I did warn him against that company,' intoned Geoffrey self-righteously. 'There were whispers in the city. That's why I took my money out.'

'But you didn't warn him soon enough, did you?' Louise still felt angry about it. 'You made sure you got your money out before telling John, and by then it was too late.'

'But I didn't tell him to invest what money he had left in Hinks and Hillier for your pension, did I? Anyone who read the financial papers would have known not to do that.'

'I'm sure John did what he thought best, but you knew he never read a financial paper. He wasn't that kind of person. He was too trusting because he was a good man,' said Louise defensively. 'But that's all water under the bridge now,' she added. 'No point in even thinking about it.'

'Anyway, now you've started in business yourself, I only hope you've got a good accountant,' said Geoffrey sullenly. 'These small business ventures can be fraught with booby traps for the uninitiated.' Nothing, it seemed, would make Geoffrey look on the bright side.

'Is your middle name Eeyore?' snapped Louise.

Geoffrey looked blank, and Jane unexpectedly giggled. 'I don't think he's read *Winnie The Pooh*.'

'The bank manager is being very helpful at the moment,' said Louise pouring herself another sherry. She could see why Jane was so addicted to the sherry bottle; Geoffrey was enough to drive anyone to drink. Jane should leave him, as she was always threatening to do. But Louise knew she never would. She put the bottle back down in the grass, pointedly not offering more to Geoffrey.

Maggie came outside to join the luncheon party obviously still annoyed with Louise as she glowered at her and flounced petulantly over to a chair near Geoffrey. She'd changed for lunch into a fitted dress. It was brilliant yellow, decorated with intricate mirror work, and showed off her good figure and perma-tan to an advantage. But nothing, Louise noticed, could disguise the fact that her skin had wrinkled into brown crêpe with age. She looked at her own arms, slightly tanned from working in the garden, and well rounded and decided that maybe there was no advantage at all in being stick thin if it meant that you looked as if you were wearing a brown paper bag over your bones.

Maggie fluttered her eyelashes at Geoffrey, who responded with a coy smile. 'Shall I refill your empty glass?' she asked.

Although seething, there was nothing Louise could

do to stop Geoffrey having more sherry. 'Mutton dressed as lamb,' muttered Jane to Louise, nodding at Maggie as she passed her the bottle. Maggie poured herself and Geoffrey a generous measure of sherry.

Penny arrived and dumped Jacob, who had just woken up, on to Maggie's lap where he proceeded to try and pick off the mirrors with the determined dexterity that only small children possess. 'You can have him, Maggie, while I get his lunch ready.'

Maggie had other ideas. After prizing Jacob's podgy fingers from her dress she put him in his high chair. 'I can't cope with a child at the moment,' she announced theatrically, turning to Geoffrey and putting a hand to her forehead. 'Not after the news I've just had.' Jacob roared with frustration at being separated from the Maggie and the mirrors, but ignoring the noise Maggie firmly strapped him in the chair.

Jane, and Geoffrey looked interested. 'What news?' shouted Jane above Jacob's roars.

'It's Seth,' sighed Maggie, throwing her head back and closing her eyes as if in anguish. 'He's decided to come back to England and spend the rest of his life with me.'

'What about his work?' asked Penny, coming out of the kitchen and hastily putting a bowl of pizza pieces in front of Jacob, who stopped roaring immediately and began eating the pizza.

'He says he's made enough money, and he's feeling old and tired. He's going to retire and live quietly in England with me.'

'Where?' asked Louise. An ominous feeling of apprehension began to settle over her.

'Lavender House, of course,' said Maggie. 'I shouldn't have told him how wonderful it was here living with you and the grandchildren. I really don't want to be saddled with an old man at my age, but it looks as if I'm going to be.'

'And what age would that be?' shouted Jack through the window, 'or are you stuck at thirty-two like most actresses?'

Maggie ignored him.

Louise felt both flattered and angry. Flattered that Maggie was enjoying herself so much that she wanted to stay, but cross at the thought that she assumed the two of them could just move in and stay forever. 'Well, I'm not sure the children will always be here,' she said cautiously, 'because, of course, I expect Penny and the children will be going back to London at the end of the summer. Sam has to start pre-school. So you will want to be back in London as well to be near Penny and David.'

'Oh no,' replied Maggie firmly. 'Seth will be much more manageable down here, and the great thing is I don't have to do anything, not even think about getting a cleaner in. All that is taken care of here at Lavender House, and when I get the chance of some work it's not a problem. I can just pop up to London or wherever the location happens to be.'

'And don't worry about Sam, Mum,' said Penny who'd overheard the conversation. She put down a large pie on the table. 'This is the first one, another to follow.'

'Why shouldn't I worry about Sam?'

'Because I've booked him in for pre-school here; they had vacancies at East Willow church school, so I've put his name down. I can stay on and be your chief cook and bottle washer, with Jack in charge, of course.'

'Of course, the real problem is I don't think I'm ready yet for a full time relationship,' muttered Maggie, petulantly tugging at one of her gold hoop earrings. 'It can get so boring.'

'You've never tried it, so how can you possibly know,' snapped Louise, beginning to feel incredibly bad-tempered. Suddenly it had transpired that Maggie and Seth would be permanent, and Penny also intended making Lavender House her permanent home without ever thinking to mention it to her. Things were getting out of control. 'I'm trying to run a guest house,' she said, 'I expect people to come and go, not stay permanently, and I certainly don't want it full of family members.'

'What's wrong with family members if they pay their way?' demanded Maggie.

As she couldn't think of an answer to that, Louise heaved a sigh of irritation.

'Yes, I agree,' said Jane loudly.

'With what?' asked Penny and Louise together.

'With what Maggie said about full-time relationships getting boring. It's true. It's the routine I can't stand. After a few years you know what they eat, what they drink, and when they want their meals. I'm always cooking the same thing as Geoffrey will never try anything new, and his taste in clothes is awful.' Everyone looked at Geoffrey in his bright green golf shirt and too tight beige trousers. He opened his mouth to say something, but Jane, given courage by several glasses of sherry was in full swing, and there was no stopping her. 'If you think that's awful,' she said, waving an arm in his direction, 'you should see his underwear. He will insist on wearing Marks & Spencer boxer shorts a size too small. They are disgusting; everything hangs out, like a couple of bags of wrinkled nuts.' She clenched her hands, every bit as dramatic as Maggie at her best. 'I can't tell you how I long sometimes to get a pair of scissors and snip the bloody things off.' Geoffrey moved uneasily in his chair and put a hand protectively in his lap as Jane moved across to him, so that she was standing menacingly above him. 'Yes,' she said. 'Married life is boring, boring, boring!'

By now everyone was staring at Geoffrey who had turned beetroot red and was looking extremely worried as he choked on the last of his sherry. Wiping his mouth with the back of his hand, he shuffled as far back in the chair as was possible. 'Do you mean to say you find me boring?' His voice was querulous.

'Yes,' said Jane, 'I do. And don't wipe your mouth with your hand like that. That's another thing I can't stand.'

Oh dear, thought Louise, Jane's had far too much sherry, and it looks as if she's going to hit him if I don't do something. 'A glass of wine anyone,' she said brightly, opening a bottle of white wine Penny had brought out. 'And do have a piece of this spinach pie, Geoffrey. It's absolutely delicious.' Hastily cutting a wedge and passing it to him, she dragged Jane off to one side. Anything to get the pair apart. Everyone was gazing open mouthed at Jane and Geoffrey.

Geoffrey took a mouthful of pie, and at that moment Jane broke from Louise's grasp and lurched back over to him. 'I hate you,' she said.

'Well, I'll be damned,' Geoffrey brayed, spraying chewed pieces of spinach and pastry in all directions.

'And don't talk with your mouth full,' shrieked Jane, her voice on a rising note of hysteria. 'That's another thing I've always hated about you. Quite apart from the fact that you are hopeless in bed.'

Sam looked very interested. 'Mummy says I am very good in bed,' he announced loudly. 'Because now I'm in a big bed, and I don't get out.'

'I can't be that bad,' Geoffrey shouted back at Jane, 'otherwise Sharon wouldn't be so keen on me.'

'Aah! So you *are* having an affair.' Jane's voice shot up several decibels.

'Only a little one. And it's finished now. Everyone is entitled to the odd fling, especially if they're married to someone like you.'

'Only a little one! Well, I'm not surprised about that. That's all you're capable of. A little one!' shouted Jane. 'Did you pay her?'

'Yes … no … I did, but I … anyway I'm still with you,' Geoffrey's voice tailed off. He stood up and tried to look dignified, which wasn't easy as he had a large piece of spinach stuck to the front of his stomach. Louise thought the colour went well with his shirt.

She passed him a serviette and pointed to it. 'I think perhaps,' she said, quietly but very firmly, standing up and indicating the door into the kitchen from the garden, 'you should go inside.' Geoffrey obediently followed her pointing finger, and after a moment's hesitation Jane did as well with Louise bringing up the rear. Once they were inside, Louise slammed the door shut, then went across and closed the kitchen window as well. She turned to the pair. They were standing either side of the large table looking like a couple of prize fighters sizing up the oppo-sition and deciding where to land the first blow.

Luckily Jack was nowhere to be seen, having done the cooking, Louise presumed he must have gone back to his room, or into the garden by the conservatory door at the other end of the kitchen.

'How dare you air your dirty washing in front of my family,' said Louise. She was trembling with anger, but managed to keep her voice calm and businesslike. 'You can both leave now, this minute, and don't come back until you've sorted yourselves out, one way or the other.'

'How can we sort it out,' quavered Jane, suddenly

changing back into her usual needy, insecure self. 'What shall I do?'

'I don't know, and what's more, I don't care,' said Louise, for once saying exactly what she felt, instead of trying to smooth things over and be understanding. What was the point, she thought. She'd never really understood Jane and Geoffrey's relationship anyway, and if she had any sympathy at all it was for Jane. God only knew what Geoffrey was like as a husband, but he was Jane's husband, not hers, and Jane was the person who had to deal with him.

Walking through the kitchen into the hall she opened the front door. 'Goodbye,' she said firmly.

'Goodbye.' Jane sounded more plaintive than usual as she slunk through the door onto the gravel at the front of the house. She took a few uncertain steps towards Geoffrey's gleaming jaguar, and then turned back. 'Can I borrow your bicycle?' Louise nodded, she could understand Jane not wanting to ride with Geoffrey, and in view of the state they were both in it was probably safer that way. Louise had visions of Geoffrey crashing the car in a rage. Jane took the bicycle, which was still leaning against the bay tree at the end of the wall where Louise had left it the previous night, and wheeled it across the gravel. 'You are so lucky, Louise,' she said tearfully. 'You've got your family all around you and you've got Jack to look after you.'

'Jack doesn't look after me,' said Louise. 'I look after myself, and for goodness sake, Jane, stop being so pathetic. You're not a fool, you could easily look after yourself, if that's what you want.'

At this point Jack arrived and stood behind Louise. 'What's this all about?' he said. Then he saw Geoffrey.

Louise didn't actually see the moment their eyes met,

but she sensed it. She also sensed that something momentous had happened. She'd thought before that perhaps Jack knew Geoffrey from what he'd said, but now she was absolutely certain of it. Jack put his hand on her shoulder and squeezed hard. Instinctively Louise knew this was not a squeeze of comfort, but a gesture of something she didn't understand. In fact, ridiculous though it was, she sensed that Jack wasn't even thinking of her at all; there was something between him and Geoffrey flowing like an electric current. And it wasn't pleasant.

'That's right. You tell Jane what to do,' Geoffrey said to Louise, then he paused and glowered at Jack, and added in a low voice which had a menacing ring to it, 'And you'd better take care to look after yourself, Louise. There's a lot about him you don't know. Don't think that because Jack is good in bed he's good at everything else.'

Louise exploded. 'I don't sleep with Jack, not that it's any of your business anyway.'

'Can't think why he's hanging around then,' jeered Geoffrey, but although he was being aggressive, Louise had the strangest feeling he was worried. 'I'll tell you one thing though.' He leaned in close to Louise, his alcoholic breath making her feel sick. 'Your John might not have been very bright when it came to investing money, but he'd never have stood a chance with Jack O' Leary on his tail. He'd have been hung, drawn and quartered.'

Louise felt a creeping panic. 'What do you mean?'

Geoffrey laughed again, leaning closer with the dogged determination of a drunk. 'Ask him. Go on, just ask him.'

Louise gave him a violent push. 'Go away you hateful man. You're drunk and disgusting, and I do think Jane should leave you. You don't deserve her. '

At this point Jane took off on Louise's old bicycle,

crunching through the gravel as she pedalled furiously down the drive. 'I am leaving you,' she shouted back at Geoffrey. 'I'm packing up and going now.'

'Oh no!' Louise put her head in her hands. She knew what it meant. It meant another bedroom in Lavender House was going to have a semi-permanent resident.

CHAPTER
~ FOURTEEN ~

ONCE THE WARRING couple had departed, Louise turned and looked at Jack. His expression was inscrutable. She looked away then stole another glance at his profile, and came to the conclusion that he was looking decidedly shifty. She burned with longing to ask him what Geoffrey had meant. Did he mean John had done something wrong, or that he was involved with Jack in some way? He'd never mentioned a Jack O'Leary to her. Never. Not once during all their married life and she'd have remembered a name like that, it was not a name one came across every day of the week.

'The food will be spoiling,' he said quietly, avoiding looking at her directly. 'Let's join the others and eat.'

'But, Jack, I …' her words were a waste of time and trailed off into thin air as Jack was already striding away towards the dining table in the shade of the fig tree. Louise gave up and followed him. She had the feeling that even if she had managed to ask him something he would have evaded the question. Maybe he might tell her one day, when he was ready. It was then, something, she'd known all along, but had never actually acknowledged, struck her. The reality was that she knew nothing about Jack, only what he had chosen to tell her and that was very little.

Lunch was strangely subdued. Even Maggie had been shocked into silence by the ferocity of Geoffrey and Jane's row. 'At least I get on with Seth,' she muttered to Louise, adding sotto voce, 'in small doses. It's the large dose I'm worried about.'

Louise glanced at Maggie and was surprised to see real panic in her eyes, and realized that she was nervous about Seth joining her in England. Not knowing what to say, she hesitated then said lamely, 'Well he is your husband. You must have married him because you wanted him in large doses at the time, and because you loved him. Just as Jane must have loved Geoffrey once.'

'Yes,' said Maggie doubtfully. 'I did love Seth.' There was a long pause, and then she said eventually. 'At least, I think I did. But I also think I've forgotten how to love now. It all seems so long ago, and that first rush of passion always fizzles out like a damp firework eventually.'

'All you probably need is a match to light the fire again,' said Louise. Then she thought of John. How would they have been now if he had lived? Their passion had died long before he'd had his heart attack. Sex was not the be all and end all of their lives. It was nice and satisfactory but not a raging passion. They'd been happy enough though, sometimes she'd thought they were like a couple of shire horses, harnessed together, ploughing their furrow in life, both going in the same direction, needing no instructions as their path had already been mapped out for them. Then she thought of Jack. He was the age John would have been if he'd lived, but somehow his attitude to life seemed younger and she had the feeling that if she lit a match near him he'd take off with a great big whoosh. But she didn't know for sure, it was only a thought, and now there was another side to him, the darker side of the confrontation with Geoffrey, except that Jack had said nothing. He'd remained silent. She wished she knew what it meant.

By the side of her sat Maggie, whose demeanour could only be described as melancholy.

A heavy silence hung over the table, almost like a visible cloud. Sam and Jacob were unusually quiet, as they were concentrating on the serious business of eating. 'The pie is delicious,' Louise said at last. Someone had to say something to break the atmosphere.

'I'm glad you like it.' Jack helped himself to another slice. 'Penny and I experimented with the pastry adding sunflower as well as olive oil instead of margarine. Seems to have worked well.' He too was obviously anxious to drag the atmosphere back to some kind of normality.

Penny responded gratefully. 'Certainly has, judging by the amount that's been eaten.' She began cleaning Jacob's messy tray before starting him on his pudding, and turned to Louise with a grin. 'Thank God they've gone.' She nodded at Geoffrey and Jane's empty seats and began spooning Jacob's favourite pudding, mushy banana and yoghurt, into a bowl. All Louise's disquieting thoughts disappeared as she watched Jacob, sitting in his high chair, small pink mouth open as always, waiting for the next delicious morsel. She felt a stab of sadness. Small children were so adorable, all they needed was to be loved and fed. Then they grew up and life became more complicated. Jacob and Sam were lucky, they had the luxury of a real childhood, and they were cherished with more than enough food for them to eat, unlike the children on TV, the refugees from war and famine, or those sold into slavery because their families were poverty stricken. Those children with enormous dark eyes and stick thin arms and legs moved her to tears so that she always gave more money than she could really afford to the charity trying to help them.

'I can't think what Jane sees in that Geoffrey fellow,' said Maggie cheering up a little, and dragging Louise's meandering mind back to the present. 'Pass me some more wine, will you darling?' This was to Jack who, Louise noticed, was still eating and staring thoughtfully into space. Maggie leaned forward, skinny brown arm extended, golden bangles jangling, her hand holding a large balloon glass. Maggie always insisted on drinking wine from the largest wine glasses, said she needed to appreciate the 'nose'. 'Of course,' she continued, 'she should have left him years ago. I would have done.'

'You always leave everyone,' said Penny.

'Darling,' Maggie sloshed the wine Jack had given her around in her glass, 'I only leave when I've got another better specimen lined up ready and waiting.'

'And now?' Louise couldn't resist asking.

Maggie heaved a huge sigh. 'And now, I suppose I'll have to settle down with Seth. I really can't be bothered to go chasing after men. It's all so exhausting at my age.'

'And what is that? Your age, I mean, even David doesn't know that.' Penny asked.

'A secret between me and my birth certificate.'

'Anyway, David will be pleased,' said Penny. 'The bit about not chasing after men.'

'What men?' asked Sam who was following the conversation with puzzlement.

'Here you are, darling, have a cherry yoghurt, your favourite,' said Penny quickly, plonking the pot in front of him, adding to Maggie, 'he's always wanted you to settle down.'

'Since when do you care what David thinks?' enquired Louise.

'Just out of interest, Maggie, David told me that Seth is coming over with a suitcase full of Viagra,' said Jack solemnly. 'So you'd better watch out.'

Maggie shrieked in horror, and everyone burst out laughing. The tense atmosphere of the moment before suddenly dissipated like a passing breeze.

'Getting back to Jane,' said Louise thoughtfully, 'I don't think she will leave Geoffrey. If she did, she wouldn't have the lovely house she's got, and the comfortable life that goes with it. Besides, Jane's quite a bit older than me. She's well into her fifties now, and like me, she's got no qualifications to speak of; nothing that's relevant in today's world. She did shorthand typing in her youth, but there's not much call for that now. In fact, I suppose, we're rather alike in that respect. Middle-aged and uninteresting.'

'But, darling,' Maggie exclaimed. 'You do yourself a disservice. For a start you're still young, and you've always managed on your own, because you are a writer. You've got about ten books under your belt. You are interesting, *and* you're running a guesthouse. Very successfully in my opinion.'

'Thanks, Maggie, for that vote of confidence, but it's only with an enormous amount of help,' replied Louise. She looked across at Jack. 'And I have all of you to thank for that. Also where would I be today if Jack hadn't tipped my bike into the ditch?'

'My pleasure,' replied Jack, and everyone laughed. But Louise thought he looked even more uncomfortable than he had when first meeting Geoffrey.

'Yes, what were you looking for, driving around these country lanes on that day?' asked Louise, seizing the opportunity to try and find out more about him. 'You never did tell me.'

But she was thwarted yet again, however, by Penny interrupting. 'You know, Jane makes fabulous herbal soaps, shampoos, creams and things,' said Penny, still feeding Jacob and thinking about Jane. 'She could make a reasonable living by employing some local women, collecting all the flower heads she needs to make more, and then selling them on the Internet.' She paused and looked triumphant. 'Then she could leave Geoffrey because she'd be independent.'

'She hasn't got a computer,' said Louise, 'and I doubt she'd be willing to use one. Besides she's not geared up to do it on a commercial scale.'

'Don't be so negative, Mum.'

'Also she'd have to sell an awful lot to make a living.'

'Negative again,' said Penny. 'But remember, if she left him she'd get half the house, and that wouldn't be peanuts.'

Maggie let out a long sigh of pleasure, and leaned back in the old garden chair so that she could get more sun on her already mahogany-coloured face, throwing off her wrap to expose her top and arms.

My God, her skin looks more like a brown paper bag than ever today, thought Louise, then hastily banished the uncharitable thought.

'Computers are terribly easy to use,' said Maggie airily, stretching like a cat in the sun. 'Everyone uses them nowadays. Why, even I email Seth.'

'Only when David and I set it up for you,' Penny pointed out. She looked at Louise, 'which reminds me, Mum. Jack and I have been discussing how we can advertise Lavender House, and we've decided to set up a website, to help people to find us.'

'I haven't got a good enough computer, not for stuff like that. I've only have the one I write my books on, and that's terribly old. It's suitable for word-processing, but even sending emails is often a problem. David says it hasn't got enough bites, or whatever they're called, and he's the expert.'

'We've thought of that. A new computer is coming tomorrow, and I'll set it up for you,' said Jack.

Louise felt an unexpected surge of irrational anger. 'How dare you and Penny organize everything. I'm not an idiot you know. I'm glad of your help, but I want to decide things for myself. Besides, I can't afford a new computer,' she added fiercely, 'so cancel it.'

'It's a present,' said Jack. 'My leaving present.'

'Your leaving present?' Louise felt as if he'd physically slapped her and instinctively put a hand up to her face. Of course he was free to do as he pleased, but somehow, despite everything she'd said, in truth she'd imagined him as a fixture in Lavender House. Now she suddenly felt desolate, and didn't know what to say. Finally she said, getting the words out with difficulty, trying to sound matter-of-fact and light-hearted, 'So you're going at last.' What she wanted to say was, is it something to do with Geoffrey? Because that was fixated at the back of her mind. But she didn't.

Jack cleared his throat. 'Yes, I've got to go in a couple of days, but I'll set everything up before I go. The computer will be easy to run. You and Penny won't have any trouble, and if you do you know you can always call on David. He'll come down like a shot.'

'Yes, of course he will,' said Maggie, sounding irrationally cheerful which made Louise feel even more dismal. 'Yes, he certainly would come down like a shot, and he'd be fantastic at keeping the website up-to-date.'

Louise saw that Penny too was looking dumbstruck. 'You're leaving?' she said faintly, looking at Jack.

Jack flushed and looked defensive. 'Well, you didn't expect me to stay forever, did you?'

'Yes,' said Penny, and burst into tears.

'No, of course we didn't think you'd stay forever.' Louise tried to speak like the businesswoman she was trying to be. But if she were honest, she hadn't really thought of him leaving, at least not in the foreseeable future. Maybe one day, but now that day had arrived, and she knew that life would be different for all of them. He'd become part of Lavender House, part of the day-to-day life, especially part of the kitchen where the noisy banging of pans and the sound of him chopping vegetables and herbs, mingling with his tuneless humming had been an everyday feature. Lavender House certainly wouldn't be the same without him, and where did that leave her? She'd always maintained that she didn't need, or want, another man in her life, but Jack had crept into her heart almost without her noticing it. A dream lover. But like all dreams he was about to disappear. She would be solo again, and the prospect was dispiriting.

Jack was as good as his word about the computer. He set up the website with David who came down especially to do it. Louise noticed that Penny and David were definitely warmer towards each other, which helped her disconsolate mood, although to her disappointment David didn't stay for long.

'I've got rather a lot on at the moment back in the office,' he told Louise. Then he took her hand and squeezed it. 'But don't think I'm giving up on Penny and the boys. I've got big plans and I'm going to woo her all over again.'

'You can't do much wooing from London,' said Louise. 'Long distance love never works.'

'Who said anything about long distance? Wait and see.' David sounded confident.

Jack was ready to leave. His bags were in his car, and Louise stood beside him in the turning circle of gravel in front of the house. Everyone else had said their tearful goodbyes; it was just Louise left. New people were arriving today, and there were already three other cars parked, and another tucked in at the back behind the old gardening shed. It was going to be a busy weekend, as it was August Bank Holiday, and she'd already let his room, although she felt like a traitor as she booked in the new people.

'You won't miss me,' said Jack. 'You'll be too busy.'

'I will miss you.'

'I thought you always said you didn't want a man in your life.'

'Yes, but you're not a man ... I mean, not any man ... not my man.' Louise stumbled over the words. 'You're Jack. That's different.'

'Chief cook and bottle washer, you mean.'

'No, that's not what I mean.' Louise looked at him, his dark eyes, usually twinkling with laughter, were serious. Clenching her fists she willed herself to take a step into the unknown, not caring that she might be rebuffed and made to feel like a silly teenager. 'You know that's not what I mean,' she repeated. 'I've grown very fond of you, Jack, we all have. I feel as if you're part of my family. In fact, I wish you were part of the family.'

'Part of the family as your lover? Is that what you mean?'

Louise swallowed, then whispered. 'Yes, I think

that's what I mean. But you are already married, you said so.'

'I'm not married now, but I'm not free now either. I have some things I must do, things to tie up. When I've finished, I'll come back. And if you still feel the same way, then we can take it from there.'

'I will feel the same way.'

'You might not,' said Jack very sombrely. 'Not when you find out what it is I have to do. Somehow, I don't think you'll still want me to be part of your family then.' He leaned forward and took her in a great big bear hug and kissed her long and hard. It was completely different from the other fleeting kiss, which had left her uncertain and wanting more. This was like the kiss of her dreams only much, much better. Longer, deeper, meltingly passionate. Finally, he drew away, and ran a finger down the side of her face. 'Goodbye, my darling,' he said, climbing into his car. The engine roared, the wheels churned the gravel and he was gone, leaving Louise standing with her fingers touching her lips where his lips had been only a few moments before.

She might have stood daydreaming for longer had Jane not appeared in her car almost before the sound of his car engine faded into the distance.

'I have left him,' she announced, clambering out, dragging a large suitcase from the front passenger seat. 'Geoffrey, I mean.'

As if there's any need for explanation, thought Louise, resolving to hold her tongue and not tell her sister that coming to stay with her was about the most inconvenient thing she could do at the moment. 'You do know you'll have to stay in the pottery cottage with Penny and me,' she said. 'And you'll have to sleep on a mattress on the floor in a sleeping bag. I've run out of beds and sheets.'

Jane giggled. 'It will be just like being at Girl Guide camp, except the loos will be better.'

'Loo, singular.'

Jane was not put off. 'That's heaps better than having to dig your own latrine like we did at Guide camp.'

Louise left Jane happily dragging a suitcase on wheels with one hand and clutching a holdall with the other making her way to the pottery cottage. Somehow it didn't seem right that she should be so happy; leaving one's husband after thirty odd years was a big step, not one to be taken with girlish glee. Louise gritted her teeth in exasperation. It was bad enough Jack leaving today, but Jane turning up was just one more problem she could do without. As soon as she had enough time, Louise supposed she'd have to point Jane in the direction of a good solicitor if she really wanted to go ahead with a divorce. However, Jane and her impending divorce were forgotten as she heard a car coming up the drive; it had to be her next couple of guests. She dashed into the house to tidy her hair and put some lipstick on, just to make sure she looked respectable. She wanted to look like a professional guesthouse landlady with years of experience behind her, instead of a few weeks.

Once she'd shown the new guests to their room, which had previously been occupied by Jack, and organized tea and scones for them, (Aggie Smethurst had surpassed herself that morning with golden scones risen so high they looked as if they might fly away, and yellow clotted cream which she'd also made that morning) and given them leaflets with the best local restaurants listed for their evening meal, she dashed downstairs to the family in the kitchen.

'Jane's here,' she said.

'I know all about it,' said Penny with a grin. 'I've told

Jane she can have David's Z bed, as he's having the mattress on the floor of my bedroom.'

'Oh.' Louise was totally at a loss for words at this turn of events.

Maggie was noisily loading the dishwasher with the tea things brought in from the garden. Knives and forks upside down, cups balanced at precarious angles, she will never learn, thought Louise in resignation. Luckily she hadn't yet fathomed out how to start the machine so it was always possible for someone else to reorganize it. But she was happy and beaming from ear to ear, gold bangles jangling more vigorously than ever. She was obviously pleased that Penny and David were moving closer together. Louise wondered whether David and Penny would be making love again, but that was too much of a delicate question to ask. And what about marriage? But she couldn't ask about that either, anyway she supposed that was putting the cart before the horse at the moment.

'David thinks,' said Penny, 'that if you are going to increase your business, and start keeping really business-like records like Norman Long says, the kind that will keep the Inland Revenue happy, then you need a proper office. The box room where David has been sleeping will be perfect for an office.'

'It's a bit large for my needs,' said Louise, unwilling to start plunging into proper business mode immediately. It was an unspoken thing that Jack would be on hand to help ease her into that.

'No, it's not too large. It's just right, because David is going to move his office down from London to here, so he can use the extra space.'

'Oh,' said Louise again. All this was happening a bit fast. 'But what about his clients?'

David entered the kitchen carrying a filthy Jacob

followed by an equally filthy Sam. 'They were down by the stream,' he said. 'Sam opened the bottom gate and they got out. We'll have to watch that. Could be dangerous. I'll fix that gate.'

Penny took Jacob. 'I've just been telling Mum about using the box room as an office,' she said, 'and you moving your office down here from Blackheath.'

'If that's OK with you, Louise. I can do all my own work, and manage the bookings and financial affairs of Lavender House as well. If you agree, of course.'

'Agree!' said Louise who'd been wondering when she was ever going to find time to do the paperwork in between changing sheets and tidying bedrooms. 'I'd fall down on my knees with gratitude if I didn't have to get up again. But what about your London clients and the house?'

'The house can be shut up for the time being, and most of my clients can be done via the Internet,' said David. 'Of course, I'd have to go up to town and see some of them from time to time, but most of the time I'd be here, with Penny and the boys, and you and Maggie,' he added.

'And Seth,' chimed in Maggie. 'He'll be here soon.'

'And Jane,' said Louise. 'Heavens what a mob we are.'

'The Lavender House Mob,' said Maggie, and they all laughed, and Louise found herself wishing Jack was around to share the joke.

A whole month passed and they were into September. The chickens were thriving, and so far foxes had not been a problem. Tabitha would have caught a chicken given the chance. She spent hours watching them, her tortoiseshell and pink nose pressed close to the chicken wire. The horse-chestnut tree at the side of the house began to shed its conkers, much to Sam's delight. He collected bags full of them, and then arranged them in rows on the bench outside the kitchen in order of size. Leon often came to join him, which kept Jane happy. She was seeing more of her grandson now than she ever had before, because Wendy had suddenly decided to take him out of nursery three days a week, and had passed him over to Jane to look after.

Louise was surprised. 'What does Dennis think about this arrangement?' she asked.

'I have a feeling Wendy hasn't told him, although she hasn't said so. But as Dennis is hardly ever at home it doesn't really matter. I'm happy.' Which was true. Being away from Geoffrey and having Leon around had changed Jane. She laughed a lot, and Louise realized that she hadn't heard Jane really laugh much for years.

David came into the kitchen for his morning coffee. He was now thoroughly settled in with Penny. 'I've been having a close look at your accounts,' he told Louise. 'You don't need to save money; this business is doing very nicely. You can afford to put in the double drainer now and the new stainless steel worktops in the kitchen.'

'It won't be my old comfortable kitchen any more,' Louise complained.

'True, but you've got to do it. I've had another email from the environmental health officer, as well as the health and safety people. They are coming round soon for an inspection. They've noticed that your business is taking off; therefore they're following it up. It's only because this is a small country place and everything moves at a snail's pace that you've got away without doing it for so long.'

'I'll ask Kevin if he knows anybody who …'

'No,' interrupted David firmly. 'I've lined up someone recommended by the girl at the council, that way we won't have any problems regarding the fixtures and fittings etc.'

Louise hated officialdom but had to agree David was probably right. 'OK, go ahead,' she said. 'But just make sure I know exactly when they are coming, and how long the kitchen will be disrupted. Then I'll limit the number of guests in Lavender House, or maybe close it altogether for a few days.'

David disappeared back to the office and Jane made coffee for everyone. 'I am grateful that you're letting me stay here,' she said to Louise, 'but once I've got the money side of things sorted I'll find somewhere near to rent or buy and get out of your way.'

'No rush.' Louise had got used to Jane being around. 'By the way, have you found out why Wendy has suddenly let Leon come here with you so often? And what does she think about you leaving Geoffrey?'

Jane stirred her coffee thoughtfully. 'I don't know, she's never ventured an opinion. But something's happening between her and Dennis. She's not the nervous, brittle woman she was, she's on the brink of being a human being again, almost on the point of confiding in me. At least, I think so. I know it's a funny thing to say but I find myself liking her again. Not something I've felt in years.'

Louise looked at her sister. Sometimes she did come out with the strangest things. 'Jane, how can you not like your own daughter?' she asked. 'It's not natural.'

'It's very easy when someone is horrible to you. I've never believed that blood is thicker than water. Wendy and I have never clicked, not like you and Penny.'

'We've had our fair share of misunderstandings,' Louise replied dryly. 'Life is never all sweetness and light.'

'Well, anyway,' Jane continued, 'she seems worried,

and Dennis is, of course, the smooth talking bastard he's always been.' Maggie looked at Louise and raised her eyebrows. It was unlike Jane to use such language. 'And,' said Jane reflectively, 'he is very edgy, and what's more, strangely enough, so is Geoffrey. And it's not because I've left. He doesn't care two hoots about that. It's all got something to do with money. I know it has. Geoffrey and Dennis have been buzzing back and forth on Eurostar to Brussels as if their lives depended on it.'

Maggie who'd been listening said, 'I think Geoffrey is worried because you've left him. That's why he's edgy. He wants you back. Husbands and wives should be together, it's only natural.' Maggie was suddenly turning very romantic at the prospect of Seth arriving any day.

'You've changed your tune,' Louise teased her.

'I'm mellowing, darling. It's either old age or this place. I've never felt so contented in my life.'

'Take it from me it's probably old age,' said Louise. 'Just tell me all this again once Seth has been here for a month. Then see how you feel. By the way, when is he arriving?'

'The day after tomorrow. I'm driving up to Heathrow to pick him up.'

Upstairs Jacob began to howl. He'd just woken from his morning nap. 'Oh my God,' said Penny to Louise as she left the kitchen to fetch Jacob, 'I hope Seth's nerves are good, he's going to have a hair-raising journey down the M3. Always supposing she ever finds Heathrow,' she added sotto voce.

'I heard that,' Maggie shouted after Penny's departing figure. 'Anyone would think I'm not a good driver.'

Seth arrived in the late afternoon, slightly shaky after a couple of hours of Maggie's driving.

'I could do with a large whisky and soda,' were his first words.

'Oh dear, we don't have any soda.' Louise said. 'No one has ever asked for soda before.'

'Scotch on the rocks then, a double.'

Knowing that he'd been a celebrity TV Chef, albeit it on a local TV channel in New York State, and the fact that he was married to Maggie, who, despite her age, was always glamorous, Louise had expected a distinguished looking man. Seth in the flesh turned out to be small, slightly wizened looking, bald with a very large nose, button black eyes, and a laugh which echoed around the house. Louise fell in love with him at first sight, and so did Penny.

'I told you he was nice,' David said to Penny. 'Seth, I can't think why my mother has been so obstinate all these years, refusing to live with you in New York.'

'She didn't like being kosher,' said Seth.

'Oh, I didn't know you were kosher, Maggie didn't say.' Louise's heart sank. She didn't know where to begin with kosher food and dietary requirements.

Seth tossed back his scotch and held out his glass for a refill. 'I'm not kosher; my favourite food is pork sausages. But I worked for a Jewish, strictly kosher, TV station, and if I wanted to keep my job I had to be careful.' He turned to David. 'It was very difficult when your mother came over. I had to keep her away from my colleagues and most of the social circle I moved in.'

'I can imagine.' David laughed.

Seth looked at Louise. 'So now I'm here at Lavender House, I'm free to eat anything that's going, and I will. I'm retired, and Maggie and I have got to work out how to get along with each other twenty-four-seven. But something tells me I'm going to love it here.'

'You'll be part of the Lavender House mob,' said David, 'which reminds me, Louise, the kitchen will be done next week. Brought up to EU standards,' he added for Seth's benefit. 'Health and safety and all that jazz.' He saw Louise's expression. 'Don't worry, next week I've arranged it so that we are empty of guests for the first four days, Monday to Thursday. That should give Dave Shearing and his team time to install everything and turn the gas, electricity and water back on. While it's off we can manage on some old mini gas stoves for camping that I found in the shed. All we need to do is buy a couple of gas bottles and we can cook on those for a few days.'

'Looks like you'll be having a baptism of fire,' Louise told Seth. 'Let's hope this good weather holds, because then we can cook in the garden. It'll be like being on holiday.'

CHAPTER
❧ FIFTEEN ❧

THE WEATHER WAS wonderful. Dave Shearing and his team ripped the kitchen apart in no time, and as there were no guests to worry about, the old scrubbed pine kitchen table was dragged outside and the whole family ate and cooked every meal in the garden. The dogs thought they were in heaven as they were hopelessly spoilt. In the kitchen, Louise was firm and often shut them out at meal times, but in the garden they were there all the time, noses at table height, begging from everyone who fed them titbits.

'Greyhounds have delicate stomachs,' Louise grumbled. 'They shouldn't be eating the same as us, it will upset them.'

'Rubbish,' said Penny, 'look at them, they're thriving on it. Seamus is even getting a middle-aged spread.'

Seamus looked at Louise with his soulful brown eyes; she could have sworn there was a smile on his whiskery face. Megan was more secretive and took her stolen bits of food beneath the table.

Of course being an American, Seth was a dab hand at making hamburgers; something Louise had never tried before, always thinking them junk food. But Seth's were different. Made from organic minced Aberdeen Angus beef, to his own special recipe, even she had to admit they were to die for. He also got up early every morning and made bread in the pottery cottage ancient oven, so they had crunchy fresh bread rolls to go with the hamburgers and salad, other times he made enormous cottage loaves, and when he was feeling really energetic he made croissants.

'Can I do this every day?' he asked Louise. 'I can't give up cooking. I'll go mad if I do.'

'I can't actually see them, but I think you must have wings and a halo, because you are my angel,' said Louise. 'You can do as much cooking as you like.'

'When the guests are back in residence, I'll try out some bagels on them,' Seth told her. 'You can never buy a really good bagel in England.'

Louise couldn't believe her luck and hugged him. 'Bagels it is,' she said.

Eating in the garden put everyone in a festive mood; it seemed to Louise that none of them gave Jack a second thought. Nobody missed him. But she did. She relived the kiss often, and remembered his last words, *goodbye my darling*. But why was it he'd said she might not want him to come back? Of course she did. That would never change. She couldn't wait for him to come back, and felt like a teenager who'd fallen in love for the first time.

It was on the second evening of their eviction from the kitchen when they had a barbecue going as well as the camping gas stoves. Louise was sitting on the far side of the table, with Sam and Leon, who had been allowed to have a sleepover, thinking dreamily of Jack and wondering when he would reappear.

The two boys gobbled up their hamburgers then climbed down from their chairs. 'Nanny, can we go and look for hedgehogs?' demanded Sam.

'Of course, darling. But stay in the garden. Don't open the gate.'

'They can't,' said Penny. 'David has fixed it. Go play in the sandpit.'

The two little figures disappeared down the mossy path.

It was only when everyone was eating the last of Seth's pomegranate and lentil salad that Penny decided it was time for the boys to come in, and looked for them in the sandpit.

'Oh, I told them they could go hedgehog hunting,' said Louise.

'But they went in the direction of the sandpit,' added Jane.

Penny called them. 'Time for bed, you two. I'll come and get you in a moment.' She looked at Jacob in his high chair. He'd fallen asleep with his head on the tray, his nose jammed on a piece of chicken covered in tomato ketchup.

'He looks so sweet,' said Jane. She stood up. 'If you sort out Jacob, Penny, I'll give Sam and Leon quick baths and put them to bed. It's long past their bedtime too. It's getting dark now.'

It was then everyone realized that Sam and Leon were nowhere to be seen.

Four long hours had passed since they'd started searching, and it was now one o'clock in the morning. The police had been called; Wendy had arrived in a hysterical state. Maggie was not much better, and was weeping loudly.

Seth turned out to be a tower of strength where the two howling women were concerned. He stopped Maggie and Wendy crying. 'We need an action plan, not tears,' he told them sharply. 'It's no use all us of running around like headless chickens.'

Louise tried to think straight. 'Now,' she said, 'I think Penny must stay at Lavender House with Jacob. Someone needs to be here in case the police or someone else brings them back.'

'No, I'm going out to look for them,' said Penny. 'I'll bring Jacob with me; I can still just about carry him in his hammock.'

'Right,' said Louise in a calm voice, which surprised even her. 'You keep to the garden and the outhouses; the rest of us must spread out and search the woods and fields. Everyone must have a mobile phone and a torch, so that we can keep in touch with one another. We'll shut the dogs in the kitchen, because greyhounds have absolutely no sense of direction once they're off home territory. We don't need two lost dogs as well as lost children.' So the dogs were shooed into the kitchen, given a bone each, and locked in.

Two policemen arrived at Lavender House. One of them was near to retirement and Louise knew him well, Gus Lowman. 'Boys will be boys,' he said, comfortably. 'They've gone off on an adventure to play somewhere and got lost. Sensible idea of yours,' he said to Louise, 'mobile phones and torches. Now don't go too far from each other, they may well be exhausted and asleep under a bush. I'll try and get reinforcements.'

'Someone has abducted them. You read about it all the time,' sobbed Wendy.

'Not from here, Miss,' said Gus Lowman. 'They were in the garden weren't they? They'll not be far away.'

But Louise knew from the tone of his voice that he was as worried as they were. 'I suppose you'd better phone Dennis and Geoffrey,' she said to Wendy and Jane. 'They need to know, so that they can come down and help with the search party.'

'They're both on their way to Waterloo, to catch the Eurostar to Brussels. I told them what had happened before I left,' said Wendy, blowing her nose and trying to control herself.

'And?' asked Louise.

'They said they had more important matters to attend to.'

'You mean they knew and still went?' Louise could hardly believe her ears.

'Bastards,' said Maggie and Jane simultaneously.

'Come on,' said Seth, 'let's start looking again. We'll go much farther afield this time.'

'Yes,' said Louise, worry tightening its grip round her chest like a vice. 'Sam can open the bottom garden gate now, so they could have gone anywhere.'

They split up and spread out in a line once they were outside the garden gate towards the field and the stream which lay on the far side. Louise tried to ignore the nightmarish visions of two small bodies lying face down in shallow, muddy water. A few yards away from her was Penny, then Jane and further on was Wendy, who was still sobbing. An hour went past as they stumbled over fallen branches, and down rabbit holes in the dark before eventually reaching the end by the stream. The other end of the search line had already reached their end of the stream, which snaked across the field higher up. Louise could see the lights from their torches flickering in the darkness, and could hear their voices calling to Sam and Leon.

'Right,' called Gus Lowman, 'now we've all reached the stream, we need half of you on this side, and the other half of you on the other side. We've got to make sure we miss nothing.'

Maggie plunged into the water; Louise saw the glint of her gold bangles and glittering dress in the light of the torches as she crossed to the other side. Seth went across as well as Gus Lowman. That left Louise, Jane, David, and the other policeman whose name was Colin, and Wendy, who was now weeping so much Louise doubted she was much use, on the rockier side of the stream.

'This side is more difficult so I'll stay here,' said Colin, 'Now all stick fairly close together, and you two go that way,' he told Jane and Louise. 'David, Penny and I will take her.' He nodded at Wendy, adding, 'Not that she's much use the state she's in.'

Jane and Louise set off, shining their torches into the water and along the muddy edges of the stream. It was rough and uneven because it was where the cattle came down to drink.

'We're going to find them. We're going to find them. They'll be all right.' Louise felt that if she kept repeating those words it would keep the children safe.

'I can't remember the last time I really prayed,' whispered Jane. 'But I'm praying now.'

'Me too,' Louise whispered back. 'They'll be all right. I'm sure of it.' But fear was cutting through her like a red-hot knife. They were coming to where their part of the stream gushed under the road in a deep culvert. If they'd been swept down there, who knows where they'll be now, she thought.

Suddenly, in the distance they heard Maggie scream. 'I've found them. I've found them.' She went on screaming and screaming, with the full force of her lungs, the sound searing through the darkness of the night, but they couldn't hear what she was saying. They're dead, thought Louise, hardly able to breathe. Turning, they both stumbled blindly through the mud and water towards the sound.

When they got there Gus Lowman and David had dragged them out of the water and they were lying on the bank. Maggie's screams had subsided into loud hiccupping sobs, and Wendy who'd been crying all night was strangely silent. Penny was standing still as if frozen to the spot. Louise took all this in as if in a nightmare.

'Resuscitation position,' said Gus to David, 'now tip their heads back and clear their mouths.' Together they each took one child and cleared their mouths of mud and weeds. 'Pull the chin down gently and give a breath, then start gentle compression with the heel of your hand. One, two, three, four five, then breathe,' Gus said. Together they did it, David and Gus counting together all the time.

'Are you sure this is right?' asked David frantically. 'I thought you had to blow into the mouth much harder.'

'Not with children, you mustn't be too vigorous. This is right for drowning.' But as soon as he said it, Louise began to have doubts. Was it right? She couldn't remember. But Gus was trained and must know.

Colin was on his radio. 'The paramedics are on their way,' he said. 'They won't be able to get the ambulance all the way because of the mud; they'll have to run across the field. I'll go and open the gate so they can get in as far as it's safe to bring vehicle in.'

David and Gus continued, rhythmically pressing, then stopping. 'Oh God, Gus, I do hope you are right.' David's voice broke.

'I am,' said Gus quietly. 'Just keep going.'

Louise didn't say anything. She couldn't.

Then suddenly first Sam and then Leon coughed. They coughed again, and spluttered and Sam spewed up what looked like a mouthful of mud and weed.

Penny burst into tears and both she and Wendy threw themselves down by the side of their sons.

'Steady on,' said Gus.

'They're alive,' said Maggie, sinking down on to her knees in the mud and raising her hands skyward. 'Thank you, God,' she said. 'Thank you.'

For once, no one laughed at her theatrical reaction.

'We'll keep them in for the night, just for observation,' said Dr Jenny Walters. She was the paediatrician on duty at Rumsey's small hospital. 'Children are incredibly resilient. They're going to be perfectly all right. Don't worry.'

Wendy, Penny and David were standing by the cots where the boys lay sleeping. The rest of the search party were still outside in the corridor, except the two policemen who'd gone off on another case, with the promise to come back in the morning to take a full statement.

Of course, they all wanted to come in to the ward, but Dr Walters, and the nurse on duty, were quite firm. Parents only. She was young, too young, thought Louise, suddenly feeling very old, but Dr Walters was brisk and efficient and she trusted her. By now everyone had calmed down, and the boys had been washed, put in clean nightclothes, and warmed up. When they'd arrived at the cottage hospital they'd been pale little wraiths, but now they were nicely pink, and tucked up in hospital cots, side by side, fast asleep.

'It was lucky that tonight has been particularly warm for September,' said Dr Walters.

David and Penny stood by Sam's cot, their arms around each other. Jacob still asleep in his hammock slung around Penny. 'My God, I don't know what I would have done if we'd lost him,' said David.

'Nor me.' Penny leant her head on his shoulder.

'I do love them both so much, and you too,' whispered David. 'Promise me that from now on we'll never be separated.'

'Promise,' said Penny. She looked across at the other cot where Leon lay. Wendy was standing beside the cot gripping the rails, looking at Leon, and Penny knew she was drinking in every detail of his hair, skin, eyelashes, small hands and the shape of his form beneath the hospital blankets. She was dishevelled and muddy, as were they all and her tears had smeared muddy tracks on her pale cheeks. She looked so alone, so desolate. There was no one for her to cling to, no one offering comforting words of love because Dennis was away. Money, thought Penny, money, that's all he thinks about. Before she'd got to know her better, Penny had sometimes envied Wendy's life. Lovely house, smart parties, often abroad, an expensive nursery for child care, but now she realized that she was lacking the most important thing in life. Love. And so was Leon. At least her boys had David's unconditional love, and so, it seemed, did she. She made to move towards Wendy, wanting to include her.

However, it seemed that the nurse was thinking along the same lines, as she said to Wendy softly, 'Shall I ask your mother to come in and be with you?'

Wendy nodded, and Jane came in and put her arms around Wendy and held her close the way a mother holds a small child. 'Oh Mum,' said Wendy. 'Mum.'

'There, there,' said Jane soothingly. 'Leon is safe. That's all that matters, and he's got you and me.' She cradled Wendy's head against her shoulder, and whispered, 'And everything will be all right, you'll see.'

Wendy heaved a shuddering sigh. 'I don't know about that.'

'We'll make it all right,' said Jane firmly. 'For Leon's sake, and yours, we'll make it all right.'

Louise watched the two of them through the glass door, thinking that this was the first time she'd ever seen Jane and Wendy show any real emotion towards each other since Wendy had grown up. She wondered about Dennis and Geoffrey. Why hadn't they cared enough to come back? They should be here, but they weren't, and she had a gut feeling that something was very wrong where they were concerned, and it wasn't just a couple of rocky marriages at stake.

'The two mothers can stay the night if you wish,' said the nurse looking pointedly at her watch. Dr Walters had gone hurrying off to another part of the hospital, answering a call on her pager. 'But everyone else must leave I'm afraid.'

'Can they come in just to see them quickly before they go?' asked Jane.

The nurse nodded, and Louise and Maggie were allowed in for a quick peep at the sleeping boys. Even Wendy smiled at the sight of Maggie; her once glittering dress was bedraggled and stiff with dried mud, except the end of it, which was still muddy. She was leaving a trail behind her like a snail, which caused the nurse to raise her eyebrows. Her heavily applied mascara had run giving her enormous panda eyes.

'Oh, the darlings,' she said dramatically, zooming forward. The nurse just managed to stop her putting her muddy hands on the side of the cot.

Louise covered in mud, said nothing, just breathed a deep sigh of relief, blew the two boys a kiss, and held out her hand to Jane, who took it as they left the small room; leaving the two mothers drinking a mug of Horlicks, each covered in a blanket and settled down, for what was left of the rest of the night, in armchairs one each side of the cots.

Because of the work in the kitchen, Lavender House was still without hot water, so everyone made do with a very quick shower at Pottery Cottage before falling into bed.

It was as she was sinking into sleep that Louise thought of Dennis Mills and Geoffrey. Why hadn't they returned to East Willow when they knew of the emergency? What was so urgent that they had to go to Brussels in the middle of the night? Then as usual, she thought of Jack and remembered the strange atmosphere between him and Geoffrey. He had neither denied nor acknowledged that he knew Geoffrey, and although it seemed illogical, she was sure that Jack had something to do with their disappearance.

The next morning, Louise fetched Penny, Wendy, and two still tired and rather subdued little boys back from the hospital. Everyone had their own theories as to why they'd wandered off. Penny and Wendy put them straight upstairs, as they were still sleepy, and then came back downstairs into the garden for coffee and a croissant, which Seth had got up at the crack of dawn to make for everyone.

'I think they'll sleep for the rest of the morning,' said Penny, gratefully biting into a warm croissant.

Luckily the day was another warm one, because Dave Shearing's men hadn't quite finished. 'Only one more day out in the garden, I promise,' he said. 'By six o'clock tonight, we'll be done and dusted and out of here. And that's a promise or I'll eat my hat.'

Louise looked at his greasy flat cap. 'It doesn't look very appetizing, but I'll keep you to that.'

He laughed. 'No need. You can have your kitchen back, and you'll have hot water, a good central heating system, and a kitchen that'll be passed "A1" by any environmental health inspector in the land.'

'I hope you're right,' said Louise.

'No worries on that score, it's my brother who does the inspecting,' said Dave.

'I'm all for keeping things like that in the family.' Maggie was helping Seth do a fry-up for breakfast. 'Would any of your men like a bacon and sausage sandwich to give them extra energy to finish?'

There was a chorus of 'yes,' from the kitchen, and Louise noticed with amusement that Maggie had suddenly got all domesticated since Seth's arrival. Maybe all the talk about enjoying being on her own as a woman had been a front. It seemed she liked having Seth around, and she could understand why. He might be small and roly-poly, but he was practical, cheerful and generated bonhomie, just as Jack had. The thought of Jack brought a lump to her throat, and she wished he were still at Lavender House.

But no point in thinking about that, she had other more immediate problems to solve. Norman Long, the bank manager had contacted her. You need a proper business footing now, he'd said. The thought filled Louise with dread. She was used to muddling along and so far she'd been lucky most of the time.

Penny looked at her mother, she knew about the letter from Norman Long. 'Mum,' she said, 'David and I have decided to get married. Here in East Willow church, if the vicar will let us, he should, as we are resident here at Lavender House, for the time being anyway.

'What do you mean for the time being?'

'Well, you know that old house in Waterhouse Lane,

the one that's been up for sale for ages.'

'Yes, because it's falling to bits,' said Louise, wondering what was coming next. Out of the corner of her eye she saw Maggie put the frying pan down quickly, and turn towards Penny and David, beaming from ear to ear.

'Watch out, those sausages will burn,' Seth reminded her. She turned back to her task but moved to the other side of the stove so that she could hear more easily.

'I agree it does need some renovation,' said David quickly, 'but I've looked over it several times. The original part of the house is an old forest type cottage, thick mud and wattle walls, and all the rest is made up of extensions added on at different periods. It needs some TLC and a bit of money spent on it, and then it would be perfect. It's got a lovely enclosed garden, so the children could play there safely, and hardly any traffic goes down that lane. I'm putting in an offer; putting our house in London up for sale, and moving my office, lock, stock and barrel down here. I'm going to have a wooden chalet in the garden to work from once we've got the house more or less sorted. I may lose a few clients to start with, but I'll soon build it up again, although I'm not going to be the workaholic I was. I want to see more of Penny and watch the children growing up.'

Maggie twirled theatrically. She was wearing a multi-coloured patchwork skirt, which Seth had brought back from New York, and it flew out, in a stiff circle around her. She might be old and wrinkled, but there was no doubt she still retains that touch of glamour, which Jane and I have never had, thought Louise.

'Ah, the children,' she sighed. 'How I long for the days when you were small, it seems like only yesterday and here you are, a father in your own right.'

'Long for the days when I was small!' David raised

his eyebrows and looked at her sternly. 'You never saw me. You were either on stage, or heavily involved with a divorce or a new lover, usually all at the same time. I was left to the tender mercies of whatever nanny you could hire who would put up with your idiosyncratic behaviour.'

'Darling,' said Maggie reproachfully. 'That's not true. I loved you.'

David suddenly grinned. 'I know you did in your own way. It's just that you were different from other parents, and I always wanted one wearing a beige twinset with pearls.'

Maggie shuddered at the thought.

'No divorces or lovers now,' said Seth firmly. 'Just me. Pass me those sausages. They must be done.'

Maggie meekly passed the pan containing the sausages across to him, and the pair went into the kitchen to feed the workmen. Louise burst out laughing.

'So there you are, Mum,' said Penny. 'David and I are going to get married, it's what you always wanted, and you too Jane. You were always on at me as well.'

'Strange isn't it.' Wendy's voice was very quiet. 'Everything is working out for you, and everything is disintegrating for Mum and me. Both getting divorced ...'

'But,' Louise interrupted, 'just because Dennis didn't come back last night doesn't mean ...'

'It means he doesn't care about Leon or me,' said Wendy. 'But then I suppose I've known that for a long time. I married a man like Dad. Strange isn't it, they say people do, but I never believed it'

'What exactly do you mean?' asked Louise.

'I mean that girls who have violent abusive fathers always end up with violent abusive men as husbands.'

Everyone turned to look at Jane and Wendy. 'Violent,

abusive,' Louise repeated. 'Do you mean that Geoffrey actually hit you?'

'Yes,' whispered Jane. 'And afterwards he always wanted, well you can guess.' Louise shook her head. 'Well, what I mean is, he wanted me to do strange things, which I didn't like and which frightened me, then afterwards he was nice to me. But suddenly it all stopped so I thought he was having an affair. And he was.'

Louise went to Jane and put her arms around her. 'Why didn't you tell me? I always thought you and Geoffrey were happy in an odd kind of way, even though I never liked Geoffrey. Why on earth did you put up with him, why didn't you tell me?'

'It's not the sort of thing you can tell people,' said Jane. 'Anyway, I've left him now.' She straightened her back. 'I know I'll have to find a job, and find somewhere else to live. But I'll do it, somehow.'

'Hello there.' It was the postman who'd come round to the back of the house as he always did. 'Quite a bit of mail, mostly junk I expect though.' Much to Louise's relief he made a speedy exit back the way he'd come.

'Thanks.' Louise picked up the mail and sifted through it. There was one hefty envelope containing the proofs of her book with a nice note from the editor Simon Weatherby. Louise put that to one side, heaven alone knew when she'd have time to go through that, and then there was another large, but slimmer, manila envelope. 'This one here is for you, Jane.' She looked at the back of the envelope. 'It's from Salisbury, Green and Guy, that's the big firm of solicitors isn't it?'

Jane took the letter hesitantly. 'Geoffrey must have started the divorce proceedings already. He's so clever. He'll leave me with nothing, I know he will.'

'Rubbish. The law is the law, and nowadays wives are

entitled to half of their husband's estate. So you won't be left penniless. Anyway, you can sue him for physical and mental cruelty.'

Penny nodded, agreeing with her mother, as Jane turned the letter over and over in her hands. 'Go on, open it, Jane,' she said. 'We all want to know what it says.'

Jane slit open the large envelope, and retrieved several sheets of headed paper covered with typing, underlined in red here and there. She scanned it slowly, while everyone waited breathlessly for her to speak.

Even Wendy got impatient. 'Do hurry up, Mum.'

Eventually Jane dropped the documents in her lap. 'I don't believe it,' she whispered.

Louise could stand the suspense no longer and snatched the papers from Jane impatiently and began scanning them. 'Neither do I,' she said.

'Believe what?' said Penny, David and Wendy together.

'That Geoffrey has made the house over to Jane. All she has to do is go in and sign the necessary papers and it's hers. Completely. He's also opened a bank account in her name, and put half a million pounds in it. Again, all she has to do is go into the bank and sign the relevant papers and it's hers. There's no tax to pay, as she's still his wife. He's just transferred it all, lock stock and barrel.'

'Perhaps he wasn't so bad after all.' Penny voiced all their thoughts.

As she spoke there was the sound of tyres crunching on the gravel as a car drove up to the front of Lavender House. Whoever it was went to the front door and rang the bell.

Louise went through the kitchen to answer it. Maggie and Seth were still there chatting to the workmen. The kitchen looked pretty good, but was obviously not quite finished. 'Don't waste time,' said Louise as she passed through. 'This has got to be finished and in functional mode by this evening and I shall not allow anyone to leave until it is.'

'Functional mode. What does that mean?' asked the youngest workman.

'Working order,' said Seth. 'Come on, Maggie, we'd better leave them to it.' Louise continued through to the front door, fingers crossed that it wasn't guests who got the date wrong and had arrived early. But it wasn't. It was Norman Long, the peripatetic bank manager from Rumsey.

'Oh,' said Louise, immediately worrying that she'd done something wrong, and her accounts were in a muddle. She'd been trying to do them herself since Jack had left, with David's help, but mostly on her own. 'Is there a problem? What have I done? It isn't time for the tax return yet is it?'

Norman smiled. 'Stop worrying; it's not you I want to see. It's your sister Mrs Jane Steadman, I need to see, and I believe she is staying here at the moment.'

Louise ushered him in and led the way through into the sitting room, which was still covered in dust-sheets because of the work in the kitchen. 'I'm having the kitchen remodelled *à la* health and safety, and environmental concerns and all that jazz, hence the dust-sheets,' she said, ripping off a couple from the settee. 'If you wait here I'll go and get Jane. I suppose it's about all that money her husband has deposited in her name.'

Norman coughed discreetly. 'I'm not allowed to discuss a client's business,' he said.

'No, of course not. I'll get her.'

Louise shot out into the garden. 'Norman Long, the

bank manager is here to see you, Jane. I've put him in the sitting room.'

'Oh.' Jane clutched the solicitor's papers to her chest. 'I don't want to see him on my own. I've never dealt with anything official before.'

'I'll come with you, Mum. He's bound to let me be with you, as I'm your daughter.' Wendy stood up. 'Come on. It must be important otherwise he wouldn't have bothered to come out here.'

They disappeared into the house together.

Maggie rubbed her hands together with glee. 'This gets more exciting by the minute,' she said. 'I can't wait to see what happens next. I think Geoffrey is a crook, and it's all a big tax fiddle.'

'You keep your nose out of other people's divorces and financial affairs,' Seth said sternly. 'And you can't go around labelling people crooks unless you have some proof.'

Penny, however, had no such inhibitions. 'I've always thought him a crook,' she said firmly. 'I regard anything he does or will do with suspicion.' She got up and prowled near the house. 'I can't wait to hear what Norman Long has got to say.'

'Never mind that. What I've got to do now is clear up, and begin thinking about the day after tomorrow when I've got new guests booked in. All hands to the deck.' She took no prisoners, and soon everyone was working. Aggie Smethurst came up for her Friday order for afternoon tea. 'Scones and one of your fruitcakes,' Louise told her, 'and some of your dried flower arrangements for the fireplace in the sitting room. I noticed them growing in your garden the other day, they're at their best at the moment. The colours are brilliant, just what I need in that fireplace.'

Aggie went, pleased with her large order, and Louise polished and vacuumed the hall, arranging a large vase of coral coloured gladioli from the garden in a big green vase on the highly polished hall table. They were reflected in the large mirror behind the table and gave the hall a warm, welcoming glow. Normally, Louise would have stopped and admired her arrangement, but now she could still hear a low murmur of voices from the sitting room, and it was all she could do to stop herself from going to listen at the keyhole. The curiosity was killing her. Why had Norman Long come up to the house to see Jane? Why was it he was there for so long? Why hadn't he waited for her to go into the bank in the normal way? She wondered if there was some problem. Maybe Geoffrey didn't have that much money to give, but surely the solicitors would have checked? The possibilities kept spinning round and round in her head as she went upstairs to put the finishing touches to the bedrooms.

She thought of Jane and Wendy's revelations. Up until recently, she'd always thought that they were dull and ordinary, and now it transpired their lives had been anything but. But I'm ordinary, she thought. Is the rest of the world all dysfunctional but covering it up with a veneer of ordinariness?

Jane's voice calling her, cut through her increasingly chaotic thoughts. 'I'm up here, in the back bedroom changing the sheets,' she called down. Jane arrived; pink in the face and puffing from hurrying up the stairs. 'Well?' demanded Louise. 'What was all that about?'

Jane sank down on the bed. 'I don't know where to begin.'

'Begin at the beginning and go on to the end,' said Louise impatiently. 'It's the only way.'

'You sound like something from *Alice in Wonderland*.'

'I'm beginning to feel as if I *am* in Alice in Wonderland,' cried Louise. 'For heavens sake, do get on with it.'

'Well,' Jane began.

CHAPTER
SIXTEEN

AFTER A LONG and rambling explanation, Louise managed to ascertain from Jane that Norman Long said he'd been advised by an officer of the Serious Fraud Office that they were investigating Geoffrey's financial affairs, and that he should get the money transferred by Geoffrey to Jane, signed, sealed and delivered as soon as possible. Hence his visit, as he was only going to be in the Rumsey bank one day this week, and if he didn't do the paperwork today, the whole thing might fall through, because the SFO would step in and take the money.

'He said he didn't want me to miss out on the money, and that once it had been transferred to me everything would be all right. That's what the man from the SFO had told him.'

'The Serious Fraud Office,' repeated Louise slowly. 'So Geoffrey must have been up to no good. But I can't understand why the SFO should warn the bank. Why should this man help you? Is he someone we know? Did Norman Long tell you his name?'

'Oh, yes,' said Jane happily. 'His name is Jonathan Smith, and he's not local. He's based in the international office in London. But who cares about the whys and wherefores, it's because of him, you are now looking at a wealthy woman.' She stood up waving the sheaf of papers gleefully before putting them back into the envelope. 'Now I'm off to the solicitors to make sure the house really is mine. I have to sign the papers for that today as well.'

'But what about taxes and capital gains etc?' said Louise. Tax was something she always worried about.

'Norman said there was absolutely no problem there. Geoffrey is still my husband so no tax is incurred apparently. Good job I hadn't already divorced him, otherwise there would have been.'

'You couldn't have divorced him in a couple of days anyway.'

'True. But the way I was feeling I would have done if I could. Now it seems hardly worth the bother.'

'What I still don't understand is why Geoffrey has suddenly transferred all his money as well as the house to you. I know you stormed out and said you were leaving him, but I didn't think he believed it. So why has he done this?'

'I didn't think he believed me either,' admitted Jane, 'and you know something, I still don't. But I'm certainly not going to turn any of this windfall down, and I will divorce him just to make certain that he never gets his hands on any of it again.' Jane stood up, hugging the envelope to her chest and started and humming 'Everything's Coming up Roses', hopelessly out of tune as usual. 'Oh, by the way, Wendy is going back into Rumsey with Norman to discuss her finances now she has left Dennis for good, and then afterwards she's going into Paris, Randall and Smithson, the solicitors who specialize in divorce. So will it be OK if you and Penny keep an eye on Leon for this morning? I think I ought to go with

254

her after I've finished my business about the house.'

Louise nodded. 'Of course.'

Jane stopped and paused in the bedroom doorway, where Louise was still sitting bemused, surrounded by a pile of clean bed linen. 'Do you know, I think Norman has taken quite a shine to Wendy, and she to him.'

Louise pulled a face. 'He's nice, but rather dull don't you think? Wendy's been used to the social high life as the wife of an MEP.'

'After violence and treachery, a nice dull man who is kind and caring will seem like paradise,' said Jane. 'He's just what Wendy needs; she's not the most exciting girl in the world. I suppose she takes after her father, not me,' Jane added reflectively. 'I've always had more get up and go.'

Louise hid her wry amusement, Jane with get up and go! But she kept silent, not wanting to spoil Jane's moment of triumph.

'By the way,' Jane shouted back up the stairs. 'Once I've got the keys to the house, and I know it's really, really, mine, I'll go back there. That will give you more room in the pottery cottage.'

Louise slumped back on the bed in relief. But had Geoffrey really gone for good? Brussels was only a train ride away and he could pop back up in East Willow at any moment. Louise felt worried. Lately, it seemed that she never knew what was going to happen next. Was it only five months ago she'd been sitting in the garden worrying about paying for the damaged slates on the roof, and trying to finish a book? Book! That reminded her. She'd not had a moment to do the proof editing or to write a single word for the next book, which she'd been contracted for. Somehow the book had receded to the back of her mind and didn't seem very important, but as it was being published at the end of the year, Louise decided she'd better sit up late that evening and get on with the proof editing. Not that she usually had much to do, because she was a slow and careful writer. She wondered why Dottie hadn't been on at her. She had been surprisingly quiet lately, so Louise assumed she must have bigger fish to fry, otherwise she'd be pestering her for the next one so that she could pocket the next part of the advance. If she were perfectly honest, Louise knew she couldn't possibly run Lavender House and write books. There were just not enough hours in the day. She'd have to make a decision soon, and she was pretty certain Lavender House would be her choice, although she would miss writing. Her last book had been quite serious, which was why Dottie hadn't liked it. But she had needed to write it, and her spirit had felt lighter ever since she'd finished it. It wouldn't make any money, of course, but at least it was being published, and anyway now she had Lavender House to support her, so the money didn't matter so much. Also she found that she enjoyed being at the centre of a busy life, as opposed to sitting for hours alone with a computer.

That night was their last uninterrupted meal together as a family before the next influx of guests into Lavender House. A delighted Tabitha wound her way around the windowsills, which had been denied her whilst the workmen were there; the other cats inspected the kitchen, then retreated for a night's mousing. They weren't characters like Tabitha, and were almost feral, just treating the house as a hotel whenever they needed feeding or felt like a bit of warmth in the winter. The dogs were the most pleased that everything had returned to normal, and that their baskets had been put close to the central-heating boiler again. After an inspection of all the new furniture, they collapsed grate-fully into their beds.

'These animals should be kept out of the kitchen,' said Jane, who'd never been as fond of animals as Louise, 'the environmental health people won't like cats and dogs being permanently in their beds by the stove or under the table.'

'Dave Shearing has promised his brother will give me notice when he's coming to do the inspection, so I'll evict them all then, and let them back in when he's gone.' Louise picked up Tabitha and cuddled the old cat, kissing her tatty ears; she might be small but she'd been a ferocious fighter in her younger days. She was a bag of bones now, and her days were numbered. Louise found it unbearable to think that soon she wouldn't be at Lavender House. 'Anyway,' she said putting a purring Tabitha back on the window sill, 'we've never caught any nasty diseases from our animals, and neither have our guests. People are too hygienic these days.'

Jane sniffed, but didn't argue.

The candles were lit, and the table laid with her mother's old dinner service, the one she kept for best, the rose pink one with gold edging. It gleamed in the candlelight. The only disadvantage, thought Louise, thinking how lovely it looked, was that it had to be washed by hand as it was definitely not dishwasher friendly. Sam and Leon had been allowed to stay up as they had slept most of the day, but Jacob was sound asleep, which meant Penny could relax.

It suddenly struck Louise that everyone around the table had made life changing decisions in the last few weeks and days, whereas she remained the same. Jane and Wendy had thrown off their husbands, and it looked like Wendy was about to embark on another relationship; Penny and David had got back together and so had Maggie and Seth. As for me, she reflected, letting the house is biggest thing I've done, and that has been life changing in a way, but not quite in the same league as the others.

'I'm going to cut up these chickens and feed us before they get cold,' said Seth taking shears from Louise's hand and expertly quartering the chickens. 'By the way, Maggie and I have been talking.'

'Yes,' said Louise warily.

'Don't worry, darling.' Maggie's voice came from the far end of the table. Tonight she was a glittering vision in gold again, her favourite colour. 'Seth and I ...'

'I'll say it,' said Seth sternly.

Maggie subsided in a little golden flutter. 'Yes, darling,' she answered meekly.

'Oh, how I wish Jack was here,' said Penny, echoing Louise's thoughts exactly.

'Me too,' said Jane. 'I did like him.'

'I wish I'd known him better,' Wendy chimed in. 'I only met him briefly and that wasn't under the best of circumstances. He must have thought I was an awful mother.'

'Is anybody going to listen to me?' demanded Seth. 'I was in the middle of saying something very important.' Everyone looked at him and waited expectantly.

'Well?' said Louise.

'Maggie and I would like to live here permanently as guests. We'd like to sell the London house, and live here as permanent residents. It means that Maggie doesn't have to do any housework which she's no good at anyway, but we'd take care of our own laundry.'

'There's a good launderette in Rumsey,' piped up Maggie, in case anyone thought she might actually be washing and ironing. 'I'd take everything there, or to the dry cleaners.'

'We'd pay the going rate,' continued Seth, frowning at Maggie's interruption, 'but there is one condition.'

'And what is that?' asked Louise.

'The condition is that we can eat with you in the kitchen, and not be stuck on our own in the dining room. And that I'd be allowed to cook sometimes. I should miss not cooking.'

Louise stuck out her hand towards Seth. 'You're on,' she said. 'Regard it as signed and sealed, and you can cook as much and as often as you like. The two of you will be company for me during the winter months when there are no guests, and a source of income for which I'll be grateful.'

'Louise, you need never worry about money. Not now I've got my millions,' said Jane.

'Half a million,' Louise reminded her, 'and that's got to last you. You'll need to invest it, but I appreciate the offer.'

Maggie interrupted her with a whoop of delight, and produced a magnum of champagne from beneath her voluminous golden skirt. 'I can't bear to have this cold bottle stuck between my knees for a moment longer. I'll get frostbite.'

Penny leapt up and got the champagne flutes from the cupboard, and David popped the cork.

They raised their fizzing glasses. 'Here's to all of us, the Lavender House Mob,' said Maggie. 'Everything has turned out all right in the end.'

Louise found herself wishing more than ever that Jack was there. She could almost hear his wicked chuckle and see him tossing back his champagne with a gusto that only he possessed.

Wendy refused a second glass. 'I've got to drive Leon home soon,' she said.

It was then that they all realized that everything was not quite all right, at least, not as far as Wendy was concerned. 'What happened to you this morning?' Penny demanded. 'Did you see the bank manager, the solicitor or who?'

'Both. But I'd rather not talk about it now.' She nodded in Leon's direction and lowered her voice. 'I'm OK for the moment. I've opened a separate bank account in my name and my salary will go into that. The mortgage is paid up until the end of next month. All I've got to do is track down Dennis.' She dropped her voice to a whisper. 'But I've no idea where he is, and he's not answering his mobile.'

Jane put her arm round her. 'It will be all right, dear. I know it will.'

Wendy managed a weak smile. 'That's what Norman said. He was so sweet, he said not to worry and that he'd make sure I was all right.'

The very next day, David put in an offer for the dilapidated house in Waterhouse Lane; apparently there was already someone interested in buying their house in London. Penny clapped her hands with glee as she told Louise. Suddenly she was longing for a place of her own, to be alone with David and the children. The summer had been lovely, but she missed being independent, being her own mistress, in charge of things. She always tried to consider Louise first because Lavender House was hers, even though she knew she had been rather bossy at times. And then there was David. She had persuaded herself that she was better off without him, but now they were back together working as a team, not each in their own separate worlds, she realized, and she knew David did as well, that together they made a whole. The time apart had been good; it had made them more considerate towards each other.

'I can't wait to move in,' she told Louise. 'I know it's going to be hard work getting it up to scratch, but between us David and I can do it. And next week we're going to speak to the vicar so you'll have an autumn wedding in Lavender House. A very, very quiet affair as we shall be almost broke after spending all our money on renovating the house. We're not even going to invite any friends from London; it will just be the Lavender House Mob, as Maggie calls us. Seth has offered to do the catering.'

Then Penny suddenly felt guilty. Everyone was leaving and her mother would be alone. 'I wish Jack hadn't gone,' she said.

Louise made a face. 'So do I. But he has and that's that.'

'It is strange that he left so suddenly. Then Dennis and Geoffrey disappeared at the same time. The three of them disappeared all at once.'

'A mere coincidence,' said Louise briskly, although to tell the truth, she was not sure that it was. But the connection was impossible to fathom out. Unless, and this was something she didn't want to think about, but the uncomfortable idea kept creeping into her mind, the arrival of Jack at Lavender House hadn't been accidental at all. He'd arrived to spy on Geoffrey and the rest of Jane's family, Wendy and Dennis. There was that business of Geoffrey insinuating that somehow John's money had been involved and that he'd known Jack. But when she'd tried to find out Jack had skilfully evaded any mention of Geoffrey, John or anyone else.

'Anyway,' she continued, picking up Jacob who was attempting to climb up her leg via Seamus's back. He had one leg over Seamus who was standing looking woefully resigned as only a greyhound can, 'All we can hope for is that Geoffrey isn't in serious trouble, and that both he and Dennis will turn up.'

'Wendy suspects that Dennis is involved in some fraudulent scam. She told me so the other day, and asked me to keep quiet,' said Penny.

'Well, just mind you *do* keep quiet,' replied Louise. 'One word out of place, and Dennis, being the nasty type he is, wouldn't have a qualm about taking you to court for slander.'

'Don't worry, I will. And when we're all gone,' Penny added, ending the conversation on a more cheerful note, 'you'll always have Maggie and Seth to keep you company. Besides, we'll all be in and out like so many yo-yos. You won't know whether you are coming or going.'

Louise laughed ruefully. 'Who would have thought I'd end up spending my last days with Maggie and her latest husband'

'Last husband,' corrected Penny. 'And these are not your last days. You're not old. Some gorgeous man will come along and sweep you off your feet, you wait and see.'

Louise didn't answer. She didn't want to be swept off her feet, unless it was by Jack, and that was very unlikely. Like Geoffrey and Dennis he'd disappeared into thin air, although he *had* told her he would come back when he was free. She clung on to that hope, like a child waiting for Santa Claus to arrive down the chimney.

Two whole weeks passed by in a flash. David found that moving his office to the country was much easier than he'd ever imagined. He didn't miss the pub and his mates in Blackheath, most of whom confessed to being green with envy.

Brian the barman had already left and set up home in East Willow in the cottage with his partner. He popped round to Lavender House, and drooled over Louise's old chests and huge wooden wardrobes. 'They're worth a fortune,' he told her.

'All inherited,' said Louise. 'Sometimes when I'm slaving over them with the beeswax polish I feel that I'd like to throw the whole lot out and replace it with stuff from Ikea which can be wiped over with a damp cloth.'

Brian shrieked in horror. 'Philistine! Don't you dare. But let me know if you ever do decide to part with anything.'

Louise promised she would, although she knew she wouldn't.

'And when you've got your house renovated,' Brian said to David, 'don't you even think about buying any antiques without looking at ours first.' He gave David his new card: Brian and Roger at Willow Antiques. 'Just remember we have wonderful stuff, beautifully restored, I've been to furniture restoration classes at the Courtauld Institute, so I know the business.'

David promised he'd look them up, 'Although we've not got much money, as apart from the renovations we've got to pay a big mortgage, houses aren't cheap in Hampshire.'

'Tell me about it, dear.' Brian flapped his hand expressively. 'That's why my partner and I are living in a one up and one down cottage, with the garage as the showroom. But the garden is lovely. We're going to grow our own veggies as soon as I find out how and when to plant seeds.'

*

For the time being, David moved his stuff into the box-room at Lavender House as he and Penny were still sharing Pottery Cottage with Louise until the purchase of Nurse's House was complete. That was the name on the deeds of the house in Waterhouse Lane as apparently the village nurse had been resident there for many years.

Wendy was working back at the surgery, and had taken Leon away from his expensive nursery and put him with Sam in the village pre-school for the mornings, which cost nothing, and then either Penny or Jane picked both of them up and kept them until Wendy finished work. Leon thrived on the new arrangement, and both Louise and Jane thought that for the first time in his short life, he looked happy and healthy. Jane was happier as well, but Wendy still looked permanently worried. There was no trace of Dennis, even his parliamentary secretary in Brussels had no idea where he was, and he hadn't turned up for any of the meetings she'd scheduled. The Conservative party was threatening to expel him, not that Wendy cared about that.

Jane didn't care about Geoffrey either. 'As far as I'm concerned,' she told Louise, 'he could have fallen overboard from the ferry when he and Dennis left for Brussels.'

'Except they went by train,' Louise pointed out.

'Don't be facetious,' said Jane. 'You know what I mean.'

Louise did. But it didn't solve the mystery.

On the last day of September, the weather changed from summer to winter overnight. The temperature dropped, the wind blew and it bucketed down with rain. Louise shivered as she cooked breakfast for her guests; she had

264

six in at the moment, three couples. Poor things, what would they do? She hoped they wouldn't want to stay in all day, she didn't want to have to put on the central heating yet, although she decided she would light the fire in the sitting room in the late afternoon, and invite them all back for afternoon tea at four o'clock.

When she mentioned this, they all accepted her invitation with alacrity, and then set off for Winchester, umbrellas up and raincoats tightly belted.

After preparing the fire in the sitting room, so that all it needed just before four o'clock was a match, Louise went back to the kitchen.

'How about lighting it now?' said Maggie, shivering as she and Seth settled down to read in the sitting room.

'Four o'clock this afternoon,' said Louise firmly, thinking she might as well start as she meant to go on; central heating and logs were both expensive. 'You'll have to move about a bit to keep warm, or stay in the kitchen.' She whizzed through the housework, and then opened a cookery book to try and get some ideas for cakes for the tea. To save money, she'd decided to make them herself, she'd got all the ingredients she needed according to the recipe: flour, currants, sultanas, caster sugar, margarine.

Seth came in. 'I'd forgotten how much Maggie can go on when she has a mind to,' he said. 'She's still grumbling that she's cold. I've told her to put on a cardigan, but she says they're old fashioned.'

Louise waved at the pile of ingredients on the table. 'You can help me if you like.'

'I'll make a fruit cake,' he said, 'while you knock up a soup or something for lunch. I brought in a load of vegetables from the garden this morning. You can make a nice warming soup. The children are coming for lunch today aren't they, they'll need that when they come in on a day like today, and so will Maggie and I. Then this afternoon, just before your guests come down to tea I'll make some drop scones as well. They always go down well straight off the griddle.'

Louise started on the soup and Seth, the fruitcake. Once the ovens were on, the kitchen soon became warm and cheerful. Seth whistled a jazz tune as he worked. It reminded Louise of Jack and his humming, and she felt a stab of sadness. Maggie drifted in; she'd gone upstairs and changed into a purple woollen tracksuit, offset with about a dozen chain necklaces. She sat herself down in the wicker chair by the window and looked out.

'Good heavens, it looks like a funeral procession coming here,' she said.

Louise and Seth rushed over to the window and looked out. Two enormous black limousines were rolling slowly up the gravel drive towards the house. They stopped. The door of the last one opened, and Wendy climbed out and ran weeping, towards the back of the house and the kitchen door. Maggie let her in, but she couldn't speak, only hiccup something totally incomprehensible. They all watched as the chauffeur got out of the first limousine, and opened the rear doors. Two men climbed out. They were dark suited, very official and stern looking, and both carried briefcases. They walked from the limousine towards the front of the house and rang the bell. The sound shrilled through the house, and Louise went to answer the door. It was only as she opened the door and the men were near to her that she realized one of them was Jack. But he was quite a different Jack to the one they had all known. This man's hair was short and sleek, he appeared to have lost his tan and there was no sign of the familiar stubble on his chin they'd all got used to. His blue eyes no longer twinkled.

They were stern and cold, and he seemed larger than ever, but not in a huggy-bear type way. Rather in an ominous, frightening way. Louise felt her heart pound with apprehension. She hardly noticed the other man, she was so fixated on Jack, but it registered that he was of the same ilk. A city type, sophisticated and worldly wise, and, like Jack, he was definitely not friendly.

'Are you Mrs Gregory, the sister of Mrs Jane Steadman?' asked Jack.

'You know damned well I am,' Louise replied. She was beginning to feel angry. Something was going on, something she didn't understand, but the one thing she did know was that Jack was not the man she'd thought he was. Certainly not the man she'd thought she'd fallen in love with.

'It's a necessary formality,' said the other man in a smooth voice. 'We have to establish your identity.'

'He knows my identity very well,' Louise pointed an accusing finger at Jack, and noticed that he did look slightly uncomfortable.

'It's official procedure,' said the man in the same smooth voice. 'My name is Gerrard Holby and this is …'

'I know his name,' interrupted Louise angrily.

Gerrard Holby ignored her and continued, 'this is Jonathan Smith. We are both officers of the Serious Fraud Office. May we come in?'

Although he asked in a polite manner, his tone of voice indicated he had absolutely no intention of taking no for an answer. In fact, he didn't even wait for Louise's answer, but pushed the door open wider and walked straight past her towards the kitchen where the sound of Wendy's hiccupping sobs echoed out into the hall. As far as Louise could make out between the hiccups, Wendy was saying, 'I may have to go to prison.'

As soon as his colleague's back was turned, Jack reached out and gently clasping Louise's hand, raised it to his lips and kissed her fingers. 'Everything will be all right, eventually,' he said quietly.

Louise snatched her hand away. 'How dare you touch me,' she hissed. 'How could you live in my house pretending to be one person when all the time you were another? We all thought you were a friend, I thought, I thought....' She choked on the words, then said angrily, 'Never mind what I thought, you came here to spy on me, didn't you?'

'Not you, Louise, well ... yes, that's true, originally.' He hesitated, 'But once I got to know you. Then I knew you were not ...'

'I don't care what you knew or thought of me. I just want you out of my house as soon as possible, and I never want to see you again.' Louise almost spat the words out she was so furious and hurt. 'You'd better follow your colleague, Jonathan, or Jack, or whoever you are, and I'm coming with you to find out what the hell is going on.'

Jack bowed his head, and silently walked ahead of her into the kitchen. Wendy was sitting there, surrounded by a copious amount of tissues. Maggie was comforting her and had her arms around her in a defensive manner. Louise followed, her mind in turmoil. Now she admitted it to herself for the first time. She really had fallen hopelessly in love with Jack, or rather the man she thought Jack was, and he'd said he'd come back to her. All this time, she'd been hoping he would come back one day and sweep her into his arms and kiss her the way he had the day he'd left, and then they would live happily ever after. A storybook ending, the way it happened in the best romantic novels. But now it transpired, he wasn't Jack at all, he was someone different and he had used not only her home, her friendship, her family, but her most sensitive emotion, love, to find out whatever it was he was looking for. She held back her tears with difficulty. Fool, fool, she told herself, you let your stupid heart rule your head. How could you expect anyone to fall in love with you; you may have a good figure, and your hair is still blonde, but you're a middle-aged country woman, not someone for a man like Jack.

She looked at him standing in the kitchen towering above everyone else, immaculate in his dark suit, striped shirt and dark blue tie which brought out the blue of his eyes. Every inch the city gentleman, looking as if he had just stepped out from a film set. Beside him and Gerrard Holby, we, the Lavender House Mob, even Maggie, all look scruffy, she thought miserably.

Seth quietly moved across to the stove and gave the bubbling soup a stir, then looked through the glass door of the oven to inspect his cake.

Wendy blew her nose loudly then stood up. 'Do you know where Mum is?' she asked Louise.

There was a knock on the kitchen door, and it opened slowly. Louise expected to see Jane, but it wasn't, it was Norman Long. Oh God, thought Louise, not more financial problems! But it appeared not.

'I heard the rumours that Wendy had been arrested, and I know I'm not one of the family but I just had to come and see if she was all right.' He pulled up another chair and squeezed himself in beside Wendy, putting a protective arm around her. Wendy went pink, but leaned on him gratefully and looked pleased.

Heavens, this whole scenario gets more bizarre by the moment, thought Louise. I won't be surprised if at any moment now Jane comes in on the arm of Bert Hackett, she's been buying an awful lot of eggs from him since ours have stopped laying. Her wayward thoughts were interrupted by Wendy, who repeated, 'Do you know where Mum is?'

Louise shook her head. 'I really don't know. I wasn't expecting to see her today.'

'More to the point.' Gerrard Holby had a very thin, sharp voice, and Louise disliked him more than ever. 'Do you know where her husband, Geoffrey Steadman is?'

'He's her husband, not mine. Why should I know where he is? And I doubt that Jane does either. He's very nearly her ex-husband anyway; she's in the throes of divorcing him.'

It was then that she noticed Gerrard Holby was recording everything they were saying, he had a small recording device and was holding it in his hand. He noticed Louise looking at it. 'This is all perfectly legal,' he said in his thin, icy voice. 'As an officer of the Crown I am at liberty to record our conversation.'

'You haven't cautioned us, so you can't use anything we say against us in court,' snapped Louise. She wasn't certain whether this was true or not, but she'd seen it said often enough on TV and it sounded good.

Maggie looked at her admiringly. 'There, Louise knows about these things,' she said to Wendy, giving her a comforting squeeze. 'You've got nothing to worry about. You won't be going to prison. You've done nothing wrong. None of us have.'

'Why is your sister divorcing Geoffrey Steadman?' Gerrard Holby asked Louise before turning to Wendy, 'and I understand that you are divorcing your husband, the MEP Dennis Mills as well. Why is that?'

'It's none of your damned business why either of them is divorcing anybody,' shouted Louise, a blind rush of red rage sweeping over her. She lunged towards Gerrard

Holby, nearly knocking him off his feet, and snatched the recorder he was holding. 'And you can stop using this thing.' Throwing it to the floor she stamped on it as hard as she could, sending small pieces of plastic and metal shooting in all directions across the kitchen floor. Standing in front of a very startled Gerrard Holby, she heard what sounded like a muffled snort coming from Jack or Jonathan, whoever he was. She ignored it. 'Now what's all this talk about prison, and why do you want to know about bloody Geoffrey and Dennis?'

'I've never heard you swear like that before, Louise,' said Jack

'Fuck off,' said Louise, glad to see that the previously imperturbable Gerrard Holby now seemed very perturbed indeed, and was quite pale. 'Well, don't just stand there like a couple of stuffed dummies. Somebody tell us what's going on. It's about time you started answering some questions instead of trying to give us a grilling. This isn't a totalitarian state, you know. This is England, a free and democratic country. And we want some answers, and what's more we want to be treated with respect, not like criminals.'

'Isn't she marvellous. But what does totalitarian mean?' whispered Maggie to Seth.

Jack stepped forward, and gently drew Louise away from his obviously terrified colleague. 'I think I'll deal with this,' he said.

Louise glowered at him. 'Get on and deal with it then.' She lowered her voice, but was still bristling with anger.

'Why don't we all sit down,' said Jack quietly. Obediently like small children, including the obnoxious Gerrard, they all sat down around the kitchen table. Even Louise sat, albeit reluctantly. 'I think before we begin,' he said, 'someone ought to see if that cake is ready. It smells as if it probably needs to come out now.'

Seth jumped up. 'I'd forgotten it because of all this excitement.'

'It's a disturbance,' muttered Louise. 'There's nothing exciting about it.'

Seth opened the oven door and slid a skewer into the middle of the fruitcake, then brought out the cake and put it on the side to cool. Jack waited until Seth had sat down again and then continued. 'We have been watching the financial dealings of Dennis Mills and Geoffrey Steadman for some time now; they have been moving money around Europe and opening offshore accounts. However, we could prove nothing illegal was going on because we needed dates of when they were abroad, which is why I came down here to East Willow to keep an eye on their movements, and hack into their computers.'

'Why did you come down here to do that?' asked Norman Long, who knew about computing.

'I needed to know when they were here in Hampshire, I needed visual proof, photos. Also luckily for me Geoffrey Steadman hadn't bothered to encrypt his wireless router down here,' said Jack, 'so I was able to gather plenty of useful information.'

'But why did you choose to stay at Lavender House?' demanded Louise. 'You could have stayed at the Stag and Beetle, you didn't have to choose here.'

Jack looked uncomfortable and hesitated for a moment before saying. 'I did intend to stay there, but then I met you and saw your lovely house and ...'

'Used me,' said Louise bitterly.

'Anyway, why is Wendy in such a state, thinking she's going to be put in prison?' demanded Norman, holding Wendy even tighter.

'There has never been a question of that, I'm afraid she

jumped to that conclusion herself. I suspect,' Jack looked at Wendy sternly, 'that she had an inkling that something illicit was going on.'

'I knew there was, but I was afraid of him,' said Wendy in a whisper. 'He could be very …' she gulped, then continued, 'violent at times, especially with Leon and I didn't want my son to be hurt any more than he had been already.'

Jack looked sympathetic, and so, to Louise's surprise, did Gerrard Holby who said, 'there's no need to be afraid any longer. As soon as we catch up with him he will be prosecuted and almost certainly will go to prison.'

'Prison,' shrilled Maggie excitedly. 'Will I have to go in court before a jury as a character witness?' she asked, standing up and throwing her head back as if she were already in the witness box. Louise immediately had an awful vision of Maggie floating into court in the most lurid dress imaginable, and giving an over-the-top account of the goings on at Lavender House.

'No,' said Jack quickly. 'This is nothing to do with you.'

Maggie subsided back down on to her chair looking disappointed. 'Told you so,' whispered Seth.

'Where do I fit into this?' asked Louise. 'If I fit in at all. You've told me you picked Lavender House. You did single me out, didn't you? It never occurred to me at the time, but you did find out by devious means, mostly from my daughter, about my financial situation, didn't you?'

'Yes,' said Jack. 'I did, we both did,' he nodded towards Gerrard Holby. 'It was because of the money from Hinks and Hill, which was a company fronting a money laundering operation. We've closed it down, and I'm afraid that's why you lost your allowance. You were the only person on the books receiving money from that fund on

273

a regular basis, so naturally we were suspicious. The man you spoke to on the phone was one of our men; he was manning the computers and phones to pick up anyone showing undue interest in the closure of the company.'

'You'd have undue interest if you'd lost your money,' said Louise. She was no longer angry, but shocked. Surely, John hadn't been involved in money laundering? Was every single thing she'd always held dear in her life to be shattered by these two men?

'We know now, that your husband, although involved, was an innocent party. He, himself had his money embezzled by Geoffrey Steadman,' Jack told her. Louise heard Wendy gasp. 'I'm only sorry that we have to involve any of you.' He looked across at Wendy. 'We were hoping that both of them would come back here to their wives.'

At this point in the proceedings Jane arrived, red in the face and breathless. 'There's gossip in the village,' she said. 'About Dennis and Geoffrey and at the surgery they told me that Wendy had been arrested.'

'That's not true.' Louise drew up a chair for Jane, and made her sit down. 'You've got nothing to worry about, neither has Wendy. However, it seems that both of your husbands are crooks.'

Jane drew in her breath. 'A crook,' she said thoughtfully, then gave a nervous giggle. 'Does that make me a gangster's moll?'

'I've always wanted to play a gangster's moll,' said Maggie.

'Shut up,' said Seth.

Despite everything, Louise laughed. 'Don't be ridiculous. Anyway, let's get back to the point, these ...' she hesitated, about to say gentlemen, then decided that was too nice a term to use, so said, 'these *men* thought that Dennis and Geoffrey might be hiding out with you.'

Wendy gave a bitter laugh. 'Hide out with me! Dennis wasn't even interested when Sam and Leon were lost that night, neither was Dad. They wouldn't come back when we called the police, and everyone else was out all night searching.'

'Absolutely,' agreed Jane. 'The bastards! They still don't know, or care, that they were taken to hospital and kept in for the night.'

Jack gave a horrified gasp, and reached across to clasp Louise's hand. For a moment she thought he was gasping at Jane's language, but then realized he was concerned for the children. 'My God! The two children were missing, all night? Why didn't you call me?'

Louise snatched her hand from beneath his. 'How could I call you? Have you forgotten? You did say goodbye, but that was all. I didn't know where you were, none of us did. You didn't leave a number, the mobile number we had for you didn't work. You just disappeared. It was as if you had never existed. And now I know that in a way that's true. The man we thought of as Jack doesn't exist, because none of us knew then who you *really* were.'

CHAPTER
❧ SEVENTEEN ❧

LOUISE LEANED ON the kitchen window sill looking out into the garden. Weak February sunlight illuminated the drifts of snowdrops swirling across the deep green of the lawn. A mild wet winter had made the lawn grow luxuriously, when it should have remained dormant after the long dry summer of the previous year.

This morning, despite the glorious scene outside the kitchen window, Louise felt depressed. She thought of the previous summer. What a long time ago that seemed now, and what an incredible summer it had been. From the moment that wretched letter from the insurance company had dropped through the letterbox, quite apart from her own crisis, there'd been one family crisis after another, and then one revelation after another. I suppose I was selfish living in my own little world, she thought. I should have guessed that there were problems with Jane and Wendy and their respective spouses, because the signs were there but I didn't want to see them. Louise felt guilty; Jane had tried to confide in her in a roundabout way, but she didn't want to be bothered with other people's problems and had just thought it strange and sent Jane off on her way, with a few words of useless advice.

She'd let Jane hide behind the perfect front she'd presented to the world, because she preferred to hide her own loneliness in the solitude and comfort she got from writing, except that she hadn't really realized she'd been lonely. It was Jack, damn him, who'd made her face that. I suppose we're all like that really, she thought now. Little islands on our own, afloat in a sea of people.

Until the money from Hinks and Hill had ceased to exist, she'd not really worried about money; there was always just enough to fix a slate here and there, to pay the gas and electricity and feed herself and the animals. She hadn't wanted other people's problems to intrude into her life. She wished now that she hadn't even written her last book, the one Dottie said was depressing and hadn't been able to sell to a well-known publisher. But it had been a cathartic exercise, although she hadn't realized it at the time, and when she'd finished it she'd felt a new woman. However, now she wasn't certain she wanted any of her family to read it. Although common sense told her she need not worry, none of her family was particularly into books; it was not high on their list of priorities. Besides, it would probably sink like a stone without trace, as had her last couple of books.

Dottie kept telling her she was getting too serious. 'Where are those light frothy books you wrote when I first took you on?' she said.

'I don't feel light and frothy,' Louise had replied. 'I suppose I think more about mortality and the meaning of life. Don't you?'

'Certainly not,' Dottie had replied firmly. 'I only think of the future and hitting the big time.'

She gave a rueful smile at the memory; Dottie was forever the optimist. She hadn't heard from Dottie for ages, the book had been published just before Christmas, and she'd received the small cheque which was the rest of her advance, and that had been that. She'd not written a single word since, as there was never enough time to sit down and think, although lately she had been feeling an urge to put some thoughts on paper. But Lavender House was demanding. There was the decorating and then the alterations to be supervised, and the family were equally demanding.

Penny and David had put off their wedding until the summer, much to Louise's relief. At least that was one thing she didn't have to worry about for the time being.

Jane was already divorced, and Louise had been amazed at how quickly and easily it had gone through.

'And it only cost me five hundred pounds,' Jane told Louise. 'I didn't have to go to court, all I had to do was fill in some forms as instructed by the solicitor and that was that. If I'd known it was that easy, I would have done it years ago.'

'Except that Geoffrey might have put up more of a fight years ago, and you certainly wouldn't have got the whole house, or the money.'

'True.' Jane sounded reflective but not at all sorry as she said, 'Poor old Geoffrey. I wonder how he feels now he's been caught and charged, although apparently he's out on bail and living in some penthouse by the Thames. He doesn't seem to be hard up judging by the lawyer he's hired. I suppose he's paying for it all with his offshore money.'

'No sign of Jack, or Jonathon, or whatever his real name is,' said Louise. 'He must be involved in the case, although he's never mentioned.'

'Yes,' said Jane, adding thoughtfully, 'pity you shouted at him the way you did. It was enough to frighten any man off.'

'I did it for you.'

'Never mind, you always said you didn't fancy him anyway, so it doesn't matter.'

Louise didn't answer. There seemed no point.

'I do worry a bit about Wendy, though,' Jane continued.

Wendy's divorce was proving more complex than Jane's because of Dennis' position in the EU Parliament, or rather his ex-position. He'd been expelled for maladministration, although was still, apparently, on full salary. So at the moment she was in limbo.

'Norman Long, my spotty bank manager, appears to be comforting her very well and she doesn't seem too bothered,' said Louise. She didn't mention it, but she'd noticed that Norman's spots had practically disappeared and now he appeared to be quite nice looking. She wondered whether it was the result of Jane's organic creams, or sexual satisfaction. 'They are definitely sleeping together,' she added.

Jane thought not. 'They can't be. They're not married.'

Louise roared with laughter. Her sister never failed to surprise her. 'Jane, this is the twenty-first century,' she reminded her. 'Look at Penny and David; people don't wait for marriage these days.'

Sometimes, Louise still despaired of her sister, but had to admit that she was slowly blossoming into a different woman. Gone were the Country Casual suits, and court shoes, to be replaced by jeans, T-shirts, wellington boots and anoraks. Her business, which she'd renamed 'Grass Root Remedies', was going from strength to strength; so much so that she could hardly keep up with the sales on the Internet and was paying Shelley from the village to do the packing and posting for her.

*

The trial of Geoffrey and Dennis started at the end of February. They had been charged jointly as their finances were so interwoven, according to the SFO, that it was impossible to separate them. According to the newspapers, it was likely to go on for months. The local paper, the *Rumsey Advertiser* was very excited at the beginning of the trial, and ran lurid headlines for a couple of weeks, and then lost interest as it got more complicated.

'No doubt there will be a flurry of headlines again when they are sentenced,' Louise warned Jane. She felt sorry for the jurors who'd had to sit through hours of incomprehensible financial jargon, which she and Jane had long ago given up trying to understand. But apparently it was a certainty that they'd both get custodial sentences in England, possibly followed by trials or even prison sentences in Belgium or France.

Although, as Jane had said the previous week, when they'd been sitting in the kitchen while it bucketed down with rain outside, 'Whatever happens, they won't be too bothered. These days people are let out of prison almost before they start their sentences, and once they're out, they'll collect their money from wherever it is hidden. Offshore accounts or numbered accounts in Switzerland, so Norman says; then they'll appear in some remote part of the world where they will start up businesses and do it all again.' Jane was very laid back about all of it.

'Don't you mind that he's got all that money stashed away?' asked Louise.

Jane laughed. 'Mind? Why should I? The only decent thing he did was to make the house over to me, and put half a million into my bank account. Although I'm pretty certain he did it as a tax fiddle and intended to come back and repossess it in one way or another. But he won't be able to now. My lawyers have sewn everything up so that he can't lay a finger on anything, least of all me or Wendy.'

Louise thought of her own finances, and wished she had half a million in the bank. But she didn't, so there was no point in thinking about it.

It seemed Jane could read her thoughts, because she put an arm around her and squeezed Louise. 'As I told you before, don't worry about money. You know I'll always make sure you're OK. You've only got to ask.'

Louise laughed and tried to make it sound light hearted. 'That will never be necessary. You know me. Something always turns up. I'm like a cat with nine tails.' On cue Tabitha leapt on to the table and pushed her knobbly old head against Louise's chin, purring loudly. 'All I need is some sunshine instead of this depressing rain.'

The following week, one morning dawned bright and sunny. It was lovely, crisp and inviting, and Louise firmly relegated all worries of the ongoing trial, and thoughts of Jack, which still had a nasty habit of creeping into her head when she least expected them. Today she was going to enjoy the fine weather.

It took some time to find her walking boots from the back of the hall cupboard, but eventually she retrieved them and returned to the kitchen with a spare pair of socks and the boots.

Seth came down into the kitchen, filled the kettle and started making some coffee. 'Where are you off to?' he asked, watching Louise struggling into thick knitted socks which she wore in the boots.

'I'm going to give the dogs a good long walk, something they haven't had for ages because of all the rain. In the summer I always put them in the car and take them up to Fairly Mount, especially in the evenings. It's lovely there, so quiet and peaceful and the views are marvellous. But this morning I think I'll take them across the fields to the woods.'

'Why not Fairly Mount this morning?'

'It will be too slippery; it's chalk down land and quite steep. And as it's the first fine day for ages, there are bound to be lots of rabbits about. The dogs will race after them and I'll never get them back.'

What Louise didn't say was that she hadn't walked there since Jack had left. In her mind, it was their special place, and she thought, looking back now, that it was where she had begun to fall in love with Jack. They'd never indulged in passionate lovemaking, although Fairly Mount was so remote that if they had it was unlikely that they would have been disturbed by anyone except the dogs. But apart from linked arms, and a delicious hug when he'd picked her up after she'd fallen down a rabbit hole, that was as far it had gone. Often Louise had longed for Jack to make a move because she would have responded with enthusiasm. But he never had, and now she knew why. He was working on an assignment, and she just happened to be an interesting diversion from the job in hand. She didn't let herself think about it too often, there were too many bitter and twisted people in the world, and she had no intention of joining their ranks.

'Mind if I come along with you this morning?' Seth's voice broke into her rambling thoughts.

'I'd love some company. Get your coat and let's get going.'

Putting on an old woollen jacket, Louise opened the back door and let the dogs out. They rushed forward, joyfully whirling around in circles, crushing all the snowdrops, which somehow miraculously survived this daily morning ritual.

Louise and Seth followed them in silence, hands deep in their pockets, as it was still very chilly. It was a quiet time at Lavender House now; Wendy's house had been put on the market and as she and Leon had nowhere else to go, they had moved in with Jane. Louise had moved back into Lavender House, because during the winter months there were no guests. Money was tight, but Seth and Maggie were still in residence, and Seth was very generous. Louise's once weekly organic evening dinner parties had really taken off, and were always fully booked, people coming from miles around. She'd built up quite a reputation, the whole evening becoming quite a cult thing. The local TV station had done a small piece on her organic evenings, as they called them, and she could have done more if she'd wanted. But even with the help of Seth in the kitchen, Louise always felt absolutely dog-tired by the end of the evening, and thought once a week was enough.

It was always after they'd had a really successful dinner party, and she, Seth and Maggie were sitting in the kitchen relaxing with a bottle of wine, that Louise found herself missing Jack more and more. After the SFO had finally tracked down Dennis and Geoffrey and arrested them, Jack, or Jonathan Smith as he was really called – although she could never think of him as that – had disappeared into thin air. At the beginning of the trial, Louise had scoured the newspapers to see if he was mentioned, but he never was.

'Working undercover,' Norman Long had told her. 'I doubt that Jonathan Smith is his real name; that kind of work is always done in the shadows.'

Seth and Maggie proved to be her salvation during the long winter months. They helped her decorate some of the bedrooms ready for the influx of people in the spring, and also helped her to thoroughly clean the house. She'd dispensed with the services of Mrs Dickson, who turned out to be useless.

'I can't keep her,' she told Seth. 'She always has a bad back or a bad something, and now says she's allergic to dust. Anyway the net result is she's unable to do most of the work I wanted her to do.'

'Yes, get rid of her,' agreed Seth. 'Maggie and I can help out until you find someone good enough for the spring and summer when business takes off again.'

'I love it, darling,' said Maggie. 'It's wonderful practice for when I get offered a part as a cleaner. I'll ask my agent if there are any cleaning lady parts going in one of the soaps.' She still dripped in jewellery, and for the winter had swapped her dresses and skirts for a series of brilliantly coloured tracksuits, and when cleaning, wore large orange-coloured rubber gloves.

When they went shopping together in Rumsey, Louise always thought Maggie looked like a bright flame amongst the rest of the inhabitants, who were all dressed in beige and grey anoraks as if it were some kind of regulation uniform. In fact, she had spurred Louise on to purchase a coral-coloured warm winter jacket which she wore with a vivid turquoise scarf because it made her feel summery.

'Everyone should feel summery in the winter,' said Maggie. 'It's *de rigueur*, you can't feel depressed when you feel like summer.'

Penny popped in every day, and often left Sam and Jacob to play, and when Sam came, Leon came as well. Since his father had disappeared from his life, he'd changed from a prim, rather cowed, pale child, into a normal little boy full of mischief. And although he and Wendy were living with Jane, Wendy was spending more and more time with Norman in his Victorian terraced house in the oldest part of Rumsey; sometimes she took Leon and sometimes she left him with Jane. Leon seemed happy wherever he was.

Louise knew that Penny and David were wielding paintbrushes, and plastering the walls of their house as if their lives depended on it, which, in fact it did, as they'd moved into it long before it was really habitable. But the children didn't care that there was no hot water to begin with, nor electricity and neither did Penny or David.

'It's fun camping in a big house, Nanny,' Sam told her. 'I've got my own torch because there's no light in my room.'

But at last their house was beginning to look more like a house rather than a ruin and a builder's yard, and they had the comfort of hot water, a cooker, and a working lavatory instead of a camping gas stove and a chemical toilet.

In fact, now Louise thought about it, all their lives had changed and seemed more or less sorted. Except mine, and I'm back to square one. She remembered Jane in the garden that day last spring when she'd said, 'I can't understand why someone hasn't snapped you up,' and Louise remembered replying vehemently that she didn't want to be 'snapped up' as Jane had put it.

Although now she looked back, she wondered if the rather depressing book she'd written, which Dottie had hated but sold, wasn't an indication of her inner feelings at the time that she hadn't recognized. And then, quite suddenly, everything changed. One by one people had dropped in and out of her life becoming part of the Lavender House mob as Maggie insisted on calling them. Even though some had now moved out, they were still near, and never a day passed without somebody coming to the house. Louise knew that as soon as the weather was warm enough, the children would be back playing in the jungle, which was what Sam and Leon had named the bottom of the garden. So being surrounded by family and friends, as she was, there was no reason to miss Jack. But she did, and bitterly regretted repulsing his overture when he and Gerrard Holby had first made their appearance. He'd wanted to explain, but hurt angry pride had prevented her from letting him, and after that moment there'd never been another chance.

She and Seth walked through the long wet grass across the fields and towards the woods where Sam and Leon had got lost. 'I can't help remembering when the boys got lost,' she said. 'What a night that was. But everything is sorted out now, thank goodness.'

'I don't know about that,' said Seth seriously. 'There's still one major thing outstanding, and that's Jack.'

'Oh, he's not outstanding.' Louise tried to keep the tremor from her voice. 'He's long gone. Jack is history now.' She called the dogs. 'Seamus, Megan, come here. Back home now.' She turned and would have started back towards the house but Seth put out a restraining arm in her way.

'You love him, don't you,' he said quietly. 'And you miss him.'

'I never loved him. And I certainly don't miss him,' Louise snapped. Then to her horror, a tear trickled down her cheek because she was unable to stop it. Seth put his arms around her, and Louise wept. 'I'll never see him again,' she said between sniffs, 'and I'm behaving ridiculously for a woman of my age. I'm behaving like a lovesick teenager.'

Seth held her away from him and smiled. 'Shame on you. You are a writer, you write about people's emotions.

You, more than anyone, should know that whatever age you are on the outside, inside you're still a teenager. We all feel the same now as we did when we were very young. Look at Maggie; she's a prime example. It's only recently that she's emerged from adolescence!'

Louise had to smile at his description of Maggie. It was so apt. 'You are right,' she said. 'But I have to face facts. I screamed and shouted at him when he came back and told us the truth about who he really was and why he was here, because I was so angry. He betrayed all of us, and he let me believe he really did feel something for me, but I imagine my reaction that day would have put him off for good. He did try, you know, when he and that other awful man arrived, he tried to take me aside and tell me everything would be all right, but I wouldn't listen and pushed him away. I was so furious, I couldn't think straight.'

Seth grinned. 'Yes, you were pretty ...' he hesitated and then said mildly, 'forthright.'

Louise blew her nose loudly, and then shrugged. 'That's putting it mildly. But I said what I said, I can't undo that, and he's now he's gone from all our lives. He's probably on the other side of the world chasing some other crooks and I'm unlikely ever to see him again.'

Seth gave her a squeeze. 'You never know. Life's one long round of turning corners, and you never know what or who you are going to bump into.'

Louise laughed. 'As a writer I can tell you that is a terrible sentence. But I do know what you mean.' She called to the dogs again and put them on their leashes. 'This is the time of morning, when it's sunny, that the rabbits came out for a little sun bathe and a nibble of fresh grass. One sniff of a rabbit and it is goodbye to the dogs for the day,' she told Seth. 'And I can't afford to waste time today because David's coming over to teach me some more tricks on the computer. He says there are things I ought to know in case I need to do something quickly on my own.'

'Very sensible idea,' said Seth, falling into step beside her as they made their way back across the field. 'You never know what's ...'

Louise finished the sentence for him. 'Round the corner,' she said.

CHAPTER
EIGHTEEN

THE TRIAL OF Dennis and Geoffrey continued its long and complicated progress, but it was so remote that everyone in East Willow forgot about it most of the time. Occasionally there was a small paragraph in one of the national papers, but the newsworthy element had diminished. Louise wondered what they'd both do when they got out of prison, as it appeared that they almost certainly would get a custodial sentence. It would be in some open prison, of course, and not for that long if the course of justice followed its usual pattern. Would Geoffrey come back and hassle Jane if he was hard up?

But Norman Long assured her that crooks like Geoffrey were never hard up. 'They always have money tucked away somewhere,' he said.

But nevertheless, Louise couldn't help worrying. At last her sister was happy, and she wanted her to stay that way.

Jane, however, seemed totally unperturbed. 'If Geoffrey so much as shows his nose around here,' she said firmly, 'I shall kick him out.'

These days, nothing seemed to faze Jane. She made her soaps and gels in ever increasing quantities, and had persuaded Bert Hackett to set aside another field to plant the lavender and other flowers she'd need next year. Louise noticed she seemed to be getting very friendly with Bert, even inviting him round for supper, when Wendy was out with Norman Long, which Louise thought very suspicious. Surely her sister couldn't be embarking on an affair with a man who had dirt under his fingernails? Not Jane, who had always been so fastidious about things like that, much too fussy in Louise's opinion. Then she told herself to come to her senses and stop speculating about her sister's possible love life. Anyway, thoughts of Jack always got in the way, and the only man who ever showed any interest in her as a woman was Daniel the milkman, who still hadn't had his teeth fixed.

Then suddenly, when they'd all lost interest in the trial, it came to an abrupt close. The judge, in his summing up, said as plainly as he could without appearing biased, that they were guilty of fraud on an enormous scale, and the jury agreed with him and returned a unanimous guilty verdict on Geoffrey and Dennis. The following week they were sentenced, Geoffrey to three years in prison and Dennis to five.

Jane came round that evening with all the newspapers which had given write-ups of the trial, and Louise celebrated the iniquitous pair's imprisonment by lighting a fire in the sitting room, and began opening the two bottles of red wine, which Seth had bought especially for the occasion. 'Do the room good to have a real fire going,' she said, throwing plenty of logs on. 'This room hasn't been used since the last lot of paying customers were here.'

Seth and Maggie settled themselves in armchairs near the fire, and Jane spread the newspapers out across the floor. 'Jack isn't mentioned in any of them as far as I can see,' she said.

'Of course he wouldn't be mentioned,' said Louise. 'If he was in any of the reports, it would be under the name of Jonathan Smith, and anyway he's nothing to do with us any more, so it's of no particular interest.' Louise saw Seth glance in her direction and concentrated on opening the bottles. Part of her longed for some word of him, and the other part of her wanted to banish him forever.

'I'm interested,' said Maggie.

'Tell me what the papers say.' Louise steered the conversation away from Jack.

Maggie picked up one of the papers and gasped. 'Ooh,' she said, rolling her eyes dramatically, 'it says here that Geoffrey Steadman was a notorious womanizer, and that he owned a brothel in Hamburg.' Her voice rose with excitement as she looked at Jane. 'Did you know that, as his ex-wife, that could mean that you own half a brothel? Ex-wives are entitled to half of everything. I know about things like that.'

'Really,' Jane looked interested. 'Yes, I suppose a brothel would be quite profitable,' she said slowly. 'Perhaps I should ask my lawyers to look into it.'

'For Heaven's sake, forget that,' said Louise, pulling up another armchair. 'Considering all the trouble you had with Geoffrey when you were married, I really don't think you're cut out for running a brothel.'

'What was the trouble when you were married then?' Maggie leaned forward, her nose quivering like a hound scenting something very interesting. 'Was it sex?'

'There wasn't any, that was the trouble, and now I know why.' Jane opened another paper.

Maggie gasped. 'But you had Wendy, so there must have been, you must have had, unless....'

'It was immaculate conception? No such luck. No, Geoffrey is definitely Wendy's father, but fortunately she doesn't seem to have inherited any of his traits. Only mine, and that's the tendency to pick the wrong man to marry. But as for sex, that was it, more or less, apart from the erotica which I don't really count and wasn't keen on.' Jane sighed. 'I did make an effort later on, but I left it too late. His mind was elsewhere.'

'Not only his mind by the sound of it,' said Seth who was reading one of the tabloids.

There was a knock on the door, and Wendy and Norman stood there. 'I've put Leon upstairs in your bed with a hot-water bottle and his teddy,' said Wendy to Louise. 'I hope that's all right.'

'Of course it is.' Louise moved her chair, and then everyone else moved round a bit and they squeezed on the rug with Jane who was still poring over every word. Louise went into the kitchen and came back with the wine glasses and poured everyone a generous measure.

Wendy sipped her wine and looked over her mother's shoulder at the papers. 'You don't think that they'll come back here when they get out, do you?' she asked nervously.

'I'll punch Dennis on the nose if he dares come near you.' Norman sounded fierce, but although he had improved immensely and matured in looks since he and Wendy had got together, Louise still thought he was not one of nature's best specimens of manhood. Nice but weedy, was how she'd have described him, but that didn't matter. He made Wendy happy.

'I should leave the police to deal with him, should he ever come back, which I doubt,' said Seth sternly. 'Take it from a man many years your senior; it's always best to leave these matters in the hands of the law.'

'It's a pity you didn't practise what you now preach when I first met you,' said Maggie, 'because if you had you wouldn't have got your nose broken.' She accepted a glass of wine from Louise, raising it to Seth. 'But you were magnificently brave, even though he did knock you out, and I had to pay to have your nose set. But that's another story.'

They spent the rest of the evening chattering and laughing. At least, the rest of them did, Louise sat in her chair watching the flames flickering red and yellow on the logs, wondering where Jack was.

Towards the end of March, Wendy announced that she and Leon were moving in with Norman permanently.

Jane reverted back to her usual worried self and asked Louise over to her house for tea and a discussion.

'Come straight over after you've finished walking the dogs,' she said.

Louise was surprised at the invitation as dogs were not usually welcome in Jane's house. She said they were dirty and smelly, which, as Louise always said, was not true of her dogs. Greyhounds never smelled, they were much too fussy to let themselves get smelly. Jane also accused them of being muddy, which was true after a walk at this time of year. However, given a drink, a quiet corner to sit in and they soon set about cleaning themselves with feline thoroughness, so Louise accepted the invitation, as she had complete faith in the good behaviour of Megan and Seamus. She assumed the invitation was all part of Jane's new laissez-faire attitude to life, although, apparently, this was not yet extended towards Wendy and her love life.

She'd been so busy the last few months that she hadn't visited Jane in her own home, it was always Jane coming over to Lavender House, so when she arrived at the Larches, she was surprised to find the cast-iron gates wide open. In Geoffrey's days they had always been firmly locked and one had to tap the code into the pad on the gateway before they would creak open. The garden had changed as well. Gone were the serried ranks of bushes and plants, which Louise had always hated, thinking it looked like a military parade ground, and in its place were freshly raked beds, with marker sticks showing what was planted. Calendular, *Papaver rhoeas*, *Hypericum perforatum*, and other Latin names, none of which Louise recognized but which were obviously planted with Jane's herbal business in mind. The rock garden had changed as well, a lot of the plants gone, and new ones in their places, the only one which Louise recognized, was valerian from its thick, grey-green winter leaves.

Jane came out and met her, with no comment about the dog's muddy paws. 'Bert and I have been busy as you can see,' she said. 'The entire garden is being turned over to wild flowers and herbs. It's amazing how useful they will be. I'm branching out in my products. Not just things in pots and jars in the future, but herbal pillows, cushions, draft excluders. I'm going to be the largest cottage industry in Hampshire by the time I've finished, and I'm changing the name of the house from the Larches to Toadflax Cottage.'

'Oh,' Louise was surprised and didn't think it a particularly pretty name, but was anxious not to spoil her sister's obvious enjoyment of all the changes she'd made. 'It's very …' she hesitated, then said, 'interesting.'

'I know you're not keen,' said Jane leading the way through to the conservatory at the back of the house, which caught the last of the winter sunshine. The dogs followed, and settled down in the warmest spot, and began licking their feet. Jane glanced at them, and Louise wished they wouldn't lick quite so noisily, but Jane carried on talking about the name of the house. 'I wanted something people thought unusual, and could remember, if not all of it, then at least part of the name. By the way Penny's coming over as well, because Wendy is picking up both boys from the pre-school session this afternoon, so she can collect Sam here, and at the same time she can give Wendy the benefit of her advice where Norman is concerned.'

'Personally,' said Louise, 'I think you are making a mountain out of a molehill. Wendy is quite old enough to decide what she wants to do, and if she wants to live with Norman, then so be it.' She sank down into one of Jane's over-cushioned, over-patterned, bamboo armchairs, and while Jane brought out the tea, she flipped through the *TV Times*. 'Oh that programme, *Open Leaves*, is on now. It's about books,' she said. 'Dottie told me I ought to watch it, but I'd forgotten until now. Can we have it on?'

'Of course.' But from the tone of Jane's voice, Louise knew she'd have much rather talked about Wendy or her herbs.

Louise flicked through the channels then suddenly stopped as she passed Euro News and flicked back. 'That's not the book programme,' said Jane, glancing at the TV.

'No it's the news, and I thought I saw Jack in amongst the crowd just now.'

Jane came over and perched on the arm of Louise's chair. 'How could it be Jack? It's some meeting of EU commissioners and he's not one of those.' Together they scanned the screen and listened to the commentary. It was a meeting of various EU financial ministers concerning a scandal of fraudulent claims for travel expenses, plus, as far as they could make out another scam about olive trees which didn't exist but which were being claimed for in Sicily, and the Puglia district of Italy. The word Mafiosi kept being bandied about. 'I think you were mistaken about Jack,' said Jane.

'No,' shrieked Louise. 'Look, there he is again, standing talking to that man with a big nose, the one with a cup of coffee in his hand.'

'You're right,' whispered Jane. 'And I must say he does look like a mafia gangster.'

'Rubbish, that man is much too small. He's a typical civil servant type.'

'I didn't mean him, I meant Jack,' said Jane. 'He's the one who looks like a gangster!'

Then annoyingly the news switched to sport and coverage of the Six Nations Rugby cup.

'Damn,' said Louise, and flicked through to the book programme. 'I shall go back to Euro News in an hour's time. They usually repeat everything.'

The Book Programme, *Open Leaves*, had recently changed its format, and was now hosted by a bubbly bright blonde, called Lucy Frost. When Louise switched over, she was talking about a non-fiction book on the nomadic tribes of the Kalahari Desert.

'It was so vivid,' she gushed to the author, 'I could almost feel the insects crawling up my legs.' She crossed one leg over the other, showing, thought Louise, an unnecessary expanse of thigh.

The author, Arnold Beatty, a gaunt-looking man with sunburned skin and a wispy grey beard, looked unenthusiastic at her comment. 'The insects are irrelevant,' he said. 'I wanted to give an insight into the deeply spiritual relationship which exists between the Kalahari Bushmen and their environment. The feeling that the Bushmen have the stars embedded within their souls.'

'Oh yes. Absolutely. Mr Batty er Beatty.' The girl looked flustered and leafed rapidly through the book. Louise couldn't help grinning. She obviously hadn't even glanced at it before they came on air, and was now desperately searching for something interesting to pick up and expand on. 'Ah,' she said, 'on page 796 there is an almost lyrical quality to the words, I can feel them reaching out to me, in a deep and meaningful way.'

Arnold Beatty took the book from her and looked at the page. 'It doesn't mean anything,' he said. 'It represents the moaning of the winds across the desert and is just a jumble of words. It should be read aloud, like this …'

Lucy Frost snatched the book from his hands before he had the chance to read anything, and snapped it shut. 'I'm afraid our time is up. Thank you so much, Mr Batty.'

'Beatty,' said the author through gritted teeth, 'Arnold Beatty.'

'Absolutely. Yes. Again, thank you so much for coming on the *Open Leaves* programme and enlightening us all.' With a beaming smile, she turned to the camera, which zoomed in on her and held up the book, unfortunately upside down. 'For all of you who are interested in the Kalahari Bushmen and their …' she paused for a second, then said, 'habits,' her tone inferring that they were rather nasty habits, 'this book is for you and is available from all good bookshops.'

She turned to her left, and Louise could imagine the studio staff hastily shuffling Arnold Beatty out, while the new interviewee was settled on the other side of the settee. Then she sat up and took more notice. 'Look, Jane, it's Dottie LeClerc, my agent.'

Jane brought a cup of tea over and sat in the other armchair. 'Is she going to promote your book?'

Louise leaned forward as Lucy Frost introduced Dottie. 'Every author will tell you that the most important person in their professional life is their agent,' said Lucy. Dottie tossed her hair back and pushed her dark glasses higher up on her hair, which today was orange. 'It is the agent,' continued Lucy, 'who assesses the original manuscript and decides which publisher to place it with.'

'Huh!' snorted Louise, 'if only it were that easy.'

'So.' Lucy crossed her legs the other way giving the viewers another angle from which to admire her legs. Dottie shuffled slightly in her seat, she was wearing her usual outfit, a floaty black top with lots of costume jewellery, long black skirt and boots, and was twiddling with her earrings. 'So,' Lucy repeated, 'tell me about this exciting new author you've discovered'

New author. So that was it. Louise sank back in her chair feeling disappointed. 'It can't be about me,' she said, 'because I've been with Dottie for yonks.

Then she heard Dottie say, 'this author, Louise Gregory.'

'That's me,' shrieked Louise in amazement.

'Sent me her manuscript and immediately I knew I had a winner. *Loneliness is Woman* is a book of rare literary quality, so I placed it with an exclusive publisher.'

'Exclusive publisher,' said Jane in an awed tone of voice. 'You never told me.'

'What she really means is that that she couldn't sell it, and eventually a very small publishing house, desperate to get their hands on anything, and pay peanuts into the bargain, took it. And as for knowing it was a winner, she told me she hated it, said it was depressing into the bargain and that she'd never be able to sell it.'

'Oh,' Jane was puzzled.

'Yes,' continued Dottie, tilting her head so that the camera got a better angle, 'as soon as I read *Loneliness is Woman* I knew it would appeal to women of all ages. It moves seamlessly from the trials of a young wife to those facing a woman in old age and ...'

Louise exploded. 'She said she hated it!'

'Has it got a lot of humour?' asked Lucy.

'None,' said Dottie firmly.

'Well, at least that's the truth,' snorted Louise.

'But I don't understand any of this,' said Jane.

'But don't let that put any readers out there off.' Dottie turned and smiled sweetly into the camera. 'Take it from me, a good book doesn't need humour, all it needs is to be a good read. It needs to be a page-turner. And this book has that quality in bucketfuls, which is why it has been long-listed for the Quasar Women's prize. It indicates power and remoteness.'

'A little bird tells me that it is likely to be short-listed,' said Lucy rather coyly, leaning forward and showing a generous amount of cleavage.

'Where did they get this presenter from?' asked Louise, feeling exasperated.

'Never mind her. It looks as if you will be short-listed, and that will mean more money won't it?' said Jane, who by now was very impressed.

Dottie tossed back her orange hair, and twiddled one earring furiously. 'I heard just before we came on air that it *has* been selected. *Loneliness is Woman* is on the Quasar short list and the publishers are ordering another print run.'

'Won't be for many,' said Louise gloomily.

'Whoopee,' shouted Jane. 'This calls for a celebration.' She leapt up and fell over both dogs, who had also leapt up at her 'whoopee', thinking everyone was going out for a walk again. She picked herself up from the floor as the front doorbell rang announcing the arrival of Wendy and Penny with the three children. 'You get it,' she shouted at Louise as she struggled to get back on her feet.

Much later, Louise made her way back to Lavender House, on her bicycle, which luckily had been left at Jane's house on a previous visit. The dogs loped alongside, and she very nearly ran them over several times; she was feeling distinctly squiffy from Jane's home-made wine and knew she really shouldn't have been riding or driving any- thing, although at least on a bicycle she couldn't do much damage. She thought briefly about Wendy and Norman, whom they'd hardly discussed at all. As far as Wendy was concerned it was a *fait accompli* and Jane was so excited by Louise's good luck that she seemed to have forgotten she had any objections to her daughter's domestic arrange- ments. All to the good, thought Louise, never interfere in your offspring's love life.

Lavender House was in darkness, Maggie and Seth obviously having gone to bed, and Louise felt disap- pointed. She wanted to tell someone her news, but there was no one to tell. There was a message on the answer machine from Dottie relaying the good news, with the promise of a call in the morning. It reminded her of why she'd written the book, a cathartic purging of her soul for all the important times when she'd longed to share some- thing with someone, anyone, but couldn't because she'd been alone. Even after the birth of Penny, John had been working away, and hadn't managed to get home; not his fault, it was just the way things had worked out.

The cats rushed at her, all four of them mewling noisily, as she hadn't fed them before she went out, because she didn't think she'd be long. Pouring dried biscuits in their bowls and topping up their water, she sat down at the kitchen table and thought of Jack. If she got a few reviews and there were a couple of articles in the papers he might see them. And then what? Nothing probably. He'd had plenty of time to get in touch but he never had. She had to accept the fact that he'd been a passing moment in her life. But he'd left a trail of memories that she knew would never leave her. She dithered between another glass of wine before bed or a cup of Horlicks, and then decided to be sensible and have the Horlicks.

Throwing another log on the wood burning stove in the corner, which the dogs appreciated, squeezing as close to the stove as they possibly could without burning themselves, she sat down with her hands clasped around the hot mug and gave herself a good talking to. It is ridiculous, she thought, here am I, a sensible woman mooning about a man who passed briefly through my life; and who wouldn't have been here at all if my sister and her daughter hadn't married crooks! Not an ideal set-up for a romantic liaison. Get on with your life woman. You've never needed a man before and you don't need one now.

Seamus turned over on his back; legs splayed out, totally relaxed, and began to snore loudly. That's what I should be doing, thought Louise. I should be in bed, sound asleep. Filling a hot water bottle, she climbed the stairs and settled herself in bed. Outside the wind rattled the window-panes. The weather was on the change; it looked like March was going out like the proverbial lion.

CHAPTER
NINETEEN

THE NEXT MORNING dawned calm, bright, and absolutely and beautiful. It appeared the storm in the night, which had rattled Louise's window-panes, had blown itself out. She watched the news on TV while eating a piece of toast and having coffee, her morning ritual. The weather forecast was awful, storms, thunder and lightning and snow blizzards.

'Ridiculous,' mumbled Louise to herself through a mouthful of toast. 'They haven't looked out of the window.'

Maggie and Seth were still in bed. In the clear spring light, the house looked clean and fresh, the bedrooms were all ready now for any guests who might turn up, and she even had another bedroom en-suite, Kevin and his mate having managed to squeeze a shower and a toilet into the corner of the bedroom on the far side of the house. When they'd started, she'd never thought they'd manage it, but somehow they had, and now it stood there, sparkling white, waiting for its first customers.

'They'll have to be on the slim side,' said David, when he saw it. 'Don't let this room to anyone large.'

'I can get in it,' said Louise.

'Yes, but you're slim. A man the size of Jack would never manage it.'

Louise didn't answer, and wished he hadn't used Jack as an example. She thought about their conversation now as she sat at the kitchen table. Damned man! I must not get obsessed, she said to herself, and decided to concentrate on something she'd been putting off for ages. She would try to get her English Tourist Board roses put on her sign; Norman Long, now well and truly part of the Lavender House mob said it would give her business gravitas. Pulling out all the paperwork she'd received from the English Tourist Board, Louise started ticking boxes to see if she would qualify for one rose or two to put on the board outside the gate and on the website. 'Wretched things,' she muttered eventually, and threw the mountain of paper bad-temperedly into the waste bin. 'What does it take to qualify? I've ticked a hundred boxes but the extra shower room isn't the right size to count towards a rose. I'll never qualify.' She glowered out of the window. 'Who needs roses anyway,' she said, looking at the cats, who were sitting with expectant expressions by their bowls; catching mice was out of the question when it was cold outside, they wanted fish biscuits. Louise carried on with her conversation to the cats. 'I managed perfectly well last summer without a single rose, and I'll do just as well this year. Lavender House doesn't need roses, it's got lavender.'

The cats' eyes never wavered, they were willing her to get the box of fish-flavoured biscuits out and feed them, which she did. The sound of the biscuit box had sent the dogs scuttling to their bowls, which she filled with dog biscuits. They ate quickly and untidily, scattering biscuits in all directions. She'd just finished sweeping up the stray biscuits when the phone rang.

It was Dottie. 'Well darling,' she screeched down the phone. 'What do you think about getting on the short list? Are you pleased?'

'Of course I'm pleased. I'm also amazed. How did it happen?'

'Well,' Dottie gave a wicked giggle. 'It helps that I'm very friendly with one of the judges. He might, if I play my cards right, ask me to marry him'

'But I thought they were all women?' Louise blurted out.

'Not all, darling. Now, tell me.' Dottie's shrill voice reined in Louise's wandering thoughts. 'What is the title of your next book? And what is it about? Simon Weatherby wants to know, and he says he'll put the first chapter at the back of the book in the next print run of *Loneliness is Woman*.'

Title of next book! First chapter! Louise realized she hadn't given writing more than a fleeting thought since she'd posted the manuscript of *Loneliness is Woman* off to Dottie back at the beginning of last year.

'Well?' prompted Dottie, impatiently. 'What is your working title?'

'*Love and the Unmarried Woman*,' said Louise, grabbing at the first words that came into her head. 'It starts at the end of a woman's life and works its way back to when she was young and hopeful. I thought writing the whole thing backwards in time would be an interesting angle from which to tackle the subject.' An impossibility her common sense told her, but she ignored that. She could dash off a chapter about her feelings now that Jack had gone and she was feeling bereft, yes that's a good word, remember that! Bereft. She'd worry about the rest of the book later, anything to keep Dottie and the publisher happy. 'It needs polishing up, though,' she lied, mentally crossing her fingers. 'I'm only on the first draft.'

'Fab, darling,' trilled Dottie. 'Send it to me within the next couple of weeks, and we'll take it from there. I'm going to screw a big advance out of Simon for this next book. He can afford it. I've found out he's a billionaire and has taken up publishing for a hobby. Now he's going to find out that it's an expensive hobby, but with an author like you on board, and me to lead him gently by the hand, he can't lose, and neither can I.'

Louise felt everything was moving much too fast. 'What do you mean? Lead him by the hand? You can't start an affair with him as well.'

'Who says I can't,' said Dottie, with a giggle and put the phone down.

'She's mad,' Louise told the assembled animals. 'Maybe I should get a sane agent.' But it was too late to change now; Dottie had set up the project.

Dottie's unexpected and definitely over-excited behaviour made Louise feel restless. It made her wonder if she really did want to write another book, which she knew was contrary given that it looked as if her last book was going to be a success against all the odds. But she had the strangest feeling that perhaps that part of her life had come to an end. She decided to take the dogs up to Fairley Mount for a good long walk, reasoning that she couldn't put off going there for ever just because of memories of Jack. Besides, she needed to think. She would try and work out what to do while walking the dogs, but first she'd pop in on Penny and David.

After loading the dogs into the car, she shouted up the stairs to Seth and Maggie. 'I'm taking the dogs out for a long walk, probably to Fairley Mount.'

Seth came out on to the landing, still in his bathrobe.

'Do you think that's wise? The weather forecast is awful. We've been watching it on TV.'

'Oh, what do they know,' said Louise, pointing to the window where the sun was streaming in. 'It's a lovely morning. The weather forecasters have got it wrong again. The dogs and I need a dose of fresh air and sunshine and that is what we're going to get, after I've popped in to say hello to Penny.'

'Well …' began Seth.

But Louise had already slammed the front door behind her.

Jacob came rushing to meet her when she arrived at Penny's house. He was really walking now and could cover the ground with amazing speed. Louise picked him up and kissed him. Penny came rushing after him, breathless, and wearing paint-splashed dungarees. 'I'm trying to do the last of the painting in the kitchen while David's up in London. He's sharing an office with a friend now, and pays him by the hour so it's not too expensive. Do you want a coffee?'

'No thanks, I'm taking the dogs for a walk.' Louise looked at Penny and felt relieved. 'You look happy,' she said. 'I take it everything is all right now between you and David.'

'Yes thanks, Mum, and it's due to you taking me in when I ran away.'

Louise raised her eyebrows at the memory. 'I very nearly sent you straight back, you know.'

'But you didn't. And I'm grateful because I know at that time we were struggling financially, you through no fault of your own and me because I'd walked away from David's money. God knows what we'd have done without Jack and his money. But that time away gave me breathing space, and made David see that running a big house was not an easy option. He couldn't manage it on his own, let alone with two babies to cope with.' She grinned happily. 'He's so different now. The funny thing is we don't have nearly as much money, but we do have time for each other. He helps with the children, and we've decided we're definitely getting married soon; probably the end of this month or May, no fuss and bother, just a registry office and a few friends and family.'

'Maggie will be pleased as well as me. I note she doesn't advocate the single woman status quite so much nowadays,' said Louise wryly.

Penny giggled. 'Bit difficult that, now that she and Seth have a last settled down.'

Louise kissed Jacob again, and passed him over to Penny. 'I'm off. Those dogs need exercise.'

As she left, Penny followed her and said wistfully, 'I wish you had someone special, Mum. Even Jane seems to have formed an attachment with Bert Hackett.'

'I don't need anyone,' said Louise firmly, 'and I certainly don't need anyone like Bert Hackett. Give me a break!'

Driving to Fairley Mount, she slipped a CD from the film *The Commitments* into the player, and nodded her head along in time to 'Mustang Sally'. Since David had been around she'd grown to like soul music, he was always playing it.

The car wound its way up the steep narrow road to the top of the mount. The sky was the pale blue of springtime, catkins danced on the hazel bushes lining the lane, and in the back of the car, the dogs sat up and started to take notice. They knew where they were going.

Louise parked the car in the small space reserved especially for visitors set along side a blackthorn thicket, which was in full bloom, the white flowers covering the bushes so thickly it looked like snow. She let the dogs out of the car, and they raced ahead with long, lolloping strides, ears flying back. She smiled; they loved every moment. Then she started the climb towards the top of the mount. Fairley Mount was chalk down land and the path was part chalk and part flint, a steep climb. In the field on her left, the newborn lambs were with their mothers, each one wearing a little plastic coat to protect them against the chilling wind which swept along the ridge of the hillside. Once she reached the top, Louise stood for a moment, savouring the view; it was possible to see three counties from here: Wiltshire, Hampshire and Dorset, and Louise always stopped to look. She glanced at her watch. She had nothing much to do at Lavender House, so decided to walk the long way back, down the other side of the hill, along the bottom beside the forestry plantation, then back up the hill to the car. That should exhaust the dogs.

Setting off down the hill at a brisk pace, the dogs still rushing in front of her, although coming back every now and then just to make sure she was still there, she suddenly noticed that the sun didn't seem so warm, and the wind felt keener. Before her stretched the view, a patchwork of fields, some already turning yellow where early oilseed rape was beginning to bloom, the spire of Salisbury Cathedral pointed a stone finger skywards in the distance, and the sky was still blue, not a cloud in sight. But an extra blast of cold wind, which nearly knocked off her feet, made her turn and look behind.

The contrast was frightening. Bearing down upon her and advancing at a seemingly phenomenal speed were the blackest clouds she'd ever seen, below them and before them a dense curtain of grey was moving towards her, and she realized it must be the snow that had been forecast. As she looked, she saw a jagged flash of lightning in the darkest part of the clouds, no thunder, just lightning. By now she was halfway along her chosen route so there didn't seem much point in turning back. She made a quick decision, better to go on and stick to her chosen path. Quickening her pace, she called to the dogs and put them on their leashes. Lightning meant thunder, and Megan was terrified of thunder, and one clap would be enough to panic her and then she'd blindly run, and run, and get herself lost. It had happened once before, and luckily someone had found her miles away, a quivering, terrified heap. Louise wanted to hang on to her now.

Reaching the bottom, she managed to stay ahead of the advancing storm, but when she just started back up the hill, on the path to the car, she found she was walking into the storm, leaning in against the wind in the ever-increasing darkness. She told herself that at least she was getting nearer the car, but then it started to snow. At first, large fat flakes, which stung her face, and stuck in her hair, then it came down faster and faster, a white-out. It was almost impossible to see, but Louise kept going, reasoning that as long as she was going up hill she'd be all right. A clap of thunder had Megan screaming and pulling madly on her leash, twisting in a circle and entwining Louise's legs; she and the dogs all stumbled into a thicket of small ash trees and brambles. It was then that Louise realized that she had gone too far to the right; she wasn't on the path to the car but on the other path to the top of the mount. Crouching down in the thicket trying to calm Megan, with Seamus tucking his head under her other arm, Louise had never felt so miserable and frightened in her life. How stupid she'd been to come up here on her own and to ignore the forecast, and to add insult to injury, she now remembered she'd left her mobile phone on the kitchen table. Not that it would have been of much use; the signal on the mount was poor at the best of times. Now it would be non-existent.

How long she crouched there, shivering, she didn't know. She could see through the blizzard that the snow was getting thicker and thicker. Even if she eventually got to the car, she wondered whether she would be able to get down the narrow lanes. This high down land area was renowned for the wind blowing snow into impassable snowdrifts. I could freeze to death, she thought, and then told herself not to be so stupid. People didn't freeze to death in Hampshire, she would just have to sit it out, and at least both Penny and Seth knew where she was.

'Louise, Louise, where are you?' At first she thought it was her imagination, but then the sound came again, a faint voice, torn to shreds by the howling wind and another rumble of thunder. But it was real, for there it was again. 'Louise, Louise, Seamus, where are you?'

At the sound of his name Seamus, pricked up his ears, then lunged with all his strength and made a bolt for it. The leash slipped from Louise's hand, and she burst into tears. Now she'd let go of Seamus and he'd get himself lost. Standing up, and trying to keep a tight hold of Megan's collar, Louise screamed at the top of her voice.

'Seamus, Seamus, come back. I'm here.'

Seamus came back; his ears plastered to the side of his head with snow, and close behind him was Jack.

'What the hell do you think you're doing out here?' he said, holding out his arms towards her. Louise fell into them and he held her a moment. Megan, who she was still hanging on to on her leash, squeezed in between

310

them, a black quivering, shivering bundle.

'Oh, Jack, you don't know how glad I am to see you,' Louise spluttered through a mouthful of snowflakes.

'Huh! That's not what you said the last time I saw you. But never mind, let's get out of here.'

'I'm not sure where my car is,' said Louise, trying to wipe away snow from her eyes and face without letting go of Megan. There was no problem with Seamus, now he'd found Jack, he was sticking to him like a leech. She tried to look up into his face, could hardly see, but had a feeling his expression was grim. 'How did you know I was here? In this spot?'

'Instinct and a good memory of our walks in the summer, besides Penny told me you'd come up here walking the dogs, you mad woman,' replied Jack. 'Come on. My car is only a few yards away on the main path.'

Megan was still shivering and refused to budge, so Jack picked her up. 'Hang on to Seamus and my coat,' he told Louise, and started back up the hill. Louise did as she was told, and after about five minutes they reached a Land Rover, parked precipitously on the edge of the incline. 'Get in,' said Jack. 'We'll collect your car tomorrow, or whenever the snow clears.'

Louise clambered around to the passenger side and got in. The dogs needed no invitation; once the door was opened, they were in before she was.

'I didn't know you had a four-wheel drive,' said Louise, realizing as she said it that it was a ludicrous thing to say. Jack shifted into gear and drove the vehicle back up on to the relative safety of the tiny lane, which ran along the top of the ridge.

'There's a lot about me you don't know,' he said.

'But how ...' Louise began.

'Never mind that, let's get this show on the road.' He

put on the satnav, which lit up the darkness inside the Land Rover, pushed a couple of buttons and studied it. 'Right,' he said, 'I'm going to keep on this road which will eventually take us down into Salisbury and civilization, where, hopefully, the roads will be clear.' He passed her his mobile. 'Try and ring Penny and tell her you're safe and with me.'

The journey back to Lavender House was difficult in the blinding white-out of the storm, which seemed to gather in ferocity as they made their way down the steep hillside. With the dogs shivering in the back, pushing their wet noses between her and Jack (they would have squashed on to the front seats had they been able) Louise felt both relieved and apprehensive at the same time. Here am I, she thought, I wanted so much to see him again, and now that he's here I'm afraid to open my mouth because he looks so fierce.

She glanced sideways again. His expression was still grim. 'It was good of you to come and find me,' she ventured to say at last.

'I came for the dogs,' he replied. 'I know you can't handle them when they're frightened, especially Megan, in a storm.'

'Oh!' He didn't say he'd come for her. But how and why had he been talking to Penny anyway? Maybe. Perhaps. She could always hope. 'Well, anyway ...' she began.

The Land Rover hit a boulder in the road, and lurched sideways, one wheel going down in the deep ditch at the side of the lane.

'Stop talking, and let me concentrate,' growled Jack, using all the gears at his disposal to gradually ease them out of the ditch.

The atmosphere was tense; Louise held her breath, willing the Land Rover to climb back on to the main part of the lane, which eventually it did. After that, Louise remained silent for the rest of the journey, not speaking even when they emerged from the whiteout into sleet and rain and the civilization of the outskirts of Salisbury.

Jack turned the car in the direction of East Willow. 'What did Penny say when you rang her,' he asked.

Louise had forgotten that she'd rung Penny. She was still puzzling as to how Jack had come to her rescue, and more importantly, why. Was he staying, or had he just passed by and looked in on them? 'Oh!' she said again, hastily gathering her thoughts together. 'She said she was glad that we were OK and that she'd do as you asked.' Louise frowned. 'What did you ask her to do?'

'I asked her to light a fire in the sitting room and get some hot drinks ready for us when we arrived.'

'A fire in the sitting room? That's a strange request. Whatever for?'

'Because you and I need somewhere private to sit which is warm. We need to have a long talk, and I don't want your entire family interrupting and putting their five eggs in. Much as I love them all.'

'Oh!' said Louise, unable to think of anything else to say.

'Is that all you've got to say? If I remember correctly you had a lot more to say the last time I saw you.' He suddenly grinned as he turned briefly towards her.

Louise felt her cheeks flame. 'Well, I ... er ...' she stumbled over the words she wanted to say.

'Don't tell me now. Leave it until I can hear you properly. At the moment it's rather difficult as I have Seamus's wet nose stuck in my ear.'

Louise relaxed. Yes, it could wait. She smiled, looking

at Seamus who was straining further and further forward as they got near to East Willow and Lavender House.

Louise was glad of the roaring fire Penny had got going in the sitting room. Everyone milled excitedly around them when they arrived. Maggie extravagantly kissing Jack and throwing her arms around his and the dogs' necks.

'The darlings,' she cried. 'I was so worried about them.'

'What about me?' asked Louise.

'Of course, we were worried about you as well,' said Seth. He held Louise's arm, drawing her away slightly, and added quietly, 'This is what you wanted, I think. Now take some well-meant advice. Just curb that impulsive tongue of yours and listen.'

'Yes,' said Louise meekly, wondering what it was Jack was going to tell her. After shooing everyone out of the way, Jack led the way in the sitting room and Louise followed. There was a pot of hot coffee on a tray, some cups and a still warm fruitcake, obviously made by Seth. Louise sat herself down opposite Jack. It is ridiculous to feel so nervous, she told herself, and wondered if he was nervous as well.

They both started speaking together.

'Shall I pour the coffee?' said Louise.

'It was your entire fault, yours and the Lavender House Mob,' said Jack.

They both laughed awkwardly. He *is* nervous, thought Louise and began to pour the coffee. Somehow, that made her feel better.

'What do you mean, my entire fault?'

'Not just you. Everything,' replied Jack. 'Originally I did intend to stay at the pub and carry out covert investigations into Geoffrey and Dennis' movements, and also to snoop on their email traffic and get into their computers.'

'How *do* you get into other people's computers?' asked Louise. 'I've always wondered.'

'You'd never understand, my darling. Your mind isn't on that wavelength. Anyway, don't interrupt my flow.'

He called me, *my darling*, that's a good sign, thought Louise, but remained silent.

'But then I met you,' Jack continued, 'and my life changed. I wanted to get to know you better. It was only after I started staying at Lavender House that I realized that you had been affected by the complicated financial shenanigans of Geoffrey and Dennis.'

'You mean, losing my monthly allowance?'

'Exactly! Then as Geoffrey and Dennis's affairs began to get more interesting, so at the same time did you and your family, and I'm afraid I began to do my detective work quite slowly. I didn't want the time to come when I'd finished and had to leave. But, of course, it did eventually, and I couldn't tell you why.'

'I don't see why not. Surely by then you knew you could trust me.'

'The work I do is secret until it gets to court, and even then I'm not in the limelight, I'm one of those shadowy figures you read about. That's the way it has to be.'

'All the time?'

'Yes, I'm afraid so.'

Louise frowned. Suddenly she felt doubtful. He wanted to come back into her life, she was sure of that now. But could she cope with a man who had such big secrets? Someone who would disappear but never tell her where he'd gone. 'I don't think I could live with that,' she said slowly.

'You don't have to. I've given up working for the SFO. I'm going to be a plain dull accountant, with a firm in Rumsey.'

'An accountant!'

'Yes, why not. I'm qualified. Besides I've got a job. I become a partner next week with Laverstock, Whitby and Dunn, in Rumsey.'

'That won't be very exciting,' said Louise. 'I mean you won't be going to things in Brussels. I saw you on television on the European News,' she added, 'at some big conference.'

Jack laughed. 'I think taking charge of the accounts of Lavender House, and a best-selling writer will be quite exciting enough for me.' Then he looked serious, and said gently, 'That is, if you can bear to have me around all the time.'

For a moment. Just a moment. A split second really, Louise hesitated, then she said, 'I think I could bear it.'

Jack stood up and held out his arms and Louise moved across to him to be enveloped in a great bear hug. Then he kissed her a long, lingering, deeply satisfying kiss. When they came up for air, Jack looked at her, his dark eyes smiling. 'We've got the rest of our lives to catch up on everything else,' he said.

'Mmm,' sighed Louise. 'Somehow I don't think I'll ever have time to finish another book, so I'll never be a best-selling writer. If it comes to choosing between being with you or sitting in front of a computer on my own, I know which I'll choose.'

'Me?'

'Every time,' said Louise, sliding her arms up around his neck, pulling his head down to kiss him again.

Outside in the hall Maggie had her eye glued to the

keyhole. 'They're kissing again,' she hissed. 'I think that's a very good sign.'

Seth pulled her back. 'It is a good sign. But you shouldn't be looking. Come away.'

'Yes, how dare you spy on my mother,' said Penny, grinning from ear to ear and pushing Maggie aside so that she could look through the keyhole too. 'Come on, let's go into the kitchen.'

'All right.' Maggie reluctantly allowed herself to be dragged away from the hall. 'Let's go into the kitchen and open a bottle of something in celebration.'

'The trouble with you,' said Seth 'is that you always want to open a bottle of something.'